MURDER BY BICYCLE

*Veronica Heley titles available from
Severn House Large Print*

Murder by Accident
Murder by Committee
Murder in the Garden
Murder of Innocence

MURDER BY BICYCLE

Veronica Heley

Severn House Large Print
London & New York

This first large print edition published in Great Britain 2007 by
SEVERN HOUSE LARGE PRINT BOOKS LTD of
9-15 High Street, Sutton, Surrey, SM1 1DF.
First world regular print edition published 2006 by
Severn House Publishers, London and New York.
This first large print edition published in the USA 2007 by
SEVERN HOUSE PUBLISHERS INC., of
595 Madison Avenue, New York, NY 10022.

British Library Cataloguing in Publication Data

Heley, Veronica
  Murder by bicycle. - Large print ed. - (An Ellie Quicke
  mystery)
  1. Quicke, Ellie (Fictitious character) - Fiction 2. Widows
  - Great Britain - Fiction 3. Detective and mystery stories
  4. Large type books
  I. Title
  823.9'14[F]

  ISBN-13: 9780727876089

Printed and bound in Great Britain by
MPG Books Ltd, Bodmin, Cornwall.

One

The housekeeper spread the newspaper cutting out on the kitchen table.

HANDYMAN'S TRAGIC DEATH
Popular handyman Patrick Murphy, 38, was found dead on his kitchen floor after spending the night celebrating his birthday with friends. His long-term partner, Betty Cooke, 35, said he'd often been told by his doctor to cut down his drinking. 'But he was all for a laugh, wasn't he, and perhaps it was a good way to go.'
Popular Paddy was always ready to lend a helping hand to a friend in need. Betty said tearfully, 'What I'm going to do without him, I don't know.'

The housekeeper took down her 1960s edition of Mrs Beeton's book on Cookery and Household Management, acquired at second hand when she'd got married. She turned to the section on 'Control of rodent and insect pests in the home'. She passed over the pages on which she'd pasted the cuttings and notes she'd made concerning the

5

deaths of her husband, her father and her sister ... then the dog ... until she found a clear page. She pasted the new cutting inside.

The verdicts had been misadventure, gastritis, accidental death ... then there'd been the dog, which rather spoiled her record for getting it right first time. And now Paddy: liver failure.

She was not best pleased with Paddy's death. All that care and preparation, and the wrong person had eaten the doctored rolls. She'd aimed higher than Paddy. Well, she'd have to try again, that was all.

Someone rang the doorbell, someone who meant to be answered.

Ellie was in the bath.

She rolled her eyes. It would be her dreadful daughter Diana at the door, wanting Ellie to do something for her. Or Ellie's aged aunt, who could be rather imperious.

Or maybe her nice neighbour Kate from next door? No, it wouldn't be Kate, because Kate had a key and anyway she usually came in the back way via their adjoining gardens.

Someone rang the bell again. Ellie tensed, waiting for them to go away. A salesman? Someone wanting to chop down her trees, or re-lay her front path? She was not going to get out of the bath for a salesman, no way! She'd only just got in, the water was at the right temperature and anyway, why shouldn't she enjoy a leisurely bath in the early

6

evening if she wished?

If it was anything important, they could push a note through the letter-box, or leave a message on the answerphone.

She didn't often treat herself to a bubble bath. In fact, she couldn't remember ever having done so before.

Had she been given bubble bath when her husband Frank had died? She didn't think she had, although she'd heard it was considered an acceptable present for a widow.

Anyway, the caller – whoever it was – seemed to have gone away.

Had the water temperature dropped a degree? She turned the tap on to trickle more hot water into the bath. The bubbles were beginning to subside, but she'd make the most of them while she could.

What luxury!

Crash! It sounded as if someone were trying to kick the front door in. Someone shouted her name.

Ellie shot upright in the bath.

A burglar?

Then came the horrifying sound of breaking glass. Someone was breaking into her house! SOMEONE WHO KNEW HER NAME!

Ellie Quicke was the very mildest of women, but over the last few years she had helped to solve various crimes in the community, and one or two nasty individuals had ended up in prison as a result. Could one of them have obtained an early release and come looking for revenge? She'd heard some prisoners were being freed after having served no more than a third of their sentences. Could this be one of them?

Ellie looked wildly around. Living alone, she'd never bothered about covering herself up between bedroom and bathroom. No dressing-gown hung behind the door, and she'd left the clothes she'd taken off in her bedroom. She reached for a towel to cover herself with. Could she get to the bathroom door and lock it before the intruder discovered where she was? The bathroom door was flimsy. Would it hold while she phoned someone for help on her mobile?

Panic stations! Her mobile was not in the bathroom with her. She'd left it somewhere ... in her bedroom, possibly ... but maybe downstairs in her handbag. She only used it for emergencies.

She got out of the bath, wrapped the towel around her, and pushed against the door to activate the catch against ... whoever it might be. She could hear him trying doors downstairs, looking for her.

'Mrs Quicke?'

She wanted to scream but refused to let herself do so, since it would only waste energy.

'Mrs Quicke!' He was walking around the

landing, trying doors. At last he reached the bathroom, and pounded on that door. 'I know you're here, somewhere. A neighbour saw you come in some time ago. Are you ill?'

That was an odd thing for a villain bent on revenge to enquire.

He pounded on the door again. 'Shall I phone for an ambulance?'

She tried not to sound nervous. 'I'm perfectly all right. Go away!'

'I'm not going away until I see for myself that you're all right. Come out, Mrs Quicke, or I'll have to break the door down.'

Did she recognize that voice?

She opened the door.

Ellie Quicke had been trained by her husband and daughter to believe that she'd been put into this world to serve others. It wasn't until Frank died that Ellie discovered that she had a mind of her own, that she could make friends of her own, and that she could – every now and then – do something just to please herself.

The day someone broke into her house had been a case in point. She'd spent Sunday working hard for the church, just as was expected of a comfortably-off widow. She'd promised herself a special treat on Monday and had indulged herself – feeling only a little guilty – in a day's shopping in Town. Hence the indulgence in an early evening bath, surrounded by expensive bubbles.

And why not? Hadn't she earned it?

It appeared that someone thought otherwise, as she was shortly to be called to account for everything that she had or had not done the previous day.

It had been a special day at church. Their vicar was popular and services were well attended, with some people coming from way outside the parish boundaries. That Sunday there'd been a Bring and Eat lunch for everyone who cared to stay on after the morning service, and a large number had been expected.

Ellie was there to help, of course. She'd been on the coffee roster at St Thomas' church for years. As if that weren't time-consuming enough, after her husband's death she'd also been persuaded to join the choir. Ellie didn't think she had much of a voice, but she'd spent most of her adult life doing what was expected of her, so that day she hadn't only been helping with the catering but also singing in the choir.

Nothing much had changed at church since she'd been widowed. True, they had a new vicar, Thomas; affectionately known as Tum-Tum because of his ample frontage. Ellie liked Thomas, who was a practical person with a touch of Captain Birdseye about him.

Then their old organist had died and her

place had been taken by the scoutmaster, who wasn't making too bad a job of it. Apart from that, the coffee roster was still run by tyrannical Jean who could bully for Britain, while Mrs Dawes – the stately head of the flower-arranging team – continued to tell everyone what to do and how to do it.

Looking back, Ellie couldn't think what she'd done to turn herself into Public Enemy No. 1.

She'd gone to church early to deliver the quiches she'd made for the feast, and to help Jean and that nice woman, Maggie something, to set out the chairs and tables for lunch. She'd rushed into her choir robes at the last possible minute with the aid of stately Mrs Dawes, who was an impressive alto as well as being head of the flower-arranging team.

Their scoutmaster-turned-organist had a mild manner but knew how to keep his singers in order. He'd given Ellie a black look as she was the last one to line up in the vestry.

On the dot of eleven o'clock the vicar, followed by the choir and congregation, processed around the outside of the church, singing more or less in tune, robes flapping in the breeze, with Ellie hoping not to lose any of the extra sheets of music which they were supposed to have put securely into folders, but which she had forgotten about.

Then back into the church for the special service.

Ellie tried to follow the sermon without worrying too much about whether there'd be enough food for everyone at lunch; they were all supposed to bring something to eat, but some people always forgot and you had to take that into account when catering.

Mrs Dawes harrumphed through the service, because one of the lilies in the enormous and very beautiful flower arrangement at the side of the altar had seemed to her critical gaze to be past its best.

There had been an even bigger crowd than usual in the church, with extra chairs being brought in to seat people down the side aisles. Ellie was pleased to see many people she knew in the congregation, including her next-door neighbour Kate and her husband, plus toddler; also her aged Aunt Drusilla, who rarely attended church, but had made an exception for today. And many others. A good turnout.

After the service, Ellie divested herself of her robes in a hurry and scooted round to the church hall, knowing that Jean would be more than usually sharp-tongued on these occasions and might take it out on anyone else unwary enough to offer to help ... such as that nice woman whom Jean had reduced to tears last week ... and Rose, Ellie's old friend, who was now treasured housekeeper and friend to her Aunt Drusilla.

Ellie served endless cups of tea and coffee. Faces passed before her kaleidoscopically. She responded to greetings from those she knew best, caught a glimpse of this person and that, grabbed a sandwich when she could ... and then there were the mountains of washing up and putting away ... and the leftovers to be disposed of, mostly into Jean's capacious basket. Ellie was pleased at the time to see that nothing had been left of her quiches. Later, she wished – how she wished – otherwise.

Finally the floor had been swept while chairs and tables were stacked so that the Toddlers' Group wouldn't find the place in a mess the following morning. By that time the catering team had shrunk to just two people, Jean and Ellie, because Maggie's husband removed her to get his supper ready, and dear Rose was whisked away by Aunt Drusilla, who was always careful to see that her housekeeper didn't overdo it.

Dear Tum-Tum – Thomas – had actually come in to help them do the final clearing up, and told Jean and Ellie to go home 'Now!' even before Jean had given grudging permission for Ellie to depart.

It had been a good day, and Ellie had to admit she got a certain satisfaction out of a job well done. But as she trudged back over the Green, let herself through the gate into

13

her garden and climbed the slope to her house, she was glad it was all over. It had turned hot that day.

She cast a longing glance at the garden chairs and table she'd set out on the lawn ... but no, she couldn't relax yet. The plants in her conservatory needed watering and she'd promised to take some magazines round to Mrs Dawes, who liked the glossies but couldn't afford to buy them for herself.

As she scrambled herself a couple of eggs for supper and fed her marauding tom cat Midge, Ellie decided that tomorrow would be a day of self-indulgence, a day in which she would refuse to answer the telephone or the doorbell to anyone from window-cleaners to salesmen to friends needing a sympathetic ear.

She advised Midge of her plans as he gulped down his supper. 'My ideal would be breakfast in bed, then staying there with a good book – nothing too worrying – and a box of Belgian chocolates. Only,' she sighed, 'breakfast in bed is no good at all if you have to get up to make it yourself, and the only time I ever tried that, I spilt tea in bed and there were crumbs everywhere and I hated it.

'On the other hand,' she said, removing Midge's empty dish, rinsing it out and putting it into the dishwasher, 'I could be daring for once.' She followed Midge up the stairs to bed.

'I could get up early and leave the house before anyone called. I could take the tube up to Oxford Street, and do some window-shopping. I could do with some new underwear. I could have lunch somewhere really nice, not look at the price, and pay by credit card. I could pretend that I was a Lady of Leisure. A Lady who Lunched whenever she felt like it. What do you think, Midge?'

Midge had no hesitation about carrying out his own plan for the night, which was to give himself a thorough wash, then curl round at Ellie's side and have a good sleep. Ellie left the window open so that he could get out and go hunting if he wished.

'Tomorrow,' she promised herself, 'is my treat.'

So it had been. She'd window-shopped, and then she'd gone into an exclusive lingerie boutique and tried on this and that ... which had rather gone to her head, especially when she discovered that she'd lost a few pounds recently. She'd started off by looking at some plain but practical underwear but ended up buying one set in sheer ivory satin and another adorned with lace, which she knew perfectly well she'd never have the nerve to wear but just couldn't resist. She used her credit card and tried not to feel guilty when she saw the total.

She was not the sort of woman who

normally spent much on herself, even though she could afford it nowadays. Before her husband died she'd bought her clothes in charity shops, though nowadays she did venture into department stores at sale times. She'd never been into a beauty parlour, and her short, prematurely silvery hair was trimmed by a local hairdresser when it became shaggy. She wore a pale pink lipstick and a dash of pressed powder when she remembered. That was about it.

On her way back to the tube station, a display of bath products seductively packaged encouraged her to make one last purchase: some expensive bubble bath. She wondered what Frank would have said about all this self-indulgence if he'd still been alive ... and then told herself that it was all very sad, but it was no good beating up on herself when he'd been dead for some years now.

She went home, fed Midge and ignored the winking light on the answerphone. In fact, she muted the tone so it wouldn't disturb her. Then she went upstairs to try out the bubble bath, even though it was still early evening and she never usually had a bath at that time of day ... a shower, yes, but not a lengthy bath. She wondered, idly and with a certain mischief, whether she would bother to go to choir practice that evening. She decided that she wouldn't, and that she didn't care if the choirmaster did miss her.

16

For once she was going to please herself...

...until someone rang the doorbell and yanked her out of the bath.

'Mrs Quicke! So there you are! Are you all right? Do you want me to phone for an ambulance?'

Ellie blinked. It took her a moment to work out that she knew the wild-looking young man standing on her landing. Seeing people out of context invariably threw her. Then she recognized him, but couldn't for the life of her understand what their normally mild-mannered organist and scoutmaster was doing on her landing.

'Mr Holmes? What on earth—?'

He passed his hand across his eyes, sagging with relief for some reason. 'Ah. I can see you're all right. Did you have a very bad time? Did you have to call the doctor?'

'I really don't—'

His eyes went to her bare shoulders, and she hitched the towel closer to her neck. His eyes then went to her bare legs. He was one of those people who blushed from the neck upwards.

Ellie knew she no longer had the body of a Pocket Venus – which was what Frank had used to call her in the days when they were courting – but nevertheless she didn't feel she had much to be ashamed of, either. She would have been amused if she hadn't realized that the man before her was on the verge of disintegration. Normally he presented an image of conventional young businessman, with smooth brown hair, brown eyes and carefully understated but pricey suits. Middle management incarnate. Now his hair was wild, his eyes flared, his tie was undone, and his shirt was hanging out of his trousers.

Ellie Quicke – with a sigh for her lost bubble bath – realized that it was up to her to take charge. 'I don't know what all the fuss is about, or why you felt you had to break into my house, but—'

'Sorry. I don't feel...' He sat down on the top stair, and washed his face with his hands. He actually groaned.

Ellie was alarmed. 'Are you ill?'

He shook his head, wordless.

'Oh. Well, in that case, if you'll allow me to put some clothes on, perhaps we can sort out whatever the problem is.'

He began rocking to and fro, not with his previous energy, but as if he hardly knew what else to do with himself. Ellie inched round him and into her bedroom, where she dried herself and scrambled into an elderly but comfortable blue jumper, skirt and sandals. A glance in the mirror caused her to pull a face, but a few passes with a hairbrush and a swipe with her favourite pink lipstick made her feel more presentable.

18

Reggie Holmes was still sitting at the top of the stairs when she emerged. Short of pushing him down the stairs, she wasn't quite sure how to move him on, but luckily he responded to a tap on the shoulder and a suggestion that he might like a cup of tea in the kitchen.

'Now,' she said, placing a large mug of sugared, strong tea in front of him, 'perhaps you will tell me what this is all about.'

He looked at her with deep-set, miserable eyes. 'I can't believe you don't know. There's all hell to pay, and Joyce has had a miscarriage!'

Joyce was his wife and dear Rose's only daughter, but Ellie had not previously thought the girl a candidate for maternity. Rather the reverse, in fact. Joyce was proudly progressing up the ladder at work in one of the national banks, which was, of course, commendable. Privately Ellie considered that Joyce was a shrew, and that Reggie was well on the way to becoming a hen-pecked husband.

Ellie wondered whether Joyce had got pregnant by accident, since the girl had often said that her career was to be developed before she 'gave in' to her husband's desire for a child. But whether Joyce had intended the pregnancy or not, whether she was or was not devastated by her miscarriage, it had obviously hit her husband hard.

Ellie said, 'I'm so sorry. I didn't know she was pregnant. But I don't quite understand why you had to break into my house to—'

'She only found out last week. I was over the moon, and I knew she'd come round to it once she got used to the idea, and now...'

'Drink your tea.'

He rubbed his eyes, which were red, but obediently drank some tea. 'She was up all night with it. I had it, too, but not nearly so badly, and then this morning ... I had to take her into Accident and Emergency because it was all coming away, and then ... and then ... they said they couldn't do anything, that the baby had gone and I ... I didn't know what to do.'

'Poor Joyce. How terrible for both of you. Have they kept her in hospital? Does Rose know?'

'They're keeping Joyce in overnight and she's sedated and I'm not to go in till late this evening, and they'll probably let her out tomorrow after making sure ... you know...'

Ellie interpreted that to mean that the hospital wanted to give Joyce a D&C clear-out to make sure everything was all right.

' ...and I phoned Mother-in-law, but she'd been up all night with it, too. And that terrible woman she works for ... sorry, I forgot she's your aunt, but she said Rose wasn't fit to look after anyone else, and that's when I realized other people might have

20

been affected as well, so I rang Mrs Dawes, who sounded so weak I hardly recognized her, though she said she was on the mend. She was really worried about you and asked me to make sure you were all right, so I tried ringing you but you wouldn't answer the phone. I rang Thomas, and he said he'd had it, too, but not so badly, and he'd taken old Mr Pole into hospital first thing this morning and...'

'What's wrong with everyone, then?'

He gave her a very odd look. 'You really don't know? Food poisoning, of course. They're saying it was your quiches that did it. Everyone thought you'd be bound to have gone down with it, too. But you haven't, have you?'

His expression changed from hang-dog to prosecuting counsel. 'So what have you got to say for yourself?'

The housekeeper had got the job because she didn't mind looking in on her landlady's elderly father a couple of times a day. He lived in two rooms upstairs and only ate liquidized food, so it wasn't an onerous position and allowed the housekeeper to keep on just one other carefully chosen cleaning job.

Her landlady, Ruby, ran a boutique in the local shopping centre. After work Ruby usually went straight to a wine bar, returning home late at night.

21

It suited Ruby to have someone to look after her father, and it suited the housekeeper to have a place where she could bring some of her bits and pieces and make it feel like home. The wages were good, and she had plenty of free time to concentrate on revenge.

Two

Ellie had been reaching for her own mug of tea, but on hearing this, she sat back in her chair with a bump.

Reggie's forefinger wagged under her nose. 'We were worried sick, Thomas and I, so we made a list of who was in the choir and divided it up between us. You were on my list. When you didn't answer the phone or the doorbell, I made sure you were laid out on the floor in the bathroom, sick as a dog, or maybe already gone to hospital. And look at you! Perky as Pinky!'

Ellie blinked, but he wasn't finished yet.

'There's everyone worrying their heads off about you, and you sit there as calm as you please, enjoying yourself while everyone else around you—'

'I really don't think—'

His forefinger poked her in the chest, hard.

'So why did you do it, eh? What makes you think you can get away with wholesale manslaughter?'

Ellie gaped. One minute she'd been luxuriating in a bath, pleased with herself and at ease with the world. Patting herself on the back even, after having worked so hard the day before. And now ... could it be true that her quiches had poisoned the community?

'What makes you think that it was my quiches...?'

'We all had them, didn't we? Mrs Dawes said, "Let's have some of Ellie's quiches because we know they're not shop bought." Thomas was with us at the time, and he agreed. Mother-in-law brought some over for Joyce, who hadn't really fancied anything much to eat until she was coaxed to try your quiche and now...'

'But...' Ellie didn't know what to say. Her mind went completely blank. She, who'd been supplying food for church functions for years, was now, at her age and with all her years of experience, accused of poisoning some of her best friends? She couldn't take it in.

Her phone rang again, and though she'd muted the sound, this time she heard it because she was so close. Both she and Reggie turned their heads towards it.

'What's the betting that's someone else wondering if you've gone down with it, and feeling sorry for you?' Reggie asked. 'But you're perfectly all right, aren't you! You took care not to eat anything you'd cooked!'

'I didn't have any of my quiches because I didn't have time. I got a sandwich to eat when I was washing up, but—'

'You don't mind other people getting sick, but weren't going to risk it yourself, right?'

'Wrong,' said Ellie, trying to think clearly and not succeeding. 'There was nothing wrong with my quiches. I've used the same recipe for years, and I've never had anyone complain about them before.'

'Until now. It's criminal, what you've done. What about my unborn child, eh? What are you going to do about that?'

Ellie blinked again. This situation was way beyond her. Could she really have made a terrible mistake when baking those quiches? She'd used an old recipe which was more solid than the usual modern-day ones in which you just slopped beaten egg over some kind of filling, because men in particular needed something to line their stomachs.

She'd cooked four pastry cases blind. She'd filled two with a prawn and egg mix, and two with cheese and sweetcorn and then poured a thickened mixture of evaporated milk and flour and butter over all. Had there been something wrong with one of the tins of sweetcorn that she'd used? No, she didn't think so. She'd bought the tins from the local supermarket late last week, and they hadn't been malformed or out of date or anything.

It must have been the eggs! She'd bought them from the very reliable fishmonger in the Avenue, together with the prawns, which had been frozen, and ... she couldn't think for the moment what else she'd used. She counted them off on her fingers. Eggs, milk, flour, butter, a little grated onion, pepper and salt ... how could anything have gone amiss?

The answer thudded into her brain. Either the prawns or the eggs hadn't been cooked long enough, and she'd given her friends a nasty stomach upset.

The telephone rang again. Someone was leaving a message on the answerphone. She ought really to get up and attend to it, but she couldn't move. She was staring at a scenario which horrified her: had she, by some terrible mistake, allowed the terrible bug E coli to cause Joyce to miscarry and some of her best friends to be made violently ill?

Dear Rose ... Mrs Dawes ... Thomas? Old Mr Pole, who though not exactly one of her favourite people, had not deserved to be poisoned by her cooking? She shuddered.

If she had made them ill – unknowingly, of course – then that made her culpable, didn't it?

Reggie had now got himself more or less under control, though she supposed he was probably still suffering from shock. He got up, pushed his chair carefully back under the table, and began to right his appearance. Tie: twist into an appropriate knot. Shirt: push back into trousers. Hair: smooth back.

'Well,' he said, heavily sarcastic, 'I can see that nothing I've said has got through to you, so I'll leave you in peace to think it through. Be assured, this is not the last you'll hear from me about it. Naturally, I've cancelled choir practice this evening, though I do not expect to see you in the choir in future, right? I believe your husband left you a small fortune; well, I'll be contacting my solicitor in the morning, and asking for damages, right?'

He rather spoilt the effect with that last 'right'.

Feeling numb, Ellie got to her feet to see him out. Shards of glass lay across the hall floor. He hesitated, perhaps wondering if he ought to help clear it up.

'I had to break in, to make sure you were all right. Don't expect me to apologize for that. Or pay for a replacement.'

He opened the front door wide and held it, obviously debating one final taunt. He was not a man used to hurling bad language around, but he managed to find the right word this time.

'Murderess!' he said, and banged the door to behind him.

Ellie put out a hand to prevent herself from
falling. It was she who was now in shock.

She stared at the mess in her hall without
really seeing it. She wondered if she'd fallen
asleep in the bath, and this was all a dream.
A nightmare. She thought about pinching
herself, and found herself laughing at the
absurdity of doing so ... then put her hand
over her mouth to stop herself laughing.

One part of her mind said, You're hysterical! Stop it!

Another part said, Why shouldn't I let out
a scream or two, if I like?

She put both hands to her head and held
on to it, in case it flew off and started orbit-
ing the room. She could feel a nasty headache coming on. And was that a twinge in a
back tooth?

The phone rang again.

Shaken loose by Reggie Holmes' noisy
departure, one more shard of glass teetered
in the frame, and toppled on to the floor of
the hall to join its fellows.

She knew she ought to get moving. For one
thing, she could hardly leave the house with
a broken window all night. Even if she
wasn't visited by an opportunist burglar, the
wind and rain might well sweep in ... not that
it looked like rain at the moment. It was a
warm night, with not even the slightest of
breezes to stir the air. She fancied she could

even smell her new David Austin English rose in the bed by the front door from where she stood, and the old-fashioned honeysuckle, too.

The phone stopped ringing, and she heard someone leaving a message, but she was too far away to work out who it was who was speaking. It might not be someone she knew, of course. It might be one of those awful sales calls telling her in a too-bright voice that she had been selected as a prizewinner in a competition for which she hadn't entered, and all she had to do to claim the prize was to dial such and such a number, when her trip to Disneyland/the Caribbean/ a time share in Greece would immediately become hers. And if you believe that, you'd believe anything.

Murderess!

She heard herself make a strange noise in her throat. Was she going to break down and cry? Whatever would Frank have said, if he could have heard Reggie's accusation! Why, Frank would have said...

She sat down on the chair in the hall with a bump. She couldn't for the life of her think what Frank would have had to say in the matter.

She tried to clear her mind. When she was cooking the quiches, she'd also been in and out of the kitchen, attending to the plants in the conservatory at the back of the house.

So, just to make sure she hadn't over cooked them, she'd put the timer on. Yes, she was sure she had. You cooked those quiches long and slow and thorough. And she had done so. She could picture herself hovering over the oven, waiting for the timer to ring and then taking the quiches out one by one and putting them on a rack to cool. They'd looked just fine.

If the eggs hadn't been cooked right through, she'd have seen that something was wrong.

They'd been cooked all the way through. She was sure of that.

But suppose the prawns had been off?

But they hadn't been. The fishmonger was reliable, and anyway she'd given them a sniff or two, to make sure. No, the prawns were all right.

She was sure of it.

Almost sure of it.

No, this was ridiculous. The quiches had been properly prepared and properly cooked.

Anyway, from what Reggie had said, the effects of – whatever – had only lasted a few hours. And that wasn't like E coli, or listeria, or anything else she could think of which might have been started up with poor food hygiene. It was dreadful that Joyce had lost her baby, of course, and that Mr Pole had been taken to hospital. But they were the ones most likely to be affected by a tummy upset of any kind.

No, she wasn't to blame in any way.

Unless, perhaps ... she had somehow, in some way, used something that ... what could have produced such an effect? Senna? Cascara?

She shook her head in bewilderment. She hadn't such a thing in the house. Frank had never used such things, and she hadn't, either. Nor Diana. If Frank had needed his stomach coaxing to behave, she'd bought some rhubarb, or gooseberries or other fruit, and she had never, ever, bought or used anything from the chemist to produce such an effect.

It was awful that Reggie should think her cooking to blame, but it was not so!

Ellie spared a moment to wonder, rather grimly, if Joyce would join him in mourning the loss of their child. Ellie rather suspected, from what he'd said about assuming that Joyce would soon have become accustomed to the idea of being pregnant, that the girl would have found her miscarriage a blessing rather than a curse. But, look at it whichever way you did, there was a loss to the world.

A shaft of evening light reflected off the broken window and dazzled Ellie. She had somehow to get that broken window boarded over. But she didn't have any hardboard in the house. Would cardboard do, until she could get her builder in to see to it? He was supposed to be coming round to repoint her garden wall some time soon. Perhaps he could do both jobs at once.

She looked at her wrist but she hadn't put her watch on after being yanked out of her bath so abruptly … which reminded her that the bath was still full of cooling water, and she'd left a damp towel on the floor of the bedroom, a thing you should never do. As her mother had always said, 'How can you get a towel dry if you leave it in a heap on the floor?'

She twisted round to check the time on the grandmother clock in the hall. It seemed to have stopped. Or was it really only seven in the evening? Perhaps it was. In any case, it was long past the time her builders would have downed tools for the day.

She decided that she wouldn't think about the damage she might or might not have done with her cooking, because it was too awful to contemplate, whereas dealing with something practical – like boarding up a window – might just about be possible.

Would Kate and Armand next door be able to help? Foxy-faced Armand was a teacher at the local high school, with a hasty temper and a kind heart. He'd probably help her do something to make the house safe for the night … that is, if he and Kate hadn't been struck down by the lurgy, too.

Ellie turned her head to listen for noises in the semi next door. She could usually hear the couple moving around, since part of their staircases ran up on either side of the party wall. Or she'd hear Catriona, their toddler. Silence. They must be out.

Strange, that. Armand should be back from school by now – though perhaps not, if he'd attended an after-school meeting. Kate was a self-employed financial expert and used an excellent babysitter to look after baby Catriona ... but still, it was after seven o'clock and someone ought to be home by now.

Or, perhaps – ghastly thought – they were all lying in bed next door with stomach trouble ... dying, perhaps.

Ellie shot to her feet and went looking in the kitchen for the key to Kate and Armand's back door. They had her key, and she had theirs.

Just as she found it, she heard a car draw up outside, followed by the sound of Kate coming down the drive, making soothing sounds to her toddler. Kate must have been working late and just picked Catriona up from the babysitter's. At least they were alive!

Ellie sat with her head twisted round to the wall so as to hear better, and was even more relieved when she heard Armand's voice, too. He must have been quietly working away in his study and that's why she hadn't heard him.

She felt limp with relief.

Now, perhaps, she could tackle the pile of messages of the telephone, which rang again as she reached it.

She thought, I bet that's my daughter wanting something...

It was indeed Diana. And Diana did indeed want something.

'Mother, where have you been? I've been ringing and ringing. It's all very well for you to decide not to answer the phone as you've nothing to do but please yourself all day, while I have to be out and about at people's beck and call, rushing around to make a living...'

Ellie subdued an impulse to slam the phone down. Obviously Diana was in the best of health. Diana hadn't been carted off to hospital in the middle of the night, or been suffering debilitating stomach pains. Well, Diana hadn't been at church yesterday, of course, so she wouldn't have had an opportunity to eat any of her mother's cooking.

As usual, Diana wanted Ellie to do something for her. Probably something Ellie did not much want to do.

'I went up to Town for the day,' said Ellie. 'But I'm here now. What was it you wanted?'

'Oh, it's far too late now! I had an appointment myself up in Town, a most important

33

appointment, and I needed you to collect little Frank from school this afternoon – you know he doesn't go full time until next term – and where were you when I needed you?'

'I had an appointment up in Town, too,' said Ellie, crossing her fingers behind her back. 'I could have altered it if I'd known you wanted me to babysit, but...'

'I had to call in a favour from one of the other mothers, and I must say she wasn't at all pleasant about it. As if I had arranged the appointment just to annoy her. Little Frank wasn't best pleased, either, because she never lets him play on her son's computer, just because Frank happened to have had a small accident with it last time he was there...'

Ellie tuned out the rest of the diatribe. Little Frank was four years old, and had just started in the reception class at big school. During the week he lived with his father Stewart, his father's second wife and their infant prodigy, a cooing, happy toddler who adored him. At weekends and on special occasions he went to his mother, who spoiled him, to which he reacted exactly as might be expected. When he was with his father, he behaved slightly better than most bright four-year-olds. When he was with his mother ... well ... least said.

Ellie had forgotten that this week Stewart had taken his second family away for an early summer holiday and arranged for Frank – at Diana's insistence – to stay with his mother.

Ellie told herself she ought to have remembered that. Perhaps, her over-active conscience said, you forgot because you didn't want to remember. You didn't want to give up your day up in Town to look after little Frank instead.

'I'm sorry I was out, Diana. How have you arranged things for the rest of the week?'

'If you can have him in the afternoon tomorrow and Wednesday, then I suppose I can somehow manage to cope on Thursday...'

Ellie began, 'I've got a meeting on Wednesday afternoon,' but Diana wasn't listening.

'...and they'll be back on Friday, won't they? Oh yes, and I need you to come and look at another property with me. House prices are so high at the moment that I shall need a partner for my next renovation and I need to get cracking on it. I did tell you I'd sold the last of the flats at my present place, didn't I? Perhaps Wednesday morning? I'll ring you.'

Diana rang off, leaving Ellie wanting to scream. Diana's confidence that she could earn a good living by buying, renovating and selling older properties was not shared by her family. Diana fell for every last modern fad. Diana believed in fake wood floorboarding and halogen lights in lowered ceilings; she tore out fireplaces, cornices and picture rails; she bulldozed gardens to create off-road parking spaces; she dismissed capacious sinks and put in teeny-weeny glass bowls which you couldn't wash more than the tips of your fingers in and as for kitchen units, she didn't believe in draining-boards because everyone who wanted one of her up-to-the-minute flats would naturally have dishwashers and probably not cook much, anyway.

Diana's flats were suitable settings for the upwardly mobile until they wanted to settle down, when they moved on to something better adapted to family life. It was a mystery to Ellie how Diana had ever managed to sell the flats she'd created out of the monstrosity of a building she'd bought a while back. But there; different times, different styles of décor, and at least Diana had managed to make a return on her investment in the end. Probably. So why did she need a partner for her next project? Was she over-reaching herself, as usual? Or really in trouble financially?

Ellie's tooth twinged again, and she massaged her cheek. Was she really going to have toothache on top of everything else?

Having rid herself of Diana, Ellie pressed Play on the answerphone, and was horrified to hear how many messages had been left for her.

Diana's voice came first. Of course. Ellie fast-forwarded.

Miss Drusilla Quicke's voice came next. The elderly but terrifying Miss Quicke was Ellie's aunt by marriage. For many years she'd treated Ellie as an unpaid skivvy, but recently they had become good friends. Like Diana, Miss Quicke dealt in buying up and renovating flats and houses, but unlike Diana, Miss Quicke was a shrewd investor who understood her market and never underestimated the value of original features and a bland palette of colours.

Miss Quicke's voice might be cracked with age, but she was her usual decisive self. 'Ellie, my dear. Rose has been up all night with a tummy bug and isn't fit for anything, so I've sent her back to bed. She insisted I let you know she's poorly in case I needed something, so that you could come round and look after me. But really, there's nothing I need, as I told her. I am perfectly capable of making myself a cup of tea when necessary, and you know Rose always leaves plenty of food in the fridge, though I must admit the milk did seem a little off – this warm weather, you know – so I rather think I'll pour that down the sink. Perhaps if you're passing this way later on this morning, you could drop in another pint for me? Thank you, dear.'

Another click. This time it was Thomas,

phoning from the vicarage. 'Ellie, one of the plagues of ancient Egypt appears to have hit the parish. I had it in the night, but I always keep something in my medicine chest to stop the rot so I'm all right, but I've had to take old Mr Pole into hospital, and they're keeping him in. I hear Mrs Dawes has been hit. Are you all right? If you're still in the land of the living, do you think you could pop round to see her? Catch up with you later.'

Click, click, went the answerphone.

Mrs Dawes next. Ellie hardly recognized her voice. 'Ellie ... oh dear ... I may not be able to...' The call ended there.

Ellie heard herself groan. Whatever had she done? Remorselessly, the answerphone regurgitated its messages. Diana again. Querulous, angry. That girl had been born angry.

A fresh voice. Kate from next door. 'Ellie, I'm out for the day, over at Felicity's, some tangle with her tax. If you're around, I'm rather expecting a parcel so if you could take it in for me, I'd be grateful. See you.' Kate didn't sound as if she'd been affected.

Diana again! 'Mother, ring me!'

Thomas, sounding rather weary. 'Ellie, are you all right? Reggie's been on to me to say that Joyce has landed up in hospital. Two more members of the choir have gone down with it that I know of, so I'm ringing around to see if – oh, catch you later. There's someone at the door...'

Aunt Drusilla, concerned but patient. 'Ellie, dear? Are you there? I expected to hear from you before now, but not to worry about us. Dear Rose is up and about, but very concerned about Joyce, who's been rushed off to hospital. Rose wants to be with her daughter, but she really isn't strong enough so I forbade it. I'll get a cab and take her in this afternoon, if the girl is kept in, or maybe Roy might take her...'

Roy was her son, illegitimate but acknowledged, which made him a cousin of Ellie's. Every now and then Roy asked Ellie to marry him, but she'd never taken his offers seriously.

'...I must say, we are both extremely concerned about you. If I don't hear from you within the next hour, I'm going to start ringing the hospitals.'

Diana AGAIN! 'Mother ... oh, this is the outside of enough!'

Felicity Kingsley, her pretty voice concerned. A much younger woman, recently widowed, she was a newish but very good friend of Ellie's who lived on the other side of the Park. It was her deceased husband's complicated affairs which helped to keep Kate gainfully employed.

'Ellie, I've just heard from Roy that there's some kind of bug going round at church.' Roy, apart from being Aunt Drusilla's son, was also an architect who'd done some work

39

for Felicity, and was, truth to tell, rather taken with her – as indeed he was with every attractive woman under sixty.

'Roy says dear Rose has gone down with it, too. He had a touch of it in the night and got over it, but he says she's really poorly. Are you all right? Kate's just come round and says she hasn't seen you this morning so now we're both worried about you.'

Ellie told herself she ought to be pleased that so many people were worried about her, but in reality it was just adding to her feeling of guilt.

Roy himself came on next, sounding far too hale and hearty for someone who was feeling as fragile as Ellie. 'Ellie, shall I drop by later? This cursed stomach bug is playing havoc. My mother's all right but I'm worried about Rose, she looks completely washed out. Have you heard that Joyce has been taken to hospital? I've told my mother I'll take Rose in later on today, if the doctors say it's all right...'

Diana AGAIN!! 'Mother...!' And then a lot of heavy breathing. At this rate the tape on the answerphone would soon run out. With a bit of luck.

Someone who rang and then cut off. Probably a sales call, or maybe someone who'd called earlier and hadn't bothered to leave a message, realizing that Ellie still wasn't answering the phone.

The doorbell rang. Ellie dragged herself off her chair and made it to the front door, crunching glass underfoot.

'Well!' said Thomas. 'I'm glad to see you're still in the land of the living. And how is our very own murderess this evening?'

The housekeeper was pleased with her new method of transport; it made getting about so much easier. She'd never have thought of it, if that woman hadn't come round on her bicycle trying to sell some home-made bread rolls.

'Like to try some? Fresh baked this morning?'

The housekeeper had slammed the door in the woman's face. As if she couldn't make her own bread rolls, if she felt so inclined!

But then, she'd had an idea. Wasn't there an old bicycle in the shed at the bottom of the garden here? She'd learned to ride a bike as a child, and they say you never forgot how. The large panniers front and back would hold all that she needed, and get her to and from her other job in no time at all.

Sometimes she wished she could afford a car. Her husband had had a car and had taught her to drive, but she'd disposed of the car after he … went. A bicycle would solve a lot of her problems, not least of which was helping her to keep an eye on Lady Kingsley. She'd get it out that afternoon, and see if the tyres and brakes needed checking over. Ruby would pay for that, wouldn't she?

41

Three

Thomas had intended to make a joke of calling her a murderess. Probably.

It was all too much for Ellie. She didn't believe for a moment that she had caused everyone to go down with E coli, but at the same time she couldn't help feeling that, somehow, she must have done something wrong.

There was a moment in which she could have laughed his joking tone off, but then she decided that, no, it was all too much! And dissolved in tears.

His arms went around her in a bear hug, and she clung to him, weeping into his shoulder, feeling that for once she didn't have to be a Brave Little Woman, but could do with some cosseting for a change.

'There, there! I didn't mean ... I was only joking ... Ellie, my dear!'

'Yes, yes, I know!' She was trying to be sensible, she really was, but it was such an enormous relief to be folded into a man's embrace like this, knowing that he could take care of everything, that she didn't have to worry about anything...

Except that he stopped talking. She gasped and stopped crying because ... oh dear. Or did she mean 'Whoopee!'?

There was a tense moment in which neither of them moved, and then her neighbour Kate's voice came crashing through whatever thoughts had been passing through Ellie's head.

'Ellie, are you all right? I just popped up to the car for a moment and noticed your front door was open and ... whatever's happened to the window? Have you had a break-in or something? Oh!'

The 'Oh!' was because she'd come far enough into the hall to notice that Ellie was clutched in Thomas' embrace.

For one wild moment Ellie considered hanging on to Thomas, who was not, as it happened, showing any signs of letting her go. The word would be all round the parish in nano-seconds, of course. Ellie Quicke seducing the vicar, etcetera. She couldn't allow that to happen, for Thomas's sake. Or her own.

So she did the best thing she could to scotch any hint of a rumour before it could start. She extricated herself from Thomas, and threw herself at Kate, tears spurting like crazy. 'Oh, Kate! It's just so dreadful!'

She hung on to Kate, sobbing as wildly as she could, pushing away the memory of what had very nearly happened with Thomas to be examined later, in privacy ... because he probably hadn't meant anything by it, anyway, and Kate was one of her dearest friends and was as much of a rock in times of trouble as Thomas.

'Ellie! There, there!' said Kate, dropping whatever she'd fetched from her car, and putting her arms around her friend. 'Whatever's the matter? I don't think I've ever see you cry before.'

Ellie sobbed a couple more times. 'You should have seen me after Frank died. I couldn't stop.'

'Yes, yes, of course. So what's brought this on? Have you had a burglar? Do you want me to call the police? Is someone coming to board up your window, and who did it, anyway?'

Ellie hiccupped, sought for a hankie, didn't find one, and said, 'Storm over! Excuse me while I grab a tissue. I'm all right now, really. It was just I needed to howl for a moment or two.'

Thomas had withdrawn to the kitchen, and was standing with his back to them putting the kettle on, sensible man. Kate pushed Ellie on to a kitchen chair, found the box of tissues and set it in front of her. Ellie blew her nose hard and wondered where to start with explanations. For some reason her mind didn't seem to be in proper working order. And her tooth twanged again.

She tried to appear her normal self. 'There's been a bit of a panic, Kate. Some of the people who were at the church lunch yesterday went down with the runs last night, and a couple of them have had to be hospitalized...'

'I heard about Joyce when I was at Felicity's,' said Kate. 'Roy dropped by with a couple of tile samples for her to look at, saying he was just going to take Rose to the hospital to see her daughter, though I couldn't quite make out why. Joyce isn't in any danger, is she?'

Ellie closed her eyes and sat back in her chair, waiting for Thomas to sort it out. Which he did.

'It seems Joyce was in the early stages of pregnancy and now she's lost the baby. There's a rumour going around – which I don't believe for a minute – that Ellie didn't cook her quiches long enough, and has given us all E coli. Naturally Ellie's very upset, and I made matters worse by making a crude joke about it. Tea, everyone?'

'I'm so sorry,' said Ellie to the space between them. 'I can't think what came over me, breaking down like that.'

Two concerned faces looked down at her. Thomas: bearded, dark-haired, dark-eyed, solid. A man you could trust. Kate: tall, dark and handsome without being beautiful. A

45

woman you could trust, too.

Ellie blew her nose again and said, indistinctly through the tissue, 'Reggie Holmes called me a murderess and said he didn't want me in the choir any more ... and if I over-reacted, well, I can't help it. I've worked all my life for the church, and I wouldn't ever, not ever, have done anything to ... the prawns were fresh, and so were the eggs, and I did cook the quiches long enough. I did! I've used that recipe for years. Well, perhaps not since Frank died, but ... well, you know what I mean...'

'Yes,' said Thomas, placing a mug of tea in front of her, and pushing the tin of biscuits close to her elbow. 'We know what you mean.'

'...and I've been thinking how else my quiches could have upset so many people but I don't have any cascara or whatever that stuff is in the house, because I've never needed it, and neither had Frank.' On her second repetition of this, she suddenly realized that she had once bought some senna for Diana, but couldn't remember for the life of her whether she'd ever used any of it. She'd forgotten all about it. Perhaps it was still lurking at the back of the medicine cupboard upstairs? She couldn't go and look now, especially since she'd just declared she had never bought any. She hadn't meant to lie. Oh dear...

Thomas nudged the biscuit tin even closer, and she took a chocolate digestive biscuit and passed the tin on. She knew the chocolate would do her good, though she didn't feel at all like eating. As she bit into the biscuit, she felt that distinctive twinge in her back tooth again. She really must make an appointment to see the dentist.

Kate was into her frowning, thinking mood. 'Let me get this straight. There must have been at least a hundred people there for lunch yesterday. Armand and I only stayed for a cup of coffee and a couple of sausage rolls after the service because we wanted to feed Catriona and get out for the afternoon. I saw how much food people had brought. There must have been a couple of dozen quiches on the table, besides packs of sausage rolls and bowls of salads and ... oh, enough to feed an army. Why should anyone think Ellie's quiches were to blame?'

'Because,' said Thomas, 'most people don't have the time to cook properly any more, so they buy something to bring. There's only a few people – like Ellie – who take the trouble to cook. Of course, anyone who knows anything about food will go for the home-made stuff. The choir managed to grab three out of her four quiches and make off with them, and as far as I've been able to check so far, nearly everyone in the choir has been affected.'

Ellie stifled a little wail of horror.

Kate bent her brows even further, at her most formidable. 'What happened to the fourth quiche?'

Thomas shrugged. 'That was one of the cheese and sweetcorn ones. It stayed on the food table. Jean saved a wedge for me and I had a touch of the runs but nothing much to talk about. I assume Rose had some herself, because she also went down with it.'

Ellie picked up her mug of tea with hands that she forbade to tremble. 'We know that Rose coaxed her daughter to eat a piece, and that's why Joyce ended up in hospital. Perhaps we ought to ring Rose to find out what happened to the rest of that quiche. Oh, I can't believe this is really happening!'

Kate propped her head on her fist, thinking. 'Let's get this straight. The only way those quiches could have been responsible for an outbreak of tummy upsets would be either with the prawns or with the eggs. Ellie says they were both fresh and that she cooked the quiches the right length of time.'

'I've just remembered,' said Ellie. 'I had eggs last night for my supper from the same box, and I wasn't ill. So it can't have been the eggs, can it? It must have been the prawns.'

Thomas shook his head. 'I had a wedge from the cheese and sweetcorn quiche. I didn't have any prawns, and I got the wob-

48

bles in the night.'

'So,' said Kate. 'We can clear the quiches of blame.'

There was silence while they all considered this scenario.

Thomas said, 'Come to think of it ... Reggie's talking about E coli, but in my experience that's no quick and easy thing to deal with. It can kill the elderly and put pregnant women at risk. It can lay young children low. I suppose you could have a mild strain which would make you suffer for just a few hours, but I thought it was much more powerful than that. Remember those cruise liners where half the passengers fell ill and many had to be hospitalized? This doesn't sound like the same thing.'

'You mean that someone else's hygiene rules were less than perfect?'

Thomas shook his head. 'I don't relish asking around about it, but I don't think Reggie's going to let the matter drop. And maybe he's right not to. We've got to find the source of the problem. If Ellie's quiches aren't it, then what is?'

Ellie said, in a tiny voice, 'Perhaps ... perhaps the flour I used? Were the quiches left in a warm room too long?'

'That hall is never warm enough to set bacteria breeding.'

Kate said, 'Has there ever been any trouble like this before at a parish lunch? What about

49

that gang of youths who hang around the Green outside the church all the time. Could they have got in during the service and ... oh, I don't know ... put something in the water for coffee? They'd probably think it hilarious.'

'I suppose it's possible,' said Thomas, sipping tea. 'I've had to speak to them a couple of times for creating outside the church during a service, but I didn't think there was any real harm in them. And what would they use?'

'Cascara? Senna?' said Ellie.

Thomas put more sugar into his tea. 'People were taking food into the hall for at least half an hour before the service, while Jean and Ellie and one or two others were getting things ready. During the service? Hm. I'll check with Jean to see if she locked up the hall while the service was on, because that's the only time the place might have been deserted enough for someone to have got in and done the deed.' Thomas pulled out his mobile and pressed buttons.

Ellie closed her eyes tightly. 'If Jean's gone down with it, too, and heard Reggie's story, my name will be mud and I might as well emigrate.'

'Yoohoo!' Kate's foxy-faced husband Armand appeared in the doorway, carrying their beloved daughter Catriona, who had orange goo all round her mouth; she seemed to have been fed and therefore was at ease with the world. 'What's going on? Ellie, did you know your window's been smashed in?'

Thomas moved off into the conservatory at the back of the house, to make his phone call. Kate took Catriona from her husband, wiped the toddler's face with a tissue and explained what had happened.

'Grief!' Armand was half amused and half concerned. 'Good thing we grabbed something and left early, because otherwise we'd have made a beeline for your cooking, Ellie.'

'Thank you,' said Ellie, realizing that he intended a compliment, even if it could have been worded in more sensitive fashion. 'Can I get you a cuppa?'

Armand was enjoying the situation. 'Is it safe to drink with you?'

Kate was shocked. 'Armand!'

'Oh, don't mind me,' said Ellie, trying not to become hysterical. 'I'll soon get used to being thought a murderess, and it might cut down the number of people who drop in and expect me to give them a meal at the drop of a hat.'

Thomas came back in, rubbing his beard. 'Jean's out. I'll try her later.'

'Ellie? Are you there?' A man's voice. Six foot of silver-haired charm, her cousin Roy appeared in the doorway, ushering a fragile-looking Rose into the kitchen ahead of him. 'Did you know your front door was open, and someone's smashed a window?'

Rose was some years older than Ellie, and today looked even older than usual. Armand hastened to give her his seat at the kitchen table, which was already littered with the mugs of tea that had been made that evening. Thomas abandoned his mobile phone to scoop up the mugs and wash them at the sink.

Rose patted Ellie's arm. 'Are you all right, dear? We've been so worried about you. Dear Miss Quicke didn't want me to leave the house but my tummy seems to have calmed down now, and you know, dear, that she really can't be trusted to eat properly if I'm not there to look after her, and honestly, I'm feeling quite myself again now, and I had to see for myself that Joyce was going on all right, which of course she is, and the doctors say she can go home in the morning and she's putting a brave face on it, almost too bright, if you know what I mean, dear, and really there's plenty of time for her to start a family and everyone has babies later nowadays, don't they?'

Ellie nodded, and Kate made a sympathetic noise in her throat, though both women probably had reservations about the likelihood of Joyce permitting herself to get pregnant again in the near future.

Roy took the fourth and last chair and held out his arms to little Catriona, who was a flirtatious little madam and willingly went to him. As Kate said, it took a flirt to recognize another one, and Roy was as accomplished a flirt as you could find in a month of Sundays. Ellie liked him very much, with the proviso that if he asked her to marry him again, she'd clock him one! He was far too like her poor dear Frank to put herself through that again, and in any case, he didn't really mean it.

'Ellie,' said Roy, batting his eyelids at Catriona, who batted hers back, 'is it a stupid question, but have the police been informed?'

Everyone tried to speak at once, Ellie saying that she thought it was up to the hospital or the doctors to advise of an outbreak of food poisoning, Kate saying that she didn't think the Health and Safety people would be brought in for such an isolated outbreak, and Thomas saying that surely the police wouldn't be interested when nobody had died.

'Except Joyce's baby, of course,' said Armand.

Silence set in as everyone considered this unpalatable fact.

Roy peaked his attractive dark eyebrows. 'I meant the broken window.'

'Oh.' Ellie adjusted her thinking. 'No, I won't press charges.'

Thomas nodded, fingering his beard.

Thomas was being unusually quiet. Thomas wasn't meeting Ellie's eyes. Ellie looked at him, and felt herself begin to blush. That moment when he'd had his arms around her ... she'd better not think about that now! She noticed that Kate was also looking hard at Thomas. Kate was no fool. Kate could read Ellie well, too. Ellie opened her mouth to make some comment which might distract Kate when yet another visitor tapped on the kitchen door and came in.

Enter Bill Weatherspoon, Ellie's long-time friend and family solicitor, monkey-faced and slightly old-fashioned. 'Ellie, what's going on? Did you know your front door's open and someone's broken the window?'

Six heads turned to see who had come in; seven if you counted Catriona.

'Oh!' said Ellie, hands to her face. How could she possibly have forgotten that Bill had said he was going to drop around to-night with the programme for next season's local operatic society?

She struggled to her feet while Kate, Armand, Roy and dear Rose all tried to tell Bill what had been happening. '...thinks that something was wrong with the quiches Ellie made ... my daughter lost her baby ... we can't think who might have ... it might have been the lads who meet ... everyone in the choir went sick ... it couldn't have been Ellie who...'

'One at a time,' said Bill, exercising authority. He smiled the affectionate, indulgent smile of a parent to a wayward child. 'Ellie, have you been getting yourself mixed up in something untoward again? What am I to do with you?'

'I'm so sorry, Bill.' Ellie was penitent, because it was quite true that she usually went to Bill for advice whenever she got into a mess. 'Honestly, it wasn't my fault this time. I was minding my own business, and...' She made a helpless gesture.

Bill held on to his smile. 'That's what you always say, my dear. Well, now I'm here...' He held the kitchen door open, indicating that Ellie's guests had outstayed their welcome. Ellie didn't say anything to keep them with her, so they took the hint.

Roy sighed and handed Catriona back to Armand. Roy liked children, though he'd not had any in his own short and ill-fated marriage years ago. He said he'd take Rose home if Ellie didn't want him for anything else. Ellie said that was kind of him and she was quite all right now.

Rose was still rather tearful. 'I can't help wanting grandchildren, it's only natural, isn't it?'

Ellie gave her a hug. 'You're absolutely right, Rose. Give my love to my aunt, and say I'll pop in tomorrow to see her.'

Armand said he'd got a bit of hardboard

55

that might do to secure the window over-night, and he'd be back in a tick to attend to it. Thomas wasn't meeting Ellie's eyes, but left, promising to check back with Ellie in the morning. And Kate...?

Kate examined her hands which she'd laid out flat on the table. She said, 'No, of course not,' in an abstracted voice and removed herself, too.

Ellie accompanied her visitors to the front door and closed it behind them, trying not to worry about the broken glass on the floor. She was feeling rather limp. She looked up to see Bill making his way into the sitting-room. Ellie followed him, trying to concen-trate. On the one hand she felt the need to apologize to him for his reception, and on the other she wanted to crawl into bed and howl.

'So sorry, Bill. A storm in a teacup, I think. I hope. I was just having a bath when our organist arrived in a great state, accusing me of having laced the food I'd provided for the church lunch. His wife had miscarried and he wasn't exactly thinking straight. He called me a murderess and banned me from singing in the choir. It will probably turn out to have been a prank on the part of those lads who hang around the church. Or a virus. It was all rather upsetting.' At that moment her tooth twanged again. She really must ring the dentist and make an appointment.

'What a rigmarole,' said Bill, amused. 'Well, if you haven't got choir practice tonight, I'm taking you out to eat. It's about time we had a serious talk.'

Ellie did her best not to cower. When people said they wanted to have a serious talk, it meant they wanted to scold you about something. Years of deferring to her late husband's wishes made it hard for Ellie to defend herself against this approach, particularly when she liked and respected someone as much as she did Bill.

If only he hadn't taken up his stance with his back to the fireplace! It was a meaningless gesture, of course, since it was a hot summer's evening and there was nothing in the grate but an arrangement of dried flowers. But the fact was that the authority figures in Ellie's life – her father and her husband – had always stood in front of the fireplace to lay down the law, and now Bill was doing it, too.

Perhaps because she'd had such a trying day, it made her want to giggle. She fought the impulse, because dear Bill would never have understood her amusement.

Let's face it, he was the nicest, the very dearest of her old friends. They'd known one another for ever; she'd helped him through the bad days of his late wife's long illness, and done her best to befriend his teenage daughters as they grew up.

Then again, Bill had been wonderfully helpful to her after Frank's early death, and had always been there for her when she'd got mixed up with any funny business. He could be relied upon both for good advice and for practical help. Moreover, it was fun to go out with him in the evenings sometimes to golf club and Rotary dinners. They both enjoyed gardening, and several times a year he'd take her out to a good garden centre, where they could fill the boot of his car with interesting plants.

He deserved better than that she should laugh at him now. She told herself that it wasn't every day that she was accused of murdering someone, and that that accounted for her present case of hysteria. She scolded herself. Grow up, Ellie. This is no time for silly jokes.

It didn't seem appropriate – much as she would have liked it – to ask him to hang around while she asked Diana about the bottle of laxative which might or might not still be upstairs.

Her tooth twanged again.

'Help yourself to a glass of sherry?' she said. 'If you'll give me five minutes to change, I'd love to come out for a meal.'

'Splendid.' He helped himself to sherry, and she made her escape from the room, shutting the door carefully behind her.

The telephone was in the hall, but there was an extension in the study. First things first. Her dentist had moved into bright new premises in the Avenue. He might or might not still be there at this time of the evening, but she knew from experience that when a tooth began to twinge like this, there was no point in pretending that the problem would disappear overnight. She had heard that most people waited two days – two days! – with toothache before they contacted a dentist, but she was not one of them. She went for her check-ups as soon as they were due, and never missed an appointment. She punched in numbers and waited for the answer machine to click in.

There were many other things she ought to be doing, such as contacting Mrs Dawes to see how she was coping, and checking that Joyce was coming on all right, and Diana, of course; but when you had toothache, everything else paled into insignificance.She left a message asking for an appointment urgently, and then rushed upstairs, not to change her clothes but to delve into the back of the medicine cabinet, where sure enough ... oh dear, how had she come to overlook it? There was a bottle of senna tablets, rather aged by now; in fact, well past the sell-by date. The seal had been broken. There was a plug of cotton-wool in the top, which she pulled out. The bottle seemed pretty full to her, but it was impossible to tell how many tablets might or might not have been used, since she didn't know how many there ought to be in the first place.

So, she'd lied when she told the others that she'd none in the house. Misery me. She sat on the edge of the bath, wondering what to do about it. She hadn't meant to lie. She'd genuinely forgotten that she'd got them. It would sound awful if she rang them up now, and said, Listen, I've just remembered...

And anyway, it had probably been those boys larking about.

A gentle popping sound made her look down into the bath, where the last of her beautiful bubbles were disappearing. She pulled the plug to let the water out, with regret for the time when she'd lain there, enjoying herself, little knowing what was going to happen.

She looked at the beautiful satin underwear she'd bought that day, but decided that she didn't have time to put it on. She found a pretty, wide-necked blouse and matching skirt in a subdued grey – Bill liked her to dress up a bit when he took her out – found a more or less matching pair of shoes and a rose pink cardigan, brushed out her hair, made a pass with some cream powder at her nose, decided she needed a stronger lipstick than the one she had on, couldn't find the one she wanted so made do with the pale pink one, collected her small handbag and transferred keys and cards and hanky to it, and was ready.

No, she wasn't. Back she went for her mobile phone, switching it on to see if there were any messages there. There weren't. Very few people had that number, and even fewer knew it, because they were aware that she rarely switched it on and kept it for emergency use only. As for texting! Kate next door had tried to teach her to text, but the lesson hadn't taken.

Bill had his car outside. He changed his car every two years, of course. 'Do you mind Graham's Grill?' This was the latest restaurant to open in the neighbourhood, and was supposed to be very pricey.

'Lovely,' she said, wondering if she ought to have put on something a little more up-market. Well, too late.

Graham's Grill was on the ground floor of a large Edwardian house at the end of the Avenue. The bar in the foyer had suitably murky lighting, and the menus were so large it was hard for Ellie – who was not tall – to see over them. Bill advised her what she would like to eat, and she smiled and nodded, because she really did not feel like having another argument.

The intermittent pain in her tooth was settling down to a not so dull ache. She'd have to take some painkillers when she'd eaten.

'Now, my dear...' said Bill. And at that moment her mobile phone rang. She hadn't remembered switching it on but perhaps she had done so without realizing it.

Muttering an excuse, she extracted it from her bag and pressed the green button.

'Ellie? Thomas here. I wanted to speak to you before you heard from anyone else. I've been on to the hospital about old Mr Pole. He died a few minutes ago.'

'Oh, that's terrible.' Ellie couldn't think of anything else to say.

'I'm on my way over there now. No one else knows as yet, but you'd better be prepared. I'll try to have a word with the lads outside the church when I get back, but if they won't admit responsibility and the police are brought in on it, Reggie will have his say.'

'Yes.' She thought of the opened bottle of senna, and didn't know what to do. Thomas rang off, and she shut off her mobile. Replacing it in her bag, she realized to her horror that she'd brought the bottle of senna instead of the painkillers she'd intended to take. Now what was she to do? Confess all to Bill? Yes, but ... she felt so stupid about this. And guilty. Though really she couldn't think how she could have made such a stupid mistake as to put senna in her quiches. Yet somehow, that's what had happened and she had to face facts.

Bill was looking annoyed. Quite rightly. A man didn't take a woman out to supper only to have her spending all her time on her mobile, did he?

'Sorry,' she said. 'Mr Pole died in hospital. I'm afraid some people will say that I hastened his death, because although he was very old—'

'My dear girl.' Bill took one of her hands in both of his. 'It distresses me to see you taking all the problems of the world on your shoulders. I promised Frank that I'd look after you, and goodness knows, you've managed to get yourself into some pretty scrapes since then, all because you allow people to involve you in their lives.'

Ellie opened her mouth to contradict him but the waiter deflected her attention by slipping a plate of seafood salad in front of her, which gave her time to reflect that Bill did have a point. She hadn't gone looking for problems, but when her friends had got into trouble she hadn't thought twice about getting involved.

'You're right, of course,' she said. 'But I can't sit and twiddle my thumbs when my friends need help.' The wine waiter approached with a bottle of chilled white wine. Bill tasted it, and nodded. The waiter poured her out a glass, and she tried not to flinch. Chilled wine on her aching tooth would be just too much. 'Might I have a glass of tap water, please? No ice or lemon.' The wine waiter raised his eyebrows, indicating that patrons of Graham's Grill didn't usually ask for water with their meals. Maybe she'd get it and maybe she wouldn't.

Bill squeezed lemon juice. 'I've been giving this some thought, Ellie, and I've come to the conclusion you've been rushing into all sorts of activities which are not really your scene, because you've been trying to fill the vacuum created by Frank's death. For instance, your previous vicar bullied you into joining the choir, which you've never really enjoyed doing, have you? And when I think of all the years you've spent serving coffees and teas and washing up for the church ... well, words fail me!'

'You have a point,' said Ellie, trying to think clearly over insistent toothache.

'I have a solution to offer,' said Bill, clearing his plate. 'I'm at a loose end now I've retired, and we've agreed you've far too much time on your hands ... so let's combine the two. What do you say, Ellie? We've been such good friends for years. Let's make it permanent, shall we?'

'You mean...?'

'Marriage, of course. Separate bedrooms, naturally. I could do with some congenial company and heaven knows, you need someone to look after you. Agreed?'

Chameleons could adapt themselves to blend in with their surroundings. The housekeeper decided that she would be a chameleon, too. She found a shabby padded jacket in the charity shop similar to that worn by the woman who went round on her bicycle selling bread rolls. The perfect disguise. It amused her to think that she could deliver her 'goodies' to any house in the district, and everyone would think they came from the other woman.

She'd wrapped the empty packets of laxative in newspaper and pushed them into a litter bin in the Avenue. Dropping the bag of rolls off at church had been an inspiration. That stupid vicar had taken them in himself. She hoped he'd eaten at least two. That would teach him to invite Ruby to church, making out he was really interested in her. Well, no one would visit a church where everyone fell sick, would they?

Four

Ellie sat at her kitchen table, gazing into space. In one hand she held a packet of paracetamol, from which she'd just extracted two, downing them with a glass of water. In the other hand she clutched the bottle of senna.

While she waited for the paracetamol to kick in, she marvelled at everything that had happened to her that day. She'd woken up that morning feeling moderately pleased with herself and her life. She'd gone shopping and perhaps been a little self-indulgent. And then...

Reggie Holmes and his accusation. She looked down at the bottle of senna. She'd clutched it so hard that she had difficulty in letting go. Her face burned as she remembered Reggie's accusation. 'Murderess!' He'd knocked her off balance and she wasn't sure she'd recovered yet, particularly since Thomas's embrace had introduced a new element into the confusion that ruled her mind.

Don't think about Thomas for the moment! She needed a calm space in her life before she could consider what that might mean. It had been so surprising, and yet ... no, she mustn't think about that yet. There's too much else to think about now.

Think about Bill's proposal, which she ought to have seen coming because he'd been hinting for some months that he'd enjoy a closer relationship with her. Ever since Frank had died, Bill had taken her out for meals now and then, and she accompanied him on formal occasions when he needed a partner. It had all been very low key and enjoyable. Ellie had once or twice thought about taking the next step along the road to re-marrying, but had always deferred serious consideration ... it was too soon ... she liked him enormously, but...

Then he'd come out with a proposal at the restaurant, just like that, when she was feeling really down and her tooth had been giving her merry hell and she'd forgotten her painkillers. His kindness, his loving care of her, had broken through her hard-won self-reliance, and she'd found herself searching for a hankie in her bag. In tears. For heaven's sake, why had she had to cry, just at that moment?

Bill had taken her tears as agreement that she needed looking after, and had moved his chair closer so that he could put his arm around her shoulders. Part of her had liked that, while the other part had been annoyed with herself for having broken down.

The situation had deteriorated further when two of her dearest friends passed by on their way to another table and paused to say hello, with questions in their eyes as to why Ellie was being comforted so intimately by her solicitor.

Bill had made the most of the interruption. 'Roy: well met again. Lady Kingsley. Congratulate me. I've just asked Ellie to marry me, and she hasn't said no.'

Her cousin Roy had hesitated a fraction of a second before saying, with considerable warmth, 'Well done, you two! Ellie, you've chosen the better man, I'm sure. Let's have some champagne to celebrate.'

How many times had Roy asked her to marry him in the past? Six or seven times? She'd lost count. She was very fond of him and flattered by his interest, but she'd never taken him seriously as a prospective husband. Well, it was true that she'd experienced some fleeting moments of jealousy when he'd turned his attentions to other women – which he did every now and then – but that was all.

The other woman that evening was her much younger friend, and Kate's employer, Felicity Kingsley. It wasn't surprising to find the two of them patronizing this up-market restaurant. Roy liked to go to such places and he liked the company of pretty women.

Felicity favoured Ellie with a slightly puzzled look before kissing her cheek. 'Dear Ellie, I'm so glad for you.'

'Oh, but nothing has been settled yet,' said Ellie, disengaging herself from Bill, and blowing her nose. 'Really it hasn't. I mean ... dear Bill, give me a chance to catch my breath.'

Most people wrote Felicity off as a dumb blonde, but she could be acute at times. 'Do you mean, "Oh, sir, this is so sudden"?'

Ellie managed half a laugh. 'Something like that, yes.'

Bill said, 'Nonsense. This has been on the cards for ever. You didn't say no, Ellie, so I'm taking that as a provisional yes. Roy, Lady Kingsley: will you join us?'

'Definitely champagne,' said Roy, beckoning the waiter over. 'Keep up the pressure, Bill. I've never known anyone in need of a husband as much as Ellie. I made some moves in her direction myself, but she was wise enough to tell me to go and play elsewhere. Right, Ellie?'

What could Ellie do but smile and enjoy all the attention she was getting? The ache in her tooth subsided a trifle, and she found herself liking the way that Bill looked after her. It was pleasant to be pampered for a change, and to see Bill laughing and smiling; he'd had far too little to laugh about in recent years.

She wished she'd put on a better outfit, but there was always a crumple in the rose leaf, wasn't there?

Later that evening Ellie sat at her kitchen table, half listening to the tock of the grandmother clock in the hall, clutching a packet of paracetamol, and marvelling at the way her life had been turned topsy turvy in one short day.

The future looked bright, didn't it? She need never worry about anything ever again. Bill would stop her being badgered by people to do this and that for them. Looking after her finances – which had caused her many a headache, in spite of the fact that she'd put most of her inheritance into a trust fund – would be done by someone far more competent than herself. She would be able to move from this small semi to Bill's beautiful old house with a garden that ran down to the River Thames.

She would spend time on herself and dress tastefully and expensively, as was expected of Bill's wife. Bill had plenty of money, too, and they wouldn't need to worry about scraping along on an inadequate pension. They would travel, perhaps go on a world tour. Cruises? Probably. She would be looked after beautifully for the rest of her life.

It was a most attractive proposition.

Wasn't it?

She sighed. The paracetamol was kicking in. She relinquished the rest of the packet and picked up the bottle of senna tablets again. Sell-by date: long past. They probably didn't sell senna in bottles nowadays. The bottle was nearly full. How many pills would there have been originally? She hadn't a clue.

How many tablets would have been necessary to produce such a devastating effect on so many members of the church? What was the dosage – two per night per person – but the dosage could be increased. How many tablets would it take to upset all the members of the choir plus Joyce and Rose and Thomas? There were twelve members of the choir, so ... at least twenty-four?

She emptied the bottle out on to a plate and counted. There were forty-eight pills left in the bottle and the bottle was nearly full. Perhaps there had been fifty tablets originally? Which meant that two had been used at some time. Two tablets couldn't possibly have had such a dire effect.

Therefore: this senna bottle had not been the villain in the case.

She felt herself relax a couple of notches.

She told herself that she *knew* all along that she hadn't been the one who'd interfered with the quiches. She'd been knocked off balance by Reggie Holmes, and then there'd been the toothache ... she pressed her tongue against the offending tooth and hardly felt anything. Paracetamol was a wonderful antidote to pain, provided you didn't take too many.

So if she hadn't done it, then the lads outside the church must have been the culprits. Thomas would deal with them.

Midge jumped down from the chair opposite her, where he'd been having a pre-nighttime snooze, and stretched, yawning horribly. She gave him his last dollop of food for the day and tidied the kitchen till he was ready to go up to bed.

She loved her kitchen now that it had been refitted. It was so much lighter and easier to clean than the old one, yet she had far more cupboard space and work surfaces. She had cupboards that swung out from corners, and racks of narrow shelves that pulled out on wheels. A dishwasher – not that she used that much – and an eye-level oven.

Her old kitchen had been installed by Frank many years ago and it had never been particularly clever or convenient. This one – she caressed the granite work surface with a smile – was fit for a queen. In fact, she spent a lot of time in the kitchen, sitting at one of the chairs round the glass-topped table and looking out through the conservatory to the slope of her pretty garden. More time than she spent in her green living-room which, to tell the truth, was looking a bit tired nowadays.

Perhaps she'd consult Kate and Felicity – who had both helped her redesign the kitchen – about doing up the living-room.

Oh. But if she was going to marry Bill...?

Well, sufficient unto the day. Midge led the way up the stairs to bed.

The housekeeper couldn't sleep. Over and over she replayed the moment when she'd seen Lady Kingsley crossing the road from the retirement home, waving to a friend and getting into his car. A man friend, and her with her husband not dead a year!

Lady Kingsley had taken what was rightly hers, and must pay for it. If only she hadn't used the last of her sleeping tablets on the rolls which Paddy had eaten! Sleeping tablets added to alcohol was a lethal mixture, as she'd proved in the past.

The housekeeper took an indigestion remedy, telling herself that she'd get even in time. One of these days Felicity Kingsley was going to be very very dead, and if it took a little longer than planned ... well, anticipation was a joy in itself, wasn't it?

She went downstairs and made herself a hot drink in the kitchen. She'd left a hot drink in a flask beside the old man's bed, and he was still capable of going to the toilet by himself, thank goodness. Ruby had come in an hour ago, tumb-

ling over in the hall, drunk as a newt, as usual. The drink would kill her before the old man popped his clogs at this rate.

All was not gloom and doom, though. Only that morning she'd made a wonderful discovery when turning out a cupboard in the kitchen. An old-fashioned pestle and mortar. So useful for crushing up spices – and other things.

She'd given the pestle and mortar a thorough clean and left them to drain. She wouldn't use a drying-up cloth, because that might transfer germs, and you could never be too careful when you were experimenting.

Soon ... soon...!

The phone rang as Ellie took in the milk next morning. Half past eight. She'd had to get up to take some more paracetamol in the night, and had overslept.

It was the dentist's receptionist. He was fully booked that day. Would she be able to wait till the end of the week? There was a slot on Friday afternoon free? Or, if the pain became too much, she could come in and wait for him to see if he could fit her in between other clients.

Miraculously, the tooth was hardly twanging that morning, so she said she'd take the Friday slot. She put the phone down and it rang again.

This time it was Thomas, rather more formal than usual. Ellie supposed he was embarrassed by the memory of that moment in which ... well, he'd not meant it in any romantic fashion, had he? It was just one of those men things. They'd no control, had they? She would follow his lead and pretend it had never happened.

'Ellie, good morning. Sorry to ring so early. Are you all right?'

'Yes, I'm fine. And you?'

'Fine, yes. I thought you'd like to know I went back to the hospital last night, and the nurse said there's got to be an autopsy for Mr Pole.'

Ellie winced, and her tooth twinged. If there was an inquest, then Reggie Holmes would have his say and it would all come out that he thought Ellie had poisoned the quiches. 'I'm sure it wasn't my cooking that...'

'Agreed. But something went wrong and we've got to find out what it was. I had a word with the lads outside the church last night, and they're in the clear. They claim they went to a football match in the park on Sunday morning, a local derby. I checked, and they did. And now I come to think of it, we'd have seen them if they had been around on Sunday morning.'

Ellie felt as if someone had hit her in her midriff. Obviously she'd placed too much reliance on the boys being responsible.

Thomas continued, 'Now, I know it's a

weekday and a lot of people will be going to work. Also we usually have a few people helping to tidy up the flower beds around the church on Tuesday mornings...'

Ellie had forgotten that it was Tuesday and gardening time. Everyone usually came over to her place for elevenses afterwards.

'...but I think we ought to cancel that. We've quite a few parishioners who are about during the day-time. I'm asking every-one who can make it to come to a meeting in the room at the back of the church hall today, at ten o'clock. Please spread the word around. We need to get a picture of what everyone ate. We can't have the main hall because the Toddlers' Group will be in there. Can you make it?'

'Of course.' It was a relief, really, not to have to go out gardening that morning. She really did not need her life to be any more complicated than it was already. Besides, it looked like being another hot day; too hot for serious gardening.

They couldn't meet at the vicarage because it was being rebuilt at the moment, with Thomas lodged in temporary accommoda-tion. Ellie had been wondering whether or not she really ought to go along to the dentist's and wait to be seen. Well, this meet-ing at church must take priority. She mustn't forget to collect her little grandson from reception class at noon.

Oh dear; if Reggie told his story to the newspapers ... if there was an inquest and everybody read that she'd laced the quiches with poison ... it didn't bear thinking about.

The phone rang again before she got to the kitchen with the milk. Aunt Drusilla. 'Ellie, my dear. Roy's just dropped in to tell me that you've got yourself engaged to Bill Weatherspoon. Is that true?'

Ellie groaned. 'He seems to think so, but...' She let the sentence hang.

'Hrrmph! A pleasant enough man. I knew his parents, and his first wife, of course. Old money, and plenty of it.' Miss Quicke always knew things like that. 'I had once hoped that you and Roy ... but no, I suppose he really isn't up to your weight.'

Ellie tried not to giggle. She was not a big woman, and Roy probably weighed fourteen stone and was over six foot tall. 'You flatter me.'

'I never flatter.' Which was true. 'I'd like to see the lad settled before I die...'

This made Ellie smile. Miss Quicke had no intention of dying. Since her operation for a new hip, she'd become as spry as she'd been at sixty.

'Are you trying to blackmail me?'

Miss Quicke didn't just laugh, she cackled. 'Rose says she wants to be matron of honour at your wedding.'

'Oh, but Aunt Drusilla—'

'I said she shouldn't count her chickens before they're hatched.'

'Mm. I haven't exactly said ... at least, Bill is a lovely man and I'm very fond of him, but...'

'Just what I thought. Now, changing the subject, are you going to the meeting at church today? Roy said he didn't think I'd want to bother, but I'm not having dear Rose getting food poisoning without doing something about it. Rose says she's feeling fine now, and is talking about picking up Joyce from the hospital and going back home with her, staying overnight to see that she's going to be all right. Personally, I think Joyce is as tough as an old boot, and it's Rose who could do with being looked after, because although she says she's all right, I don't think she's fully recovered yet.'

'Aunt Drusilla, are you sure you weren't affected? What did you eat at the lunch?'

'I had a piece of your prawn and egg quiche. I thought it lacked a trifle of salt, but there! I do realize it's the latest food fad to cut down on salt.'

Ellie couldn't get the words out fast enough. 'And you're feeling perfectly all right? Not ill at all?'

'Of course not. Your cooking usually agrees with me.'

'I'm glad about that.' Ellie wound up the conversation feeling a bubble of excitement.

Aunt Drusilla had eaten some of her quiche and hadn't been ill!

Ellie's hope strengthened that perhaps her quiches had not been to blame after all. The phone rang again.

Diana, at her most peremptory. 'Mother, I'm ringing to make sure you remember to pick up little Frank this afternoon, and I'm just checking my diary, and I'm free tomorrow morning at about ten. Little Frank will be at school, so I'll have an hour and a half to spare. Will you meet me there, or shall I drop by and pick you up?'

Ellie felt her tooth twinge again. She couldn't think straight when that happened. 'What's that about, dear?'

Diana had been born impatient. 'Oh, Mother, I told you! I need you to look at this house I want you to buy with me. It's ripe for redevelopment. Now the market's so flat, I think I can get it for a knock-down price. We can go halves, if you like.'

'I don't like,' said Ellie, trying to keep a civil tone. 'Anyway, I'm not in any position to subsidize you. Bill Weatherspoon's asked me to marry him.'

'What?' A long pause in which Ellie could hear Diana's rapid breathing. 'Ah, well in that case … you'll be moving out, won't you? So you can let me have your house, which is going to be mine on your death, anyway. I'll put it on the market immediately, which will

79

tide me over nicely till—'

'No, Diana. That's not what I—'

Diana had already put the phone down.

Ellie put her tongue out at the phone, knowing it was a childish gesture, but finding it relieved her feelings. Why did Diana persist in thinking the house would be hers after Ellie's death, when she was only due to inherit half under her father's will and Ellie herself had no intention of leaving her half to Diana? In fact, she'd made a will leaving it to a trust fund. And, bother it, she'd meant to ask Diana about the bottle of senna.

There'd been no phone call from Bill. Perhaps that was just as well. She really couldn't make up her mind what she felt about his proposal. Yes, she was flattered; yes, she liked him enormously ... but...

It was time to get a move on if she wasn't going to be late for the meeting.

It took some nerve for Ellie to push open the door to the church hall. She was a fraction of a minute late, due to having changed her clothes twice before deciding to wear a blue denim skirt with a pretty pink top. She wanted to appear respectable but not dowdy; a classically cut skirt to emphasize that she was a good cook, but in a modern material to make the point that she was not so ancient in years that she'd mixed senna into a recipe for quiches. The pink top was to show she didn't care what people thought about her.

'There you are, dear.' In the back row Mrs Dawes moved her chair a couple of inches along, so that Ellie could sit beside her. Mrs Dawes tended to overflow chairs. Ellie slipped into the seat with a subdued query about Mrs Dawes' health.

'All right now, dear. I think I even lost a little weight.'

The room was crowded. Had Aunt Drusilla and Rose made it? They lived beyond the parish boundaries but were regular attendees – at least, Rose was regular, and Aunt Drusilla came when she felt like it. Ellie couldn't see them. Everyone was talking at once. Thomas sat at a table up front, with one of the church-wardens on one side of him and Jean the bully on the other. Reggie Holmes was in the front row, arms folded, glaring at Thomas. (Why was he glaring at Thomas? Had he been airing his views too openly and had Thomas reined him in?)

Everyone she could see she knew by sight, and most of them she knew by name. Roy leaned back from the row in front of her to smile at Ellie and say, 'Hi!' That nice woman, Maggie something, who often helped out with the coffee rota, was sitting beyond Mrs Dawes. She smiled at Ellie, and twiddled her fingers in greeting. Quite a few members of the choir were there. Ellie braced herself to receive some unfriendly looks, and yes, there were one or two but perhaps not as many as she'd feared.

Thomas rapped on the table, and the room fell silent. Thomas had a natural gift for controlling people. 'Morning, everyone. So glad you could make it. Let us be quiet and draw our thoughts together for a moment, asking God to be with us at this difficult time...'

People bowed their heads in prayer. It was a moment of comfort in the midst of turmoil.

Thomas said 'Amen,' and cleared his throat. People righted themselves in their chairs and paid attention. 'As you know,' said Thomas, 'some of us experienced a problem after Sunday's faith lunch. For most people it was a passing inconvenience but Mr Pole had to be hospitalized and has since died...'

A rustle of dismay, but no tears. Mr Pole had not been a nice man.

'...and as he hadn't seen a doctor for some time...'

A ripple of suppressed amusement. Mr Pole had been a misogynist who'd never married, had never voted for their excellent woman member of parliament, had said he'd leave any church that accepted women in the pulpit, and had resigned from his local health practice when they took on a woman

82

doctor.

'...there will have to be an autopsy...'

'*And* an inquest.' That was Reggie, making his point.

Thomas inclined his head. 'It may well come to that, yes. At the moment all we know is that certain people who ate here on Sunday were subsequently taken ill. I've called this meeting because...'

'You are *not* going to hush this up,' said Reggie. 'I know you think that—'

'Reggie, I have every sympathy for your distress but my brief is to care for everyone who has been affected, not just for the people who attended church and fell ill but for the church itself. The thought that the papers might say people were poisoned because they went to church sends shivers down my spine.'

Reggie uncrossed and recrossed his arms, scowling. There was a solid silence in the room as people registered that this incident could indeed have some nasty repercussions.

Thomas let his eyes wander round the room. 'Whether the autopsy proves that Mr Pole died of natural causes or not, whether the police get involved or not, I personally want to find out what happened. For our sakes, for the sake of our church, we have to get at the truth. So let's put aside all pre-conceived notions, shall we, and get some facts down on paper? Agreed, everyone?'

83

Most people nodded. A few were stiff-necked, but thoughtful. One or two glanced Ellie's way. She felt herself redden, but refused to drop her head or slink out of the room, which is what she wanted to do.

Only, she really hadn't done it, had she?

'First of all,' Thomas said, 'there was a suggestion that the lads who are often to be found meeting on the Green, outside the church, might have been responsible. I wish to make it clear that they had nothing to do with it. Which means that we must try to trace where the outbreak started, ourselves.' Thomas checked that the church-warden beside him was ready to take notes.

'Now, I'd like us to make a list of everyone who was affected. We know that practically everyone in the choir ... yes, Reggie, I have your list here. Now, who else was ill after the event? If you have heard of anyone ... yes? Rose McNally, of course. And? Yes ... will you repeat that name, please?'

Other names were proffered, and somewhat to Ellie's surprise they were names she didn't immediately recognize.

Thomas checked with the church-warden: 'Have you got all that? Yes ... at the back there? Any more...? Yes ... that's more than I thought. How many...?'

The church-warden did some adding up. 'Thirty names, so far. There may be others, of course, that we haven't heard about.'

Thomas stroked his beard. 'A good round number.'

Reggie added another name, at which several people half laughed and stirred in their seats. This particular person was known as Miss Hypochondria, and adding her to the list would probably not prove anything one way or the other.

Thomas flattened out his hands on the table. 'Yes, well ... we all know that that particular lady suffers from many complaints, so—'

Reggie was ready to explode. 'Why are you wasting our time like this? We all know who did it! Why don't you just come right out with it and say you're trying to protect Mrs Quicke, which is utterly disgraceful and I'm going to the bishop about it!'

There was a general stir in the room, while Ellie felt herself lose all colour. How could Reggie! That was the most appalling suggestion! Yes, Thomas did like her, but he'd never ever ... well, not until last night, and that had been a moment of madness ... and as for suggesting that he'd lie or cheat to please her – no way!

Apparently there were still a few people who hadn't heard Reggie's theory. Several heads were turned in her direction.

'How dare you!' A magisterial voice from the far side of the room. Ellie knew that voice. She craned her neck forward to see that Miss Quicke was ensconced by the far window, with dear Rose at her side. Miss Quicke's voice could cut through steel. 'I ate some of Ellie's quiche and suffered no ill effects whatsoever! Whatever private disappointment may have come your way, young man, you have no right to slander the innocent.'

Thomas leaned forward. 'Miss Quicke: would you confirm exactly what you did eat on Sunday?'

'A slice of Ellie's egg and prawn quiche – cheese does not agree with me, so I didn't try that – and a small square of shortbread. Very pleasant. Dear Rose had the same, plus a sausage roll, but I never eat more than one piece of pastry at a time. Yes, Rose was very ill afterwards. Perhaps you should be enquiring who brought the sausage rolls?'

A stout woman with a florid complexion half rose in her seat. 'There was nothing wrong with my sausage rolls. I got them from Marks & Spencer's in the Broadway.'

'Their sausage rolls are always good,' said a thin woman with sparse hair. 'I brought some, too. I don't cook, since my hubby left me.'

Reggie wasn't giving up his vendetta easily. 'Perhaps, Miss Quicke...' and what a sneer he put into his words, '...you think to protect your niece from a law suit by lying about what you ate!'

'Young man!' said Miss Quicke, awfully. 'I am not in the habit of lying, and what is more, I do not go around making false accusations which I cannot prove. Instead of allowing yourselves to be led down blind alleys, you should all be making lists of what each one of you ate on Sunday, stating whether you were ill or not afterwards. See if you can find any common factors. Is that clear?'

'I second that,' said another well-known voice. Ellie craned forward to see her next-door neighbour, Kate, with Catriona asleep in her arms.

Thomas said meekly, 'Just what I was about to suggest. Now, not everyone could make it this morning, but with a bit of luck we can work out what went wrong. Jean here will give out paper and pens and I want you to write your name at the top of the sheet, followed by a yes or a no, as to whether you were ill or not afterwards. Below that, write down what you ate, in detail. On a second sheet, please write your name at the head, and below that, what you brought for others to eat.

'I already know that Jean, Maggie and Ellie barely had a chance to nibble anything, they were so busy looking after everyone else. What I want them to do is to settle themselves down at a table in the corner and write down as much as they can remember of who

87

brought what food into the hall.'

Ellie half expected him to say, 'I'll give you ten minutes,' like a school-teacher. But he didn't. Instead, he conferred with the church-warden, who left the hall.

Ellie clambered over legs to the small table in the corner, closely followed by Maggie. Jean thrust sheets of paper at her, Ellie delved into her handbag for a pen, and tried to concentrate. It wasn't easy.

She thought back to when she'd arrived early on Sunday morning, carrying her quiches and tea-towels, that sort of thing. She'd found a bag containing packets of biscuits and small cakes dumped on the floor just outside the door and carried that in with her. They'd probably been put there by Reggie, who would have arrived early to sort out his music for the service. Joyce didn't cook.

She wrote down, 'Ellie Quicke: four quiches. Reggie/Joyce?: two packets each of biscuits and small cakes.'

When she'd arrived, Jean had been laying white paper tablecloths on two big tables while Maggie had been hauling another table into the hall. Jean always brought crisps and nuts. When Ellie had put her bags down, she'd helped Jean lay out plates, large and small and ... then serving platters, ready for the food as it arrived. She'd put her four quiches at one end of the tables and the sweet biscuits and cakes at the other. Maggie had brought some bowls of salad stuffs: a bean salad and a mixed green salad. Plus a couple of bottles of different salad dressings. Those had gone next to the quiches.

Mrs Dawes had put her head round the door and handed in a tin containing some of her famous shortbread. Dear Rose had brought a home-baked fruit cake, weighing a ton. Rose had stayed on to help, laying out cups and saucers for tea and coffee.

When Thomas had set them this task, Ellie had at first thought it would be impossible to work out who had brought what, but over the years people did tend to bring the same things, time and again, so it wasn't as hard as she'd thought. Routine saved thinking time. Ellie's list grew.

'Time!' said Thomas, as the church-warden returned bearing a sheaf of papers. 'Now, I want you all to keep the lists of what you ate; but Roy, would you gather up the lists of what food people brought and give them to Jean? Jean, would you compare your lists of what people brought with the lists made at your table?'

There was a general shuffling around as the lists were passed to the front and gathered up.

'Now,' said Thomas, 'would you please divide into groups of three or four. We've photocopied the list of those afflicted, and each group will have one of those. See if you can spot what the victims ate that nobody else did.'

Everyone looked glum, but nobody rebelled.

Jean, Ellie and Maggie concentrated. A subdued murmur rose from the hall as everyone got down to their tasks.

Jean read out what she'd got on her list; Ellie and Maggie ticked the items off. There was just one item left on Ellie's list which didn't appear on the others.

Jean was annoyed with herself. 'I'd forgotten about them. I remember putting them out on a tray – they went like hot cakes – but I don't remember who brought them. Ah well, let's look at the lists of what people say they brought.'

They concentrated again. No one claimed to have brought the mystery items.

'I can't be sure,' said Maggie. 'But didn't Thomas bring them?'

Thomas? All three heads turned to look at Thomas just as Felicity – sitting just beyond Roy – put up her hand. 'Thomas, it sounds silly, and probably lots of people haven't put it down on their lists because they wouldn't think it important, but we have a match here – apart from Ellie's quiches, that is. People do tend to overlook them, don't they?'

'What's that?' asked Thomas, not noticeably perturbed.

'Well, someone from the choir who'd been ill said they had a bread roll—'

'Oh!' Rose bobbed up. 'I had a bread roll, too. But I don't think I wrote it down on my list.'

'So did I,' said Mrs Dawes. 'In fact, I would have had two, but Mr Pole had the last one. He said they were nice and soft, just as he liked them. Teeth, you know.'

Ellie's next-door neighbour lifted her pencil. 'They're here, too.'

Thomas turned to Jean. 'So who brought the bread rolls?'

Jean quailed. Ellie had never seen Jean quail before. The idea of accusing Thomas of poisoning church members was too much for her. Maggie and Ellie exchanged looks. Ellie half rose in her seat. 'No one thinks you made them, Thomas, but I seem to remember you bringing them into the hall. You didn't bake them yourself, did you?'

Five

Sensation! A subdued murmur ran through the room, and then there was a silence in which they could clearly hear the voices of toddlers at play in the big hall next door, and a van drawing up outside in the street.

Thomas was frowning, stroking his beard. Reggie was flexing his neck, looking this way and that, also frowning. He didn't want his nice theory being messed up by new evidence.

'Bread rolls?' said Thomas. 'No, I didn't bake any bread rolls. I did have one, yes. It was good. Freshly baked, but I don't recollect...'

Ellie prompted him. 'You brought them in while we were setting up. Don't you remember? In a plastic bag?'

Thomas's face cleared. 'Oh, that! The bag was just outside the door here, and I thought the donor had been in a hurry to get into church, perhaps had to look after an elderly relative or a child, and been in too much of a hurry to hand it in properly. Yes, I picked it up and brought it in. Jean said to dump it on the table, and I did. Does anyone know who brought it?'

Silence. Heads were shaken all round.

'If we could find the bag they came in...' said Jean.

Maggie scotched that one. 'Dustbin day today, and they've already been and gone.'

Jean didn't like this. 'The rolls all went. Every last one of them. There were thirty. Oh.' Realization struck. 'And we've got thirty people who were ill afterwards.'

Reggie was loath to give up his vendetta. 'Thirty-one. It needn't have been the rolls. It could just as easily have been the quiches.'

Roy lifted his fistful of papers. 'There's nothing else that matches in my batch. Two members of the choir had quiche, but no roll. And they were perfectly all right afterwards.'

'Same here,' said Kate, cuddling Catriona, who had now woken up and was looking around, bleary-eyed. 'But we've got someone here who had a bread roll and a piece of quiche, and went down with it.'

Felicity was biting her forefinger, worrying away at some thought or other. Ellie tried to catch her eye, but didn't succeed.

Miss Quicke got to her feet by numbers, using her stick for best effect. 'Well, I had quiche but no roll, and no trouble. Rose had quiche, sausage roll and bread roll, and she was up all night. I suggest that if there aren't

93

any other pointers, we start looking for who-ever brought the bread rolls and started all this pother, and dismiss the charges against my niece.'

Thomas smoothed out a grin. 'This isn't a court of law, Miss Quicke, but I take your point. You agree, Reggie?'

'I ... you haven't proved anything, one way or the other.'

Thomas ignored that. 'Now, who do we know who bakes their own rolls?'

'I've got a bread-maker,' said a buxom young mother, 'but I don't make rolls. I don't know anyone who does, apart from the shops, that is.'

Jean shook her head. 'Those rolls weren't shop-bought. They were home-made. They weren't an even enough shape for shop-bought.'

Felicity was tugging at a strand of blonde hair. She made as if to speak, then subsided again.

'There is someone,' said an elderly woman at the back. 'She goes round on her bike, ringing doorbells and offering freshly baked rolls for sale. They're not bad. I've had them a couple of times.'

'Oh. Her.' A neighbour nodded. 'Yes, but she doesn't come to church. At least I've never seen her.'

'I've seen her around on her bike...'

'She doesn't come every week, but...'

'I never buy at the door.'

Thomas brought the meeting to order. 'This is important. Does anyone know the name of this woman, or where she lives?'

Some people shook their heads. 'Never asked her...'

'She never said.'

Ellie looked at Felicity, who was now biting her lip and gazing at the floor. Did Felicity know something about this woman? And if so, why wasn't she spitting it out?

Thomas said, 'It's most important that we find this woman, and soon. We've experienced for ourselves the damage she can do with her baking. She's got to be stopped before she kills someone else. If you think of anything – anything at all – that might help to identify her, I need to know straight away. Can you all ask around, neighbours, friends ... see if anyone can find out who this woman is, and where she lives. Perhaps she's given out a business card to someone? Or left a telephone number?

'As soon as we know who she is, rather than give her name to the police I'll pay her a visit, see if I can find out what went wrong. Suggest she stops selling her home-made rolls till she's had a proper check-up. She might well be a carrier of salmonella or E coli, but completely unaware of the damage she's done. If the police do get involved, that's another matter, but until then I suggest that we keep it quiet. We really don't want this getting into the press, do we?'

'Agreed ... yes, of course ... I might ring my friend over by the park, see if she knows ... you're right, Thomas.'

Reggie stood up. 'If you're wrong, Thomas, then God help you, for I'll not forget.'

Thomas didn't even wince. 'Quite right, Reggie. We need people like you, to keep us on the straight and narrow. No hard feelings?' Thomas held out his hand, and with some reluctance Reggie shook it.

'Meeting closed,' said Thomas. Most people poured out of the small hall into the foyer and set off for home, but Ellie, Maggie and Jean began to stack chairs against the wall. There'd be a dancing class coming in that afternoon. The rooms in the church hall were rarely left empty for long. Felicity picked up her chair and moved towards the wall, but didn't deposit it with the others.

Kate signalled to Ellie. 'Are you going straight home?' Ellie nodded. Kate was the most level-headed of all her friends and Ellie would have welcomed a word with her, but Catriona was beginning to wail, and with a shrug and a 'Catch up with you later?' Kate took her daughter away.

Ellie went on stacking chairs and collecting the papers that people had discarded at the end of the meeting. Thomas put his hand on Reggie's elbow, and slowly walked out with him, listening the while to the younger man's decreasing volume of complaints.

Roy helped to stack chairs, retrieving handbags and stick for his mother and Rose. 'Ellie, I'm going to take Mother back home, and then go with Rose to the hospital, see if we can retrieve Joyce. Felicity, do you need a lift anywhere?'

'Oh. No, thanks, Roy. See you later.' Felicity finally managed to put her chair on to a nearby stack, but still didn't depart with the others. Jean held the door open, impatient for everyone to leave. Ellie took Felicity by the elbow, and steered her out of the door.

The housekeeper watched next-door's cat convulse and die. My, that was quick! Wasn't nature wonderful? She hadn't realized that so little of something which was so easily available would kill. It was always hard to gauge how much she ought to use. The encyclopaedia in the rarely used front room had been most unhelpful in that respect. She'd better bury the cat before its owner started looking for it.

Felicity Kingsley could sometimes give the impression of being a brainless bimbo, as a consequence of marriage to a particularly unpleasant man who'd done his best to kill her spirit.

Ellie was one of the few people who recognized the girl's native intelligence. 'Felicity, I can see you're worried about something. Come back for a bite to eat?'

Felicity fell into step beside Ellie. 'I don't know whether to say anything or not. There was a woman who came round on a bicycle selling bread rolls when my husband was alive. I often bought them. They were good when eaten fresh, and no one was ever ill afterwards. She's been round to my new house a couple of times since I've moved, but now I'm on my own I don't eat so much bread and I haven't bought anything from her.

'The thing is, Ellie, that I can't believe it's her fault. If I point people in her direction, then I'd only be making mischief and damaging her trade. Maybe she needs the money from selling her rolls to make ends meet.'

Ellie considered what they'd learned that morning. 'It does look as if it was the rolls which made people ill. Perhaps she's a carrier and doesn't realize the harm she's done. We've got to find her and stop her doing it again, or she'll get into real trouble. If you know where to find her...'

'Oh, I don't.'

Ellie gave Felicity an old-fashioned look. It sounded to Ellie as if Felicity might have spoken the absolute truth, but perhaps not all of the truth. 'What's her name?'

'I don't know. You're on the wrong track. She's neither evil nor senile. She's just an ordinary middle-aged woman – older than me, anyway.'

'You used to have rolls from her on a fairly regular basis. You were a good customer. Perhaps she gave you a business card, so that you could order more from her?'

'She may have done, but if she did I never used it. I kept all the tradesmen's cards in a big pot in the kitchen at the old house, and threw them out when I moved. She used to come round and ring the doorbell every so often, perhaps once a fortnight, and I'd buy rolls from her most times. I never knew exactly when to expect her but that didn't matter because I always kept plenty of bread in the freezer.'

'Did she have a regular day of the week to call on you?'

Felicity puckered her brow. 'I think it was in the middle of the week, but not always on the same day.'

'Was she heavy-set, or thin? What sort of bicycle did she use? How did she dress?'

'How should I remember? She was ordinary size. Built a bit like you, I suppose. Short dark hair. She usually wore trousers and a padded jacket. Dark colours.'

'You must have looked at her card when she gave it to you. Does she live locally?'

A shrug. 'I told you, I'm not sure she ever gave me a card, and if she did I can't remember that I took any notice of it.'

A lie? Ellie opened the gate into the bottom of her garden, and led the way up the path. Midge bounded out of a flower bed and got to the back door before them. Ellie unlocked the door into the conservatory and hooked it open ... it must be over thirty degrees in there. She'd forgotten to open the windows before she went out, so did so now.

'Felicity, if we don't find her, the police will have to be brought in. Surely it's better if we locate her first, tell her what's happened, and get her to clear things with Health and Safety? If it's not her fault, then we can tell people to go on buying her rolls. If she's responsible – well, the sooner she's stopped, the better. So how do we find her? Coffee? A sandwich?'

'It's a bit early for lunch, and I usually only have a yoghurt, anyway. She's not been round to see you?'

Ellie patted her tummy. 'I seem to remember getting a flier from her through my door a couple of times, but I'm trying to lose weight so I threw them away. I've got some plain yoghurt in the fridge. I usually mix some fruit in it. Is that all you eat for lunch?'

'Well, Roy says that...' She glanced down at her slender figure. 'He can be tactless, can't he?' She used almost exactly the same tone of voice as Ellie did when she talked of Roy, a mixture of fondness and exasperation. But was there a hint that she'd been hurt by Roy's careless comment? Ellie rather hoped not, for Felicity's sake. Roy was not a good long-term risk for romance.

Ellie said robustly, 'There's nothing wrong with your figure.'

Felicity grimaced. 'He was admiring a sixteen-year-old with a twenty-inch waist at the time.'

Ellie dumped a large carton of yoghurt, some spoons and some bowls on the table. Roy could be tactless, but he could also be warmly generous. She urged Midge off a chair so that Felicity could sit at the table. 'I'll tell you one thing about Roy. When I was skint and thought I'd have to go out to work to keep this house, he offered me a job even though he didn't need anyone working for him then. His heart's in the right place, as they say.'

'I know.' Felicity made a visible effort to throw off her preoccupation. 'Now, what's the plan for you and Bill? May I be bridesmaid, or matron of honour, or whatever? May I come shopping with you to buy your outfit?'

'Don't rush me,' said Ellie. 'Or I'll back off, right?'

The problem with using poison was getting the proportions right. Strong tastes had to be disguised, somehow. Should she use sweet or sour

101

next time?

She'd already decided not to use paracetamol; it was easy to get hold of but it took too long to take effect, and there was always the risk that the victims would realize what was happening and get themselves pumped out at hospital before they could suffer much damage.

She had decided – with reluctance – not to use sleeping pills again. They had been useful in the past, but to get any more meant having to register with a new doctor, and she wasn't too keen on doing that. No need to leave a paper trail to her new address.

Ruby had some sleeping pills, of course. The housekeeper decided to save those for a rainy day. How lucky she was that there was a garden in her present place. Plants had so many uses, didn't they?

Someone put his finger on the bell-push and kept it there.

Ellie started. She'd been happily dead-heading some trailing geraniums in her conservatory while letting her mind wander over the problem of how to find the lady with the bread rolls. She'd completely forgotten until that moment that Bill had said he'd take her out to lunch that day. Immediately her bad tooth twinged.

She glanced down at her denim skirt and pink T-shirt. It had been all right for the meeting at church, but it wasn't smart enough for lunch at the places Bill liked to eat.

She scurried through to open the front door, wondering where she'd left the paracetamol. She knew she was going to be scolded – oh, in the very nicest way of course. And then she remembered that she was supposed to collect little Frank from nursery and look after him that afternoon. She glanced at the clock. She was going to be late to collect him!

Bill pressed a delicious little nosegay of freesias into her hand as she opened the door, but his smile vanished as he took in her workaday appearance. 'I did say twelve o'clock, didn't I?'

'Yes, but ... oh, do come in. What beautiful flowers! There's an emergency. Diana needs me to collect little Frank from nursery and look after him this afternoon. His father and Maria are away this week, so ... would you mind terribly if we put our meal off for a couple of days?'

Bill came into the hall as Ellie distractedly sought for her handbag, which was not where she thought she'd left it ... and had she any painkillers in it? Yes? Keys. Yes.

'Why do you let Diana push you around so much?' Bill was carefully hiding his annoyance at this change in his plans, but it was leaking out around the edges.

'I suppose because I feel guilty. If I'd only

103

stood up to her while she was growing up, maybe she wouldn't take me for granted so much nowadays.' She picked up her cardigan and threw it over her shoulders. June winds could be as sharp as March, and after a brilliant morning the sky was clouding over and the barometer in the hall was sinking towards Rain. 'Do you want to walk me over to the school?'

He was not amused. 'Suppose I take you over there in the car, we pick up the lad and take him down to the river, let him chase seagulls or something. Give us a chance to talk properly.'

'I'd love to, but it won't work. Frank's usually tired when I pick him up from school, and really crotchety. I don't want to expose you to that. I'll bring him back here and feed him carbohydrates, and then let him be quiet for a while. He insists he doesn't need a rest after lunch, but of course he does. He'd be fit for company about four. Shall I bring him over to you then for an hour before Diana collects him?'

She pulled the front door to behind them, checking once again that she had her keys on her. She'd only just checked, hadn't she? Yes, there they were.

Bill did his best to smile. 'I suppose I'll have to get used to a different timetable. My girls haven't seen fit to get married and have babies yet, so I'd better get in training. Get in the car and we'll collect him.'

She did so, feeling meek. There was a lot to be said for having a man taking charge of things.

Bill drove smoothly but rapidly back up to the Green and around the church, stopping just beyond the pedestrian crossing outside the school. 'I'll wait for you here, and you can give me lunch for a change.'

'I was going to give him baked beans on toast, but I suppose I could do you an omelette.'

Bill shuddered, but did wait.

Frank was fractious, as she'd anticipated. He didn't know why Ellie had come instead of his mother. He didn't want to get into a strange car with her, and he wasn't going to let her tuck his shirt into his trousers or brush his untidy hair or wash his dirty face; no way. Sometimes Ellie could charm him into a good mood, but today she was on edge and found it difficult to be patient with him.

Bill seemed to expect they'd eat at the dining-table in her living room, but she automatically laid up for them in the kitchen. By the time she'd put baked beans on toast in front of Frank, and dished up an omelette and a green salad for the grown-ups, her tooth was aching and she was feeling worn out. Bill was putting a good face on it – she had to give him full marks for that – but he didn't know how to talk to little Frank, and it was clear he didn't enjoy eating in the kitchen.

Ellie bridled a bit. Her new kitchen was lovely. And convenient. But then, it wasn't what he was used to.

She felt she had to apologize to him. 'So sorry, Bill. What a fiasco. What with the drama at church ... we've all got to look out for this woman who's been going around selling suspect bread rolls...' She tried to make a joke of it, but could see she wasn't getting the right reaction.

Bill said, in a tight voice, 'I really do think, Ellie, that you might start thinking about yourself for a change, instead of running around after other people who wouldn't lift a finger if you were in trouble.'

'Oh, I don't know. I think they would. And it would be really serious if the papers got hold of it, and created a scandal about people being poisoned at church.'

Bill compressed his lips. Ellie remembered, too late, that Bill attended an extremely old and beautiful church near Kew Gardens. Would he want her to go there when they were married? *If* they married. Probably.

Oh. This meant she'd have to give up going to her own church, which had been part of her life ever since she and her husband had moved to this house so many years ago. She wasn't sure how she felt about that. Or how she felt about Bill, either, come to think of it.

Frank thrust his plate away from him. 'Don't like that. I want some ice cream.'

Bill admonished. 'My mother used to say, "I want, never gets."'

Frank stared at him, a mulish expression growing on his face. He opened his mouth to say something rude, but Ellie got in first.

'What's the magic word, Frank?'

He almost decided to have a tantrum. His colour heightened ... but just in time remembered that Ellie didn't give in to tantrums. He said, 'Please.'

Ellie gave him a scoop of ice cream and offered to make Bill some good coffee, if he'd like to wait for her in the sitting-room. Which he did.

Ellie coaxed Frank up the stairs into the room kept specially for him, and saw him happily playing with his own little computer. Usually she read a picture book to him at this time of day and didn't let him play on the computer till later, but today she had Bill to look after as well.

Oh. Wasn't Bill meant to be looking after her? Mm. No, when they were married, he'd expect to be fed and to have his clothes laundered and his house cleaned. That's what men of Bill's generation expected of women. In return you got looked after yourself. Sort of. You didn't get fed and have your clothes laundered and the housework done for you. Or you might, come to think of it, get the housework done for you ... but there was an unwritten agreement about who did what in the house. A cave-man sort of agreement. He's the hunter-gatherer, and she does everything else.

She shoved the dirty plates and saucepans into the dishwasher while the coffee perked. It would be rather like looking after her dear dead husband all over again – except that Frank would have wanted a three-course meal waiting for him when he came in from work.

Probably it's what Bill would expect, too.

Well, she could do all that standing on her head, couldn't she? Then she could look forward to some congenial company, and not having to worry about getting the boiler serviced or remembering to pay the bills. She'd be given treats, and taken out and about and ... surely it would be worth it?

Or would it? If she had to make up a balance sheet, weighing up who got the most out of a relationship, then she wasn't sure marriage to Bill would work out in her favour. No.

She took the coffee in to Bill, with one ear cocked for sounds from above. Perhaps little Frank would fall asleep over his computer, which had been carefully screened to cut out unsuitable programmes.

Bill had his coffee black. She put two sugars in hers and added milk.

Bill steepled his fingers. 'My dear Ellie, how pretty you're looking today.'

Ellie burst into tears. She hadn't intended to. She was mortified. She reached for a hankie, a tissue, anything. She hiccupped and she wept.

'So sorry, Bill ... didn't mean ... it was just...'

She howled into her hankie. Bill moved to sit beside her on the settee, and put his arm around her, making clucking noises.

'Oh, how silly of me. How embarrassing. But it's been so long since ... possibly not since ... and my dear Frank, although ever so ... but he never...' She blew her nose and mopped up. 'You must think me completely mad.'

'I only said what I've been thinking for years. Ellie, my dear! I think you're the prettiest, most desirable, loveliest little woman that—'

She tried to laugh. 'Oh, Bill. Don't overdo it.'

'I've hardly started.'

He was holding her just a fraction too tightly. She didn't want to move into his shoulder, precisely, but she didn't want to hurt his feelings by moving away, either. She stayed very still, and he seemed to get the message for he relaxed his arm about her shoulders.

'I mustn't rush things, what?'

She kept her eyes down, but produced a smile. 'Something like that. I'm very fond of you, Bill. You know that. But...'

'But at our age there's a lot of things to be thought through before we plunge back into matrimony. Yes. I've been thinking about it for quite some time, but I gather that you haven't.'

'Y-yes. A bit. But I didn't get very far. Dear Bill, so much has happened to me since Frank died, what with setting up the trust fund and sorting out Aunt Drusilla, and fending off Diana and looking after little Frank and somehow getting mixed up in other people's problems...'

'And coming to me every time you got into difficulties.'

'Yes, I have, haven't I? It's been wonderful to feel that you were always there and would help me no matter what. I've missed my own dear Frank enormously, and there's been times when I've wondered if I could cope with ... whatever problem it was that life threw up at me, but I've made some good friends, too, and life has been ... well, not easy exactly ... no, not easy at all sometimes, come to think of it. But very *interesting*.'

Bill laughed, and patted her knee. 'That's what I admire about you, Ellie. You never let anything get you down.'

She produced a watery smile. 'Oh, I don't know.'

'I phoned my daughters last night and broke the news to them that I'd proposed to you, and that you hadn't turned me down outright. I don't see that much of them nowadays, with one living in Scotland and the other in Leeds. I think they were rather surprised that their doddering old father was thinking of getting married again...'

Ellie interpreted this to mean the girls were alarmed to think that their father might leave his money to a step-mother when he eventually passed on.

'...but said they thought it was a good idea, particularly as you weren't some equally doddering old lady...'

Ellie had no difficulty in interpreting this, either. The girls thought that a younger step-mother could take over the nursing of their father when he got to the stage of being incontinent or terminally ill.

'...and they're going to try to get down to visit me again soon. They remember you with fondness, of course...'

So they jolly well should, thought Ellie, remembering the hours she'd spent listening to their teenage angst, and sitting with their dying mother. She'd been fond of them both, in a way, while finding their self-absorption somewhat trying.

'...and they asked me to send you their love and best wishes.'

'Their filial blessings,' said Ellie, rather

111

sharply for her.

'What?' said Bill, not quite connecting. 'Oh. Yes, I see what you mean. I hope Diana takes it as well.'

'Diana is thrilled,' said Ellie, grim-faced. 'She's always looking for funding, and thinks she'll get her clutches on this house if I marry you.'

Bill was alarmed. 'Ellie, under her father's will, she only gets half the value of the house when you die and you've made a will leaving your half to a trust fund, so ... Suppose you let me deal with Diana in future.'

She drew back. 'She's my responsibility, Bill.'

He twinkled at her. 'I've helped you deal with her in the past.'

That was true. She got to her feet and smoothed down her top, glancing up at the ceiling. Little Frank had been very quiet for some time. Uncharacteristically quiet. Grown-ups worried when children were that quiet for so long ... unless he'd fallen asleep, of course. 'I must look in on my grandson.'

She went up the stairs as quietly as she could, in case he really was asleep. The door to his room was open. He wasn't inside. Oh.

The door to her bedroom was shut, although she'd left it open. She tried to open the door, and found it was stuck ... or that something had been pushed against it.

Frank had been strictly forbidden to go

into her bedroom, so what was he up to? She knocked on the door. 'Frank, are you in there? Open up!'

A muffled wail was the only reply. Ellie turned the handle and pushed again. The door opened half an inch, but something was blocking it on the other side.

There was a shriek from little Frank. 'You can't come in! I want my mummy!'

Was she going to have to break the door down to rescue him?

The housekeeper had decided that with this splendidly overgrown garden at her disposal, she had no need of man-made poisons. A number of good old-fashioned plants and shrubs were poisonous. She missed her old garden, of course, but she'd never been able to feel the same about it after Sir Arthur Kingsley wrecked it when she got behind with the rent. But this one! Her lips twitched into what was almost a smile.

She went upstairs to the room over the kitchen which was now hers. She would have a little lie-down before she prepared something for the old man's supper. Ruby would have hers at the wine bar as usual. Drawing the skimpy curtains, the housekeeper looked out at the neglected garden. Perhaps she'd clear another patch of weeds tomorrow, to make the cat's grave less obvious.

Six

'What's the matter?' Bill followed Ellie upstairs to discover what was going on.

Frank shrieked, 'Go away! Go away, I say! I want my mummy!'

'He's shoved something against the door on the inside,' said Ellie, failing to get the door open more than another inch. 'See if you can shift – whatever it is.'

Bill tried, and failed. 'Do we send for the fire brigade?'

'Let me have another go.' Ellie inserted her hand and wrist in the narrow gap, and felt around. 'He's jammed a chair under the door-knob. Frank, do you hear me? Let us in, there's a good boy.'

'I'd tan the hide off him,' said Bill, more or less under his breath.

'I heard that!' yelled Frank. 'I'm not letting you in. You get my mummy, do you hear?'

'I can't, dear,' said Ellie, keeping calm. 'You know she's busy this afternoon. Now, if you don't want to come out, then that's all right by us. We'll go downstairs and get ourselves a drink and a biscuit, and you can stay there till you're ready to join us. All

114

right, Bill?'

'What I'd do to him!' said Bill, not bothering to keep his voice down.

Frank gave a piercing shriek. 'Don't leave me!'

'Then pull the chair away from the door.'

Pause for thought. 'If I do, you won't let *him* come in, will you?'

'No,' said Ellie. 'I'll ask him to go downstairs and wait for us. Right?'

Bill went back downstairs, muttering that children needed to be taught their place. Ellie didn't try to make excuses for Frank's naughtiness, though it did occur to her that Bill was not the ideal person to deal with a small child's tantrums.

She pulled the door towards her until it clicked shut, and in a moment she heard the chair being removed from under the door knob. Frank took a flying leap back into her bed as she opened the door, but not before she'd caught sight of his face. He hid under her duvet, but she gently drew it back to appreciate the full glory of his war paint.

'I thought it was face paint, like we have at playschool on special days,' he said, beginning to sob. 'But it hurts!'

Ellie bit her lip to hide a smile. 'Come into the bathroom and we'll see about getting it off, shall we?'

He'd used up all her lipstick, both the pale pink and the darker rose. That would come off with soap and water. But he'd also used almost the whole of a bottle of nail varnish which she'd bought in a mad moment and never used. As it dried, it had puckered the skin on his face. No doubt it did hurt. There wasn't much of her make-up left on the dressing-table, though a liberal amount was on the duvet cover and pillow, on Frank, and on his clothes.

It was going to take some cleaning up. She called down to Bill that there was an emergency and he'd better leave her to deal with it. Bill didn't argue very much. He said he'd half promised to look in on work that afternoon, so if she didn't need him any longer...

'I don't want him to see me!' said Frank.

Ellie sighed. 'If you will do silly things, Frank, you have to take the consequences, but in this case Bill has more important things to do than make fun of you, so ... let's get you cleaned up, shall we?'

Luckily she kept a drawer full of spare clothes for him at her house.

An hour later, a subdued boy had been cleaned up and inserted into clean clothes, while Ellie stowed everything he'd stained into a large bag to be taken into the cleaners. What Diana was going to say about that, Ellie didn't want to imagine. It was true that you really couldn't take your eyes off a child of that age, even for a minute.

'Come along, Frank. Let's take this bundle

to the shops. Perhaps we can call in at the library on the way back, get you some more books to read.'

'Don't like books. Don't want to go. Can we have chips at the café?'

Ellie was too exhausted to argue. 'Maybe. Get your jacket and we'll be moving.'

'Don't want to...'

He caught the look in her eye, and got his jacket. His shoes were a disgrace, but Ellie didn't keep a spare pair of shoes at her house, so he had to wear what he'd had on when he'd decided to paint himself up as a tiger. Diana would be livid about his shoes, and no wonder. They cost a bomb nowadays.

As they were going out, they met Kate just leaving, also on her way to the shops. Catriona was in her big buggy, so Kate put Ellie's bundle in the tray at the back. Frank, unusually subdued, walked beside them, with one hand on the buggy.

'What...?' asked Kate, in a low voice.

'Don't ask,' said Ellie. She wrenched her mind away from the horrors of the past hour. 'Let's talk about something else, shall we? The price of cabbages. Your latest library book. The woman selling bread rolls.'

'Yes, well, I might have come across something there. You know how it is when you're working full-time; you don't get to make friends locally. When I had Catriona and started to work part-time, I started meeting one or two other youngish mothers at the new café in the Avenue. After having worked in the City all those years, it's a completely new world to me. We actually talk about what washing powder we use, and where to get the best-value baby clothes. That sort of thing.

'I remember a couple of my new friends talking about the woman who went around selling bread rolls a while back, saying her stuff was good and, though it was a bit of a nuisance that you never knew when she'd be coming round, they often bought off her. So I thought I might pop along to the café – that's the new coffee bar that's opened on the other side of the road to the Sunflower restaurant ... lots of young mothers use it, because there's nice low sofas inside and they don't mind children so long as they don't get underfoot when they're carrying hot drinks around – and see if anyone I know is in there and can tell me about her.'

'I'll join you,' said Ellie. 'I think Felicity knows where to find the woman, or how to find her, more likely. But Felicity doesn't think she's the kind of person who'd suddenly start making such terrible mistakes with her baking, and though Felicity isn't exactly...'

'Brain of Britain? She strikes me as being pretty shrewd, though no academic, of course.'

'Precisely. I'm inclined to respect her opinion. So if we can find this woman and get her to take some kind of health test...'

'My feelings exactly.'

Frank announced, 'I want a chocolate milk-shake and a chocolate muffin.'

The two women both looked at him, with eyebrows raised.

Frank reddened, but eventually decided that he'd have to give in. 'Please.'

Ellie stopped holding her breath. Helping to bring up Frank was a tiring business. Kate was frowning, looking down at Frank's shoes, dappled with colour.

Ellie said hurriedly, 'Tell you later. I'll drop off my stuff at the cleaners and be with you in a tick. Come on, Frank. Hold my hand crossing the road.'

When Ellie did get to the new café, she found Kate was sitting between a couple of young mothers. Catriona was being bounced on the knee of a smartly dressed young black woman, and Kate was giving a bottle to a very young baby who obviously belonged to the third member of the party, a redhead. All three were talking a blue streak and Kate was giving her friends all her attention, so Ellie decided it was best not to join them. She took Frank off into a corner and provided him with what he wanted, while treating herself to a café mocha with cream. She felt she deserved it.

As one young mother left the circle around Kate, another took her place. Several long phone conversations took place; what did they all do before mobile phones were so popular?

Meanwhile Ellie was joined by Anita, whom she'd known from before the time when her husband died, when they'd both worked in the charity shop in the Avenue. Both of them were delighted to catch up on the gossip. What was Madam – who ran the shop inefficiently – up to nowadays? Did she really say that? Well, I never!

With enormous enjoyment they caught up on the news, thoroughly aired the latest scandal, discussed the fall-out from the weekend at church – Anita's mother had gone to the lunch but not been taken ill, though she knew someone who had. They talked about where they were going for their holidays that year and wasn't it a pity about Joyce Holmes' miscarriage, but there was plenty of time for her to have another, wasn't there.

Finally Frank – who'd been reasonably quiet, playing with some of the indestructible toys provided by the coffee shop – suddenly announced that he'd had enough and wanted to go home. Ellie decided discretion was the better part of valour, and agreed they should go, only picking up some vegetables and bread on the way home. Before she'd reached the end of the Avenue, Kate had caught up with them. 'Sorry,' said Kate. 'It felt a bit rude to exclude you, but...'

'There's a generation gap,' said Ellie. 'They wouldn't have talked so freely if I'd joined you.'

'I'm older than most, but sometimes they remember it and sometimes they don't. I did get round to asking about the woman who sells bread rolls, and someone knew a girl whose aunt she is—'

'Aunt?'

'Yes. She's Julie's aunt. Julie wasn't there, but one of the others knew about her, and phoned Julie and asked her. I said I was planning a big party and wanted somebody who could prepare the food for me. None of them are church-goers, as it happens, so they didn't know about what happened on Sunday. I've got the name and telephone number of the culprit. A Mrs Rivers. I asked where she lived, but my contact had come off her phone by that time and I didn't want to push too hard. We should be able to sort it from the phone book.'

'You are brilliant, Kate. I got a bit of gossip, too. The handyman-cum-gardener who worked at Felicity's old house – that big monstrosity at the bottom of the hill, you know? He was found dead last week. The inference is that he'd got drunk once too often. Anita says it was in the local papers, but I must have missed it, somehow.'

Kate looked puzzled. 'But what connection...?'

Ellie grimaced. 'I know, I know. For one dizzying moment, it seemed to me that there might be a connection, because Felicity used to buy bread rolls from this woman – what's her name, Rivers? – in the past. But he didn't die at Felicity's old house, and I'm sure there's nothing in it.'

'I respect your intuition,' said Kate, 'but surely ... no, it's just a coincidence.' At this point Catriona began to show symptoms of restlessness and Kate hastened her step. 'I must rush.'

'What's Mrs Rivers' telephone number?'

Kate was almost flying along the path. 'I'll drop it in to you later.'

It was no use trying to catch up with the much younger Kate, particularly with a tired little boy in tow, who was beginning to whimper.

'I want my mummy.'

'Let's sing along,' suggested Ellie.

'Won't! Carry me!'

'You're much too big to be carried, Frank. Look, isn't that Mummy's car ahead?'

Fatigue forgotten, Frank ran on ahead of Ellie, who caught up with him just as he was preparing to dive across the main road and managed to grab hold of his jacket before he committed suicide under a bus. 'Frank, how many times have I told you not to run into the road?'

'I hate you!' shouted Frank. Once across the road, he slipped out of Ellie's grasp and sped along to where his mother was getting out of her car. 'Mummy, Mummy, Mummy! She was all horrible and she scrubbed my face, and made me wear these horrible old clothes and then she made me walk all the way to the shops and all she wanted to talk about was people killing one another with cakes and—'

'WHAT HAVE YOU DONE TO YOUR SHOES?' demanded Diana, fending him off. Diana was all in her favourite black, power-dressed to impress. She was getting too thin for beauty, and spending time at the hair-dresser and manicurist to compensate for the loss of the good looks she'd had in her youth. 'Mother!'

'I know,' said Ellie, putting into practice the old adage that attack was the best form of defence. 'You turn your back for five minutes, and he's ruined his clothes and a complete set of bed linen. The dry cleaners say they're not too hopeful of getting the stains out, and I shall have to get myself some more lipstick and nail varnish, not to mention the stains on the carpet. I'll send you the bill for everything, shall I?'

'WHAT?' Diana gaped.

'She made me,' said Frank, turning sullen. 'She was talking to that Bill and sent me up to bed and she never came to read me a book and I was tired of the computer which doesn't have any good games on it, not games where you can kill people, anyway, so I went into her bedroom just to have a look around, and she shouldn't have left me alone all that while.'

'Bill wanted to talk to me,' said Ellie, opening her front door, 'about...'

'Which reminds me,' said Diana. 'I've put your house on the market. Even in this slow-down, it should sell pretty quickly.'

Ellie suddenly felt extremely tired, but she'd told Bill she'd try to deal with Diana herself and she must try to do so. 'You know very well that your father left his half of the house to me for life. After I die, you get his half, but not mine. You've had a copy of my will. You know exactly where you stand. Besides, it is by no means settled that I'm going to marry Bill.'

'You'd be a fool not to,' said Diana, ignoring the first part of Ellie's speech. 'He's bound to leave you a lot of money when he dies, and since he's older than you, you should come out of it pretty well.'

'His two daughters might well disagree with you.' Ellie threw down her keys and dropped her handbag on the hall chair. 'That's enough, Diana. It's been a long and tiring day, for me and for little Frank. Why don't you take him away and feed him?'

Diana fidgeted. 'I was rather hoping you could find something in the fridge for him tonight. I have appointments booked, and I thought he could stay overnight with you.'

Ellie was inspired to lie. 'Sorry. I'm out tonight myself.'

'But I was relying on you to—'

'You can't have it both ways. Either you want me to spend time with Bill with a view to marrying him, or I continue to be your unpaid nanny and look after Frank.'

'If you put it like that...'

Ellie closed the front door in Diana's face and set her back to it. The hall was darker than usual, because of the boarded-over window. She must get her builder on to the job. The answerphone light was winking. More disasters, no doubt. Too bad. Ellie wasn't playing.

The flap of the letter-box lifted, and a piece of paper floated to the floor. Ellie nearly let it be, but then stooped down to pick it up. It was from Kate, with Mrs Rivers' telephone number on it.

Ellie smoothed the paper out and took it over to the telephone, which rang again just at that moment. Aunt Drusilla.

'Ellie, are you free this evening? I think it's about time we have a family conference. Rose is preparing a light supper for us. Can you make it?'

'I suppose I could, but—'

'Don't bother to dress up. Oh, and by the way, Rose is perfectly all right again now, though that's more than can be said for that selfish daughter of hers, who hasn't so much as asked her mother how she is.'

'Joyce is out of hospital, then?'

'Only a little the worse for wear, and making a meal of it. If you ask my opinion, she's trying to make her husband feel guilty so that he won't expect her to get pregnant again too quickly. Half past seven, right?'

'Right.'

Ellie put the phone down, and listened to her messages. Nothing from Thomas. Several people from church asking if she was all right and detailing their own recovery from a bout of sickness. A cold sales call. Nothing much.

Ellie dialled the number she'd been given. The phone rang and rang. Nobody picked it up at the other end. Finally an answerphone kicked in. Ellie hesitated. What sort of message could she leave? Either she'd frighten the woman to death, accusing her of mass food poisoning, or ... no, this would have to be done in person.

She got out the phone book, and turned to the R section. There was a surprisingly small number of people called Rivers, and it didn't take Ellie long to see that N.D. Rivers could be found at the phone number provided by Kate. The address – just the other side of the

126

Avenue. It wasn't precisely on the way to Aunt Drusilla's, but it wouldn't need much of a detour to call in there.

First she had to put clean sheets on her bed and see if she could get the stains out of the carpet ... and then she'd have to change. It was all very well Aunt Drusilla saying not to bother dressing up, but it had not been a good day – and here her tooth twanged again, reminding her of her other problem – and she would rather like to get out of these clothes and into something which would boost her morale.

Perhaps she'd try on her new underwear. Well, why not?

She had an apricot and white top with a matching apricot skirt which had a built-in swirl to it. Her legs weren't bad. Perhaps she'd take some good high-heeled sandals to change into when she got to Aunt Drusilla's.

As she tackled the stains on the carpet, she found herself worrying about that poor handyman of Felicity's who had met an untimely end. Where was last week's local paper? She usually put newspapers and junk mail into the green box in the porch for re-cycling. Of course Kate was probably right, and it was nothing but a coincidence that Felicity's one-time gardener – what was his name? Something Irish? Probably 'Paddy'. Yes, Paddy – should have been found dead one morning, just as Felicity's dog had been.

Or rather, her husband's dog. Only – and here Ellie sat back on her heels to consider the matter – the dog had been poisoned.

The word 'poison' hadn't been mentioned in connection with Paddy's death, had it?

The stains came out of the carpet pretty well. Ellie tackled making the bed with clean linen.

What an unpleasant man Sir Arthur Kingsley had been, and what a relief – though of course you weren't supposed to say so – was his death in a car crash. He'd abused Felicity both physically and mentally, reducing her to a quivering, dowdy wreck. Since she was responsible for her difficult mother's residential care and had no money of her own, he'd assumed she wouldn't leave him. Not a nice man, no.

Felicity had perked up no end since he hadn't been around to criticize her all the time. Their big house had been far too large for her on her own, so she'd sold it and moved to a much smaller one overlooking the park. Encouraged by Ellie and Kate, she'd bought a wardrobe of new and becoming clothes, and had her hair restyled and highlighted.

Ellie wondered if Felicity had heard about Paddy's death. Felicity was a tender-hearted soul and would grieve to hear about it. Well, she hadn't mentioned it, so it was odds on that she hadn't heard.

Ellie glanced at the clock, took a couple of paracetamol and shed the day's clothes. She got under the shower, wondering whether or not she ought to say something to Felicity about Paddy. Probably not.

She slid into her new underwear – yes! It made all the difference to the way she felt. Put on the apricot and white outfit, brushed her hair out, found some sandals that she could walk in without killing herself, dabbed pressed powder on her shiny nose, and found the butt end of a good lipstick, which was all that Frank had left her. Memo: buy another one, perhaps a shade darker? Small handbag: keys, money, diary ... what did Aunt Drusilla want, anyway?

Ought she to phone Bill before she went out? No, better not, or there might be an argument about the way her family wasted her time.

Down the stairs. Had she time to ring her builder? No, they'd have closed for the day by now.

The sky was definitely getting overcast. Bother. She picked up an umbrella and a soft cream-coloured jacket. Shoes? No, she wasn't going back to change them. She set off at a good pace, round the Green, and down the Avenue a way ... cross over opposite the bakery and then along the residential road to the junction ... turn right ... look up the numbers of houses. Big old houses, these. Most of them were divided into flats and ... yes, this was the house in which Mrs Rivers lived.

It was a stark, red-brick Edwardian house with bays bellying out and a good wide off-the-road parking space in front. No garden. Three bell pushes, and the bottom one was labelled 'Rivers'.

This was all too easy. Ellie wondered if she should just ring Thomas and tell him she'd found the woman. He could deal with her from now on. But she'd forgotten to put her mobile phone in her handbag, and as she was here now, she might as well make contact.

Ellie rang the bell and waited. Nothing happened. Then she heard halting footsteps as someone crossed a tiled floor in the hall and came to the door.

'Yes?' It was an elderly man with sparse white hair and sagging face, leaning on a zimmer frame. He did not look welcoming.

'Oh, I'm so sorry to drag you to the door,' said Ellie. 'I was looking for the Mrs Rivers who sells bread rolls in the neighbourhood.'

'My wife's out.' His manner was not welcoming.

'Oh. Well, my name's Ellie Quicke, and I wondered whether ... what time should I call to catch your wife in?'

'Don't bother!' He shut the door in her face.

Ellie took an involuntary step backwards. What rudeness! First she was angry. How dare he! And then she shrugged and even tried to laugh. What did it matter, anyway? She'd get Thomas to deal with the woman tomorrow.

She wondered if he'd been so rude because he knew his wife had sold suspect rolls. Was it guilt that made him shut the door in her face? Well, Thomas could sort it out tomorrow.

On to Aunt Drusilla's. In addition to her own semi, Ellie had inherited a large Victorian house when her husband died, but his aunt had always lived in it, and would probably die in it, too. Ellie had never wanted to live in it herself, and was happy that Miss Quicke should see her days out in it, provided she maintained it properly. Roy, being an architect, had made himself useful by dividing the big house into two and updating all the facilities, so that dear Rose could also live there in comfort while attending to Miss Quicke's needs.

Miss Quicke herself continued to occupy all the main reception and bedrooms, while allowing Rose to enjoy herself filling the once bare garden with flowers. Miss Quicke was as careful of Rose's well-being as Rose was of hers, and had even added a conservatory on to the back of the house, to allow Rose to indulge her passion for plants.

Roy had taken over the old coach-house, turning it into pleasant living quarters for himself, plus an office. Over the last couple of years, he and his mother had gone into local housing development schemes, with Roy providing the architect's skill and Miss Quicke overseeing the money side. As Miss Quicke had observed, 'Roy is good on the broad sweep of ideas, but needs to be watched on the detail.'

As Ellie rang the bell and let herself into the tiled hall, she was looking forward to Rose's cooking, and hardly considered what shocks Miss Quicke might have in store for her.

'There you are, my dear,' said Miss Quicke, materializing in the doorway of the huge drawing-room. 'I'm glad you came early, because I wanted a word with you before the others arrive.' Leaning only slightly on her stick, Miss Quicke gestured Ellie to an antique but comfortable armchair.

Ellie came to full attention. Miss Quicke did not summon people to her presence without having an agenda. So what was up this time?

'This tiresome business at the church lunch,' said Miss Quicke. 'It's been a minor inconvenience, as it happens, but it could have had major consequences. It gave me pause to think what might have happened if ... you understand me, I'm sure.'

'"In this life, we're in the midst of death" sort of thing?'

Miss Quicke nodded. 'Suppose I had been affected, at my age? My digestion has always been weak, and hasn't become any less so with age. I must consider the future and the future needs of my family and those I care about. Which leads me to the reason I called you. You've had an offer of marriage from Bill Weatherspoon. Are you, or are you not, taking it seriously?'

The housekeeper hadn't cycled past her old house for a while. It was too painful, and she had to take indigestion remedies afterwards for her heartburn. She could get all the information about Felicity Kingsley that she needed at work. But now that she was well on the way to planning her next murder, she found herself going that way more often.

She got off her bike on the park side of the pavement, and fiddled with the brake pads to give herself an opportunity to observe what was going on. She hardly recognized the place nowadays. Felicity had had builders pulling it about, replacing all the windows and having the woodwork painted white instead of that nice dark green she had had.

There were masses of red and pink geraniums in tubs on either side of the porch. Hanging baskets, too. Most untidy.

The lawn at the front, which had once been the

housekeeper's pride and joy, had been torn up and pergolas set in an expanse of flagstones, with climbing roses and clematises sprawling all over the place.

No restraint at all!

The single garage had been pulled down and rebuilt as a double, while the up-and-over door had been replaced with one of those fidgety electronic affairs that were always going wrong. That was a pity, because it was easy to stage a suicide in a garage if you could get access to it. But she'd used that method to get rid of her late husband, and it wouldn't be a good idea to try it again. Well, not at the same address. No.

A powerful-looking car drove up to the house, and the driver sounded his horn. Felicity rushed out of the house and banged the front door to behind her. She got in the car, gave the driver a light kiss on his cheek, and off they went. It was the same man who'd picked her up from the retirement home the other day. Roy, his name was. An architect. The hussy.

At work the staff had nicknamed Felicity's mother 'Milady'. Sarcastically, of course. Milady liked Roy, didn't she? Tried to make out he'd visit her even if Felicity didn't drag him along. Stupid woman.

The woman who had once lived in Felicity's house ground her teeth. She got back on her bike and pedalled off, planning a special treat for Felicity.

Seven

Ellie repeated her aunt's words. 'Am I going to marry Bill? Perhaps I ought to, but I'm just not sure.'

'Has your affection for my son Roy anything to do with your hesitation? Because if so...'

'No.' Ellie was quite sure of that. 'He's a dear man, and I'm very fond of him, but I couldn't possibly marry him.'

'In a way I understand that, but I'd like to hear the reasons from your own mouth.'

'Because he wants everything his own way, because he's too like my own dear Frank.' She shrugged. 'I couldn't settle down to being the sort of wife he needs, always putting him first and myself last. I'm sorry, Aunt Drusilla. I've had that sort of marriage before and I don't want it again. Besides...'

She stopped, rethinking what she'd been about to say.

Aunt Drusilla raised her eyebrows again.

'Roy's got into the habit of asking me to marry him, but he doesn't mean it. He still plays the field. I think he's really scared of getting married again. And if he did, he wouldn't want someone like me. Not really.'

Aunt Drusilla hooded her eyes. 'Who would he want?'

A name popped into Ellie's head, but she rejected it straight away. 'I really don't know.'

'Don't you, my dear? Well, run along now and tell Roy and Felicity that supper's ready. Then see if Rose needs help with the dishing up.'

Roy and Felicity? Felicity was in her late thirties and Roy was in his mid fifties. Although he was a trifle older than Ellie, his earning capacity was good, he was in excellent health and looked younger than his years. Miss Quicke couldn't possibly mean...? Could she?

Ellie found Felicity poring over some plans with Roy in his office, and had to admit that they looked good together, both being tall and well-built. But the age difference! They were comfortable as friends; Roy had designed the rebuild and updating of Felicity's new house, while she'd taken an interest in his work on the vicarage site which he was currently developing in partnership with his mother.

Felicity got on well with Miss Quicke, enjoying her eccentricities and appreciating her good qualities. But that was no basis for marriage, was it? Besides, Felicity knew Roy's weaknesses too well to take him seriously as a husband ... didn't she? And after her first disastrous marriage and the miscarriage which had put paid to any hope of having children, would she really want to risk it?

And he? No, he wasn't looking for another wife, after the very different but just as painful bout of wedlock with a young flibbertigibbet which he'd experienced first time around.

Yet Ellie continued to wonder about this through the delightful light supper served up by Rose, while Aunt Drusilla supped something which looked disgusting from a bowl. Afterwards, Ellie was told to help Rose clear away and put the dishes in the dishwasher, leaving Felicity and Roy alone with Miss Quicke.

Obediently, Ellie carried dishes out to the kitchen. 'What's she up to, Rose?'

'It's not for me to say.'

'Come off it, Rose. She's trying to fix Roy up with a wife.'

Rose sniffed. 'She's been needling him for a couple of days, wanting him to ring up this old flame and that, asking him if he'd like her to invite so and so around. Roy just laughs, says he's not thinking of getting hitched again.'

'Softening him up,' guessed Ellie. 'She asked if I'd consider marrying him, but she didn't really mean it. And before you mention it, yes, Bill did ask me to marry him, and I'm considering it but not ready to come to a decision, right?'

They stacked dishes. Eventually Ellie said, 'Do you really think ... Felicity?'

Rose folded her lips tightly, which meant that she was thinking along the same lines.

'The age difference!' protested Ellie.

'Her first husband was much older than her. Maybe she likes it that way.'

At which point Felicity erupted into the kitchen, cheeks on fire and blonde mane flying. 'I'm so angry, I could spit! Ellie did you know what she was going to say?'

Ellie avoided Rose's eye. 'No. Tell me.'

'Eeek! I could kill her! I'll walk back with you, if you're ready to go.'

Roy came quietly into the kitchen behind her. He looked concussed. 'Felicity, don't rush off like that. I mean ... what she said ... just a joke, surely ... she couldn't have meant ... I can see you're all upset. Shall I take you home?'

'Your mother doesn't make jokes.' Felicity's nostrils flared, and she gave a little gasp. Now she looked as if she was about to cry. 'Oh, out of the way, Roy. No, don't touch me! I couldn't bear ... and I don't want you to see me home, either. Ellie, are you ready?'

Felicity didn't wait for Ellie but dashed out of the house. Ellie exchanged meaningful glances with Rose, collected Felicity's hand-bag and her own things from the hall, and hurried out after her. By this time Felicity was halfway down the drive, arms clutching her shoulders, muttering to herself. She paused as she reached the road, and Ellie caught up with her there.

Felicity did some deep breathing exercises. She brushed her hands down over her arms – was she feeling chilled in the night air? Was it going to rain? Felicity hadn't brought a jacket, had she? She started walking beside Ellie. 'You know what she wanted?'

Ellie shook her head.

'She wanted ... that old witch wanted ... I can't believe it! You won't, either, when I tell you.'

Ellie remained silent. There was genuine shock here, but also ... why the threat of tears?

'I mean ... Roy! Of course he's as nice as pie, but he's as daft as a brush sometimes, and has no common sense whatever! He's no intention of getting married again, and if I ever did think about it – which I've no inten-tion of doing, believe me! – not after Arthur – and I know Roy far too well to even dream of ... well, I wouldn't, would I?'

'Roy's asked you to marry him?'

'No! That horrible woman – how dare she! – told him it was about time he made an honest woman of me! As if! I mean ... how dated! Oh, I'd laugh myself silly, if it weren't so pitiful! The old have no idea, none! His face!'

A car crept along the road, keeping pace with them. Roy opened the window.

'Felicity! Ellie! Come on, I'll give you a lift.'

'Get lost, you!' Felicity raised her fist to shake it at him. Ellie thought that for two pins Felicity would have a tantrum there and then on the pavement ... if it weren't for the fact that she'd been brought up to repress her own feelings and never make a scene in public.

Roy wasn't giving up. 'Look, you don't want to take any notice of my mother—'

'I'll scream at the top of my voice if you don't go away and leave me in peace!' Felicity meant it, too.

Ellie bent down to talk to Roy through the car window. 'Leave her be. Let her calm down. Ring me later.'

Roy looked upset, too. 'I can't leave her like this.'

'I'll see her safely home.'

Felicity crossed the road without looking in either direction. Ellie scooted after her, making an apologetic gesture to the motorist who'd had to stand on his brakes to avoid them. Ellie looked back at the corner, but Roy had stopped his car and was standing beside it, not knowing what to do, looking after them.

Felicity ploughed ahead down the road, not looking where she was going till they reached the Avenue, and she stopped, bewildered. 'Wait a minute. My handbag!'

Ellie handed Felicity her handbag. 'Here. Fancy a coffee at my place?'

Felicity shuddered. 'No, thanks. I just want to be on my own. I'm not fit company for anyone at the moment, am I? I've just realized. I didn't bring the car because Roy picked me up this evening. I'll get a cab home. I don't fancy walking across the park alone at this time of night.'

'I'll come with you.'

'No, I'll...' Felicity began to laugh. There was a note of hysteria in her laughter, but then it became more natural. 'Sorry, Ellie. I'm behaving really badly, aren't I? I'll call for a cab, drop you off at your place and then I'll take it on to my house, right? No sense in both of us getting worn out just because ... just because.' She took out her mobile and phoned for a cab.

Reassured that Felicity was now in control again, Ellie allowed herself to be inserted into a cab and dropped off at her house ... only to wonder, as she felt in her handbag for her key, why there was a woman's bicycle propped up against her porch.

Bicycle. Woman selling bread rolls. The food-poisoning carrier?

Oh.

She also wondered why there was a light on in her living room. True, the sky was overcast, making it necessary to turn on lights inside houses a little earlier than usual, but she hadn't left a light on when she went out. Had she? Had she been so rushed that she'd turned one on ... no, she hadn't. Of course not. So who...?

There was only one answer. Diana had always had her own key, of course. Ellie had asked for it back some time ago, but it had crossed her mind at the time that Diana might have had a duplicate cut, and that it might be wise to get the locks changed. But she hadn't done it. Too much else to think about.

So what was Diana doing in her house at this time of night? She looked back up the garden, half-expecting to see an estate agent's board advertising that her house was for sale. Diana had pulled that trick on her once, but surely she wouldn't do it again?

No board.

Good.

She let herself into the house, only to be confronted by a middle-aged, dark-haired, hard-faced woman sitting on her hall chair. Sitting in the doorway to the kitchen was her cat Midge, waiting for his last feed of the day. Midge was supposed to be a good judge of character, but didn't appear averse to being in the company of this stranger.

The door to the lounge was closed, but it sounded as if more than one person was holding a conversation there.

Before Ellie could speak, the woman got up from her chair, and launched into a tirade. 'Mrs Quicke, right? How dare you go round telling people that my rolls put people in hospital? What harm have I ever done you, that you go around ruining people's reputation? Do you realize that I've lost half my customers because of you? Then you have the nerve to get my poor husband to come to the door, and attack him as well! There's nothing whatever wrong with my rolls, do you hear?'

Ellie blinked. 'Are you Mrs Rivers?'

The woman snorted. Ellie had heard of people doing this, but had never actually seen it done before. Mrs Rivers made a sound down her nose just like a horse. 'As if you didn't know!'

'Well, actually I didn't—'

'When my husband told me, when I got back after the second day of having my rolls thrown back in my face, I couldn't believe it! "That Ellie Quicke!" he said. "Came round wanting you. I bet she's the one spreading rumours about you. Bringing the police into it, I shouldn't wonder!" I said to him, "This is the outside of enough," I said. "Who does she think she is, ruining a poor hard-working woman's reputation?"

'I said to him, "Did she have the effrontery to leave a card?" "No, she didn't," he said. "Well," I said, "that won't stop me finding her and giving her a piece of my mind," I said. "It's an odd enough name. I'll bet I find her in the phone book." And so I did.

'And he said, "Now don't you go stirring up no more trouble." Because he'd like it if I sat home all day and waited on him hand and foot, of course he would, and it would drive me silly, instead of getting out earning my living. But I said, "I don't like taking the bike out at night, because the battery's going flat on the front light, but it's not that dark yet, and I'm going to have it out with her, face to face!"'

'Yes, but—!'

'So I came here and your daughter said I could sit here till you got home, and I said I would, if it took me all night, and I'm here to tell you that I'm going round the solicitor's first thing in the morning. I won't have you frightening off my customers, and traducing my reputation, and bare-facedly coming to my door to upset my husband. And that's final.'

'Yes, but—'

'I'm a woman of my word, I am! First thing tomorrow, you can count on it!' She swept past Ellie, wrestled the door open as if daring it to fight back, and slammed it to

144

behind her.

Ellie sank into the chair Mrs Rivers had vacated, and said 'Phew!' softly to herself. She felt as if she'd been mugged. It might have been amusing if it hadn't been so horrible. That woman! Ugh!

How dared she? And then Ellie remembered Felicity's defence of Mrs Rivers, and had, reluctantly, to agree that while the woman might be awkward and aggressive, she felt secure in her innocence. Which didn't mean she wasn't a carrier, but it did mean that she would take some convincing of the fact, if she were.

Ellie could picture Mrs Rivers' life: middle-aged, probably without college or business education, saddled with a disabled husband ... she'd got out of the house and done something to earn some money. She probably didn't earn very much, probably not enough to pay income tax, but it would be enough to give her something in hand, to prove to herself that she wasn't completely defeated by life. Yet.

Midge jumped on to Ellie's knee and began to butt her with his head. Automatically she began to stroke him.

If Mrs Rivers really did lose all her customers through this incident, it might reduce her to a state of seething discontent, sitting at home, waiting on a demanding husband hand and foot. A prospect which would sour most people. A prospect that Ellie quite saw would be horrendous to a woman of Mrs Rivers' type.

Ellie started. Raised voices were coming from her sitting-room. For a while there she'd forgotten about the possibility of having uninvited guests. Midge jumped off her lap and made for the sanctuary of the kitchen.

The lounge door opened, and a young couple stood there, smiling, with Diana behind them.

For a moment Diana looked shocked at seeing her mother there, and then she put on a bright voice, 'Hello, Mother. I thought you said you were out this evening. I didn't expect you back just yet. We have good news; these good people think our house is just what they're looking for.'

'Really?' Ellie rallied her faltering spirit. 'Are you sure you remembered to tell them about ... no, you told me not to mention that, didn't you?'

'Now what?' Diana's dark brows twitched.

The young couple looked from Ellie to Diana and back again, their contented smiles fading.

'Well,' said Ellie, trying her best to look guilty. 'You know what you said about the boy next door...'

Diana turned to the young couple with a light laugh. 'My mother's dreaming. There is no boy next door.'

'If you say so, dear,' said Ellie. 'Only, I really think it's wrong not to tell people.' She switched her eyes to the hardboard over the broken window.

The young couple fidgeted. Diana looked thunderous. 'Mother...'

Ellie produced an innocent smile. 'Such a strange combination of letters, isn't it? ASBO? I can never quite remember exactly what it means...'

'Mother!'

The young couple looked at the boarded-over window, and jumped to the conclusion that it had been smashed by a lout on an Anti-Social Behaviour Order.

Conferring without words they shuffled towards the door, the man saying, 'Yes, yes. We'll be in touch soon, yes, of course, very soon.'

They pulled the front door to behind them.

'How could you, Mother!'

'Your keys to this house, please, Diana. Do tell me how you managed to get that poor young couple to call.'

'I put the house on the internet, of course. When you said you were going to be out tonight, I brought Frank over and put him to bed here, and I've been showing people round all evening. Two have promised to make me an offer tomorrow.'

Ellie felt extremely tired. 'Keys, Diana.'

'Mother, you're not being at all reasonable.'

'If you don't give me your keys, then I'll have the locks changed tomorrow.'

'You promised to come with me to visit a house I want to buy tomorrow.'

'Forget it. You're on your own.'

Diana looked at her watch. 'I have another client due, just about now. You won't show me up in front of him, will you? I can always spin them a tale, say someone else is making a bigger offer, if anyone gets back to me.'

'I'm tired of playing games. Tell them the house has already been sold, if you wish. Tell them to go to Jericho, but get out of my house. Now!'

Diana pouted. 'You wouldn't turn your only daughter out—'

'Try me.' Ellie's tone was grim. 'My keys, please.'

Someone rang the doorbell. 'Please, Mother.' Diana found it difficult to plead, but managed it, after a fashion.

The doorbell rang again. From upstairs came a wail. The noise had awakened Frank. Ellie hesitated, wanting to go to the little boy to reassure him – and yet unwilling to let Diana travel any further down the primrose path. While she dithered, Diana sped past her to the door, opening it with a 'Come in, do! What, is it raining? What a shame. But do come in.'

Frank's wails gathered strength as no one came to soothe him. Ellie climbed the stairs, resigned to dealing with him first. Frank liked to have just a low-powered light on his bedside table when he slept at Ellie's, but Diana had forgotten to turn it on. This might, Ellie thought, have helped to disorient him when he was woken by the noise downstairs. She found him standing beside his bed, knuckling his eyes. She hushed him, switched on his bedside light, put him back into bed and covered him up.

'Read me a story. Haven't had my story tonight.'

Ellie could hear Diana showing another possible buyer around. Could she face yet another scene with a buyer? She really wasn't up to it. She got out Frank's favourite book and began to read to him, keeping her voice soft and low, reading more and more slowly. He snuggled down, listening. She paused at the turn of a page, and he opened his eyes wide. 'Go on.'

She read another page, and watched his eyelids droop ... and his whole body relax.

She slid the book on to his table, and inched herself off the bed ... only to have the overhead light switched on and the door to the landing thrown wide open, as Diana said, 'And this is the third bedroom – or study, if you prefer.'

Frank started awake and began to cry.

Ellie lost her temper. 'Diana, this is the outside of enough. Get out of my house – NOW! If you want to take your son with you, then that's all right by me, otherwise you can leave him here till tomorrow morning and get him in time for school. DO YOU HEAR ME?'

The potential buyer was a youngish businessman judging by his suit. He looked from Ellie to a fuming Diana to a wailing Frank and to his credit, he smiled.

'So sorry to interrupt. I know how difficult it can be to get children to sleep at nights.' He switched off the overhead light himself, and turned back to Diana. 'You should have warned me. Now, how recently has the place been re-wired?'

Ellie found her leg tightly clutched by an extremely upset little boy. She lifted him up into her arms, groaning a little at his weight, for he was a big boy for his age. 'There, there.' She rocked from one foot to the other, trying not to listen as Diana showed the man round the upstairs rooms.

'...and of course a loft conversion would add considerably to...'

'There, there,' murmured Ellie into Frank's ear. 'There, there.'

Frank gulped. 'Want a drink.'

'I'll put you back to bed and get you one, all right?'

'Don't leave me!'

'I have to, if you want me to fetch you a drink.' Ellie had an idea. 'I'll call Mummy to get you a drink, all right?'

Frank nodded. Ellie went out on to the landing with Frank in her arms. 'Diana, your son wants a drink, a bedtime story and a kiss.'

'I'll be up in a minute...'

Ellie began to descend the stairs, with great care, still holding Frank. 'I think you'd better take over. He may need changing, too.'

Diana's face was a picture. The potential buyer, sitting in the big armchair, grinned. 'Home from home, eh?'

Ellie transferred her burden to Diana, and watched her leave the room. Then she looked around for Diana's handbag, opened it, and took out several bunches of keys. Luckily they were all labelled. Most were for the flats Diana had been doing up and selling. Just one was labelled with the number of Ellie's house. So Diana *had* copied her original bunch of keys and kept quiet about it. Ellie slipped them into her pocket.

The potential buyer raised his eyebrows. 'What's going on?'

'My daughter has been taking liberties, I'm afraid. This isn't her house; it's mine. She would like me to hand it over to her to sell, but I'm not playing. I'm afraid she brought you here under false pretences, and I'm removing my keys so that she's not tempted to do it again.'

He pinched his chin, assessing her. 'I shall check with the land registry tomorrow.'

'Do that. Did you hear about this house via the internet?'

He nodded, and heaved himself out of the chair. 'Caveat emptor. Buyer beware. It's a nice house, could do with some modernization, loft conversion, throw the kitchen into this living-room, make it L-shaped, add a wet room and another bathroom, of course. My card.' He handed it over.

She read it and laughed. 'You're an estate agent, too? And Diana didn't realize?'

'It amuses me to see what the opposition are trying to do. Very often they don't know how to sell privately and that's where I step in. So if ever you feel like selling...'

She nodded. 'If ever I do. It was nice meeting you. Let me show you out.'

'That window,' he indicated the boarded-over window in the hall. 'Better have that seen to before anyone else comes round. Pretty garden, what I could see of it. Any time you want a free valuation...'

'Thank you.' She was still smiling as she closed the door on his heels. As Diana was still upstairs, Ellie found pen and paper and in bold letters wrote: SOLD! She found some Blu-Tack and stuck it to the outside of the front door.

She switched off all the lights in the sitting-room, went into the kitchen, put the estate agent's card on the table and made herself a cup of hot milk, which she took through into the conservatory. She didn't know whether she wanted to laugh or cry.

She turned on only one soft indirect light, and sat down to watch the goldfish swimming lazily around in the water feature, trying to relax. There was a growl of thunder in the distance, and a spatter of rain on the conservatory roof. She closed the windows she'd opened earlier. A storm might clear the air.

She heard Diana come down the stairs – far too swiftly to be carrying a heavy little boy. She heard the tap run in the kitchen. Then Diana went back upstairs again.

Ellie sipped her drink, closing her eyes. What could she do to get Diana off her back permanently? What should she do to help Felicity and Roy – because it was clear to her, as an outsider, that they had both been really distressed by Miss Quicke's interference in their lives. What should she do about Mrs Rivers, poor woman?

What should she do about Bill? She smiled. It had been pleasant to be complimented like that. What would Bill have done if he'd been faced with Mrs Rivers tonight ... and then had to cope with Diana and her clients...? And a very wet and smelly small boy in the night?

Ellie began to laugh. What a very odd day it had been, to be sure.

Diana came down the stairs again, and threw some things into the washing machine. Ellie heard her say, 'Oh, no!' Presumably Diana had spotted the estate agent's card.

Diana appeared in the doorway. 'An estate agent?'

'A nice man, I thought. He's checking who owns this house with the land registry people tomorrow. Can you be prosecuted for giving false information on the internet?'

'What did you tell him?' The voice was ragged.

'The truth. Why should I lie for you?'

Diana lowered herself into a chair. 'Because...' She couldn't finish. Perhaps even she couldn't quite bring herself to admit that she was a liar. She produced a tear. 'I need the money.'

'Mortgage your flat.'

'I have. I have to build up some capital for my next venture.'

'Get a job. Perhaps that estate agent would take you on.'

'Mother, you aren't being serious! I'm in real trouble!'

Ellie sighed. 'Diana, it's about time you grew up and took responsibility for your own actions, which includes taking responsibility for your son. I'll look after him for you when

I can, but you must understand that there are times when I can't. Tomorrow is one of them. I have a business meeting in the afternoon with my trustees, dealing with applications for money from people who are far worse off than you. So I can't have Frank then. As for helping you buy another house to develop – forget it.'

'I can borrow money against my share of this house.'

'Which won't be yours for maybe twenty more years. You probably could borrow against that, if you went to loan sharks. At a punitive rate of interest. And don't even think of forging my signature to make your dreams come true. Understood?'

'How could you! As if I would!' But they both knew that she had done just that in the past.

'Shut the front door quietly when you leave,' said Ellie. 'I don't want Frank being woken up again.'

For once Diana was unable to continue the argument. She left the house, closing the front door quietly. The cat Midge – who disliked and feared Diana – reappeared through the cat flap, looking for the last feed of the day. Ellie obliged, and they went up to bed together. She left her bedroom window open. It was still very hot, and the threatened storm had failed to materialize. She would sleep with just a single sheet over her. And

155

pray for a happy outcome for Mrs Rivers ... and Aunt Drusilla and Rose ... and Felicity ... dear Lord, please keep an eye on us tomorrow...

'Strong drink was raging.' The housekeeper didn't know where the words came from, but she thought they described Ruby's life to a T. It was disgraceful how that woman neglected her father. Luckily he seemed happy enough with the television on all day, and a constant supply of hot drinks at his side. So long as he could get along to the toilet on his own, everything would be all right.

The housekeeper had never been one for a tipple, and marriage to a man fond of drink had merely reinforced that view. The loss of control shown by a drunken man or woman disgusted her ... not that she was complaining, under the circumstances, since it suited her very well to have the run of the house and kitchen.

She set the pestle and mortar on the table. It was a little early for laburnum seeds to have ripened, but this particular tree had blossomed early, and with a little searching she'd found enough for her purpose. Of course they'd be riper if she waited another few weeks, but she'd waited long enough, she thought, and one tiny dose had worked on the cat.

She pounded the seeds into a paste, and set them aside while she prepared the dough for her rolls.

Eight

Ellie spent a wretched night, partly because of the heat, and partly because she felt she'd been too hard on Diana, who did seem to be in real trouble. Ellie couldn't remember Diana ever crying before. It was one of the girl's good points, that she never used tears as a weapon. Ellie threw her pillow out of bed and tried to sleep lying flat. Then she got up for a drink of water, put the pillow back on the bed and had the sheet just covering her legs, with her feet poking out at the end to keep cool.

Nothing much worked.

Midge got cross with her and plopped himself out of the window to go hunting. Ellie put the light on and sat up in bed, with the refrain from 'Money is the Root of All Evil' running through her head. If she hadn't inherited all that money from Frank, and if she hadn't put it into a trust fund for charitable purposes ... if only Diana could be trusted! But there it was ... she couldn't.

Ellie flounced around the bed, trying to find a cool spot and failing. There was something Thomas had said in church on Sunday ... what was it? Something about never lending money, but giving it instead. The words 'Neither a lender nor a borrower be' came into Ellie's head, but she rather thought that was Shakespeare and not the Bible. It came to the same thing. Money was the root of all evil.

She dozed off and woke with a raging toothache. Took some painkillers. Lay in bed waiting for them to take effect.

Suppose she were to give Diana half the value of the house now, instead of making her wait for it till Ellie was dead...? But given the current high price these houses were fetching, how could Ellie raise so much without cleaning out the trust fund ... and the other trustees wouldn't let her do that, would they?

Perhaps it would be worth it, though. She could get Diana to sign a waiver or something, to say she'd received all the money due to her under her father's will. Except that there was no guarantee the price of these houses wouldn't rise again, and then Diana would want more...

Suppose Ellie were to take out a mortgage on the house and give Diana the money that way...? Only, how was she supposed to pay the mortgage? Would it even be possible, in her fifties, to get such a mortgage? Ellie turned over again.

Or, she could marry Bill and sell the house and settle with Diana that way. It was the perfect solution.

Well, it didn't actually *feel* perfect, because it was going against the terms of the will, and dear Frank had known what he was doing when he made the will. But it might answer. She would ask Bill about it in the morning. He was absolutely right, and she did need someone to look after her in these matters. And it would be very pleasant to have his company all the time, and be taken out and about, and paid compliments...

Perhaps.

She was heavy-eyed in the morning; her tooth was killing her and little Frank was cranky. It took all her patience to get him washed, dressed and fed. She rang the dentist's surgery at half past eight and heard there was a cancellation at a quarter to eleven, if she could make it. She accepted with relief.

By the time she'd seen Frank safely into the playground, she felt in need of strong coffee. Normally she'd go round to the Sunflower Café and indulge, but she felt too 'scratchy' to sit quietly by herself. She couldn't relax. She needed to talk to someone, but it had to be someone who had no personal interest in the tangled relationships and dodgy doings around her.

Of course Thomas would be too busy at this time of day. Probably.

She really didn't want to be seen calling on him in his temporary accommodation, and yet of all the people she knew, she respected his judgement the most.

But, he might be pottering around the flower beds at the church, and if he was there – and he probably wouldn't be, although it was a fine morning and he often spent time sitting on a bench, talking to all and sundry as they crossed the Green – then perhaps she could stop and chat for a moment.

She must forget the moment when he'd embraced her a little too wholeheartedly the other night. They'd laugh about that some day. What a thing! As if it had meant something, which of course it hadn't.

Yes, he was there, chatting to a young mother who had a toddler in a buggy and was clearly about to produce another baby any minute. He was probably too busy to talk to anyone else. No, he was waving to the toddler as the young mother moved off, and now he saw Ellie, and she could easily pass on by with a cheerful 'hello' ... except that he looked as if he were blushing, which surely couldn't be the case. Could it?

He said, 'I hear congratulations are in order. Bill's a fine man.'

'What?' She was so nonplussed, she found herself blushing, too. 'Oh, no. I mean, there's

160

nothing settled, and really I wish people wouldn't...'

'Oh. Really? I heard ... really?'

'Really not.' She took a seat beside him. 'Thomas, may I talk at you for ten minutes, and ask you not say anything at all till I've finished? It's not about Bill, it really isn't. It's just ... everything's such a muddle and just telling you about it – and some of it you need to know anyway.'

He gave one of his mellow laughs. 'Start at the beginning, woman.' He sat back, folding his arms across his ample frontage. Relaxing.

Ellie relaxed too. 'First of all, about the rolls. Yesterday Kate and I did some asking around, and discovered the name of the woman who goes around here on her bicycle selling home-made bread rolls. I checked in the telephone book and discovered where she lived and...' Ellie gave him the gist of her conversation with Mr Rivers, and then told him about Mrs Rivers' visit to her that night.

'...and you see, Thomas, I tend to agree with Felicity, who's known the woman for years and used to buy off her when she was in her old house. Mrs Rivers may be this and that; she's aggressive and probably not over-intelligent, but I'm sure she's conscientious and careful when she cooks. I don't think she's the source of the trouble.'

Thomas stroked his beard. 'Now there's a turn-up for the books. Because, you see, I've

161

been trying to remember if I saw somebody delivering the bag of rolls to the church hall and I think I did. It was only a glimpse, mind, but as I bent down to pick up the bag I turned my head to see if I could catch whoever it was, to thank them. And I'm pretty sure that in that moment I saw a woman riding away on a bicycle.'

Ellie blinked. Oh. Then Felicity had been wrong about Mrs Rivers, and so had Ellie.

Thomas said, 'Give me her address, and I'll pay her a visit. Perhaps she's had a bout of tummy trouble herself and is contagious. Or maybe something got tipped into the dough by accident and she's too scared to admit it.'

'I suppose it's possible, but she's been making and selling her rolls for years, and presumably knows all about hygiene. And why should she start making mistakes now? All right, if she did make a mistake then I agree she ought to be stopped from selling stuff, because who knows what might happen in the future?'

Thomas nodded. 'There's another possibility. She told you her husband would like her to give up her sales round to stay at home and look after him all day. Do you think he'd be capable of doctoring her dough, so as to force her to give up her work?'

Ellie shrugged. 'I suppose he might.'

162

'Very well, I'll pay them a visit. What else is on your mind?'

Ellie hesitated, then laughed. 'This is confidential, Thomas. And please don't laugh. My aunt has been match-making, and thoroughly upset everyone in the process.'

Thomas' eyebrows peaked. 'You and Roy?'

Ellie felt herself colour up. 'No, no. I wouldn't, and he talks a lot but doesn't really mean it. No, it's...'

'Felicity?'

Ellie stared. 'Has Aunt Drusilla been talking to you about it?'

'No, no. It's just that it crossed my mind a while back. They are very much at ease with one another. They spend a lot of time together. She's helped him a lot with the work on the vicarage site, and he's very good for her, don't you think?'

Ellie shrugged again. 'Somehow, I'd never imagined ... there's the age difference...'

Thomas peaked his eyebrows at her, meaning that he didn't think it a great barrier.

'...and he's always been such a playboy...'

Thomas shook his head. 'Terrified of getting trapped into marriage with the wrong woman again.'

'Then there's ... well ... her health...'

Thomas nodded, meaning that Felicity had confided in him about it. Felicity had had a nasty miscarriage in the early years of her marriage to Sir Arthur, and had been

163

told it was unlikely that she'd conceive again. 'I gather Sir Arthur was not the kindest of husbands, and it might be that with a more – how shall I put it? – a more considerate husband, she'd be quite all right.'

'That might very well be,' said Ellie, in a tart voice, 'but in the meantime they're both very distressed. Felicity left in tears. Roy tried to calm her down and she wouldn't have anything to do with him. He was supposed to ring me about it last night, but didn't. I expect he went to the golf club and sat at the bar all evening. I'm not sure what to do. And don't say "Do nothing", because I feel I'm the only person everyone can talk to about it.'

'Hm. Roy pops round to the building site almost every day. Maybe I'll wander over there in a bit, see if he wants to open up.'

Ellie relaxed. 'Thanks, Thomas. Now if you can only sort out my daughter's problems...'

He stood, shaking his head. 'It would take a wiser man than me to deal with your daughter; there's none so deaf as those who won't listen. I'm sorry, Ellie, but I can't help you there. Perhaps Bill...?'

She sighed. 'He's offered, but somehow ... no, she's my responsibility. There's a temptation to give in to her, to let her have what she wants if she's really in financial difficulties. But with another part of my mind I know that she'll never be satisfied and that if I gave in to her now, she'd be back next week or next year, asking for more.'

Thomas said, 'Emotional blackmail.'

Ellie grimaced. 'You can say that again. Do you know something? I'm beginning to get really angry with her. Isn't that awful? But I have a horrible feeling that if something or somebody doesn't stop her in her tracks, she's going to end up in court for fraud.'

'At which time you'll ride to her rescue?'

Ellie pulled her sweater around her shoulders. The sky was becoming overcast again. Was it going to rain properly this time? 'No. I rather think I've had enough.'

An elderly woman in an electric buggy drove up, hailing Thomas with her stick. 'Thomas ... a word with you about that neighbour of mine.'

Ellie left them to it, striking out in the direction of the park. She hoped it wouldn't rain, as she'd come out without an umbrella.

She found Felicity in her front garden, tying up some strands of clematis which had come adrift. Felicity was dressed any old how in T-shirt and jeans, but now that she bought her clothes in better-class shops, even in casual wear she managed to look elegant. She also looked as heavy-eyed as Ellie felt. 'Care to join me for a cuppa? It looks as if it's going to rain.'

'I like what you've done to the front garden.'

'The back's a mess, still. I knew exactly what I wanted to do at the front, but I really don't know what to do about the back.' Felicity led the way through the hall to the kitchen-cum-eating area. Roy had done a good job extending what had once been a poky little kitchen into a large 'garden' room, with huge French windows on to the garden and a range of modern, minimalist fitments for the production of food.

Ellie caught her breath. An opened packet of home-baked bread rolls was sitting on the granite work surface. Crumbs showed that Felicity had eaten at least one.

'Now don't you start!' Felicity switched the kettle on, and banged a couple of mugs down. 'Mrs Rivers came round this morning early, almost in tears, asking me – as one of her oldest customers – to help her. She's lost more than half her customers because of the wicked lies people are telling about her, and could I help by telling people her rolls are all right. I said I would. I was so sorry for her that I bought a pack, even though I'll probably have to give half to the birds ... unless, of course, you'd like one.'

Ellie patted her tummy. 'Daren't. But Felicity...'

'Was it wise? Yes! There's a time when you've got to stand up for what you believe in, and I *know* she's all right and that her stuff's all right. I suggested that if she had any over, she deliver them to the retirement home where my mother lives. I said I'd pay. Don't say I can't afford it, because of course I can. I'll tell the staff that it's all right when I go there this afternoon.'

Felicity's mother was an unpleasant faded beauty who had lost nearly all use of her legs due to an accident she'd had when drunk. She needed full-time care. In Ellie's opinion – and that of everyone who cared for Felicity – Felicity looked after her difficult mother far better than she deserved.

Ellie seated herself at the breakfast table in the bay overlooking the back garden, which did indeed look as if it could do with a make-over. Talk about drab!

'You're right, of course. If Mrs Rivers has suffered, then we must all do what we can to put matters right, but Thomas is pretty sure it was a woman on a bicycle who delivered the doctored rolls to the church hall. He's going to visit Mrs Rivers today.'

'That's ridiculous!' Felicity was sullen. She poured boiling water on to ground coffee and dumped the cafetiere in front of Ellie. 'It's him who's made the mistake this time, not her.' With an air of defiance, she took another bread roll, buttered it lavishly, and began to eat.

'Mm. We wondered if perhaps her husband might ... by mistake...?'

'Ridiculous!' Felicity slapped the sugar

basin in front of Ellie, and put out an artificial sweetener for herself.

Ellie said nothing to that. Felicity sat, crossed her legs and uncrossed them, gazing out at the garden. 'What would you do with this part of the garden? You designed Kate's, didn't you?'

Change of subject. Ellie stood up to inspect the garden, which had been laid out years ago by someone without a drop of imagination. A patch of grass occupied most of the space. In the middle of this apology for a lawn was a square yard of badly laid crazy paving around a cement plinth from which a birdbath or sundial had long since vanished. Narrow flower beds edged the garden under the fence, with a pathway of cracked cement flagstones dividing them from the lawn. The plants looked as if they'd had it, except for a thicket of something which Ellie would classify as a weed, though serious gardeners might not agree ... oh, and a patch of mint.

To make matters worse, one side of the garden was shaded by a thickly overgrown privet hedge from next door.

A couple of drops of rain hit the window, with considerable force. 'Do you want to grow fruit and veg? Have a water feature?'

Felicity depressed the plunger. 'Roy been on to you, has he? Not that I care.'

'Do you want a bird-table? Do you get

many squirrels round here?'

Felicity fished a paper tissue out of a box and blew her nose.

Ellie reached for her. 'Oh, my dear...'

Felicity fended her off. 'Don't touch me, or I'll cry.'

Ellie poured coffee for them both. It began to rain heavily. 'Let's get some ideas for your back garden down on paper, shall we? What I'd advise is that you put the existing plants, lawn and paths into a skip and start afresh. Now, how low-maintenance do you want to get?'

The rain cleared up an hour later. Before she left Felicity's, Ellie rang Diana's mobile to remind her to be sure to collect little Frank from school.

Diana objected. 'I can't possibly leave...'

'Sorry, Diana. I've got a dentist's appointment.'

Ellie called a cab to take her to her dentist in the Avenue. Mr Patel had recently moved into shop premises which had been marvellously transformed with a bright modern layout, lots of glass and all modern bits and pieces.

Of course the first thing he said when he'd looked at the aching tooth was, 'You've lost a bit of filling,' and the second was, 'Soon deal with this. Just a spot of anaesthetic here ... and here.'

While the injection took effect, he asked how she'd been. She'd been going to him for years, and they were comfortable together. Because it was much on her mind, she told him about the suspect rolls, making light of it because she didn't want him to think anyone attending her church was automatically going to get food which would make them ill.

'Panic over, though,' she said. 'We think we've nailed the culprit, a woman who goes round on her bicycle. Thomas – our vicar, you know – is going to see her about it today.'

'You don't often see women on bicycles nowadays, do you? It's mostly teenage boys and young men. Or older men going down to the allotments. Though I do have a woman on my books who comes by bike. Is the tip of your tongue feeling numb yet?'

'Mm. Not quite. And her name's not Mrs Rivers?'

He lifted his drill. 'No, her name isn't Mrs Rivers. Shall we make a start? Raise your hand if you can still feel it.'

Ellie closed her eyes and prepared to endure, though really Mr Patel was extremely good and always gave her more anaesthetic if she needed it. It helped to pray a bit during treatment. Dear Lord, please. Something on those lines. Or, Lord have mercy...

When she was free to sit up and rinse out

her mouth, she came back to their original conversation. 'The woman I'm thinking of lives locally, not far from the Avenue. Is your client local?'

'No, I don't think you could say she's local.'

Which meant that there were at least two women going round on bicycles, or maybe – horrors! – even more than two. It was true that, in that neighbourhood, most women walked to the shops with their baskets on wheels, or took the family car. And if they had children in tow, they took the buggy and piled the shopping on that. Ellie personally didn't know anyone who went around on a bike ... oh, except poor Gladys at church who was more than a little strange and pushed her bike around rather than riding it.

But there could well be more, people she'd never even met. In which case, they'd suspected Mrs Rivers quite wrongly, and the poor woman had been losing her customers for nothing, and this was all quite dreadful.

Oh dear. And Thomas was going to visit Mrs Rivers today and accuse her of ... oh dear! Could she intercept him before then?

She paid her bill and went a couple of doors along to the new coffee shop, getting out her mobile. She tried Thomas's number, but he wasn't in his office nor in his temporary accommodation. She left messages but he probably wouldn't get them until after he'd seen Mrs Rivers. The only people who had his mobile number were the church-wardens and the secretary in his office, so she couldn't reach him that way.

It was just after eleven. Her mouth was still feeling dead, but she managed a cup of coffee sort of sideways on. Next anxiety: would Diana remember to pick up little Frank from school? Ellie had a vision of the little boy standing by the school gates, forlornly waiting for someone to collect him. Should she ring Diana again?

No, better not. Diana would only say that if her mother had finished at the dentist's, she did think Ellie could stretch a point and collect him herself, as she, Diana, was tied up with meetings all day, and what she was going to do with Frank, she couldn't imagine!

It was emotional blackmail, but very difficult to deal with when a small boy was involved.

Ellie steeled herself. She was not going to give in to pressure from Diana. Instead, she'd have a word with her aunt. The sky had cleared. The rain had cleared the air and it would be a pleasant walk to her aunt's place.

Rose opened the door, and said Miss Quicke was at home but had someone with her.

'Dear Rose, how are you now? You look

better. And Joyce?'

'Back at work, would you believe. Have you come about...?'

'Who's that, Rose?' Miss Quicke appeared in the doorway of her dining-room – now mostly used as an office for her business empire – ushering out a rather cowed-looking young man who was perspiring as he stuffed papers into his briefcase. No doubt she'd been giving him a hard time about something.

'Have you come for lunch?' Miss Quicke crossed the hall in front of Ellie, her stick punctuating every second step she took. 'Don't stand there, dithering, Ellie. Into the drawing-room, if you please. Sit, sit! I don't care to have a crick in my neck, looking up at people.'

Ellie sat. 'Not lunch, no.'

'Well? Cat got your tongue? Roy been on to you, has he?'

Ellie shook her head.

Miss Quicke leaned back in her chair. She hooked her stick over her arm, but it dropped to the floor. Ellie made as if to retrieve it, but Miss Quicke stopped her, leaning back in her chair and closing her eyes. Suddenly she looked much older.

'You think I shouldn't have said anything, but I'm not turning up my toes without making sure he's going to be properly looked after.'

Ellie kept her tone light. 'Felicity is distressed.'

'Humph! Roy's a fool if he doesn't know how to deal with that. You must admit, they're well suited. He'd have been safe enough with you, but if you don't want him then Felicity will do very nicely. She likes a father figure, and he likes a pretty young thing. She doesn't lack for common sense and would see he didn't go overboard financially. Good hips for child-bearing, too, if I'm any judge of the matter.'

'Dear aunt, please don't get your hopes up. Felicity had a miscarriage when she was married to Sir Arthur, and it's unlikely that she'll conceive again.'

The old woman's mouth worked. 'I didn't know that.'

'Roy may not know it, either.'

'They're fond of one another, though?' For once, Miss Quicke sounded unsure of herself. 'They're well suited, aren't they?'

'I don't think either of them realized just how fond they were of one another, until you forced the issue.' Ellie acknowledged to herself that some part of her had been flattered by Roy's attentions, and that she had been just the teeniest bit cross when he'd transferred his interest to Felicity. She sat on that bit of herself. 'Yes,' she said, 'I do think they are well suited.'

'Well, we must hope and pray,' said Miss

Quicke. 'What about you and Bill?'

'So much else is going on ... I haven't had time to think much about it ... Diana is...' She shrugged.

'If a man's proposed marriage and you haven't had time to think about it, then you're not in love with him and it's not going to happen.'

'Maybe you're right, but I don't think either of us expects a grand passion at our age.'

'Nonsense! You're a mere chicken!'

Ellie looked at her watch – would Diana collect Frank at twelve or not? – retrieved her aunt's stick, laid it against the table at her elbow, gave her a light kiss, and said she'd have to be off. She got as far as the driveway when Roy came rushing out of his office in the old coach-house.

'Ellie! Rose told me you were here—'

'I'm in a rush—'

'Then let me drive you wherever—'

'I've got to be at the school gates to make sure Diana picks little Frank up at twelve.'

He steered her into his car, and she was happy enough to be given a lift. He looked much as usual, she thought. That silver hair and the startlingly blue eyes made him look Irish, though he wasn't. He had great talent, considerable charm, and was devoted to his mother and to Rose. He'd made a bad choice in his first marriage, but there was no reason why he shouldn't marry again. He could move in with Felicity in a house he'd renovated for her, and his rather cramped quarters in the coach-house could be turned over to his expanding business.

'Tell me what to do, Ellie.'

'What do you want to do?'

'Why did she fly off the handle last night? It was only a joke on my mother's part, wasn't it? Was it a woman's thing? And if so, is she going to be all right in a day or two?'

'How do you feel about her?'

'I thought we had a good thing going, and I don't want to lose it. When my mother said ... I'd just never thought of her that way. You know me. I'll flirt with any pretty woman, but I've never seriously considered marrying again.'

Ouch, thought Ellie.

'I thought Felicity felt the same way. She's extremely pretty and charming and capable, of course. Delightful company. We've got to know one another well, what with this and that, and she really appreciates my mother, warts and all. I thought it was ideal for both of us.

'I hadn't realized that the amount of time we've been spending together might make other people think ... and then my mother said that ... and like a fool I stood there with my mouth open instead of turning it off as a joke. I can see that Felicity might have expected me to speak up for myself, but ... I was so surprised! How can I put it right? She won't even open the door to me, or speak to me on the phone.'

'Where did you go last night?'

'To the Club after a while...'

Check, thought Ellie.

'...but it all seemed so trivial. Everyone laughing and ... noisy ... I can't stand noise when I want to think. I drove over to Felicity's and rang her on my mobile, but she can see who's ringing on her phone display, and she wouldn't take my calls. I wanted to go and knock on the door, but I didn't want to frighten her so late at night. I sat outside her house in my car for ages. I might have stayed there all night, if a police car hadn't driven round and I thought she might have called them, saying I was stalking her or something.'

'What would you have said, if she had picked up the phone?'

'I thought we could have had a laugh together about it. Only, this morning it occurred to me that Felicity might have felt offended by my mother's suggestion. I got a bouquet of red roses this morning as soon as the shops were open, and took it to the house. I heard her come to the door, but of course she could see it was me because I'd fixed up a spy hole for her. She still wouldn't let me in.'

'There weren't any roses on the doorstep when I got there.'

'Do you think she put them in the dustbin?' He parked the car on the Green. 'What do I do now? I don't understand her.'

Ellie craned her neck to see the school gates. Parents were beginning to collect their children. Was Diana there?

'Ellie, this is important!'

'Sorry.' She tried to concentrate, realizing that what she said next might influence all their lives. Miss Quicke might have started the ball rolling, but Ellie strongly suspected that the older woman was relying on Ellie to see the romance through.

Ellie had to recognize that she'd felt more than a twinge of jealousy when Roy had started squiring Felicity around. If she worded her advice in such a way that Roy would be frightened off Felicity, he'd return to dancing attendance on Ellie, which would be extremely pleasant for both of them. But wrong.

She thought, Dear Lord, give me the right words to say.

Her mind cleared. 'Roy dear, perhaps we've both forgotten something important. Felicity had a bad time in her first marriage, as you did in yours. Arthur abused her, you know, mentally and physically.'

Roy drew in his breath sharply, and hit the steering wheel. 'Yes, of course. Poor kid.'

Ellie tried to see what was happening at the school gates. The swarm of mothers and au pairs collecting children seemed to have cleared, but she hadn't noticed Diana among them. 'I think I'd better just pop across and see...'

Her mobile phone rang. A voice with a distinct wobble in it. Felicity. 'Ellie, is that you? Could you come over, straight away? I – I don't know what to do.'

Felicity wasn't one to cry wolf. This must be an emergency. She'd eaten one too many of those bread rolls? Fallen over and hurt herself? Accidentally cut herself with a kitchen knife? 'I'll be right over, but I have to see if little Frank is waiting for me first.'

Heavy breathing. Something that sounded like a sob. The phone clicked off.

'Was that Felicity? Is she in trouble?' Roy switched the ignition on.

'Yes, but we have to check on Frank first...'

The housekeeper sang in a rusty voice as she cleaned the kitchen. At last! This time there could be no mistake. Goods delivered to the door just in time for the postman to take them in. Revenge was sweet! She would sleep well tonight.

Nine

Ellie rushed to the school gates. Perhaps Frank had been collected earlier. Diana could easily have picked him up before Ellie and Roy arrived ... or even managed to whip him out quickly while they'd been talking about Felicity.

He was still there, looking forlorn. Sniffing a bit. 'Mummy didn't come.'

'No, love, she got held up in a meeting. I'm here instead.'

'You're late.' Another sniff. But he put his grubby hand in hers.

'I had toothache and had to go to the dentist.'

He scowled. 'I've been to the dentist. I'm not going again, ever.'

She didn't argue, but urged him towards Roy's car. Frank hung back. 'What's he here for?'

'He gave me a lift. We've got to go round by Lady Kingsley's house.'

'Don't want to. Want my lunch.'

Ellie suppressed an urge to shake him. 'In a minute. Just get in, like a good boy, and

180

we'll whiz round there in no time at all.'

'Hi, Frank,' said Roy, starting the engine. 'Had a good time at school today?'

'I want my mummy.' Frank sniffled.

Ellie and Roy exchanged glances. Diana had loathed Roy from the moment he arrived back in his mother's life, thinking – quite rightly – that Miss Quicke would prefer to leave her vast fortune to a charming son who hadn't a fortune-hunting bone in his body, rather than to a money-grabbing and disagreeable great-niece.

Roy had at first been bemused by Diana's hostility but now regarded her as a tiresome but unimportant irritant in his otherwise smooth life. To give him his due, Roy had never held a grudge against little Frank and would even put himself out to entertain him now and again.

They drew up outside Felicity's house, which looked as neat and tidy as usual. Ellie dithered. 'Do you want to come in? Would you be willing to look after little Frank for half an hour, take him for a pizza?'

Roy looked longingly at the house. 'I really do want to talk to her, but ... if you think it's best, I'll take Frank off your hands for a while.'

'I won't go with you!' shouted Frank. 'I want my mummy!'

Felicity opened the door and stood there, looking forlorn. Was she crying?

181

Roy leaped out of the car, and ran down the path to her. 'My dear girl, whatever is the matter?'

'Oh, Roy!' Felicity dissolved into his shoulder, as his arms went around her. Ellie wondered if she should make herself and little Frank scarce, though as she couldn't drive she wasn't sure how she was going to manage it.

Felicity lifted her head, pushed Roy away from her, and beckoned to Ellie. 'Please, Ellie. I don't know what to do.'

'I've got little Frank with me.'

'Bring him, too.' She vanished inside the house, with Roy's arm around her shoulders.

Ellie hauled Frank, protesting, out of the car, and banged all the doors shut. She hoped they'd lock themselves – they probably wouldn't and the car would be stolen while they were in the house, but Roy obviously wasn't thinking about security, so ... 'Come along, Frank. Let's see if Lady Kingsley can find something for you to eat.'

'Want a pizza.'

'Tough. This is an emergency.' She half pulled, half led Frank into the house. The door was open to the kitchen, and they went in.

The plastic bag of home-baked rolls from Mrs Rivers was still on the work-top, open, though much depleted. A tub of low-fat butter and a knife were next to it. It looked as if Felicity had eaten several more since Ellie left.

Next to it there was another plastic bag, also containing home-made rolls!

Felicity was blowing her nose on a tissue. 'The postman rang the bell because he had a catalogue which wouldn't go through the letter-box. He handed me that bag of rolls as well. He said a lady on a bike had just left it on the doorstep.' She took in a deep breath. 'I think someone's trying to make me ill!'

'Surely not!' Roy was shocked, disbelieving.

Ellie wondered if Felicity was right. She groped for a chair and sat down, looking at the two bags. One was from Mrs Rivers; they knew that. The other one must be from ... someone else. Mr Patel was right. There was more than one lady riding around locally on a bike.

'My dear!' Roy got Felicity sitting on a high stool and ran a glass of water for her. Ellie noted that he was being more capable than usual.

'I'm hungry!' stated Frank.

'I'll get you something in a minute, Frank,' said Ellie.

Felicity pushed her hair back from her face. 'Of course he must be hungry, poor little chap. I think I've got some peanut butter spread in the fridge.'

'Don't like peanut butter,' said Frank.

183

'You do, Frank,' said Ellie. 'I gave some to you last week and you ate it and asked for more.'

Felicity wasn't listening. Visibly trembling, she hauled herself to her feet and got a jar of peanut butter out of the fridge. She took some sliced bread out of a bread box and a knife from a drawer, and proceeded to build Frank a sandwich.

'The thing is, I didn't know which lot was dodgy. I'd eaten three – no, four – of Mrs Rivers' rolls. I hadn't had any ill effects, but ... well, I thought it best to put my finger down my throat and make myself sick.'

'Understandable,' said Ellie, wondering if Felicity was going to cut herself while making a sandwich for Frank, but thinking it best to let her try to behave as normally as she could. 'You didn't touch the others, did you?'

'I wasn't thinking straight when I made myself sick. It was just a reaction, probably quite stupid, because I'm sure Mrs Rivers doesn't mean to harm me.' Felicity cut the sandwich into four, put it on a plate and shoved it in little Frank's direction. 'After I'd been sick, I had second thoughts. I'd probably got upset for no good reason, because it might have been Mrs Rivers herself who came back with a second bag of rolls for me, if she hadn't sold all she'd come out with this morning. That made me feel better for all of two minutes.

'Only, when I looked carefully, I could see that the two bags are slightly different. Mrs Rivers had ten rolls in hers; the other has eight. I opened the second bag to count the rolls and to see if there was anything else which would help me tell them apart. One bag is freezer quality – Mrs Rivers. The other isn't. In fact, it looks to me as if the other is that thin sort you get from the bakery in the Avenue when you ask for your bread to be sliced.'

Ellie nodded. Roy hovered at Felicity's shoulder.

Felicity continued, 'Also, I think they've been baked by different people. Mrs Rivers' are more regular in size and shape. The others seem to be dusted with flour, which Mrs Rivers doesn't do to hers.'

'Don't you think you should go to Casualty, be pumped out?' asked Roy.

Felicity did some deep breathing. Ellie steered her into a high stool nearby.

'I'm all right, really,' said Felicity, looking as washed-out as anyone could without actually fainting. 'It was just the thought of someone wanting to harm me that did it. I know in my head that Mrs Rivers' rolls are all right. But to realize that there are *two* people going round with rolls ... sorry, I over-reacted.'

'I think you were very sensible,' said Ellie.

185

'Now you just sit there quietly, and I'll make you a nice cup of camomile tea and some dry toast.' She busied herself putting on the kettle.

Roy got out his mobile phone. 'I think we should bring the police in on this.'

Felicity said, 'I thought about telling the police. I suppose they could do fingerprints and stuff. The postman handled the second bag, and so did I, but I suppose they could look for other prints. Only, what will we say to them? That we're afraid someone's put something dodgy in the second lot of bread rolls? Then they'll ask why would we think that. And we'd say, "Because someone doctored the bread rolls at the faith lunch at church, or spread them with E coli, or whatever."'

'Just because it sounds trivial,' said Ellie, putting bread into the toaster with one hand while pouring boiling water on to a teabag in a mug with the other, 'doesn't mean that it oughtn't to be reported. For one thing, what started as a bit of mischief might escalate into something worse. I agree, Roy; call the police.'

Roy moved to the windows to get a signal on his mobile.

'What it is,' said Felicity, accepting the mug of hot tea handed her by Ellie, 'is that they might think I'm being paranoid. I mean, I probably am.'

'Imagining someone's trying to harm you?' A cold chill ran down Ellie's back. Was she, too, getting over-suspicious? The bread popped up out of the toaster.

'Paranoid,' repeated Felicity. 'As in, someone tried to kill my husband, didn't they, with a poisoned pizza left on the doorstep? Oh, I know they only succeeded in poisoning our dog, but Arthur had the pizza analysed and there were enough sleeping tablets in it to have killed two men, never mind just one small dog. We never really did get to the bottom of that, did we, because of everything else that happened about then, and because Arthur had so many enemies that it seemed pointless when all that happened was that our dog died?'

Sir Arthur had made more enemies in his lifetime than you could count on the fingers of both hands, but he'd actually died in an accident in his car one wet night. There'd been nothing suspicious about his death, although it had been hailed with relief by a considerable number of people – including his wife.

Ellie cut the toast into soldiers, and handed it on a plate to Felicity.

Felicity sipped tea while Ellie wondered if she should mention the item of gossip she'd picked up in the café the previous day. According to her informant, Paddy something – who'd been employed by the Kingsleys as part-time gardener and handyman – had come to an untimely end some time back.

Ellie opened her mouth to speak of this, and shut it again. 'Untimely death' did not mean murder. Doctoring or infecting bread rolls did not mean murderous intent, either. Probably the two things were not connected, and there was no point in dragging red herrings across the trail.

Felicity's eyes were enormous. 'Ellie, you thought you knew who might have tried to poison Arthur, even though they only got his dog?'

Ellie nodded. She'd suspected a poor mouse of a woman whom Sir Arthur had turned out of her house for non-payment of rent. The woman had disappeared from sight, and Felicity had agreed with Ellie that the accidental poisoning of a dog hadn't warranted a police investigation.

Felicity tried to chew some toast, and gagged. 'Tell me I'm not being paranoid, Ellie. This is the house that my husband turned her out of. I'm living in what was once her home.'

Roy turned from the window. 'As we thought, the police don't think this is a serious incident. They say they haven't anyone they can spare to come here. They want us to go down to the station to make a complaint, and to take the evidence with us.'

Felicity, Ellie and Roy looked back at the counter. One bag of bread rolls had disappeared. The plate of peanut butter sandwiches lay untouched on the work surface, and Frank sat on the floor under the table in the window, butter smeared round his mouth, stolidly eating the last of a bread roll, an empty plastic bag at his side!

Felicity started to laugh. Hysteria! She clapped both hands over her mouth and closed her eyes, rocking to and fro on her stool.

Ellie's immediate impulse was to clout young Frank. He'd been given perfectly good food to eat, and instead had gorged himself on suspect rolls.

Only, of course, you couldn't clout a child nowadays, or you'd be had up for abuse. She tried to keep her voice down to normal levels. 'How many rolls have you eaten, Frank?'

'I've had enough of them. Can I have some pizza now?'

'We'd better make him be sick,' said Roy. 'Or would it be better to take him to Casualty and get him pumped out?'

Frank howled. 'You're not making me sick! I'm not going nowhere!'

Ellie's phone rang. She snatched it out of her bag.

Diana calling. 'Mother, where are you? Have you got Frank with you? I called at the school and they said you'd already gone! I thought you said—'

'I've got him here with me at Felicity's,' said Ellie, trying not to panic. 'He's just eaten something rather dicey. He might be perfectly all right, but we don't want to take any chances. We could try giving him an emetic, or take him to Casualty...'

'What?' Diana screeched. 'You've given him something to upset him? How could you! Put him on the phone, at once!'

Ellie handed the phone over to Frank. 'Mummy wants a word.'

Frank started crying. 'Mummy, Mummy, don't let them make me sick!'

Everyone could hear Diana's voice, sharp and agitated. 'Of course not, sweetheart. I'll be right over. Don't you get yourself upset.'

'That's not likely,' said Roy, sotto voce.

Felicity gurgled, trying not to laugh, trying to control herself.

Ellie took the phone back from Frank. 'Diana—' The phone went dead.

Three adults looked down at the small boy, who scrambled backwards under the table. 'Won't!' he said. 'And you can't make me.'

Ellie said, 'Felicity, how many rolls did you eat?'

Felicity's voice trembled, but she managed to reply. 'Three. I put four more out for the birds, because there were far too many for me to eat. That left three. There were ten in

190

the bag. If it's any help, he only seems to have eaten Mrs Rivers' rolls.'

Ellie considered Frank's mutinous expression. In the past he'd proved he could make himself sick whenever it suited him. Perhaps she could make him be sick now. Ellie crouched down, reaching her hand out to Frank. 'Frank dear. What you've eaten may give you a bad tummy pain. Felicity made herself sick, when she ate some. We're worried that it might make you feel bad, too. Do you think you're clever enough to make yourself be sick now?'

'No,' said Frank. 'I want some pizza, and I want Mummy.'

'If you don't,' said Roy, joining in, 'we'll take you to hospital and they'll put a tube down your throat and pour stuff down you to make yourself be sick, whether you like it or not...'

Frank wailed, and turned his head away.

Ellie said, 'Really, Roy. We don't need to frighten him.'

Felicity decided matters. 'Leave him be. If he wants to have a tummy pain, then he can have one. I don't suppose he'll be sick for more than a couple of days.'

Frank wailed again, but this time he crawled out from under the table and started to cough. Ellie, aware that he was an expert at projectile vomiting, seized his arm and half pushed and half carried him to the downstairs loo. And almost made it.

By the time she and a chastened Frank returned to the kitchen, Roy was lifting the suspect bag of rolls into a large carrier bag, using a pair of kitchen tongs so that he didn't leave any fingerprints. Felicity came in from the garden, wearing rubber gloves and carrying the original plastic bag received from Mrs Rivers. A few crusts were all that was left of the original contents.

'Shall I take them to the police for you?' Roy said, looking at Felicity.

Felicity went a shade paler, if that were possible. 'No, I must go myself. The rolls were meant for me, and they'll want to know why I've been targeted.'

'My dear,' said Roy, putting his hands on her shoulders, 'would you object if I came with you?'

'Thank you, Roy. I'd like that.'

Ellie reflected that there was nothing like being confronted with a common enemy to bring people together. Roy and Felicity were looking at one another now as if there had never been any embarrassment between them.

Frank plonked himself down at the table. 'I want some pizza. Now!'

Ellie looked at her watch. 'Heavens! I'd quite forgotten. I've got my old friend Gilbert and Kate coming round at two ... my trustees, you know? It's been arranged for ever. Felicity, you ought to eat something ... and Frank, too. Felicity, how about you coming to stay with me for a while?'

Roy firmed his grasp of Felicity's shoulders. 'I was going to suggest you move in with my mother for a few days. How about it, Flick?'

Ellie's eyes rounded. *Flick!* She'd never heard Roy use the pet name before, but Felicity wasn't shrugging him off, so presumably she didn't mind. Perhaps Roy and Felicity were a little further on down the road to marriage than Ellie had thought.

'I'm hungry,' whined Frank. 'I want something, now!'

'Yes, of course. How about the peanut butter sandwich Felicity made for you?'

Frank's lower lip came out. 'Don't like peanut butter.'

Ellie dithered, wondering whether she could get Gilbert and Kate to come later ... only Gilbert must already be on his way over from his present parish in the east of London ... and Kate would have arranged for Catriona to go to a babysitter, and Ellie ought to be there, right now! Though Kate had a key, and could let Gilbert in.

Felicity slid out of Roy's hands, not rudely, but in gentle fashion. 'Thanks, Roy. It's quite true I don't want to be alone, but I hate the thought of being run out of my own house. Come with me to the police, and then I'll decide what to do.'

Someone leaned on the doorbell while pounding on the front door. Everyone jumped.

'Diana!' said Ellie, checking the clock against her watch and looking round for Frank's jacket, which he'd dropped somewhere ... remembering that Roy had left his car unlocked outside ... would it still be there?

She let Diana into the hall. Frank ran to his mother and buried his head in her black skirt. 'Mummy, Mummy, she made me be sick!'

'What's going on!' demanded Diana. 'What have you been doing to my child? There I was, going half out of my mind, thinking he'd been kidnapped from the school gates—'

Ellie snapped. 'Nonsense, you were late. We waited till he was the last one in the playground—'

'—and all the time, so irresponsible! Just like you to—'

'Diana,' said Ellie, 'take him. He's yours. He needs feeding, and I'm late for an appointment.'

'Not so fast! You can't just—'

'Roy, could you run me back home before you—'

'—walk away from your responsibilities...'

Felicity picked up a bunch of keys. 'We're

on our way out, Diana. I don't know where you're going but I'm taking Ellie home and then joining Roy at the police station.'

'Thank you, Felicity,' said Ellie. 'Cheer up, Frank. Your mummy's here now and will get you a pizza, I'm sure.'

Roy held the door open for Diana. 'You know where the police station is, Flick?'

Felicity nodded, somehow managing to propel Diana and Frank out of the house before her. Ellie checked to see if Roy's car was still there, and unvandalized. Luckily it appeared intact. Felicity clicked the garage door open and smoothly backed her little car out. Ellie got in and they drove away, leaving Diana to turn on her son and scold him.

Ellie watched mother and son till they turned the corner. 'If I had my time again, Felicity, I would have stood up to my husband more. And Diana. I'm sorry about that scene. You could have done without the extra fuss.'

Felicity snorted with laughter. 'You know, I think we panicked, all of us. I'm sure Mrs Rivers' rolls are all right.'

Ellie permitted herself a small smile. 'Perhaps they are. But it's best to make sure. Will you ring the retirement home and tell them not to give out Mrs Rivers' bread? We can't risk more elderly people being made ill, can we?'

Felicity couldn't stop laughing. 'It's probably too late. They have their dinner early, don't they?'

'They might save them for tea.' It crossed Ellie's mind that Felicity might well not be upset if her extremely tiresome mother spent the night on the loo.

Felicity sighed. 'Yes, of course I'll ring them as soon as I've dropped you off. And you're quite right. I don't want to be on my own in that house. I do love it, and don't want to leave it. I don't want to go to Miss Quicke's because it might give her the wrong impression...'

'Yes, Flick,' said Ellie, demurely.

Felicity grimaced. 'As a nickname, it's better than some, don't you think?'

'Yes, dear. I'll be in all afternoon and evening. Come round for supper and tell me what you've decided.'

The housekeeper dismounted from her bike and wheeled it through the side gate into the shed at the back. She padlocked the wheel, and made sure the shed was locked after her. You could never be too careful, could you?

She made herself a cup of herbal tea, wondering how long it would take for Lady Kingsley to die. The housekeeper wished she could be there to see it ... but there, that would have been too risky, wouldn't it?

Sleepiness, nausea and vomiting, convulsions and coma. Excellent.

196

This time the dusty encyclopaedia in the front room had been most helpful. She thought she must be the only person who'd consulted it for years.

She did hope that using vanilla essence in the dough had disguised the taste and smell of the pounded-up laburnum seeds sufficiently.

Ten

Ellie was exhausted. Dealing with paperwork always did that to her. While her husband had been alive, he'd dealt with business matters while she'd run the house for him and Diana. She'd never had expensive tastes, was no gambler, bought most of her clothes in chain stores, had never learned to drive a car – though she'd tried – and didn't want to move from her neat little semi in the suburbs. The money dear Frank had left her was far more than she'd ever need, and with Bill's approval she'd put it into a charitable trust fund.

Kate next door, being something of a financial wizard, had joined the board of the trust, and seemed to know by osmosis which of the many applications for funds was genuine and which were not. The second trustee was the Reverend Gilbert Adams, who'd occupied the vicarage locally till the bishop removed him to a larger parish on the other side of London. He always joked that Kate was the head, Ellie was the heart, and he was the soul of the trust; though his wife said that with his large appetite, he was more like the stomach!

Be that as it may, by the time five o'clock arrived and the last piece of business was put to rest, Ellie was exhausted. Gilbert had to rush off for another meeting but Kate stayed on, saying that her babysitter would be keeping Catriona till six.

Ellie realized that she was probably feeling faint because she hadn't eaten since breakfast – and that seemed a long time ago. Before the dentist, even!

Before ... lots of things.

Kate stretched out her length, arms above her head, closing her eyes. Then she sat up, looking alert. 'Now, Ellie. Let's get down to business.'

Ellie glared. 'What have we been doing all afternoon?'

'Oh, that. Not exactly life or death, was it? I'm talking about this nasty business of the bread rolls.'

Ellie lost her composure. 'Kate, I have had a very tiring day. I haven't eaten properly since last night, I've had a session at the

198

dentist, tried to deal with the fall-out from Aunt Drusilla's ill-considered match-making, calmed Felicity down when she thought she'd been poisoned, rushed to collect Frank from school because Diana was late, cleared up when he threw up and tried to get my head round matters of high finance all afternoon ... and you want to talk about dicey bread rolls?'

Ellie didn't even begin to mention that she'd got up that morning secure in the belief that she was a much valued and sought after woman in Roy's estimation, and had learned that she came way below Felicity in his league table. That stung, even though she knew it shouldn't. She wasn't really jealous of Felicity, was she? No! But there were other things on her mind ... including Bill, and Thomas ... don't think about Thomas.

'All right,' said Kate, dimpling. 'We won't talk about bread rolls, yet. I suggest we find something for you to eat, and then we can talk.'

Ellie was working herself up into a temper. 'You say that so easily. "Find something to eat." I'm tired of "finding something to eat" for all and sundry. In a minute Roy and Felicity will be descending on me, for "something to eat". I have nothing suitable in the fridge or the freezer, and I'm not putting myself out to cook for you or anyone this evening, right?'

Kate laughed. 'Good on you, Ellie! Stick to your guns. How about I get Armand to fetch Catriona from the babysitter – he should be home from school about now – and I'll take a swing by the chippie. One medium piece of fish and a small portion of chips do you?'

'Too fatty on an empty stomach,' snapped Ellie. And then managed to smile. 'Sorry, Kate. How about some Chinese instead? Easier to digest. I'm worried sick, if the truth be told. We've all concentrated so hard on bread rolls that I think we're missing the bigger picture.'

Kate nodded. 'You're thinking what I'm thinking? After you told us what happened at church, I got out the notes I made on the poisoning of the dog at the Kingsley's last year. No one else seems to have made the connection ... except you.'

'Felicity worked it out today. It terrified her, as well it might. Oh, here's some money. Go and get me some food. If the others want some when they arrive, they can phone for a pizza or something.'

Kate departed. Ellie had meant to defrost some meat from the freezer and cook herself a proper meal that evening, but she was too hungry and too tired for that. She made herself a cuppa and wolfed down several chocolate digestive biscuits. She began to feel marginally better.

She attended to the messages on the answerphone. First was Bill. She'd hardly thought about him all day. She felt guilty that she hadn't called him as he'd asked her to.

'Ellie, my dear. I'd hoped to hear from you before now, but … I know how difficult it can be when you're looking after Frank … what a little scamp he's turning out to be—' Ellie thought that only Bill would think of calling Frank 'a little scamp' '—and I do think it's about time Diana made proper provision for him to be looked after outside school hours. But that's not what I was ringing about. I was racking my brains for a little treat for you. How about tea for two at the Ritz? Normally they're booked up for months ahead, but they've a cancellation early tomorrow afternoon, so I'll pick you up at one, shall I? You won't need any lunch beforehand, I gather. We'll leave the car at the station and go up by tube, right? So, unless I hear from you…?'

Very nice, too, thought Ellie. I've never had tea at the Ritz before. What shall I wear?

Next was Thomas. 'Ellie, I've been to see Mrs Rivers … well, actually she wasn't in at first, so I had a chat with her husband, and then she returned.' A sigh came down the line. 'I didn't get your message till I got back. What a muddle. I might drop round and see you this evening, if you're in.'

That made three people looking for someone to cook their supper for them. Tough!

The doorbell rang. Ellie expected to see Felicity and Roy on the doorstep, but it was an unknown middle-aged couple with paperwork in their hands.

'Are we too early? Our appointment to view was for six o'clock.'

Ellie said, 'I never buy at the door,' and considered slamming the door in their faces. She saw the notice she'd put on the door last night had disappeared. It might be wind that had done it. Or it might be Diana, still trying to sell the house.

The couple looked puzzled. 'Have we come to the wrong house?'

Ellie told herself it wasn't their fault that they'd been misled. She said, 'Sorry, this house is not for sale.'

'Oh, but—'

'But me no "buts",' said Ellie, exasperated beyond the bounds of normal courtesy. 'This ... house ... is ... not ... for ... sale. Go and sue my daughter for trying to force me to sell, if you wish, but don't bother me again, right?'

So she did slam the door, only to have the bell rung again a minute later. And this time it was Felicity and Roy, both looking exhausted.

'Ellie, thank heaven you're in. What a dreadful day,' said Felicity.

'The police are idiots,' said Roy. 'We had to wait ages to speak to someone above the person on the front desk, and then they didn't take us seriously.'

Felicity flopped down on the settee in the living-room and eased off her shoes. 'I'm absolutely hollow. Is there anything to eat?'

'Tea and biscuits,' said Ellie. 'And not too many of them, either. Kate's just gone to fetch me some Chinese food. I could ring her, ask her to bring some for you as well.'

'I could murder a steak,' said Roy. 'How's about you and I go down to the Carvery, Flick?'

Felicity closed her eyes. 'Oh, I couldn't move. I'm totally whacked out. Chinese would be all right, though.' She opened her eyes again. 'Ellie, the police think I'm making it all up. You don't, though, do you?'

'No, I don't. And it may be worse than you think,' said Ellie.

The doorbell rang. Another couple, both women this time, wanting to look at the house.

Ellie didn't bother with the niceties this time. She said, 'It's been sold, already,' and would have closed the door in their faces, except that she saw Kate getting out of her car, laden with bundles.

Kate said, 'I bought enough for four or five, just in case.' She gave an enquiring look at the would-be viewers of the house.

'Diana's trying to sell the house over my head,' explained Ellie.

Kate nodded, knowing Diana of old.

Ellie took the bundles into the kitchen and laid them out on the table. 'You are brilliant, Kate. Roy, Felicity: see what Kate's brought. Everyone dig in.'

The doorbell rang again. 'I'll go,' said Kate, and came back with Thomas.

Ellie didn't meet Thomas' eye, but gestured for him to draw up a stool and join them at the table. Everyone tucked in, saying 'Mmm' now and then. Midge arrived and squawked till he was fed with left-over scraps.

Ellie dished up ice cream and maple syrup for afters. Kate put on the kettle for coffee.

'I feel better,' said Felicity. 'At least, I would feel better if—'

'That's what we're here to discuss,' said Ellie. 'Let's take coffee into the other room. Hardly any washing up, thank goodness.'

Another trip to answer a couple of would-be buyers at the front door. Diana hadn't had the grace to show up and turn them away ... what was Ellie going to do about Diana?

'I'll speak first, if I may,' said Thomas, 'because I'm due at a meeting at eight.'

The cat Midge jumped on to his knee, and he began stroking him. 'I went to see Mrs Rivers this morning about the rolls. I was trying not to prejudge her but, not knowing any better, I was pretty sure that we'd found the source of the problem. She was out, and her husband was almost hysterical because he kept getting phone calls from people cancelling their orders. He's severely disabled and they're making ends meet with difficulty, but he hasn't applied for any number of grants that he should be getting. I spent some time talking to him about them and promised to send him the forms. Then Mrs Rivers arrived home. An angry woman. She said she'd managed to offload the rest of her rolls at the retirement home and—'

Felicity clapped both hands over her mouth. 'Oh, oh! I ought to have phoned to warn them not to ... and I usually call in there on Wednesday afternoons. What was I thinking of? Oh dear! Oh, this is awful!'

Thomas looked up at the ceiling, and Roy looked down at the floor. They wore identical expressions of concealed amusement. Felicity's mother was infamous for trying to flirt with male visitors. Midge decided to sit on the coffee table so that he could survey everyone from a central viewpoint.

Thomas patted Felicity's knee. 'No harm done, if Mrs Rivers' rolls are on the up and up. It was a kindly thought of yours to get her to take them there.'

'Yes, but suppose—' Felicity was beginning to shake again.

'Stop it!' said Ellie, in what even she recognized as a fierce voice. 'What I mean is,' she said, more quietly, 'that we all got in a state and didn't know which rolls were all right this morning. It was all right to over-react then, but we don't need to worry about it now. Mrs Rivers is in the clear.'

Everyone looked at Ellie with varying shades of doubt and relief. Ellie said to Thomas, 'Just to fill you in … Felicity receiv-ed a second batch of rolls this morning, which were definitely not from Mrs Rivers. The postman said they were delivered by a woman on a bicycle. Roy, take it from there.'

Roy put his hand on Felicity's knee – the opposite knee to the one which Thomas had patted. 'I phoned the police, they told us to go in and make a statement, and to take the suspect rolls with us. We gathered up a few crusts that were all that was left of Mrs Rivers' bread, and took both lots in. By this time Felicity was convinced that the same person who'd poisoned her husband's dog last year was now targeting her...'

'The police didn't believe me!' said Feli-city, shifting her leg so that Roy's hand fell off. 'Yet I'm sure I'm right.'

'Yes, I think you're right,' said Ellie. The doorbell rang again. 'Kate, tell the others why, while I deal with the door.'

This time there were three people at the door; mother, grandmother and small child. 'So sorry,' said Ellie. 'The house has been sold.'

She went upstairs to Frank's room. Surely she'd seen some chalks there? Ah. Fine. She chalked a notice on the outside of the front door.. S.O.L.D. Perhaps that would deter more visitors.

Back in the living-room, Kate was talking about the research she'd done for Ellie on poisons and poisoners: '...and this Mrs Alexis fitted the bill perfectly. Felicity asked me to help her sort out her husband's affairs, deal with the tax man, keep an eye on his financial portfolio and the properties he owns. I keep all the records in my study next door, so it wasn't difficult to trace Mrs Alexis' descent into poverty.

'I found her rent book easily enough. The house – that's the house Felicity is living in now – was rented to a Mr Alexis, some twenty years ago when rents were a lot cheaper. Now, of course, a three-bedroom detached house overlooking the park would be astronomical to rent. The rent book gives their jobs at the time they took on the property; he's down as being manager of a Greek restaurant, and she as part-time cleaner.'

'Really?' said Ellie. 'Who'd have thought it. Her house wasn't too clean when I saw it.'

'Cobbler's children?' said Kate. 'She probably hadn't enough energy to clean her own place after cleaning other people's all day. Anyway, the rent was paid promptly right up to the time that he died about ten years ago, and after that...' She threw up her hands.

'I suppose she simply hadn't enough coming in to pay regularly. And of course the rent was going up all the time. Somehow she managed to keep going until last year when things came to a head. Sir Arthur lost patience and had one of his staff lay her front garden waste as a horrible warning.'

'I remember that,' said Thomas. 'I called and tried to talk to her about it, but she said she didn't want any help, that she knew what she was doing.'

'That's when I called, too,' said Ellie. 'She was very odd. Sort of dingy, living in the past, perhaps? Everything in the house was shoddy, depressing. She was no lover of beauty, that's for sure. She was ... preoccupied, I suppose is the best way to describe her manner. She couldn't wait to get rid of me.' Midge jumped up on to Ellie's knee, and she let him settle there.

Kate sighed. 'I suppose she was one of those people who goes over and over things in her mind, building up a head of steam, justifying their actions and not able to see anyone else's point of view. She probably convinced herself that Sir Arthur deserved to be punished for treating her so badly, although in law...' Kate shrugged.

'I thought she tried to kill him with a poisoned pizza and missed,' said Ellie, 'but by the time we finally got round to looking at her, she'd done a moonlight flit, leaving no address.'

The doorbell rang again. Ellie gave a little scream of rage. 'I can't go. I've got the cat!'

'I'll go, shall I?' said Roy, and left the room.

Ellie said, 'If it is the same woman – and of course we can't be sure about that – I thought she'd left the neighbourhood for good. Sir Arthur was dead, and there didn't seem any point in pursuing her for killing his dog. It never occurred to me that she'd try to do something similar again. It didn't even occur to me when people went down with food poisoning at church...'

'Well, it wouldn't, since you were being accused of it,' said Kate. 'But after a while, thinking about it and trying not to see co-incidences where they don't exist, it began to worry me. I started to poke around to see if I could discover where she'd gone. There's nobody of that name in the tele-phone book. She's not on the electoral register anywhere in the borough; though as she moved last autumn she could easily have slipped through the net on that one. I don't think she's old enough for a retirement home, and she's not registered with any cleaning agency ... you remember she took cleaning jobs before? But I did find—'

Roy erupted into the room, looking furious. 'Anyone know where that bitch Diana is hiding out? She's told someone they can have first refusal of this house—'

'I'll deal with it,' said Thomas, and went out with Roy.

Ellie pressed her hands to her cheeks. 'What am I going to do with Diana?'

Kate said, 'Get a restraining order on her. It's the only thing she'll understand.'

'But if she breaks it, she could land up in court.'

'It might be the only means of convincing her she can't always have her own way.'

Thomas came back in with Roy. 'Sorted,' he said, and resumed his seat.

'Where was I?' said Kate. 'Oh, yes. I did some Googling and paid a visit to the back files of the local paper. There's a report of a Mr G. Alexis being found dead of carbon monoxide poisoning in his garage ten years ago almost to the day. It must be the same one. The verdict was accidental death, owing to the garage door having slammed shut on him while he was drinking wine and working on his car.'

Felicity's mouth made a soundless 'Oh! In my garage?'

Roy patted her hand. 'Remember your garage has been completely rebuilt since those days.'

'You don't think she murdered him?' said

Thomas, peaking his eyebrows.

Kate shrugged. 'What do you think?'

'No proof,' said Ellie. 'Anyway, why should she have killed him? I mean, I can understand why she wanted to get back at Sir Arthur, and in a way I can understand why she might want to hurt Felicity, because Felicity is now living in her home, but why kill her husband, who was the breadwinner of the family? Killing the breadwinner meant she eventually had to lose her home. And why poison people at the church? And what about poor Paddy?'

'Paddy?' Felicity went white. 'I know someone called Paddy. Surely, you don't mean the Paddy who used to be so helpful around our old house? He's not dead, surely?'

'Sorry, sorry, I shouldn't have come out with it like that,' said Ellie. 'Yes, he is, but it may have been natural causes. Put your head between your knees. That's the way.' She heaved Midge off her lap, and helped Felicity to put her head down.

'I'm all right,' said Felicity, after a moment. 'It's just that this is all a bit much to take in.'

Thomas was stroking his beard. 'Aren't you taking all this too seriously? So, there have been a number of incidents, accidents, call them what you will, connected with this woman. But I can't believe that she is a serial murderess. I'm forcibly reminded of Typhoid Mary – before your time – who was

211

a carrier of typhoid. People died all around her and everyone thought she'd murdered them. She was hanged for it, and yet she was innocent.'

'Yes, I know,' said Ellie, unhappily. 'It's just gossip, and coincidence. Too many accidents. Probably. I've got nothing to go on. Except that,' she steeled herself to face derision, 'I've met the woman and although she looks at first sight like a little brown mouse, I can well believe she's capable of anything!'

No one laughed, as she'd thought they might.

Kate said, 'I trust Ellie's instinct.'

Thomas nodded. 'I trust her instinct, too. If she's right, then Felicity really is in danger. On the other hand, even if this Mrs Alexis has put something in the rolls today, it may only be laxatives and that's not enough to justify us crying "Murder!"'

Felicity threw back her shoulders. 'It was something stronger than laxatives in the pizza which poisoned Arthur's dog. I realize it may just be laxatives in the second batch of rolls today. But suppose it's not? Can we take the risk? Anyway, we'll know for certain when the police analyse them.'

Everyone nodded. Ellie said, 'And until then? Felicity, will you stay here with me for a few days?'

'While we gather as much information as we can,' said Kate.

The doorbell rang again. And whoever was ringing kept his finger on the bell.

Roy cast up his eyes. 'I'll go.'

Ellie began gathering coffee mugs together to take out to the kitchen. Thomas looked at his watch, exclaimed that he was late, and got to his feet. There was a lot of shouting going on in the hall, and Roy returned, looking flushed.

'It's a couple who were here earlier, insisting that the house is not sold, and that they have every right to—'

Kate said, 'This time I'm going to deal with it.' She went out.

Ellie rubbed her forehead. 'Is it me going mad, or is Diana orchestrating this from somewhere nearby? Perhaps from her car? So many people calling at regular intervals, and some of them returning? This persecution of hers seems utterly trivial but it's wearing me down. Sooner or later I'm going to have to let them in, aren't I?'

Thomas looked at his watch again, and said, 'Roy, let's see if we can find Diana and tell her to stop it. If Ellie's right, she's parked just down the road somewhere. My meeting can wait.'

Roy agreed, and they went out, looking grim-faced.

Felicity had picked up Midge and was hugging him. For once Midge allowed what he would normally regard as an insult. 'Ellie, what am I going to do?'

'Stick it out,' said Ellie. 'But take precautions.'

'What precautions?'

Kate returned, laughing. 'I've called up the cavalry. In other words, my beloved husband is out there now. He can shout louder and knows more threatening language than they do! It comes of being a teacher in a tough secondary school, I suppose. Now, Ellie, I don't think you should stay here tonight. Move in with us? It's chaotic, what with Catriona tending to wake up at all hours, but...'

'She can stay with me,' said Felicity, before Ellie could decide what she wanted to do.

'Good idea,' said Kate. 'Now, shall I help you wash up?'

'I'll do it,' said Felicity, as Midge took a flying leap from her arms to the back of the settee.

'Then I'll go and put Catriona to bed. Armand always keeps her up far too late. See you in the morning.'

Ellie said, 'I don't want to go anywhere.' She took the mugs to the kitchen, and began piling dirty cutlery and mugs into the dishwasher.

Felicity followed, wrinkling her brow. 'That hall window of yours hasn't been mended yet, and Diana isn't going to give up easily. Suppose she tries something in the middle of the night? Roy put in a good security system at my place. It really would be better if you came to stay with me until you can get the locks changed here and have the window replaced. And it would keep me sane, if you were with me.'

She started stacking the empty Chinese food containers, to put in the dustbin.

Ellie sighed. 'I hate being driven out of my home.'

'I feel the same. But my house is like Fort Knox compared to this place at the moment.'

Ellie could see the logic of it. 'Very well. I'll come. Thanks.'

Felicity put her arm around Ellie's shoulders and gave her a hug. 'And we'll both go on a diet and lose a couple of pounds and then go shopping, right?'

The front door banged and Roy returned, without Thomas. 'Diana was in her car just down the road, just as you said. Frank was on the back seat, playing with a computer game. She was encouraging a couple who'd been here earlier, telling them to try the house again. Thomas read the riot act to them and pointed out that what she was doing was fraudulent misrepresentation. The couple scarpered at once, looking scared. Diana tried to object, and Thomas raised his voice to drown her out. She was clutching a clipboard which I took off her ... how she squawked!'

He dumped it on the kitchen table. 'See, this is a list of the people she's been interesting in this house. She screamed that I was stealing her property, and Thomas told her what she's been doing tonight is far worse. I'm going to photocopy everything and let her have it back tomorrow. I told her that if there's any more trouble, her paperwork goes to the police.' He laughed. 'I tried to take her mobile phone off her as well, but she screamed fit to pierce your eardrums and Thomas told me not to.'

'Good for you and good for Thomas,' said Ellie.

'He's just great, isn't he!' said Felicity, rinsing her fingers under the tap. 'And now, Roy, you be on your way. Ellie is going to lock up here and come home with me, because she can't stay here with that window inadequately boarded over like that. It's far too easy to smash it in. I have a bad feeling about Diana – pardon me, Ellie, but I do. I can just see her breaking in tonight and getting hold of more keys or vandalizing the place or something. Oh, I don't know what she'll do, but I don't think you ought to be here when she comes.'

Someone used a key to let himself in. Armand from next door, lugging a carrier bag full of school work and a duvet. 'Kate thinks you shouldn't sleep here tonight and I agree. I'll sleep on your settee, look after the house for you. At least I can get my marking done in peace and quiet.'

Behind him came Thomas, smoothing out a grin. 'Roy, you will make sure Diana gets her property back tomorrow...?'

And behind him came Bill Weatherspoon, icily not amused. 'Are you having a party, Ellie? Why haven't you been answering your phone? Don't tell me you've got yourself mixed up in yet another neighbourhood spat?'

For a moment everyone froze, and Ellie registered that her very good friends and neighbours were not best pleased at Bill's intrusion. Then everyone spoke at once.

'So sorry, Bill. I had to go to the dentist and then...

'I must rush ... the meeting must have started...' Thomas disappeared.

Roy waved the clipboard. 'Diana's been at it again. Look!'

'Ellie's coming to stay with me...'

Armand powered his way through to the kitchen and switched on the kettle. 'OK if I make myself a cuppa, Ellie? And yes, I'll remember to feed Midge before I doss down for the night.' Then to Bill, 'Who are you? Another of Ellie's men friends?'

Ellie hastened to smooth over what was developing into an awkward situation. 'Bill, this is my wonderful neighbour Armand, from next door. Armand, this is my very good friend, who is also my solicitor, Bill Weatherspoon.'

'What is going on?' Bill's mouth turned down. 'Ellie? I told you I'd deal with Diana.'

'So you did,' said Ellie, trying for a meek and mild tone, while part of her wanted to scream at him that they were managing perfectly well without his aid ... though perhaps they weren't managing all that well, come to think of it. 'Everything rather got out of hand, Bill, but it's all settled down now. I'll tell you all about it when we meet tomorrow. I'm looking forward to it immensely.'

Bill lightened up, and smiled. 'So that's all right, then?'

'It's more than all right, Bill.' She was touched by how little it took to make him smile, and took his arm as she walked him to the front door. 'Thanks for caring, but we really are coping. Roy, you're on your way out, aren't you? Your mother will be worrying about you. I'll be quite safe with Felicity, now.'

Bill managed a kiss on her cheek. Ellie had the impression that Armand might be making faces at Bill behind his back. He could be such a child sometimes!

She eased Roy and Bill out of the front door, and set her back to it. Felicity and Armand were both doubled up with laughter, and she would have joined them if she hadn't thought it might be disloyal to Bill.

'A bit po-faced, isn't it?' That was Armand.

Felicity said, 'I know he's been awfully good and helpful to you. But Ellie, he'll make you give up all your old friends if you marry him.'

Ellie hadn't faced that one, and had to concede that Felicity had a point. But she wasn't going to slag Bill off behind his back. 'My life would be a lot quieter without you lot dragging me into trouble. Felicity, it won't take me a minute to throw a few things into a bag. Armand, that cat's already had plenty to eat so don't let him fool you.'

They left Armand settling down to his marking, and drove back to Felicity's. In the dusk her front garden was full of scent from the honeysuckle and roses. Felicity stopped the car just short of the garage. She fingered the gadget which opened the garage doors, but didn't operate it. Was she scared of using her garage?

'You've made this front garden delightful,' said Ellie, in encouraging tones.

'I'm not going to be driven out of it,' said Felicity. She operated the switch to open the garage door, and drove in. As she opened the front door and led the way into her house, she said, 'Do you know, you're the first person I've had to stay here with me? Brand new duvet on brand new bed. How about that?'

Mrs Alexis spoon-fed the frail old man. He'd taken a sudden turn for the worse and needed an arm to get to the bathroom now. His appetite was poor, too, but he liked her home-made soups. His daughter Ruby didn't seem to care whether he lived or died. Of course, a pillow over his face while he slept would put him out of his misery. Easy as pie. But he was more use to his house-keeper alive than dead, wasn't he?

In fact, she was getting almost fond of him. He was so pathetically grateful for the little she could do for him and it was nice to be appreciated for a change ... though of course if she didn't look after him, they both knew that he'd be at the mercy of whatever carers the council might see fit to pro-vide – or worse, have to be packed off to an old people's home. And what would Ruby do then? Would she sell up, or keep the house – and the housekeeper – on?

Was the house in his name, or that of his daughter? It might be worth finding out.

The housekeeper was looking forward to the next day, when she'd be getting some good news about that stuck-up Kingsley woman. Perhaps when she'd finished feeding the old man, she'd take a spin on the bicycle round by her old house. It wouldn't do any harm, would it, and she'd like to see how things were developing.

Eleven

Felicity had given Ellie a prettily furnished guest bedroom with en suite, but she did not sleep well.

Nor, it appeared from the blue shadows under Felicity's eyes at breakfast time, had Felicity. 'Did you sleep well, Ellie? No need to answer. I heard you moving around in the night. This business is getting us all down, isn't it? I kept having nightmares about being stuck in the garage with the car pumping out exhaust fumes ... stupid, stupid!'

Felicity had opened the French windows on to the back garden and went to stand there, nursing a cup of coffee.

Ellie lied, 'I'm fine.' A radio was perched on the work surface, delivering unremarkable music and doleful news items.

'Another fine day is forecast, though we could do with some more rain, really. What would you like for breakfast? The full English?'

Ellie shuddered. 'Coffee and toast. Fruit juice if you've got any. Armand would have phoned if anything had happened, wouldn't he?'

At that moment a phone rang somewhere in the house. Felicity snatched up her landline. It wasn't that. She sought for her mobile and found it in the hall in her handbag. It wasn't that.

'My mobile!' Ellie ran up the stairs and found it in her handbag, lost in the duvet which she'd thrown back over the bed. By that time it had stopped ringing, but there was a voice message on it. Armand.

'Not to worry, my dear.' Armand sounded remarkably lively. 'I'm just off to school, but thought you'd like to know someone tried the old fishing rod trick at two o'clock this morning. You know, pushing a cane with a hook on the end through the letter-box, trying to pick up any keys that might be left on the hall table? I was fast asleep but Midge objected to this long stick invading his space and had a right go at it. What a champ he is, eh.'

'Oh.' Ellie sat down with a thump on the nearest chair.

'...but not to worry. That cat's such a weight, he snapped the tip off the bamboo cane, hook and all, and made such a row that he woke me. Whoever it was had gone by then, so I gave Midge a double helping of cat food and he slept on my stomach for the rest of the night. OK?'

'Did you report it to the police?' said Ellie, though of course Armand couldn't hear her.

'Oh, and I reported it to the police, but they said that if the chap had gone, they'd just come round some time to get a report. Said we were lucky. Said never to leave keys on the hall table. So I'm off now. Back this evening for the next instalment. Don't forget to get that window mended.' End of message.

Ellie took the mobile downstairs with her to tell Felicity what had happened. 'I do usually leave keys on the hall table, only of course last night I brought them away with me.'

'Diana thought you'd be there, and so would the keys. Which meant she could lift them without making a noise.'

They contemplated Diana's persistence with distaste. 'Breakfast?' said Felicity.

As she sipped her second cup of coffee, Ellie said, 'Are you all right, Felicity? Want to talk about it?'

Felicity returned the question. 'Are you all right, Ellie? Do you want to talk about it?'

Ellie shook her head. 'I have to ring my builder, then see if Kate is available to let him in to repair that window ... perhaps get new locks, what do you think? Then I have to find something decent to wear to the Ritz this afternoon. What do you wear to the Ritz? Do you want to visit your mother at the home?'

Felicity sighed. 'I don't want to do anything except go back to bed with a box of chocolates and something light to read.'

'You were keen to get on with designing a new layout for the back garden yesterday.'

Felicity waved her hand at her neighbour's overgrown bushes which overshadowed one side of her garden. 'What's the point? Half my garden's in shade from mid-morning on. My neighbour won't give me permission to cut back her hedge, even if it has grown too tall and overhangs my fence.'

'Come off it,' said Ellie. 'You've a right to cut back anything overhanging your garden, provided – and here's the fun bit – you give your neighbour back everything you cut off.'

Felicity was not listening. 'I'm scared, Ellie. It took me ages to work up enough courage to get the milk from the front doorstep this morning. I kept thinking someone was going to take a pot shot at me from the road.'

'I don't think she'd do that. If you avoid gifts of food left on the doorstep, you should be all right.'

'What about the husband who died in the garage? What about Paddy? How did she get to him? Why did she doctor the rolls for church? How long is it going to take the police to process those rolls? And what if they do contain laxatives? Will the police take it as a joke, or take it seriously? Am I going round the twist?'

'Yes and no.' Ellie decided not to tell Felicity to pull herself together. It never worked. 'Suppose we do something about it ourselves?'

'How?'

'Visit your neighbour, for a start, and ask what she knows. She must have lived here a long time, judging by the state of her hedge. Let me see; we'll roll up to apologize for all the mess and inconvenience she must have suffered when you were pulling this house apart and rebuilding it, and don't tell me she didn't suffer some inconvenience because all builders make mess and noise.

'Then we'll go on to talk about your plans for the garden, and how you hope it's not going to be too stressful for her to have this side of her hedge cut back. Perhaps you can even offer to help her with the cost of having her whole hedge trimmed, if you think it's become too much for her to handle by herself? She is by herself, is she?'

'Oh, Ellie! You are so ... so *sneaky*!'

'Am I really, dear?' Ellie was so gratified, she went pink. 'Isn't that nice.'

'There's something in Shakespeare about "taking arms against a sea of troubles". I had to learn it at school.' Felicity showed faint signs of animation. 'Is that what we're doing?'

'Certainly we are. First I must ring my builder.' It was Thursday morning, wasn't it?

It was so easy to lose track of the days when you were staying with someone else. Thursday mornings at home meant watching out for Mrs Dawes, who always took a flower-arranging class at the church hall that day, and who would often pop in to have a chat with Ellie afterwards. Thursday afternoons used to mean looking after little Frank, but ... well, not this week, anyway. How pleasant routine seemed, in retrospect. Ellie punched in the numbers for her builder.

The woman next door was a faded little thing. Caring for the house and an indolent, elderly husband seemed to have become rather too much for her in her eighties. Everything in the house looked clean, but as things had broken they had been neither mended nor replaced.

She ushered them into a sitting-room which contained a lot of heavy old-fashioned furniture, and introduced them to her husband, whom she called 'Father'. Ellie and Felicity were waved to an extremely hard settee covered in brown moquette.

Felicity apologized – almost grovelled – for all the annoyance she'd caused her with the rebuilding ... er, Mrs...?

Their hostess thawed visibly. 'Do call me Maisie. Now you've explained everything so clearly, yes, there was a lot of noise and dust, you wouldn't believe how much dust, but there, Father always says you can't make an omelette without breaking eggs and I suppose you couldn't help it, really, though with Mrs Alexis having been there for so many years, I suppose we ought to have known that something would have to be done when she left, oughtn't we, Father?'

'Where's my elevenses, eh?' snapped Father.

'Oh, yes. I must get on, I really must,' said Maisie, flapping the duster she'd been holding all the time, and making no move to the kitchen. 'I do appreciate your coming round to apologize but there's no need, not really, though it was awful at the time, as I said...'

'And you won't mind if I cut your hedge back on my side? It does take so much light from my garden, you see,' Felicity prompted.

'Oh, the hedge? Yes, Father tells me we can't stop you doing what you want on your side, and really it was only because I was so upset about the dust and that ... and he told me afterwards that I shouldn't have got so upset and told you not to touch it. Father always used to cut the hedge, you see, and then the boys when they came used to help him, yes, and one of them bought him an electric thing but it was far too dangerous and I was ever so glad when Father's arthritis stopped him from using it, and of course the boys would cut it if they lived nearer, but they had to move where their jobs are, doing very well, both of them, but that means...'

'The hedge,' prompted Felicity. 'Would you mind terribly if I got someone to cut your side as well as mine? It would be doing me the greatest favour, it really would.'

'Oh, I couldn't...' she looked at Father, who'd subsided in his chair and was now hiding behind the spread of a newspaper, ' ... oh, but if you really wanted to ... what do you think, Father?'

Father grunted, which they all took as assent.

Maisie brightened up. 'Well, I must get on, and now you've explained everything, it's made all the difference, and having the hedge cut for us, well, I don't deny it would cheer me up no end, don't you think, Father? I always say that having a good neighbour is a blessing...'

Ellie leaned forward. 'I suppose Mrs Alexis also found the garden difficult to maintain after her husband died. Did he help her much about the house?'

'Him, no! Father used to say he only married her so's they couldn't send him back to Greece when his visa ran out. Father used to call him a greasy wog layabout, though I always used to say to him that he shouldn't say such things, but it's quite true, Mr Alexis did smell of garlic and that oil they always

228

use in the cooking, can't stand the stuff myself and it upsets Father's stomach something wicked. But there; you shouldn't speak ill of the dead...'

'He died at home, did he?'

'In the garage, would you believe! Right up at the side of our garage, as it might be, though Father gave up using our car some time back when his sight got so bad. But it makes you think, doesn't it, that if we'd been using our car then, we might have smelled the exhaust or whatever it was, though the garage door did close tightly and that was the problem, wasn't it? That the door jammed shut on him while he was working on the car. He was three sheets to the wind, as Father said, at the time. Is it three sheets to the wind, or have I got it wrong? Maybe it's four sheets to the wind ... now I've forgotten what I was saying.'

'The poor man was drunk, you think? Probably didn't realize what was happening.'

'Ye-es.' Maisie didn't seem convinced of that. She gave her duster a flap. 'They say he'd tried to open the door from the inside with a length of wood or something, but couldn't manage it, poor thing, though of course if he hadn't had drink taken, he wouldn't have let the door close on him like that, would he?'

'Was the door always awkward?'

'N-no. Not that I know of. Though we

wouldn't know, really, would we, what with not being on such terms as to enquire. Father not liking to have to kowtow to a greasy foreigner as he called him, and me having had my nose chopped off short when I offered to help her, Mrs Alexis, with her shopping after he, her husband that is, gave her a bloody nose and a black eye ... that is...'

She looked nervously at her husband, who barked out, 'My elevenses, Maisie!'

'Yes, yes. I must get on.' She dithered herself over to the door, gesturing Ellie and Felicity to follow her. 'Mustn't gossip,' she hissed at them in the hall. 'But we think, Father and I, that he was knocking her about something cruel at the time ... and she slept right through it that night, didn't miss him not coming up to bed or anything. Makes you think, doesn't it!'

'Did you tell the police?'

'Me?' She looked frightened, darting a glance at the sitting-room door. 'Father said not to interfere, and we didn't know anything, really. Not for sure. And we were sorry for her, of course. Besides, it was an accident, wasn't it? Well,' she said, brightly, 'Must get on. We're so glad you dropped round.'

Ellie waited to have the giggles till they were approaching Felicity's front door. 'How to kill and get away with it!'

They both stopped and looked at the

porch. It was empty. No bag of rolls. No post. Felicity smiled thinly. 'Mrs Alexis might have had provocation, but it was still murder, wasn't it?'

'Not proven,' said Ellie. 'I think I'd give her the benefit of the doubt – as Maisie did – if it weren't for the other rumours about her.'

As they let themselves into the house, a phone rang. Ellie and Felicity scrabbled for their mobiles in unison, but this time it was Felicity's landline which was making the noise.

Felicity grabbed the receiver, and sat down to listen. 'Yes, Miss Quicke, I'm quite all right ... no, I know you asked me to call you Aunt Drusilla, but...'

Ellie went through into the kitchen, wondering what Miss Quicke would be saying, but thinking it only polite not to listen too obviously. She opened the French windows and stepped out into the garden. Some sparrows squeaked and flew up into the overgrown bushes ... were there birds' nests in there? Had the young flown yet?

Felicity followed her to the window, frowning. 'That was your aunt. She ... I can't believe this ... she wanted to apologize for upsetting me. I don't know what to think. It must have cost her something to apologize. She seemed really upset that I was upset. She wants me to keep on visiting her.'

Ellie suppressed a grin. She hadn't realized

Miss Quicke was capable of apologizing to anyone. Perhaps she was learning to be diplomatic in her old age. Ellie found, to her surprise and relief, that it no longer hurt to think of Felicity and Roy getting together. Good.

Felicity was distractedly opening the fridge and freezer. 'What shall we have for lunch?'

'I mustn't have any, because of tea at the Ritz.'

'I'd forgotten.' Felicity took a deep breath. 'Ellie, you'll think me an utter coward, but I don't want to stay here in the house by myself, I don't want to go into the garage by myself, and I don't want to visit my mother by myself, either. Would you come with me to the retirement home, and then ... oh, I don't know ... I'll go clothes shopping or something ... perhaps visit Kate ... till you get back, and then ... you will come back here tonight, won't you?'

Ellie thought longingly of the peace and quiet of her little house, and the conservatory across the back of it where the plants could do with being watered in this warm weather. She must make time to attend to them before Bill collected her. She said, 'Of course. Shall we go?'

The private retirement home had a pleasant outlook and was well run. It took a pleasure in providing its 'guests' with single rooms en suite, with good food and even the occasional sherry before supper. The fees were, of course, astronomical.

Felicity's mother, though now hardly able to walk by herself, continued to spend more money on her appearance in a month than her daughter did in a year. She despised the other residents of the home and barely spoke to them.

Felicity parked in the bay at the side of the home, and got out. She had bought a bunch of roses for her mother on the way in, and a box of chocolate truffles. Ellie hadn't brought anything, knowing it was unlikely Anne would pay her any attention.

Felicity was nervous. 'I ought to have come yesterday. She'll have missed me.'

Ellie followed her into the hall. The door into the office stood open, and a middle-aged woman sat inside, checking on visitors. The manageress.

Felicity straightened her back with an effort. 'Oh, I'm glad you're here. Did Mrs Rivers bring you some rolls yesterday? I said I'd pay. Were they ... did they ... were they all right?'

The woman didn't smile or thank Felicity. 'I wish you'd warned me they were coming. I already had rolls on order for the residents' lunches.'

'Oh. Yes, of course. How stupid of me.' Ellie held back a sigh. Felicity could still be reduced to schoolgirl status with a well-timed criticism.

The manageress relented. 'They seemed very nice. I think the residents enjoyed them. Mrs Rivers brought another lot around today, and I've told her that if she can provide me with them every day including Sundays, I'll make use of them, provided the bills go to you. I've already cancelled my order to the bakery.'

'Oh. Yes. Thank you. I mean, that's quite all right.' Felicity must know she was burbling like a child, but didn't seem able to help herself.

Ellie took Felicity's elbow and steered her into the common room, where the residents sat around in high-backed chairs with electrically operated seats to hoist them to their feet at lunch-time. Anne was sitting in the bay window as usual, with a rug over her legs, turning her head to see who had come.

Felicity hung back for a moment. 'So Mrs Rivers is definitely in the clear, if everyone enjoyed the rolls. No one seems to have suffered ill effects.'

'True,' said Ellie. 'Come on. Your mother's looking for you. Get it over with. And remember, we have to leave in twenty minutes.'

Anne had seen them. 'So there you are, Felicity. You do look a mess. You might take a little more care of your appearance, I must say. Why didn't you bring that nice Roy with you? He always appreciates my company. What happened to you yesterday? I was waiting for you all afternoon. I would have thought you could spare the time to visit me when I'm stuck here...'

A dowdy little woman in a bright yellow tabard and cap crossed the hall as they went in to sit with Anne. The woman was carrying a bottle of disinfectant and a rag, on her way to clean up after a resident who'd had a little accident. She stared at the group in the bay window. The sun caused Anne to reach for her film-star style dark glasses, turned Felicity's hair to different shades of gold, and touched Ellie's silvery mop with highlights.

The manageress came out of her office. 'Betty, haven't you finished the bedrooms yet? It's nearly time to start serving lunch.'

Mrs Alexis scurried into the lift, the doors shut, and she disappeared from sight. Felicity and Ellie had their backs to her, and would probably not have recognized her in that outfit if they had seen her.

But she'd seen them all right.

Going to the Ritz for tea was a trifle overwhelming for someone like Ellie, who enjoyed going to the Carvery as an occasional treat. She'd worn the second of her new sets of underwear, with her lacy rose-pink top over a silvery-grey swishy skirt and high-heeled sandals. Her legs were pretty good for her age, she thought, and she wouldn't have to walk far so it would be all right to wear the sandals.

Tea at the Ritz was laid in a slightly over-decorated pink and gold room to one side of the foyer, with a woman in a black evening trouser suit playing a grand piano, double tablecloths on all the tables, and waiters in proper black and white.

The centrepiece on each table was a three-tier cake stand; ground floor sandwiches – without crusts, of course – first floor fruit scones, with clotted cream and jam in separate serving dishes plus thin slices of heavy fruit cake, top floor what Ellie supposed must be called 'fancies' ... fancy cakes and shapes, fruit in 'boats' of light pastry, prettily arranged slices, charmingly decorated.

She tried not to gawk as she took in the delicious spread before her. My, was she hungry!

'What tea would madam like?' A hovering waiter. A long list of teas available, plus an amusing piece of verse about the pleasures of taking tea at the Ritz.

'Earl Grey with lemon, no milk,' said Bill, deciding for her.

Ellie was so intimidated by her surroundings that she didn't object to his ordering for her. What was in those sandwiches?

'Ham, smoked salmon, egg, chicken,

cucumber with cream cheese...' the waiter intoned.

Ellie reached for one, only to find that Bill had misinterpreted her movement, and captured both her hands in his.

'My dear, I've been thinking about this moment all day. To see your eyes light up, to give you some enjoyment in life. I can't tell you how much I'm looking forward to giving you treats throughout our life together. Have you ever been taken to the races? Goodwood and Ascot? Or Henley? Perhaps I can even swing it for you to go to a Garden Party at Buckingham Palace?'

'The Taj Mahal by moonlight?' said Ellie, trying to lighten the tone. She tried to withdraw her hands, but his grasp tightened.

'Why not?' he said. 'Why not, indeed? I never got there with my first wife, but who knows what's in store for us now?'

Those sandwiches! Her tummy would be rumbling soon, if she didn't get something to eat.

Mrs Alexis took off her tabard and cap and hung them up on the hooks at the back of the kitchen. Cook was fitting dirty plates, knives and forks into the dishwasher. There was just one bread roll left on a side plate.

Mrs Alexis tore it apart and thrust the pieces in the bin.

'Those rolls aren't bad, from this new supplier,'

said Cook. 'You haven't eaten your lunch. Don't you want it?'

Mrs Alexis shook her head. 'It would choke me.'

Cook shrugged. 'Suit yourself.'

Mrs Alexis had sat on her rage all morning. She took a couple of indigestion tablets for the bile rising in her throat. She took the padlock and chain off her bike and wobbled out into the road.

How had that bitch survived? There'd been enough poison in the rolls to kill two or three adults. Somehow, she'd escaped ... again.

Or perhaps Lady Kingsley hadn't fancied rolls this morning and had saved them for her tea. All might not be lost. She would cycle round there again this evening, see if she could find out what was going on.

Twelve

The waiter released the tension by bringing the tea.

'Shall I pour?' Ellie said, and this time managed to release her hands. 'A slice of lemon, very weak, no sugar or milk, right?'

Bill beamed at her. 'I hope you're hungry. Ordinarily, I never eat tea, but I think I can force myself to have a nibble today.' He took one tiny sandwich and put it on the edge of his plate. 'No more trouble with your tooth today?'

Ellie's inner ear was acute, and translated this as, 'Did ickle oo have any more painsy-wainsy with your pretty little toothy-pegs?'

She smiled and handed Bill his cup. 'Mr Patel was very good.'

'Oh, do you go to him? I go to the chap on Haven Green, myself.'

Ellie nodded, getting the point. The 'chap on Haven Green' only took private patients, while dear Mr Patel still had a number of National Health patients although all new ones had to register as private. She took two sandwiches; smoked salmon ... yum. Cream cheese and cucumber, in some special bread ... yum.

'Now,' said Bill, 'I'm sure you're dying to tell me all about your latest little problem, so let's get that out of the way, shall we?'

She bit back the words 'Don't be so patronizing.' She said, 'It's not such a small matter. Felicity is terrified. You see...' Ellie told him what had been happening, while getting through six little sandwiches, each one more delicious than the last, and beginning to spread jam and cream on the two halves of her scone.

'A storm in a tea-cup, my dear,' said Bill, appreciating the pun as he passed her his cup for a refill. 'Lady Kingsley is not perhaps the strongest of characters. Surely she isn't falling to pieces because she thinks someone's going to put laxative in a roll and force it down her throat?'

'We don't know exactly what it is the woman's being using. But it isn't only that.' Ellie poured tea, wondering if Bill would like to let her have his scone as well. 'We think she—'

'This woman who left the neighbourhood ages ago...'

'Yes, she might have. But on the other hand, who else would—'

'A practical joker, of course. Someone at your church, probably. He's a pretty odd chap, that present vicar of yours, isn't he?'

'Thomas?' Ellie leaned back in her chair, remembering how Thomas never judged, but always helped when people were in trouble. That he made himself available to all and sundry ... and some of them were very sundry indeed. That he could always be relied on for practical help. That he was a rock. That he had ... well, she mustn't think about that now or she'd get all flustered and spill her tea ... whoops!

Nearly!

Concentrate, Ellie.

'...and as for the rumours that you've dug up, well ... nobody could take them seriously, could they?' He took the last scone, put jam on it, but no cream. How could he eat a scone without cream, particularly when there was plenty of cream still in the container?

'You may be right,' said Ellie, politely. 'But whether the threat is real or imaginary, it's left Felicity in a bad way.'

He patted her hand, indulgently. 'Now, tell me what you want to do about Diana.'

'Oh. Well, she's been trying it on again. Kate suggested I get a thingy to stop her coming anywhere near me or the house; you know the proper name for it, I'm sure.' She was annoyed with herself that the right word had eluded her. She did know it. It would come to her in a minute. Her momentary lapse would only reinforce Bill's patronizing attitude towards her. 'I thought I might threaten her with it, which would mean, of course, that I'd no longer be able to look after little Frank after school. That might bring her to her senses.'

He raised his eyebrows. 'You wouldn't allow me to...?'

'No. This one's on me. I promise I'll scream for help if I need it. I have good friends who...'

'Yes, yes.' He took a slice of fruit cake, cut it into tiny squares, and popped one in his mouth.

Ellie had a vision of Thomas sitting on the other side of the table, munching away. By now he'd probably have asked for some more sandwiches – the waiters were bringing round a tray with second helpings – and he'd have got through the lot, making appreciative noises throughout. How he'd have enjoyed it, though it was extremely unlikely – given his austere way of life – that he'd ever think of spending so much money on a tea break. If he'd have been sitting opposite her, he'd have wanted strong dark tea, with milk and two sugars and no lemon. Of course, he really ought to lose some weight...

...and Bill really needed to put some on. Being hugged by a skeleton was not ... she cut that thought off. Whatever was the matter with her today? She eased a lemon slice on to her plate. So light! Was there another flavour lurking there, apart from lemon?

'What I thought was,' said Bill, dabbing his mouth with his serviette, 'that you and I should get our diaries out, and settle on a couple of nights a week and most of each weekend to start with, when we could do things together. I know you want to take it slowly, and I respect that.' He took a deep breath. 'The thing is, Ellie, and I'm sure you don't mean it, but you're so busy with your church and your little committees that you're hardly giving me a chance to ... if you know what I mean?'

She was touched that this clever man

should show vulnerability.

'Dear Bill. I don't mean to be elusive. I suppose you're right, though. I did rather look for things to occupy my time after Frank died. Then I have had to consider Diana and my grandson, the trust fund and friends. I suppose I like to be useful to people because it makes me feel I'm still of importance in the world.' She fished for her handkerchief. 'Silly me! Take no notice.'

The waiter hovered. 'Is madam ready for her crème brûlée?'

'Yes, yes,' said Bill, waving him away. 'Now this is just what I mean, Ellie. I won't have you upsetting yourself thinking that no one cares for you, when here I am asking you to marry me and...' To the approaching waiter, 'No, no. Not yet.'

Ellie allowed the waiter to take her plate, as a glance around showed her that some people had already left the tea-room. 'I like crème brûlée, don't you?'

'What? Oh, I suppose so.'

The waiter presented them with small dishes in which reposed the Ritz's version of crème brûlée: fruits on top of a warm creamy mixture. 'Nice,' said Ellie, thinking that she really preferred a crème brûlée where you had to smash the crust on top immediately it arrived, or you couldn't get at the custard beneath.

'Yes, yes,' said Bill, pushing his aside half

eaten. 'So how about it, Ellie?'

The waiter presented Bill with a folder and he put a platinum card into it.

Ellie told herself not to promise more than she could easily give. 'Monday nights would be fine. You're quite right about the choir practice. I was bullied into joining, and I never enjoyed singing there, though I enjoyed the company.'

Bill took out a gold pen, and clicked it open. 'I'd like you to come to my church this next Sunday, if you will. The Georgian church by Kew Gardens, you know? We get a very decent sermon and there's a paid choir, of course. Then we could have lunch at the restaurant opposite. I'll have to book a table, of course, but I think you'd find the food acceptable.'

Ellie opened her mouth to object to this plan, and then closed it again. Bill was right; they must spend some time together if they were to foster their relationship, and if she married him then of course she would be going to his church in future. For one wild moment she pictured everyone at 'her' church turning shocked and disappointed faces towards her, and mouthing the word 'traitor' ... or should it be 'traitress'? She liked the word 'traitor' much better than 'traitress', which somehow sounded like 'seamstress'. Or 'laundress'.

She pulled herself together. 'That would be

lovely, Bill. Will you pick me up, or shall I meet you there?'

'I usually have a late breakfast on Sundays, don't want to hurry it, digestion, you know. Suppose I pick you up at ten in time for the service at half past?'

The waiter returned Bill's card, the formalities were completed, and Ellie went down to the powder room. All pink. Of course. With Victorian fashion prints on the walls and an array of lotions and creams to use after visiting the facilities. Ellie looked in the mirror and asked herself, *What have you agreed to?*

To which she replied, It's about time you moved on, girl.

Yes, but ... her reflection argued. *Is this the road you really want to take?*

How can I tell till I've tried it? It's a very pleasant road.

So's the primrose path, and you know where that leads!

I'm very fond of Bill.

I suspect he's fonder of you than you are of him. Which means that if you allow him to think you're seriously contemplating marriage with him, he'll be shattered when you break it off.

Who says I'm going to break it off?

Gut reaction, ducky. Mind your step.

Oh, get lost!

Ellie had promised Felicity that she wouldn't be late, but would meet up with her at Ellie's house early that evening. Bill dropped her off with a peck on her cheek, saying it was a good thing she'd got that window repaired. So the builders had been and gone. Good.

Ellie let herself into her house, appreciating the pleasure of being alone and not having to worry about anyone else's feelings. She had the maddest impulse to run through the house yelling loudly – about nothing at all, really. Of course she didn't do it. Behaviour like that belonged to schooldays, when you shot out of the school gates yelling with joy at being away from teacher's eye ... and of course it was ridiculous to compare Bill with a teacher.

She dropped her keys on the hall table. Then remembered that that wasn't a wise thing to do, and put them in her handbag which she took through into the kitchen. On the way she picked up the bill which the builders had left for replacing the window, and noticed that a broken piece of cane, with a hook on the end, had been propped against the stairs. Whatever would Diana get up to next?

Midge appeared. He'd want feeding, of course. She fed him.

She said, 'Ooof!' to herself, relaxing, slipping off her high-heeled sandals and padding into the conservatory without even bothering to find her slippers which were somewhere around, probably up in her bedroom but maybe not. The light was flashing on the answerphone, but she ignored it for the time being. She opened the back door into the garden to let fresh air in, and set about watering her plants. On warm sunny days like this, she sometimes watered twice a day.

She'd tried all sorts of exotica in her conservatory and most of it had exceeded her expectations, particularly the bougainvillea, which had spread along wires all over the roof ... a glorious mat of colour.

The earth in the containers was dry and one or two of the plants had begun to droop. In this weather they'd need watering again tomorrow morning, which was another reason not to go back to Felicity's tonight ... except that she'd promised and, despite what Bill had said, Ellie did feel Felicity had reason to be afraid. In fact, the more she thought about it, the less inclined she was to accept Bill's judgement in the matter, reasonable as it might seem to anyone else.

Someone was coming up the garden path: Kate, helping Catriona to stagger along.

'Thought I heard you,' said Kate, pausing to let Catriona coo at a ladybird on a leaf. 'How did it go at the Ritz?'

'Wonderful tea. I ate everything in sight but I don't feel bloated.'

'Time for a cuppa?'

Had Kate got something on her mind?

Ellie put the kettle on, while Kate carefully helped Catriona to climb the steps into the conservatory. There were tables and chairs in there for adults, plus a low stool next to a cupboard containing some children's toys, but what Catriona really liked was to watch the goldfish swimming in the ornamental lead tank. She would watch them for ten minutes, with any luck. Sometimes she tried to catch them with her fat little hands, but had never succeeded. She had to be watched all the time, of course, in case she fell in or emptied water all over herself.

'So what's the news?' Ellie put a mug of tea in front of Kate.

Kate folded herself into a chair and then stretched out, long legs in jeans, loose top. 'Either I'm imagining things, or she's done it twice before.'

Ellie lowered herself on to a chair. 'Mrs Alexis? Done what?'

'I keep telling myself that accounts don't lie, though of course I know perfectly well that figures can be made to dance up and down and do the can-can in skilled hands. But she's not skilled, is she? I mean ... the amounts are so ... petty!'

'Begin at the beginning.'

'Yesterday I pulled out the rent book and looked at it, right? Well, this morning I got out the back files on rented accommodation, searching for ... I didn't know what. Some-

248

thing. The files contain references, correspondence, that sort of thing. Of course Sir Arthur didn't deal with such everyday matters. He had people to do that for him. But the facts are there.

'When Mr Alexis applied for the tenancy, he had a full-time job as manager of a Greek restaurant. I turned up his references, which were OK. She didn't produce any references, but then she didn't need to, did she? It was clear that he could afford the house on his income, and that was all that was needed. The rent was paid monthly, on the dot right up to the time he died...'

'Or was killed.'

Kate queried it. 'You've come up with something?'

'Tell you later. After he died, she had difficulty making ends meet, right?'

'After he died she had the tenancy transferred to her name alone. Her letter applying for sole tenancy is also on file. To back it up, she stated that there was some insurance money to come and she was going to take on another part-time job to make ends meet. Rental payments continued for about a year, more or less on time, give or take a day or two. Then there was a gap of about three months. Reminders were sent.'

'The insurance money ran out?'

'Possibly. Sir Arthur was reasonably patient, but at the end of five months he threatened to take her to court ... and she paid up. The lot. With one cheque.'

'Where did she get the money?'

'There's a letter on file explaining that her father had died and left her some money. She doesn't say where he lived, or what his name was. We don't even know what her maiden name was. Of course, his death may have been from natural causes. You could say it was a lucky accident for her. Parents do pass on, eventually, and there's absolutely no reason to believe there was anything sinister about it ... except that the pattern was repeated four years later.'

Ellie blinked. 'Another convenient death?'

Kate nodded. 'Famine and then feast. Presumably she was living on whatever she inherited from her father for a couple of years, and then the money ran out again. After some six months of making excuses, she cleared the arrears saying that her sister had died and left her some money. The wording in both letters was almost identical.'

'She was not highly educated, I'd say. Perhaps there's nothing in it.'

'Three convenient deaths?' Kate raised her eyebrows, then swooped on Catriona, who'd been dabbling in the water with an expression of bliss on her face.

Catriona squawked, but was mollified with a mug of milk and a biscuit. Kate kept her child on her knee, her somewhat hard face softening as she rocked Catriona to and fro.

Ellie wandered over to her beloved geraniums, dead-heading spent blooms and removing yellowed leaves. 'Felicity and I called on one of her neighbours this morning and learned that her husband's death was more than convenient. It seems he was knocking her about something chronic, which was why – reading between the lines – the neighbours didn't say anything when he died.'

'The verdict was misadventure.'

'Mm. It might well have been true, or she might have been able to help him to die accidentally. Perhaps he passed out from drink in the living-room and she dragged him into the garage, turned on the car engine, slammed the garage door down, and left him to die. The neighbour said he may have made a feeble attempt to open the garage door with a piece of wood, but failed.'

'If he was that compos mentis, couldn't he have turned off the ignition and then just waited for someone to let him out?'

'He might have been too drunk to reason that way. She might have placed something against the door to stop it opening, and then removed it in the morning when she went to look for him.'

Kate stared. 'Ellie, I'm glad you've no reason to murder anyone. You'd be far too good at it.'

Ellie went pink. 'Thank you, dear. But I

expect, you know, that the police didn't look too closely at the detail, seeing how much wine he'd drunk, and not knowing that he'd been knocking her about.'

'I'll have another look in the files tomorrow, see if there's anything more to be gleaned.'

'The neighbours are the best bet. Maybe I'll try the ones on the other side tomorrow.'

Catriona threw her mug on to the floor and Kate got to her feet, carrying the little girl. 'Time for supper and bath. Armand may be late tonight.'

Something in the way she held the child made Ellie suspicious. 'You're pregnant again, aren't you?'

Kate looked smug. 'I had a bet with Armand that you'd have tumbled to it before now. Come along, Catriona. Time to go.' She negotiated the steps down to the garden with care, then turned to lift the child's hand in a wave. 'Say goodbye, Catriona. And thank you for having me.'

The child waved and grinned a glorious, wide grin. She was a nice child, friendly and responsive, unlike what little Frank had been at that age. Ellie loved her dearly ... which was not to say that she didn't love her grandson, because of course she did. Just not in the same way.

Ellie stood at the door, waving till the pair had reached the bottom of her garden and turned left to access their own. As she did so, the doorbell rang behind her. One long, steady ring. Diana? She usually rang that way.

Midge exited the conservatory in haste. He hated Diana.

Ellie cupped her hands around her mouth. Kate was walking up her own garden path and should be able to hear her. 'Kate, what's the name of the restaurant that Mr Alexis was at?'

'Acropolis. In the Avenue.'

Acropolis? Ah, yes. A double-fronted restaurant with plants almost obscuring the windows in front. A slightly old-fashioned look. Ellie had never been inside because her husband hadn't liked Greek food and she wouldn't have liked to go into such a place on her own.

The doorbell rang again, impatiently.

Ellie considered not answering it. Let Diana stew. Only, of course it might not be Diana. She checked that she looked all right in the mirror in the hall, and opened the door.

Diana barged past her. 'Mother, what do you think you're doing! Trying to ruin me? I'm going straight to the police from here to file a complaint against Roy for stealing my clipboard and trying to mug me for my mobile. In fact, I rather think I'll sue. He's deprived me of the tools of my trade, made me lose face in front of my customers and lost me the sale of a house—'

'Make up your mind who's the villain, me or Roy. What I'd like to know is, how did you ever think you'd get away with it, getting people to call here to look at the house like that?'

'Oh, Mother, you'd soon have changed your tune when you heard how much money you were going to get from the sale. Nobody turns down half a million! Well, of course you'd only get half, but ... doesn't that sound a good sum?'

'No,' said Ellie, trying to keep calm. 'I prefer my house, thank you. Now, do you want a cup of tea? Oh, and where's little Frank? I hear you kept him out of bed late last night. Ought I to alert the Social Services?'

'If you'd been looking after him as you should—'

'Now who's talking?'

'—giving him bad food to eat...'

'Poisoned, actually.'

Diana gaped. 'What...? What do you mean ... poisoned?'

'The rolls had been tampered with. Possibly it was only with something to give him a tummy ache, but it might equally well have been sleeping pills or paracetamol, or something worse. He was given perfectly good food to eat but he chose to eat something he'd been forbidden to touch.'

Diana collapsed. 'Is that true? He said you hadn't told him not to.'

Ellie sat down, too. 'Mm. You may be right. We gave him some good clean food to eat, but we may not actually have pointed to the rolls and told him not to eat them instead.'

'So you admit that you allowed my son to eat something which could have put him in hospital?'

'As it turned out, there was nothing wrong with the rolls he ate, though we weren't sure about that at the time. He stole them, and sicked them up. Sufficient punishment, don't you think? Do you want a cuppa?'

'No, I ... no! I came here to...'

'To try to make me take the blame for your misdoings, just as you've tried to make me take the blame for what Frank did yesterday? Well, I'm not playing. Roy may have been a little over-enthusiastic, taking your clip-board. But at least he managed to stop your harassment of me. Yes, it was harassment. So, have you come to collect the evidence of your attempted break-in last night? I see it's in the hall. Armand was staying here last night, by the way, and he informed the police about it.'

Diana gave Ellie a bold, defiant look. 'What are you trying to pin on me now?'

Ellie sighed. 'Have it your own way. If you want the evidence, then take it. I assume that since this is Thursday, you've managed to get rid of Frank by dumping him back on his father and Maria. Did they have a good holiday?'

'How dare you talk like that, as if I'm not devoted to the child.'

'When it suits you, yes. Now, if you've nothing else to say...'

'I'm facing bankruptcy, and all you can do is—'

'Employ a good accountant. Sell that absurdly expensive car of yours. Get a job. But don't expect me to bail you out.'

'If you'd only let me have half the value of this house, which is what my father intended...'

'No, he didn't, Diana. He was fed up with your extravagance before he died. He'd bailed you out several times and given you good advice, which you ignored. If he'd wanted me to give you half the house now, he'd have put that in the will. He didn't. He wanted me to have it for my lifetime ... and don't start thinking of ways to bump me off because too many people – including Bill Weatherspoon – know what you're like.'

Diana squeezed out a tear. 'If you're going to marry him, what does it matter what happens to this house?'

'If I marry him – which is by no means certain – then I shall rent this house out and it will serve as my pension.'

'Let me rent it out for you. At least then I'd

get a fee for arranging it.'

'Which part of the word "No" don't you understand? What's more, I'm considering taking out an injunction against you coming anywhere near this house in future, or trying to sell it by any means whatever. I'll look after little Frank one afternoon a week as before, collecting him from school and delivering him to your place at six o'clock, and that's it. Understood?'

'Mother, you can't—'

'Can and will. Now if you don't mind, I need to change because I'm going out for the evening.'

Diana burst into noisy tears. Surprisingly, Ellie felt nothing but irritation. She dumped the box of tissues at Diana's elbow, and Diana grabbed a couple.

Ellie wondered at herself. How had she become so hard?

'Mother, please! I beg of you.' The tissues came down from the eyes. Crocodile tears, weren't they?

Ellie marched out to the kitchen, collected the mugs which she, Kate and Catriona had been using earlier and dumped them in the dishwasher. Then she began to wonder if she hadn't been too hard on Diana.

The doorbell rang. A rather tentative ring. Felicity?

Felicity, making excuses for herself even as she edged into the hall. 'Am I too early? I've been helping out with the toddlers at church, because they're a bit short-handed, and oh, they are so sweet. Thomas sends his love. I told him you were out living the high life with Bill. Oh! Diana? Sorry, I didn't realize...'

'Diana's just going,' said Ellie, with a firmness that surprised her. 'Diana, don't forget your piece of cane, will you?'

'You'll regret this,' said Diana, stalking out without the piece of cane.

Felicity said, 'Sorry, did I interrupt?'

'No. She always throws a temper when she can't get her own way. Are you hungry? I thought we could go to the Greek restaurant for a meal this evening.'

Mrs Alexis helped the old man to the toilet, and changed the pad in his chair. A good thing he hadn't been in his bed at the time. He ought to be having proper carers coming in to look after him a couple of times a day. She'd mentioned it to Ruby this morning, but Ruby had said she was sure Mrs Alexis could manage for the time being, and come to think of it, she really didn't want strangers coming into the house, poking around and asking questions all the time.

The old man was pathetic. He was the very opposite of her father, who'd been a right old tartar in his day. It was off with his belt and get you behind your legs the moment you did anything wrong. And then, after her mother died ...

well, best not to think about that now.

'Would you like some chicken soup for supper?'

He nodded. His hand shook as he reached for the remote control for the television and turned the sound up.

She could sprinkle something on his soup to make him sleep well tonight. She needed time to think what to do about Felicity. People who wronged her never got away with it. She'd proved that, over and over again, hadn't she? Felicity had been lucky so far, but her luck couldn't last for ever.

Felicity ought to have had some of the poisoned pizza she'd left at the big old house, and instead the dog had eaten it.

Then the handyman Paddy had taken the rolls she'd left in the porch for Felicity to eat ... and he'd died instead.

There was still hope, of course. Felicity might not have fancied the latest batch of killer rolls for her breakfast, but might eat them later on. There was always hope.

And if this didn't work, she'd think of something else. She'd had plenty of experience at getting rid of people who upset her, after all. Why should Felicity be any different?

Thirteen

The Greek restaurant had looked inviting enough, though there were no other customers when Felicity and Ellie arrived and took a table at the back. The menu was daunting, but at least someone had taken the trouble to translate the Greek dishes into English.

Ellie smiled at the dark-haired middle-aged man who came to enquire if they'd like a drink first. 'What do you recommend? This is our first visit, you see.'

He poked his pen at an item at the top of the list. 'Why not try Meze, which is a bit of everything? And for wine...'

'Why not? But no wine,' said Felicity. 'I'm driving.'

'Meze, and a glass of water,' agreed Ellie. 'I've lived here for years but this is my first visit. It's been a Greek restaurant for a long time, hasn't it? I think I was introduced to the manager at one time. A Mr Alexis. Did you know him?'

He smiled, removed the menus. 'Perhaps before my time? Under new management, you know.'

'How long have you been here, then?'

'One month, only.' He departed.

Felicity bent closer to Ellie. 'It's no good. Nobody will know anything.'

'Wait and see. When people start up restaurants in London, they usually recruit from among their own families. Perhaps someone will remember a friend or relative who *can* give us some background on Mr Alexis.'

The first of many small dishes arrived. With identically wary expressions, Ellie and Felicity tasted, looked relieved, and polished off their first course. The little dishes kept coming ... and coming ... and coming.

More customers came in. Ellie recognized moussaka when it was wafted past her, and some kind of kebab, but for the rest, she tasted and ate and enjoyed without always being able to identify what she was eating.

'I don't think I can manage another mouthful,' said Felicity, easing her waist-band.

'Madam enjoyed?' An older waiter this time, coming to remove the last of their dishes.

'Very much,' said Ellie, and tried again. 'Were you here before the change in management? I was wondering if anyone knew a past manager here, a Mr Alexis.'

He shook his head. 'Maybe my brother

knew him, one time. My brother is chef in daytime at café next door. He lives here seven eight years now.'

Felicity sighed. Not long enough.

Ellie smiled, and asked for the bill. 'Thank you. You've been most helpful.'

'Wish they had. Been more helpful, I mean,' said Felicity.

'We had to eat.' Ellie, too, eased her waistband. 'Do you think he means that little café that's tucked on at the side of this place? I thought it was a greasy spoon. I've never been in there, either. Perhaps I'll try it tomorrow.'

'What's the use if the chef's only been here for seven or eight years?'

'You never know till you've tried. Come on, Felicity. They need our table.'

Felicity pulled out her mobile, made a face and deleted whatever message flashed up. 'I wish he'd take a hint.'

'Roy? '

Felicity didn't reply, but held the door open for Ellie to leave. They walked back to the car in silence. It was a fine evening, and Felicity's front garden looked a picture, but Felicity hesitated when she turned the car off the road. Was she going to suggest leaving the car out on the driveway so that she wouldn't have to use the garage? No. She faced her fear and conquered it, tightening her lips as she drove into the garage. She helped Ellie out, and got the door shut.

There was a sheaf of flowers in the porch. Red roses. From Roy?

Felicity opened the front door and walked into the house, ignoring the flowers. Ellie picked them up, took them through into the kitchen, found a vase and put them in it. It wasn't possible for her to let flowers die for lack of water.

Felicity didn't comment, even when Ellie carried the vase into the pleasant sitting-room and placed them on the coffee table.

'It's only half past seven. Is there anything on the box?' Felicity leafed through the *Radio Times*, without giving it her attention.

'We could try next door. Not Maisie, but the other side.'

'I was thinking,' said Felicity, twisting a lock of hair around her fingers, 'that when Maisie gives up and they go into a home or something, maybe I'll buy their house, modernize it and rent it out. Or sell it.'

'Spoken like a true entrepreneur. Come on, let's pay a visit next door.'

Felicity swept the red roses out of the vase. 'I don't suppose they'll know anything, but we'll take the roses as a peace offering, shall we?'

'What did you do with the ones Roy sent you yesterday?'

Felicity shrugged. 'In the compost. He'll get the message soon, I suppose.'

They pulled the front door to behind them, and walked down to the road, turned right and went up a very different front garden path.

This neighbour's house was brightly painted in pale blue and white. The architect had been influenced both by Swiss cottages sporting lots of gingerbread around the eaves, and by an Edwardian liking for comfortable bay windows below. It was somewhat larger than Felicity's. So far, so 1920s.

The garden had obviously had a make-over from someone who'd charged an enormous sum to cover the place with decking, rocks, pebbles and clumps of grass. There wasn't a flower in sight.

'Truly awe-inspiring,' said Ellie, ringing the doorbell, which produced a tune which she couldn't for the moment identify. 'What sort of terms are you on with these people?'

'Smiling and nodding. They were away most of the winter in South Africa or New Zealand, perhaps both. '

The door opened on a woman who was perhaps in her fifties, but who, with the aid of expert help, was defying the years with some success. 'Lady Kingsley, what a nice surprise! Do come in. Are those flowers for me? How thoughtful. I'll get my housekeeper to put them in water for me.'

Their hostess ushered them through into a cavernous sitting-room furnished in minimalist fashion, which didn't really suit the style of the house but was clearly to their hostess's taste. White everywhere, walls, floors, shag rugs, upholstery. A trickle of water running down a sheet of metal – stainless steel? – along one wall. No books. Magazines, of course, and the biggest TV Ellie had ever seen, tuned in to a game show.

Their hostess was bronzed, rail thin, the cords of her neck standing out, her head looking too big for her body. Her nails were long and manicured. Ellie wanted to sit on her own hands, which showed signs of hard wear from the gardening she did.

'Suzie, this is my good friend, Mrs Quicke,' said Felicity, trying a low chair. 'She's staying with me while we try to work out what to do with my back garden. I couldn't begin even to think about it till I got my neighbour to agree to have her hedge cut back, but at last she's agreed, so we can make a start. I wanted to warn you, and apologize in advance, because we'll probably be making a bit of noise, tearing up the old and putting in the new.'

Their hostess pointed the remote at the television to mute the sound. 'I must give you the name of the little man who did ours. He's hideously expensive, of course, but right up to the minute.'

She picked up the glass from which she'd been drinking, only to realize she hadn't offered her guests anything. 'Do you fancy a little something?' She gestured to a fully fitted bar which made an incongruous note in one corner. 'I'm into red, myself.'

'No, thank you,' said Felicity.

'Well, just a small one,' said Ellie, thinking their hostess might be more comfortable if they joined her in a drink.

Suzie refreshed her own drink and issued Ellie with a large glass of red wine. 'My husband's out, I'm afraid. I'm the typical golf widow. As to what you do in your garden, well, it won't make any difference to us as we're off to Mauritius again soon. A bit too hot at this time of year, of course, but my husband has business interests out there, and beggars can't be choosers.'

'Delightful,' murmured Ellie, assessing the rings on their hostess's fingers as being worth a king's ransom. Well, a princely one, anyway. 'The thing is that although Felicity has done wonders with the house and front garden, she does find it a little ... well, almost spooky ... looking at the back garden. It reminds her so much of the previous owner.'

Suzie raised both hands in horror. 'Say no more. I said to my hubby only the other day, what a let-down for the neighbourhood that garden is, when it could be made well, really quite delightful. It's not as large as ours, of course, and you won't want to put in a swimming pool as we did, but a good garden designer can work wonders. I do so know what you mean about Mrs Alexis. It was a positive disgrace, how she let that place get so run down.'

Ellie sipped wine. 'We gather she couldn't really help herself, after her husband died?'

Suzie folded her lips, and shook her head. 'My lips are sealed.'

Felicity's voice trembled. It was probably left-over emotion from all that had happened that day, but it did sound as if she was genuinely upset. 'You'll laugh, but I honestly feel, sometimes, as if she's haunting the place, still. I keep looking over my shoulder, thinking she's staring at me from the park.'

'My dear!' Suzie was delighted. 'Well, of course, in this day and age ... but I do understand what ... she was the most extra-ordinary ... I said to my dearest one – this would be way back last summer – that I understood what people said about witches casting the evil eye...'

'You think she was a witch?' said Ellie, interested.

'Well, I suppose not, not really. But when she looked at you with those pale eyes of hers...' Suzie shuddered. 'My mother felt the same way, before she passed on, of course.'

'Your mother didn't like her?' Ellie tried not to sound eager.

'She liked the old man, all right, Mrs Alexis' father. We didn't have anything to do with them while he – the husband – was alive. I mean, perfectly polite, of course, but they weren't exactly the sort of people you invite to play bridge with, were they? I suppose he'd made the journey from Cyprus to London when he was a young man, and I think she was a Londoner born and bred, but they never went anywhere to broaden their horizons. So parochial!'

'How did your mother get to know Mrs Alexis' father?'

'My mother was something of a goer in her day, bless her. Been all over, married three times, and still got the men looking at her legs. My beloved husband used to joke that if I ever let myself go, he'd divorce me and marry my mother ... ha, ha, ha.'

Felicity and Ellie smiled and hoped they'd made the smile convincing.

'And then,' said Suzie, draining her glass and refilling it, 'Mr Brand – Charlie – came to stay with his daughter next door for a while, and my mother – who'd said she was only going to come for a week – ending up staying for a whole month. Cancelled a cruise, would you believe, just to enjoy a little romance with Charlie. Oh, a right pair they were, strutting around, throwing their money about – not that I grudged my mother a penny, because she'd earned it ... from her three husbands, you know. Charlie had his little bit saved, too, and they were out morning, noon and night, till you'd have thought they were teenagers instead of in their seventies as they were.'

'What a lovely time they must have had,' said Ellie, sipping wine. 'Did they think of marriage at all?'

'Charlie did, but my mother wouldn't consider it. Not after three goes at it. Said she couldn't bear nursing another old codger to the grave. She was very loyal, you know. Never let another man put his arm around her waist till the last husband was in his grave.' Suzie gave a great sigh. 'We won't see her like again, as my dearest one says.'

'So what happened to spoil the dream?'

'Charlie died. Got a flux. Mother was beside herself, didn't know whether to laugh or cry. Mostly cry. She was very fond of Charlie, you know. He seemed to get better, and then he got worse and he was fretting to be back in his own place, where his other daughter could look after him. He was dead within the week, so sad.

'Mother was heart-broken, but ... well, she'd been through it all before, hadn't she? She said she was going to pick herself up, dust herself down and start all over again. She went back to her place, but before she could even fetch her cat from the kennels, she had a stroke and died. Right as rain on the Friday, dead on Saturday. It was a good way to go. I hope I get taken the same way.'

'What a shame,' said Felicity.

'No heel-taps,' said Suzie, downing the last mouthful.

Ellie set her own glass down, half finished. 'Where did Mr Brand come from?'

'North London somewhere, I believe. Edmonton? No, Chalk Farm, I think. Quite pleasant, of course, but not Ealing.'

'No, indeed.' Felicity got to her feet. 'Well, thank you so much for...'

'A pleasure. Do you have to go so soon? My husband won't be back for hours.'

'I'm afraid we must. I do hope you have a wonderful time in ... where was it? Mauritius? Maybe by the time you get back, the garden will be transformed.'

'Banishing all ghostly shades, what?' Suzie laughed rather too loudly as she showed them out.

'Phew,' said Ellie, under her breath, as she led the way back. 'Chalk Farm. Charlie Brand. And a sister. It's something to go on.'

Felicity wasn't listening. 'How long do you think he's been sitting there? No, don't look now. It's Roy, in his car on the other side of the road. Do you think he's going to come over now he's seen us? I don't want to talk to him, Ellie.'

'Perhaps you ought to, to clear the air.'

Roy was on their heels as they reached the front door. 'Felicity ... Ellie. Are you all right? I've been so worried about you.'

'We're fine,' said Felicity, letting them into the hall.

'Did you get my roses? I left them in the porch. I wondered if you'd like to come out for supper? You like Graham's Grill, don't you, where we were the other evening?'

Felicity shook her head. 'Thanks, Roy, but we've already eaten. Is your mother all right?'

'Yes, but ... look, could we just talk? We've always been such good friends.'

Ellie said, 'Don't mind me. I'm just going next door to have another word with Maisie for a moment. Won't be long.'

So saying, she shot out of the front door before Felicity could grab for her, and almost ran down the front garden. There was Roy's car parked on the other side of the road. How many times had he parked there this last couple of days, trying to catch sight of Felicity? Ellie wondered if Felicity had noticed the car each time and perhaps subliminally had been aware that he was watching out for her. Perhaps that was why she'd said she felt spooked in the house.

Ellie looked away, and then – was that a flicker of movement behind it? – looked back at the car. There was someone standing on the far side of it, almost hidden. Not a tall person. No. A brown little person, who was staring at her with unblinking pale eyes.

Ellie found she'd shifted her hands to her

heart, which was beating rather too fast for comfort.

She knew that face, that woman. Mrs Alexis, who had once lived in this house. Mrs Alexis, who was probably responsible for the delivery of suspect bread rolls to Felicity's house. A woman who might or might not have assisted her husband and, possibly, her father into the next world.

A woman who had a grudge against Felicity that was leading her to haunt the place?

Mrs Alexis was no longer staring at the house but at Ellie, who felt a chill pass down her back. Mrs Alexis was not just noticing Ellie, but taking notice of her.

Her stare was flat, like that of a toad. There was no emotion behind it.

It was almost as if she were a machine, recording information about someone – something – that stood in her way.

Ellie found herself short of breath. How did the woman do it? She was a titchy little thing, even compared to Ellie, who was not tall. Yet there was a quality of concentrated menace emanating from her that caused Ellie to feel afraid.

At once, Ellie scolded herself. She wasn't afraid of Mrs Alexis. Surely not! Ridiculous!

The sun had gone behind a cloud, that was why she'd shivered.

Except that the sun was shining as brightly

as ever.

And still the woman stood there, looking at her.

Ellie wondered if the woman knew who she was, and where she lived ... and told herself that she was being absurd. How could the woman know her name or where she lived?

Except that ... somewhere recently ... now where was it? ... Ellie had caught sight of this woman in another context. She pummelled her brain, but couldn't come up with the answer.

Roy came out of the house behind her. 'Can't you make her see sense, Ellie?'

She took her eyes off Mrs Alexis for a moment to register that Roy looked wretched, and when she looked back the woman was cycling off down the road.

'What sort of sense do you want her to see, Roy?'

'I can't work. I'm worrying myself sick about her. I don't know what's the matter with me. Usually, if a girl says she's had enough, I'm only too happy to look elsewhere, but Felicity's such a ... so vulnerable, and yet so determined ... I want to pick her up and run off with her to some uninhabited island where nothing could ever upset her again.'

'You want to marry her,' said Ellie, in a matter-of-fact voice.

Roy stared at her. 'God help me, I rather think I do. But...' He swung round to look back at the house. He passed his hand over the back of his neck. 'I don't suppose she's ever thought of me that way. I mean, older than her, and a bit shop-worn, wouldn't you say?'

'It's more than possible that she can't have children.'

'Ah, poor kid. Does she think that would make a difference to me?'

'She might. And Arthur's legacy ... he was a foul husband.'

'The poor, poor kid. How can I get through to her, Ellie?' He didn't seem to expect an answer, but continued to stare at the house.

Ellie meanwhile was trying to follow another line of thought. Mrs Alexis had been watching – or at least studying – the house where Felicity lived, which added weight to the suspicion that it was she who'd been trying to pass off some nasty product of her own baking on to Felicity. No one knew where she was now living so couldn't ask her what she was up to.

'Roy!' She grabbed his sleeve. 'Follow that bike.'

'What?' Roy was still looking back at the house.

Ellie shook his arm. 'It's important, Roy. I just saw Mrs Alexis cycle off, and if we hurry we can catch up with her, find out where she lives. Come on!'

'Mm? What? We can't leave Felicity on her own.'

'Roy, please! Just for once, don't argue!'

'Yes, but ... I can't see that ... oh, very well. I'll just pop in and tell Felicity that...'

Ellie felt like screaming. 'Roy, she'll be miles off by now! Will you please...!'

'Oh, very well. But if she's miles off, I can't see that ... where are my keys? Did I leave them in the car ... no, here they are. Are you sure that you don't just want to tell Felicity ... she'll wonder what's happened if we both suddenly ... oh, all right! I'm coming!'

Ellie tried not to worry as Roy fumbled the key in the lock, looking back at the house. No Felicity came to the windows. Ellie fastened her seat-belt, while he sighed and pulled at his, finally realizing he'd trapped it in the door and having to reopen the door and pull it free.

Ellie closed her eyes and prayed for patience.

He started the car at last, and said, 'Where to?'

'Just drive along, pause at the next road off to the right, see if you can spot a cyclist.'

'What? Any old cyclist? Keep your hair on, I'm looking, I'm looking. I suppose it wouldn't be a bad idea to ... is that her? No it's a man on a motorbike. Drive on to the next? How's your eyesight?'

'Good enough. She hasn't kept on the road round the park, I don't think. Somehow I thought she must live the other side of the Avenue, though I really don't know why. Yes, I do. My dentist said she didn't live nearby. Or, to be accurate, he said he had a client who rides a bike and who lives a little way off. He didn't even say what her name was. It could be another person altogether.'

Roy paused at the next intersection, looked, and drove on again. 'Why don't you ask him where she lives, then? Though, come to think of it, he probably wouldn't want to tell you. Ethics and all that.'

They had come to the end of the park and could turn either right or left – or go straight on. 'Turn left,' said Ellie. 'If she's on the other side of the Avenue, then this is the way she'll have gone.'

Roy went slowly on, pausing at each little intersection. There was a fair amount of traffic on the roads for mid-evening. They spotted a couple of cyclists: one was a woman with a small child on a carrier on the back, one a young man with racing goggles on. Ellie reflected that it was like buses; you waited ages for one, and then several came along at once. Why hadn't she noticed before that there were so many people riding bicycles on the road?

Ellie began to worry about having left

Felicity on her own. Roy had been right; they ought to have gone back to tell her where they were going.

'Coming up to the Avenue,' said Roy. 'The traffic lights are against us. Do you want to go on?'

'Yes,' said Ellie, crossing her fingers. 'Please.'

They drove up and down a grid of roads, pausing for intersections as before. A lot of cars were parked in these roads. Commuter land. People driving back from work. They moved into an area of larger, detached houses with their own driveways.

'Nothing,' said Roy. 'Give up?'

Ellie nodded. 'Yes. Thanks, Roy. I know you thought it a wild goose chase, but it seemed to me that if only we could find out where she lives, we could talk to her, get her to stop this persecution.'

'I wouldn't call it persecution exactly, Ellie. I understand that you think she might have bumped off her old man, and I agree that just recently she's played a nasty trick or two with the bread rolls, but you've really no grounds for saying that she killed that handyman, Paddy or whatever his name was. I can see why Felicity is getting a bit edgy about it, but you can't really call it persecution.'

'You don't know what we found out since yesterday. After her husband died, she struggled to keep up the payments on the house and was bailed out by her father's death – just as he was on the point of getting hitched again. She also came into money from her sister's death rather conveniently, although I don't know whether she was on the scene at the time or not.'

'Circumstantial evidence.'

'I know, I know. But if I were Felicity, I'd be screaming for protection, too.'

He turned the car round. 'We'd best get back. I'm sure there's nothing to worry about, but ... surely, we can leave it to the police to sort out? They'll analyse those rolls and if they find anything toxic, then they'll get on to it, and find her in no time. Even if it's just laxatives in the rolls, they'll have a chat with her, make her stop it.'

'If it is her we saw watching the house,' said Ellie, feeling depressed. 'And if it's not too late to stop her trying again.'

Roy was magnanimous. 'I'm sure it's her. You're usually right, Ellie.'

Ellie felt like crying, but didn't. Now she worried that in their absence, something might have happened to Felicity. But at least Roy was wasting no time in driving straight back.

They reached Felicity's. In their absence, she'd drawn the curtains. Roy looked longingly at the house. 'Will you tell her, from me, that ... you'll know what to say.'

'Tell her yourself.'

'She won't even pick up the phone when I ring.'

'You didn't know what to say, before. Now, you do.'

He got out of the car and walked across the road to Felicity's front door, leaving Ellie to get out, slam the door and hope it was self-locking. Hadn't he ever heard of locking car doors after people got out?

The door opened on the chain. Ellie was close enough to hear Roy say, 'Marry me?' And then the door slammed shut again.

Ellie cast her eyes up to the evening sky. What sort of proposal was that?

Roy stood there with a sick look on his face. Ellie rang the doorbell three times, and said, 'Open up, Felicity. It's me, Ellie. I'll tell this big oaf to make himself scarce, shall I?'

The door opened fully. Felicity grabbed Ellie and drew her inside before slamming the door shut in Roy's face.

Felicity was crying. Had been crying for some time. She threw herself at Ellie, sobbing. 'She's out there, watching me, I know it! I can't do anything without her seeing me. Tell me what to do.'

Betty Alexis cycled back home, thinking furiously. Who was that woman in Felicity's garden? She'd seen her before somewhere ... ah, she had it. She'd visited Milady at the home once or twice with Felicity, keeping her company. Yesterday, too. Staying with Felicity, someone had said.

Surely she'd seen her before somewhere? Hadn't the woman come round to view the house months ago, before the move? Calling herself ... no, it had gone. She'd said she was looking for a house for her mother. Obviously she'd been spying the house out on behalf of Felicity. Lying and cheating, like all her cronies. They all deserved to die.

The question was: how?

It had been easy enough to kill that monster, her husband. He'd only married her to get a British passport and it hadn't taken long for him to show his true colours, whoring and tippling ... some sleeping pills in his bottle of wine when he went out to potter with the car had been almost enough to kill him, heavy drinker that he was. She'd waited till there was no more movement to be heard in the garage, then gone out to turn on the ignition in the car and bring down the door, jamming it shut with a couple of wedges she'd bought to keep the kitchen door from flying open.

She hadn't expected him to move after that, but apparently he'd half come to and tried to open the door from the inside ... and failed, luckily. She'd slept soundly that night, and removed the wedges in the morning when she went out to find him. The car had run out of fuel by that time and he was quite, quite dead. Misadventure.

She couldn't try that again, not in the same house.

His money had lasted her a good while, though. Then she'd had to think about how to get some more, and invited her father to stay, in spite of what he'd tried to do to her after her mother died ... well, best not think about that now.

She'd asked him to move in with her, share expenses. That way she could keep the house on. But he'd refused. Said he was settled with her younger sister, who was also a widow. Then he'd shown his true colours, taking up with the woman next door, old enough to be his mother, and three times a widow to boot. He'd even talk-ed of marriage.

Well, she'd had to put a stop to that, hadn't she?

It hadn't taken much laxative to set him off with a bout of gastritis. Then his ulcer had perfor-ated. Finish. Just as well that he'd gone back home to be nursed by his beloved Daisy before he copped it. A pity he only left Betty half his money, though, because it hadn't lasted that long.

She couldn't bear to lose the house, but couldn't earn enough money to keep it. Then she'd had a stroke of luck; Daisy had a nasty fall down the stairs and Betty had gone to stay with her for a few days to look after her. She'd given Daisy every opportunity to save herself. If only Daisy had agreed to move in with her ... but there; it was not to be. And really, sleeping pills dissolved

*very well in a night-time drink, didn't they?
Daisy had been so disorientated when Betty got
her up in the night, saying she thought she heard
a burglar ... one little push had been all it had
taken ... arse over tip ... screaming her head off
till she lay in the hall, legs and arms all over the
place, with her head at a strange angle. Dead.*

*Betty had screamed, too, of course. And run out
into the street in her nightie, screaming that her
sister had fallen down the stairs. Misadventure.*

*And that was where the luck had run out,
because Daisy had made a will after their father
died ... could she have suspected something? ...
and left almost everything to charity. Betty had
never understood how Daisy could have done
that. Wasn't blood thicker than water? What
Betty did get kept her going for a while ... and
then ... and then Sir Arthur had turned nasty
and wrecked the garden and she'd made a
solemn vow, with her hand on her Bible, to serve
him out for what he'd done to her.*

She'd tried, hadn't she?

*More sleeping pills in the pizza which the dog
ate.*

*And the very last of them in the rolls which
Paddy had eaten.*

*She'd thought the laburnum seeds would do the
trick. The cat had died, but still Felicity lived!
And what about that companion of hers, that
older woman who'd stood and stared at her in the
garden just now?*

What was she to do about them? Answer; she

282

must change her method, try something else. Watching the old man's telly while she fed him the other night had given her an idea.

All it took was a waste rag, some paraffin and a couple of matches. Fire in the night. Lift the letter-box, light the rag and thrust it through into the house. Down drops the fiery rag and ignites the flooring inside. Swiftly the flames travel along the floor, up the legs of the furniture, reaching the mats, the carpets, the upholstered furniture ... and blocking the stairs so that Felicity would not be able to escape ... and she'd scream and scream and scream ... and die!

If workmen had still been at the house, a fire could pass off as an accidental spark starting a blaze. As it was, a blazing rag through the letter-box could be set down to youths larking around, especially if she faked a call first to the police to complain about a fictitious gang of youngsters up to no good in the park opposite. No one would suspect her. No one knew where she lived. No one would ever connect her to a fatal fire on that side of the park.

Very well. Fire it was to be. She thought there might be a can of paraffin in the gardener's shed. She must look it out tomorrow.

Fourteen

Ellie held Felicity tightly. 'Calm down.'

'I can't, I saw her. It was her, wasn't it?'

'Yes.'

Felicity shuddered. 'I don't think I ever saw her before. I mean, I hadn't anything to do with her being turfed out of this place, and when I came to look at the house, she'd long since gone and the builders were in. I never saw a photograph of her, or anything, did I? Tell me I'm not imagining things.'

'You're not. I came to see her here, before she left. A little brown mouse of a woman, I thought, and dismissed her from my mind. Come into the kitchen. I'll get you a drink of water.'

Felicity began to laugh. Hysteria. 'I shut the door in Roy's face, didn't I? Did you hear him? Did he really say...? Oh, this is just so funny.'

'Sit down for a moment, while I see if he's gone yet. We could do with some help.'

'Not Roy. Don't let him in. I couldn't cope.'

Ellie nodded. She could see that Felicity

couldn't cope.

Ellie seated Felicity on a kitchen stool, put a glass of water in her hand, and went back to open the front door. Roy was halfway down the garden path, hands in pockets, looking lost. He raised his head when he saw Ellie, and she beckoned him nearer.

'She saw Mrs Alexis watching her, and it's upset her. I don't think you should come in just now. Perhaps tomorrow?'

'What can I do?'

'You could try the police, see if they've got any results from the analysis of the bread rolls yet. Tell them we think it's Mrs Alexis and that she seems to be watching this house. Say we've tried to trace her, but haven't had any luck. It's at the back of my mind that I've seen her somewhere recently ... perhaps in the Avenue? Anyway, it would be good to alert the police that we're taking this seriously.'

'Stalking would be serious, but it takes more than a couple of sightings to complain about it to the police. Are you sure I can't do anything else?'

'I won't leave her.' Ellie closed the door on him, and set her back to it. There was a deadlock on the door. She turned it. And a bolt, top and bottom. She shot those home, too.

Felicity had calmed down a trifle. She was pulling down the blinds at the French windows in the kitchen. 'I'm sorry. I'm all right now.'

She didn't look all right.

Ellie wondered if she should suggest going back to her house for the night. Would Diana try to break in again? Possibly. Would Armand or Kate feed Midge?

'I must make some phone calls. Will you be all right for a few minutes?'

Felicity opened cupboards. 'I'm going to do some baking. Take my mind off things. Do you like chocolate cake? Silly question. Everyone likes chocolate cake. Or perhaps I'll make some quiches ... egg and bacon quiche do you?' She began to laugh and clapped both hands over her mouth. 'Perhaps not quiches. What about some bread rolls?'

She was holding down hysteria. Just.

Ellie got out her mobile. She tried Kate first. The phone rang for some time, until the answerphone clicked in. Ellie started, 'Kate, this is Ellie...' And then Kate picked up the phone. 'Yes?' She sounded out of breath.

'Sorry, Kate. Ellie here. I'm still over at Felicity's. We've had a bit of a scare. Mrs Alexis has been round here, watching the house. It's upset Felicity, so I'm staying on. Do you think you or Armand could feed Midge and...'

'He's sitting on our kitchen table at the moment. Must have worked it out that you weren't going to be around this evening. Armand's out at a meeting, but when he comes back I'll go round and draw your curtains. Anything else?'

'If you could throw some water around in the conservatory...?'

'Consider it done. You say Mrs Alexis has been watching Felicity's house?'

'We've discovered a bit more about her past. Her maiden name was Brand. Her father's name was Charlie. He was paying court to a widow until he died, all of a sudden. There was a sister – don't know her name. Possibly lived in Chalk Farm. I don't know how she died or whether Mrs Alexis was party to the death, but we have to bear in mind that she did benefit from it.'

'I'll see what I can find out tomorrow. Sleep tight.'

Felicity started to sing, in a wobbly voice. Keeping her spirits up. She clattered pots and pans around, making noise. She put the radio on.

Ellie went into the living-room to make her next call. 'Thomas, please pick up. Don't be out at a meeting. Be there, please! If only I had your mobile number!'

He wasn't there. The answerphone clicked in, so Ellie left a message. 'Thomas, Ellie here. I'm at Felicity's. She's frightened. We spotted Mrs Alexis watching her house today. Roy and I tried to follow her, but lost her so we still don't know where she lives. You've met her, haven't you? When her garden was ruined? There's something at the back of my mind, I'm pretty sure I've seen her somewhere locally, serving in a shop? Changing books in the library? I can't pin it down ... but I wondered, have you seen her at all?'

Ellie didn't know how to end the conversation. Best wishes? All my love? Oh, what nonsense.

She ended the call and dialled Bill's number. He picked up, but was clearly watching television – she could hear the solemn tones of a newsreader – and not pleased to be interrupted. 'Sorry, Bill. Ellie here. I just wanted to let you know that I'm staying over at Felicity's for the moment. And to say how much I enjoyed tea at the Ritz today. It was quite something.'

Was it really only that afternoon that she'd had tea at the Ritz?

'Taking it easy tonight, are you?' said Bill, fondly.

Ellie set her teeth. She told herself that he didn't mean to be so condescending. He was just being ... well ... thoughtful for her well-being. 'Something like that,' she said. 'Are you watching television?'

'Catching up on the latest announcement from Downing Street. I don't suppose you're watching, are you?'

288

No, thought Ellie. I'm having the screaming abjabs, looking after Felicity, who's got
them even worse than me, and if I told you
about them, you'd only laugh and say I was
making a mountain out of a molehill. She
asked, 'What colour do you vote?'

'I've always been a Liberal, like my father
before me. Naturally.'

Naturally. Ellie felt like telling him – not
that he'd asked – that she always voted for
the Monster Raving party. She understood
that he'd expect her to vote his way in future.
It was, of course, a small price to pay for
domestic harmony.

'Well, goodnight then, Bill. I don't want to
keep you from your programme.'

'Goodnight, Ellie. Glad you're being looked after. Give my regards to Lady Kingsley.'

Lady Kingsley was breaking eggs into a
bowl, singing loudly. She'd got flour on her
T-shirt already. Ellie found an apron and
managed to insert Felicity into it without
breaking the flow of what she was doing.

An announcer on the radio said, 'And now
for the weather forecast.'

Ellie felt extremely tired. Felicity said,
'Cooking always perks me up. I can go on for
hours, now. Fancy a snack, Ellie? How about
a bacon sandwich and some coffee?'

Ellie resigned herself to a late night.

When she finally got to bed, she spent

some time going over what had happened that day. She'd forgotten to bring her Bible with her, so couldn't find any comforting words to read, as she often did just before she went to sleep. But she could pray, and did.

Dear Lord Jesus, we're in such distress ... so many of my friends and my family are in trouble, and I don't always do or say the right thing ... give me the right words to say. And protect us from all evil, amen.

Nothing happened during the night. Roy returned from a frustrating visit to the police station, where nobody seemed to know anything about Felicity and Mrs Alexis, and worse, didn't want to go to the bother of finding out. He spent the night in his car across the road, falling asleep now and then but waking up at least once an hour to check that everything was as it should be in Felicity's house.

Midge spent the night lying across Armand's stomach, about which he complained bitterly without taking any action to remove the cat.

Ellie missed her own bed, her cat, her bedroom. But slept better than she had expected.

Felicity cooked till after midnight, sat down to drink a cup of hot milk in her sitting-room, and woke up in the same chair hours later, stiff and sore.

Nothing happened that side of the park.

Friday morning. Felicity was slow, bleary-eyed. Ellie took in the milk and papers. She saw Roy asleep in his car on the other side of the road, and told Felicity, who said, 'What does he think he's playing at?'

'Guard dog,' said Ellie. 'Rather touching, don't you think?'

Felicity growled in her throat, then laughed. 'Well, we're all still alive, so I suppose that proves something. What does he want for breakfast?'

Ellie went out to the car and tapped on the window till Roy woke up. 'Coming in for breakfast?'

Roy staggered out of the car, getting his circulation going again, feeling his unshaven chin, looking about as unheroic as a man can.

Ellie prodded him up the driveway. 'You'll feel better with some coffee inside you.'

Felicity had put some lipstick on since Ellie went to fetch Roy. A good sign, thought Ellie, steering Roy into the downstairs cloakroom, saying she'd see if she could find him a razor. Felicity bagged up the cakes and quiches she'd made the previous night, to dump in her freezer.

Breakfast was a silent affair, with Felicity avoiding Roy's eye, and Roy trying to keep his eye off her. Ellie thought of lots of things to say, and kept quiet. There was such a thing as being too chatty at breakfast.

Eventually Roy said, 'I did try the police again last night. No one knew anything. What do we do now?'

Silence. Ellie could think of several things to do, like emigrating, changing her name and going to the North Pole for a while.

Roy said, 'Shall I help you wash up, Felicity?'

'I know you. You'd only break something. Besides, I've got a dishwasher.'

He tried on a smile. 'I only break stuff when I don't want to be helpful. I'll stack dishes, you clear the table, right?'

Ellie murmured that she must make some phone calls, and escaped to the sitting-room. Was that the time? Almost ten! How time flew when you were watching a courting couple make fools of themselves.

She got through to Kate, who'd been up for hours. Catriona always got them up at six.

'Midge is perfectly all right. Catriona keeps taking her toys to show to the cat, who's sitting in a semi-circle of things to play with. Armand's gone off in a temper. Double something or other with his most unfavourite class. I took in your milk and papers and drew back the curtains. No post, except circulars. Oh, and I watered in the conservatory, also the Bizzy Lizzies in the back garden, which were looking a bit droopy. There's some messages on the answerphone but I haven't touched it.'

'You're wonderful.'

'Hmph. How's Felicity?'

'Damp, but drying out. Roy's gone all protective. Sweet.'

Kate screeched with laughter. 'Well, what you really wanted to know was if I could find anything out about Charlie Brand and daughter. Nothing doing, I'm afraid. I can do some more research but frankly I'm not sure it would help. Let the police dig around there if they wish. They've got the resources for it.'

'I tend to agree. What we really need to know is the whereabouts of Mrs Alexis, and what she's up to. I've seen her somewhere, you know ... locally.'

'Shopping?'

'Mm, no.'

'At church?'

Ellie half laughed. 'No, I don't think so. Something in the Avenue. I have it.' Ellie hit her forehead. 'I was in the queue at the Post Office and she was in the other part of the shop. I remember now that she looked at me as if she might know me, and so I looked back at her. It was only for an instant, mind. Then I had to move on, and lost sight of her. The thing is, I know so many people around here by sight, because of having worked in the charity shop for so many years, that I thought nothing of it.'

'It confirms that she does live locally. Do you want to try your dentist, see if he'll come up with an address?'

'I know what he'll say...'

Kate cried out, and dropped the phone. Several anxious moments later, Kate picked it up again, and now she was nursing a sobbing toddler. 'Sorry, Ellie. Not Midge's fault. Catriona mistook Midge for a playmate and when he'd had enough and jumped up on to the windowsill, she tried to follow and fell over.'

'Oh, I am sorry.'

Kate was impatient. 'Far worse happens at sea. Are you going to be home for lunch? Share it with me, if you like.'

'I'll ring you.'

Ellie rang off, and looked out of the window. Roy and Felicity were in the back garden, looking at the overgrown hedge. He raised his arm as if to put it round her shoulders, but dropped it again before she realized what he'd been about to do.

Ellie turned away from the sight, and dialled Bill's number ... and then killed the call before she could get through. Bill wasn't going to help her on this one. She felt a little guilty that she was still involved when he'd made it clear he wanted her out of it. What was it he'd planned for this weekend? Going to the races? Or was it Henley? Or Wimbledon, or cricket ... or any number of other interesting events that she'd never in her wildest dreams thought about. And didn't care all that much for, anyway. Yes, on occasion perhaps she'd thought it would be exciting ... but how could she dress up and wear a big hat and high heels and go off for a day's self-indulgence when her friends were in trouble?

She punched in another number, and this time Thomas answered.

'Hi, Thomas, Ellie here.' She was all bright and breezy.

'Ellie, got your message. Are you all right? What's happening?'

'Oh, we're all right. Just got a little spooked last night, that's all. Mrs Alexis was casing the joint ... I mean, she was standing in the road opposite looking at us. Panic over. The thing is, I'm pretty sure she's local. You met her once, didn't you? When you called on her after the garden was trashed. Have you come across her since?'

'I meet so many people. Ellie, you don't sound ... are you all right?'

'A little too bright and breezy, you mean? I'm scared half to death, if the truth be known. That woman sends shivers down my back. I've done a bit of digging, and so has Kate and ... but I don't want to keep you...'

'Friday's my day off, remember. Take all the time you want.' A bell rang, not far off. 'Did I say this was my day off? Someone's at the door. Look, I'm popping into the retirement home to see someone this morning...'

Ellie was amused. 'I thought you said this was your day off.'

'Well, yes, but...' He half covered the receiver to shout to someone, 'Hold on a minute.' Then came back to Ellie. 'How about meeting me for lunch? If I go out, no one can come pounding on the door. Twelve o'clock somewhere in the Avenue?'

'All right. There's a new café at the side of the Greek restaurant. I haven't tried it yet. How about that?'

'Great.' The phone crashed down, and off he went.

Ellie went to see how the love-birds were getting on. Not all that well. They were sitting at the kitchen table, looking out at the back garden, and not talking. Only, his hand was half covering Felicity's as it lay on the table. He removed it when Ellie came in, and so she pretended not to notice.

How to get rid of them? In the nicest possible way, of course.

Felicity toyed with a lock of hair. 'I must wash my hair. I must look a mess. Then I thought perhaps I could get a couple of quotes to do something about the back garden. I like what Ellie's suggested, but...'

'I'll help,' said Roy. 'The man you used for the front is probably the best, but...'

'Shouldn't you be at work, Roy?' said Ellie. 'And have you rung your mother? She'll have noticed that you've not been home all night and must be worried about you. Why don't you take Felicity back home with you, let Rose make a fuss of her? She hasn't been sleeping well, so Rose can put her to bed in the spare room for an afternoon nap. She'll be safe there, till the police get on top of things.'

She wanted to add that they both looked as if they could do with a nap that afternoon, but thought it might not be tactful to do so.

'I don't want to leave here,' said Felicity, 'and of course Roy must go back to work.'

Roy put his hand over hers again, and this time she didn't remove it. 'Come back with me now. It's true I've got a meeting I should go to this afternoon. Then, if you want to come back here tonight, I'll come back with you...'

'I'm not having you sleep in your car again. What will the neighbours think?'

'Haven't you a spare bed?'

'Ellie's in the best spare room. I suppose I could put you in the little room.'

'That's settled, then.' Ellie was keen to get home, to see to Midge and the garden, and take an indigestion tablet ... all this anxiety played merry hell with your digestion. She'd also quite like to have a quiet half hour with the papers and a cup of better coffee than Felicity had provided ... where did she buy her coffee beans?

Then she would walk up and down the Avenue, to see if she could spot a little brown woman intent on murder.

The problem with changing methods was that she had to locate fresh tools for the job. Sleeping pills had been to hand on the bedside table when her husband was alive, and they'd served her well for a number of years. Laxative you could buy over the counter at any chemist or supermarket. The laburnum seeds had been to hand in the garden.

The old man had some sleeping pills, of course, and so had Ruby. But Betty Alexis had tried twice now to get doctored food to Felicity and neither time had it worked. The hussy was too well guarded or too suspicious or ... just plain lucky. Perhaps she was on a diet and that's why she hadn't eaten the food specially prepared for her; she was thin enough, in all truth.

As she cycled off to work, Mrs Alexis went over her new plan again. Yes, there was an old can of paraffin in the shed, just as she remembered. But it was far too large and rusty to be suitable for the job she had in mind. The rust had almost worn through the metal. If she put it in the pannier of her bike, jogging it along the streets might make the rust patches so fragile that the paraffin would start leaking out.

And that would never do. She couldn't risk anyone smelling paraffin on her or her bike just after Felicity's house had been attacked.

She'd seen on the news how rioters started fires with bottles of paraffin. Molotov cocktails, they'd called them.

Suppose she got hold of an empty bottle somewhere. They were always throwing them out from the kitchen at the home. Then she could decant paraffin into the bottle ... it mustn't have too wide a top. Perhaps a ketchup bottle?

Fill it with paraffin, push a J-cloth halfway in, so that it went down into the liquid, but half stayed outside to act as a wick ... strike a match, throw it at a window...

Yes! That would be better than pouring it through the door, because a window had curtains which would catch alight much more quickly than flooring.

She would do it that night, when it was dark.

Ruby wanted Mrs Alexis to give up her job at the home altogether, so that she could spend more time looking after the old man.

Ruby didn't want her father to go into a home, because – and here Mrs Alexis allowed herself a small smile – Ruby didn't own the house; the old man did. And if he had to go into a home, the house would have to be sold over Ruby's head, to pay for his keep. It wouldn't suit Mrs Alexis, either, because she'd have to find somewhere else to live. Well, life would be a lot easier if she didn't have to go out cleaning every morning. She didn't need the gossip at the home to keep up with Felicity's activities any longer because tonight should finish that job.

So, why not? Yes, she'd give up the job at the home today.

Fifteen

It was going to be another warm day. At home Ellie changed into a pale blue dress with a pretty neckline and short sleeves ... and her best set of new underwear, for some reason.

Thomas was prompt. Of course. He wasn't wearing his dog collar today, but an open-necked sports shirt in a dull red, over jeans. The jeans were possibly a trifle on the tight side but then, as Ellie very well understood, clothes did tend to get a bit tight as you grew older.

The café seemed popular enough, being half-full of men and women – mostly older types without children – indulging in pasta. The décor was modern wood-and-glass, the floor tiled. Everything looked scrupulously clean.

'I'm hungry. What a day,' began Thomas,

eyes devouring the menu. 'You'll feel better when you've eaten.'

Ellie relaxed. 'Do you really have to leave your place on your day off, in order to get some peace and quiet?'

'Woman, I've been known to drive down to the river and sit in the car listening to tapes, just to get away from the phone.'

'I'm sorry, I shouldn't have rung you.'

'My dear, any time.' He put out his hand as if to pat hers, but took it back just in time.

Ellie bent her head over the menu. 'I must admit, I'm hungry, too.'

'I could murder a full English breakfast, which I see they serve all day long. But I suppose I'd better have something sensible. And don't suggest a salad, or anything else healthy. It's my day off, remember?'

Ellie smiled, and they both ordered a pasta dish.

'Spill the beans,' said Thomas. 'And then I'll chime in with my bit.'

'Well, this is what we've discovered...' She brought him up to date, concluding with, '...and Roy's taken Felicity back to his mother's, rather like a retriever handing a pheasant over. No, that's unkind. But she's safe for the moment.'

'The police?'

'I don't think they'll take it seriously till they've analysed the bread rolls Mrs Alexis delivered yesterday morning, and I can't blame them for that. They don't know her history, and of course it's all circumstantial. You're quite right and we shouldn't jump to conclusions. But if you'd seen her staring at me last night ... I suppose you could say she's a tiny bit dotty.'

'No, I wouldn't say that. I rather think I may have found her for you, by the way.'

The waiter removed their plates. They ordered coffee.

'I can't bear it,' said Ellie. 'I've been racking my brains to think where I'd seen her, and you just...'

'She's working as a cleaner at the retirement home in the mornings. Betty Alexis. Let me explain. I usually visit the home in the afternoons, but last night there was a message on the answerphone, asking me to visit this morning as one of my parishioners was poorly and they thought he'd be whipped off to hospital any minute. So I went in early – far earlier than usual – and saw my old friend.

'He was in his room, of course. He hadn't got up. I don't think I've ever had occasion to go into the bedrooms upstairs before. Downstairs, yes. But not upstairs. Just as I was coming out, I spotted someone I hadn't seen before, going into another of the residents' bedrooms. If you hadn't reminded me, I don't suppose I'd have thought anything of it, but as it was I hung about for a bit, wondering if I was seeing things but pretty sure I wasn't. She didn't come out, so I went down to have a chat with Felicity's mother, Anne...'

'Who would have been delighted to see you.'

He grinned. Put two sugars into his coffee, and added milk. 'People are usually glad to see me, when they don't get many visitors. Anyway, Anne confirmed that the home does employ a cleaner in the mornings, and her name is Betty. That's all that Anne knows, or cares to know, about domestic help. So I popped into the office and asked about this Betty and where she might live. They looked it up. She'd given her address as the house Felicity now occupies. So that's Mrs Betty Alexis.'

'Thomas, you are wonderful! Come to think of it, I don't think I've ever been to the home in the mornings, either. So near, and yet we never knew she was there.'

He laughed. 'Sugar for you?'

'Yes, please. Two. And milk. We should celebrate.'

'What would you like to do? Go to the pictures? Take a ride out into the country and find a cream tea? Poke around junk shops?'

Ellie put her elbows on the table, and rested her chin on them. 'What I would really, really like is to sit in my own garden with a mug of iced tea and do absolutely nothing for a change. Of course I know very well that if I sat down in my garden for two minutes I'd spot something that needed doing, a weed, something that needed tying up, and I'd get up to attend to it. It's just a fantasy.'

'Substitute beer for iced tea, and that's my fantasy, too.'

'We could go to Kew Gardens for the afternoon?' said Ellie. 'Or is it too hot?'

'We could buy straw hats in the charity shop, stroll around for half an hour, ignore the hothouses, and finish up with tea at the Maids of Honour...'

'Yum. I love their pastries.'

'We should be ashamed of ourselves, after what we've just eaten.'

'Duly ashamed,' said Ellie. 'But I expect we could manage a pastry or two if we force ourselves to walk lunch down first.'

His mobile phone went off. He listened, frowned, nodded, beckoned the waiter over for the bill. Sighed. Said, 'Of course,' and shut the phone up.

'It's your day off,' reminded Ellie, wondering if anyone apart from the church-wardens had his mobile number.

'Mm. A boy from our youth club has just got himself arrested, taking and driving a car away; his mother wants me down at the police station to see if I can get him off with a caution.'

Ellie lowered her eyes to hide her disappointment. 'Of course you must go.'

'Same time, same place next Friday?'

'I'd like that, but...' she remembered Bill and his plans. 'I don't know if I'd be free. May I ring you?'

His face closed down on her. She flushed, and felt guilty. Then she got cross. These men were so vulnerable!

Thomas paid the bill and left. Ellie signalled to the waiter that she'd like another cup of coffee, which she'd pay for herself. She felt she could do with a little thinking time and this was as good a place as any in which to think. She didn't have to meet up with Felicity till evening, and it seemed too boring for words to go back home and spend time gardening and washing and dusting.

The coffee came, and she sat back, idly letting various possibilities come to the forefront of her mind. Should she spend the afternoon going over to Chalk Farm to see if she could discover more about the long-departed father and sister of Mrs Alexis? No, not really.

She could revisit Maisie and see if she could dig up more scandal about the old days. But again, the prospect did not appeal.

She might drop in on the dentist and ask if he or his partner would give her the address of their client who went around by bicycle ... only she'd seen for herself – once she started looking – that there were quite a few women around who used bikes. Not as many as men, of course. But there it was.

It was marvellous that Thomas had managed to find out where Mrs Alexis worked. The police would be interested, wouldn't they? Though it would have been even better if he'd discovered where she lived now.

Suppose Ellie were to drop round to the retirement home this afternoon? Someone was bound to know where she lived now. And that would tie everything up neatly.

She beckoned to the waiter, and asked to pay for the extra coffee. He was a youngish lad, British born but possibly of Greek extraction. As he fumbled with her change, Ellie remembered that the chef here was some relation of the man who had owned the Greek restaurant next door. She also remembered that he probably hadn't been around long enough to have known Mr Alexis. Still, it did no harm to ask, now that she was there.

'Would it be possible to have a word with Chef?'

The waiter gave a hunted look around, and disappeared. Well, trade had slackened off now that most people had finished their lunch.

A middle-aged dark-haired and dark-skinned man appeared, wiping his forehead as he removed his cap. 'You have complaint, miss?'

'No, no, indeed!' Ellie was horrified. 'Everything was lovely. It's just a personal matter. I was trying to find someone who might know a Mr Alexis, who used to own the restaurant next door, only it's under new management and...'

'Alexis!' The man looked as if he'd have liked to spit, if he hadn't been brought up properly. 'I remember that name. He give my father much grief! That man was distant cousin, right? I remember him from when I was a child. He boasted to customers how he owned the restaurant. It was true, he had some shares, but he was only manager, that's all. His wife, she make trouble, saying she was part-owner when he died. My father had to be very tough with her. She a mad woman, you know?'

'Yes, I know,' said Ellie, intrigued.

'So when he died, she made bad scenes. My father had to pay her off, buy her shares, you know? It was like she jinxed us, yes? My father died, and my eldest brother took his place here, but I had to stay in Greece to learn to be chef there. And now, many troubles for our family, my brother also is dead with four young children, so we sell next door and I work here only.'

So that was how Mrs Alexis had kept the house on after her husband died. 'Thank you,' said Ellie.

'She cause more trouble, even now?'

'Yes, but I hope we can put a stop to it.'
'I wish you well. She is a mad woman, that one.'

Ellie left the café and wandered along, paying more attention than usual to the people in the Avenue. She didn't see Mrs Alexis, but when she came abreast of the dentist's, she saw something which made her choke with laughter. A young woman in her twenties rode a bike off the road, and chained it to a stand on the pavement. The bicycle was bright red and had a child seat on the back. The woman was blonde with a fly-away mane that reminded Ellie of Felicity. She was wearing a stylish knapsack on her back. She went into the dentist's, and through the window Ellie could see the receptionist greet her with a smile.

Was this the customer Mr Patel had been referring to? It looked rather like it. Well, what a good thing Ellie hadn't tried to get the client's address out of him.

Still laughing to herself, Ellie found she was walking away from the Avenue. She concluded that she was on her way to visit the home. Well, why not? If she could get Mrs Alexis' new address out of them somehow, they'd be that much further on. Armed with that, perhaps Thomas could visit the woman and tell her to stop it. Or words to that effect.

The only snag was that the doors to the home were shut, with a notice saying that visitors should please avoid the rest hour after lunch. Ellie quailed and half turned to go. Then straightened her shoulders and rang the bell. She was not a visitor, and she was there on business.

A heavy-set, middle-aged woman with thinning hair came to the door. Competent. Probably a qualified nurse. 'Visiting hours are—'

'I know,' said Ellie, inserting herself into the hall. 'I'm not a visitor. I came to have a word with whoever's in charge.'

'She's off this afternoon, and I'm standing in for her, sort of. Do you want some details about accommodation for a senior person? I'm afraid we're completely full at the moment, but...'

'Could we go into your office? It's about Mrs Alexis.'

The woman flushed. 'Oh, her! Good riddance, if you ask me.'

'She's gone?'

'Left this morning. Sudden like. Doesn't care what sort of a mess she leaves us in. Come this way. Don't want to wake anyone up, do we?'

The office was small, claustrophobic. A small fan tried to stir the air. The woman held out her hand, indicating that Ellie should sit on a chair beside her desk. There was all the usual office furniture; telephones, computer, filing cabinets ... and a locked trolley which would contain medicines to be handed out each day.

'I'm Mrs Duncan.'

'Mrs Quicke. Ellie Quicke. I visit sometimes with my friend, Lady Kingsley.'

Mrs Duncan's expression softened. 'A very nice lady. Fancy her fixing us up with a supply of home-made bread rolls for free!'

'Indeed. The thing is that Mrs Alexis has started playing some rather nasty tricks on Lady Kingsley—'

'She hasn't, has she? Whatever next?'

'Lady Kingsley doesn't want to upset her mother by talking about it, but—'

'I should imagine not!' Mrs Duncan could see why Felicity wouldn't wish to make a fuss in front of her mother.

'—we thought, Reverend Thomas and I, that if we could talk to Mrs Alexis and get her to stop it, the police might not have to be involved.'

Mrs Duncan nodded. 'We've got her address here...' She called up a file on the computer screen, fidgeted with the mouse, and said, 'That's odd. This is her old address, yet I'm sure she moved late last year.'

She scrabbled around among some papers on the desk, and found one covered in a scrawl. 'Ah, here it is. No, that doesn't help. This is a note of what we owed her, cheque made out this morning, all in order except ... ah, "Mrs Alexis calling next week for her cards". Now, I wonder why she didn't leave a forwarding address.'

'Perhaps,' said Ellie, 'she doesn't want us to know where she lives?'

'Well, now ... I think Sandra gave her a lift one day when it was raining hard and Betty couldn't bring her bicycle ... hold on a minute, I'll see if Sandra's around. I know she's doing teas today.'

She wafted herself out. Ellie resisted the temptation to fiddle with the computer herself. After all, if it had the wrong address on it, then that's all the information it would be likely to give.

Mrs Duncan returned with a heavy-breathing ginger-haired adolescent, who presumably was old enough to drive but didn't look it.

'This is Sandra. Tell her about when you gave Betty a lift.'

'I took her down to that church that isn't a church no more, you know the one? Hanwell way. She said not to take her any further, so I didn't. She never even thanked me, and it hailing and spitting like the end of the world.'

'You don't know which road she lived in?'

'She never said, though I did ask ... thought to do her a favour, didn't I? Fancy her letting us down like that today, without giving us no notice! Says she's got a better job, full-time looking after someone that appreciates her, which she says is more than we do, and she's right there, ain't she!'

'Did she give you any other clue about where she lives?'

Sandra shifted her bulk from one foot to the other, chewing gum? 'There was something. Not about her, about her landlady. Got it! We was talking about getting some party gear and someone said what about the clothes shop in the Avenue, not the charity shop, but the posh one. Ruby's, it's called. We were saying what time it closed, seeing as we'd have to go after we finished work here, and Betty said the shop closed as soon as the pubs opened, and she should know because the woman who owned the shop was her landlady. Does that help?'

'Thanks, Sandra. Best get on with the teas now.' Sandra took herself off.

Mrs Duncan mumbled something to herself, diving into the papers on the desk again. 'Hold on a minute, Mrs Quicke. I might have something, somewhere...' She accessed a different programme on the computer. 'Ah, there it is. I thought I recognized the name. Ruby isn't a common name nowadays, is it? Someone called Ruby Hawthorne asked last week about accommodation for her elderly father. It seems the terms were rather beyond what she'd expected, so the matter wasn't taken any further. Just a note made that she'd made the enquiry. Do you think it could be the same person?'

'What's her address?'

'That's strange. The address is that of a shop in the Avenue. No home address.'

'Perhaps she doesn't want her father to know that she's been making enquiries?'

'True. That happens. It can be a shock to older people when they realize their children want to put them in a home.' She reached for the telephone directory. Sought for Hawthornes. Shook her head. 'Nothing. It must be her married name. Her father's name could be anything.'

'Then I might as well potter along to the shop, see if I can have a word with her.'

There was a stir outside. Someone was bumping a trolley along the hall. 'Would you like to stay for a cuppa? I'm sure Anne would be delighted to see you.'

Ellie grinned. 'Thanks, but no thanks.'

It was cooler outside the home than within. A brisk walk back to the Avenue, and Ellie was dying for a cup of tea in a cool room. She went straight to 'Ruby's', a mid-terrace shop with 'boutique' written all over it. Ellie wondered how the powerfully built Sandra had got on, if she'd gone shopping here. It didn't look as if Ruby's dealt with clothes over size sixteen.

Ellie, of course, was sixteen up top and

eighteen below. But she wasn't going to buy anything, was she?

She pushed open the door and met a blast of cool air. The fan here was much larger and infinitely more capable of cooling the air than the one in the office at the home. There were no customers.

A carefully blonded woman was sitting behind a minimalist ebonized desk. She wore black, with rings on her right hand but none on her left. An expensive watch was on her right wrist, too. Was she, perhaps, left-handed? Divorced?

There was no cash till in sight. Presumably only credit cards were allowed here. The clothes were in restrained colours, mostly black. Shoes, handbags on one stand. Jewellery laid out under glass. A stunning black evening dress with a plunging neckline occupied the centre of one wall. Ellie gaped at it. However did it get held up? By faith and without safety nets?

'Can I help you?'

'I rather think you can. Is there somewhere we can talk privately?'

The woman was amused. 'I don't close till half past five.'

'Then as you have no customers at the moment, perhaps you can find me a chair, and we can talk here. It's about your cleaner, Mrs Alexis.'

The woman's face became watchful. 'What

314

about her?'

'May I sit down for a minute?'

Eyebrows raised, the woman fetched a stool from a changing cubicle at the back of the shop, and placed it for Ellie.

'Thank you. It's very hot, today, isn't it?'

'So, what can I do for you? You said you came about my cleaner. I'm afraid she hasn't any time to spare to help you out, Mrs...?'

'My name is Mrs Quicke, Ellie Quicke. No, it wasn't that. I've come across Mrs Alexis in another context, a rather worrying one.'

Ruby's voice sharpened. 'What other context? She's not in trouble, is she? I've always found her perfectly satisfactory. She looks after my elderly father for me, you see.'

Ellie found the idea of Mrs Alexis being left in charge of a vulnerable old man alarming. 'Forgive me. I shouldn't interfere, I know, and it really is none of my business, but are you sure that's a good idea?'

'How dare you come here and...!' The woman checked herself. 'Unless you have some very good reason why ... do you know something that I...? Has she a police record? I think perhaps you'd better explain yourself, Mrs ... er...'

'Quicke. Yes, I suppose I'd better. The police are involved, but ... let me start at the beginning. Lady Kingsley is a friend of mine, and—'

315

'Who?'

'Felicity Kingsley. You don't know the name?'

The woman shook her head.

'Mrs Alexis used to rent a house from Felicity's husband, Sir Arthur Kingsley. She couldn't keep up the payments and had to leave. Some nasty tricks were played on Sir Arthur at the time – such as leaving him a pizza laced with sleeping tablets. We believe Mrs Alexis was responsible, but as he died in a car crash and Mrs Alexis moved, nothing was done about it.

'Only, Felicity wanted a smaller house after her husband died, so she took over the one Mrs Alexis had been renting, and it seems that Mrs Alexis bears a grudge, for lately she's resumed her campaign ... this time against Felicity. You know nothing about this?'

The woman's brow furrowed. 'What sort of campaign?'

'It started with what at first seemed to be just a nasty practical joke. She delivered some dodgy bread rolls to the church for a lunch party last weekend...'

'Really?' Operations on the nails were suspended. 'That's odd. I was thinking of going to that. Their nice vicar, Thomas something, got talking to me one day just outside my shop and invited me but ... I don't know why, I didn't go.' She shrugged. 'Not really my scene.'

'Oh,' said Ellie, her heart beating faster. 'We couldn't understand why we'd been targeted, but perhaps, if you told Mrs Alexis that you were thinking of going...?'

'I may have done. Yes, I think I did. She was on at me to take my father out for a meal that Sunday; as if he'd have enjoyed it, which he wouldn't. He hasn't eaten anything solid for months. You think she was making a point, trying to put me off going to church?' A light laugh. 'As if I would.'

'I don't know why she did it. It caused a lot of trouble. An elderly man with a weak stomach died, and a young woman miscarried. There was some confusion because another quite innocent woman had been going round selling rolls, and we all thought it might be her who'd played the trick on us, until Lady Kingsley was given two lots of bread rolls in one day, and began to put two and two together.'

The woman got up, went behind a curtain and switched a kettle on. 'Tea? Coffee? A cold drink?'

'Tea would be wonderful.' She thought with regret of having tea at the Maids of Honour in Kew, and how pleasant that would have been. Ah well.

Ruby said, 'I knew nothing of this. It's ... worrying.'

'Nobody imagines you did. But we're trying to find Mrs Alexis and ... well, tell her to stop it, really.'

'To stop what, exactly?'

Ellie went pink. 'Put bluntly, Felicity thinks the woman intends to kill her.'

Ruby cracked out a laugh.

'I know it sounds stupid. But when you take her background into consideration, it begins to make sense.'

'She had perfectly good references when she came to me. One was from the retirement home and another from a woman whose house she'd been cleaning for years. I checked and there was absolutely nothing to indicate the woman was in any way unsuitable. I'm divorced and work all hours, so I had to be careful, because I need someone I can trust to look after the house and see to my father. He won't hear of a carer coming in from the council. Mrs Alexis is the answer to my prayers.' The kettle boiled and Ruby retreated, to return with a couple of glasses of hot water in which tea bags were floating. No milk. No lemon. No sugar.

Ellie was grateful for what she was given.

Ruby sipped tea, frowning. 'You mentioned her background. What did you mean by that?'

'Well, it's all circumstantial, and perhaps you won't think it important, but ... you know the Greek restaurant here in the Avenue? Well, some ten years or more ago...'

Ruby's eyes widened as Ellie gave chapter and verse of Mrs Alexis' interesting career to date. After a while, Ruby took out a tissue with a hand that trembled, and pressed it to her lips. 'Say that bit about her father's death again.'

Ellie obliged.

'And the sister, too?' Ruby had gone very pale. 'I don't believe it.'

'I said it was circumstantial.'

Ruby stood up with an abrupt movement. Started to say something, and stopped herself. Let her eyes go round the shop.

She went over to one of the rails of dresses, and gave a couple of garments a twitch. She gazed at the wall behind the evening dress for a moment, then said, 'Circumstantial, as you say. You haven't any proof, have you?'

Ellie shook her head. 'Not till the police get those bread rolls analysed.'

'Suppose they're laced with ... what did you think she might have used? Senna? She was just playing a practical joke, wasn't she?'

'That may be true, but there was a lethal dose of sleeping tablets in the pizza which killed Sir Arthur's dog.'

'A dog!' Ruby swept her hand along the rail dismissively. 'So the poor woman is a little touched with all the misfortunes that have come upon her. If that's all...'

'Well, lately she's been watching the house – Felicity's house. It's disturbing.'

'Really? I wonder when she has time to do that. Are you sure?'

'Yes,' said Ellie, through clenched teeth. 'I'm sure.'

Ruby flounced back into her chair. 'This is absurd. I've left my father in her care for months, and there's never been a whisper of anything wrong. He actually likes her, for heaven's sake, whereas if I do anything for him, he grumbles that I do it wrong. She's always there when I get home, and I never get home till late...'

After the pubs close? thought Ellie.

'...and there's nothing, absolutely nothing to show that she means me harm, or my poor father. She's been wonderful. I can't believe ... no, I really can't believe that there can be anything wrong with her. I won't believe it. Why, I've asked her to give up work at the home so she can help out with my father more—'

'She left the home this morning, and isn't going back.'

'Well, that's the first good news you've been able to give me. I suppose,' sarcasm to the fore, 'I should be grateful. Now if there's nothing more, I'd like you to leave.'

Ellie realized she'd failed in her attempt to get through to the woman. She got to her feet. 'I understand your reasoning, but please do think over what I've said. I really don't think she is to be trusted.'

'I disagree.'

'Well, if you could just give me your address...?'

'Certainly not. I'm not having you bothering my housekeeper, and that's flat.'

'When the police have analysed the bread rolls—'

'If they find anything untoward, no doubt they will have the courtesy to let me know. Until then, don't hold your breath.'

Ellie tried one last time. 'May I leave you my phone number, so that you can contact me if—'

'If you don't leave immediately, I'll call the men in from the betting shop next door, and they'll run you out into the street.'

Ellie left, thinking she ought to have handled Ruby more tactfully. Perhaps if Roy had been with her and done his charm act, Ruby might have listened. Perhaps. Or Thomas. Either of them would probably have made a better job of it.

There hadn't been a single customer in the shop all the time she'd been there. Ellie felt like kicking the door in. Or something. Anything.

She stood outside, wondering ... thinking over what had been said. She became increasingly sure that somewhere in that conversation, she'd lost momentum. There had been a moment when Ruby had been aghast at Ellie's revelations, and then ... and then ...

it was as if a switch had been thrown and Ruby had decided for some reason that she was not going to listen to Ellie, but was going to back Mrs Alexis.

Because it would have been inconvenient to have to sack the woman? Probably.

Did that mean Ellie could give up? Well, no. It didn't.

She went half a dozen doors along to the charity shop, and peered in. If the difficult manageress – known to her staff as 'Madam' – was in, then Ellie wouldn't stop. But if she were out, as she often was ... yes! And even better, Anita was on duty, together with another woman Ellie used to work with in the old days.

Ellie pushed the door open and went in. There were more ways than one to skin a cat.

Mrs Alexis took great care filling the bottle with paraffin. She hadn't stayed long enough at the home to get one of their bottles, but there were always some to be found dumped in the litter bins along the Avenue. This one she'd found outside the wine shop. Splendid. She used a cooking funnel to fill it with paraffin.

Afterwards, everything stank of paraffin. She'd have to wash her hands carefully. The funnel? She'd put that in the trash.

She screwed the top back on the bottle and made sure it wasn't leaking. The paraffin looked a little dirty, but no matter, it would do the job.

She put the bottle in a dark carrier bag in her basket on the bike, together with a box of matches and a J-cloth. Then she washed her hands with care, and went up to see how the old dear was doing. His colour was good, and he asked for some more of her chicken soup for supper. That was a good sign. He'd last for months at this rate – which suited her just fine.

Perhaps she'd give him a sleeping tablet in his late-night drink ... and if Ruby came in early enough, she'd get one, too.

It wouldn't be any good going out till way after midnight, till all the pubs had emptied out and the streets were quiet again. Perhaps about two o'clock in the morning? She'd set her alarm for two, anyway. She was looking forward to it.

Sixteen

Ellie walked into the charity shop at five, noting that Ruby was closing up her boutique early.

The people who worked in the charity shop could have staffed MI5 without needing to be trained. They knew all about their neighbouring shopkeepers, and far more than their customers suspected about the lives and problems of everyone who shopped in the Avenue. If they had ever wished to turn their hands to it, they could have made an excellent living by blackmail.

But, with the glaring exception of Madam – whose snobbery and inefficiency were a byword – they were good-hearted men and women, working unpaid and often unthanked for charity ... and also, let's face it, for the fun of being 'in the know'.

'That Ruby?' said Anita. 'You want to know about her? Where shall we start?' And to a customer, 'Now, now. You know we can't reduce our prices any further. This is a charity shop, remember.'

Anita left one of her mates in charge of the till, and beckoned Ellie through to the back room where they were sorting and pricing the piles of stuff which were given them by the public. 'Take a seat, if you can find one. Here, move that pile of clothes ... that's it. Oh, this is Mae. New since your time. Mae, this is Ellie. She used to work here. She wants to know about Ruby.'

'Why Ruby?' asked Mae, a buxom wench with golden curls, sixty if she was a day.

'Ellie's our chief finder outer,' explained Anita. 'On the track of something nasty, are we, Ellie? Well, now. What do we know about Ruby? To start with, Ruby is something of a mystery woman. The word is that her father bought her a long lease of that shop some years back, after she got her divorce through and he went off to Australia – the husband, that is. Not the father. He's loaded, we think.'

'What's the father's name, do you know?'

'Um ... Mae, you used to work in the Post Office and saw all sorts. Do you know what Ruby's name was before she got married?'

Mae said, 'Never heard it. Never laid eyes on her till after the divorce, when she suddenly arrived, lease in hand, so to speak.'

'Where does she live, then?' said Ellie.

'Now then, where does she live?' wondered Anita. 'She runs that nice little Peugeot, keeps it out front where she can see it all the time. Where does she live, Mae?'

'Hanwell way, some place? One of those big houses which are usually chopped into flats, though I don't think hers is, the way she talks about it. Lady Muck, tries to be. Can't blame the husband for getting away.'

Anita seized a needle and thread and began sewing a leg back on a soft toy which looked as if it had been attacked with a sharp knife. 'Now, who would know?' She repeated herself. 'Who would know? Ricky, at the beauty parlour. I'm sure she goes there. It's the most outrageously expensive place in the Avenue.'

She handed the partly mended toy to Ellie and delved for a mobile phone in her handbag. 'Ricky, is that you? Anita here. Can you talk for a moment? Got a small query. Do you know where our Ruby hangs out...' She shrieked with laughter. 'Apart from the Red Lion and the Duke of Kent, that is. No, I mean, what hole does she crawl back to when the pubs throw her out? ... Oh, the wine bar in the Broadway, is it? I knew you'd know where ... Hanwell, we thought. Somewhere down near the Butts, the really posh bit ... mhmm ... no! Who told you that?'

She shrieked with laughter again, and was still shaking as she switched her phone off. 'He says he thinks her shop is a front for money-laundering for the Mafia, because she never seems to have any customers, but the stock keeps changing.'

Ellie smiled, but shook her head. 'Now come on. That's actionable.'

'Only if it's a lie. Anyway, Ricky says he's seen her car in the Butts once or twice. He comes up that way from West Ealing, and if the main road's gridlocked he goes through the back doubles.'

'Narrows it down,' said Mae, taking the mended item out of Ellie's hands, and sticking a price on it.

'So it does,' agreed Ellie. 'Many thanks.'

'Any time. Care to come back to work here? One hour, two hours a week? Full time?'

'In some ways I wish I could. I miss the shop – and all of you.'

'Get along with you. Give our love to Thomas.'

'I will.' Thomas did get around, didn't he?

Time to check in with Felicity and Roy. Wait a minute ... she quickened her pace ... Kate had said something about messages on Ellie's answerphone that morning. She'd better get home and check them, and feed Midge and water the conservatory and garden. The rain the other morning had done some good, but it wasn't enough to keep the plants going. It was very hot in the sun and the annuals in her garden would be feeling it. Felicity would be fine with Aunt Drusilla for a few hours.

Ellie's house seemed undisturbed as she let herself in. There was a frou-frou of mail inside the front door, but nothing to worry about. Midge – how did he manage to appear just as she returned? – arrived to wind himself around her legs. Armand or Kate had probably fed him but he would now demand to be fed again, just to make a point.

Yes, the answerphone light was winking.

She fed Midge first, then watered the conservatory and turned the sprinkler hose on in the back garden. She could hear Catriona chirruping in Kate's garden and, looking through the gap in the hedge, saw that Kate and another youngish mother were watching over Catriona and a similar size small boy.

Kate's garden had once had a large water feature, but a covered sandpit under an awning now stood in its place.

Finally Ellie got herself a cool drink – she always kept a jug of water in the fridge, with slices of lemon floating in it – and listened to her phone messages.

The first was from her builder, saying he was about to go off on his holidays and he'd do the repointing of her front wall when he came back, if that was all the same to her. It was.

Then Bill. 'Ellie, are you there? It's ... what time is it? ... half past nine on Thursday night, a bit late to ring but I assume you're not in bed yet.'

No, thought Ellie. I told him I was at Felicity's, but he's forgotten that, hasn't he? Uh oh, wait a minute, he probably hasn't got my mobile phone number.

'Anyway, what I wanted to say was that I'd just remembered I'm at my junior partner's for supper tomorrow night, Friday. He knows about you, of course, and wondered if you'd like to come along as well. I'll pick you up at seven, shall I?'

Click, end of message.

Ellie said 'Eeek!' She consulted her watch. Was she really supposed to be going out for supper tonight? It was nearly six now...

Another phone message. Aunt Drusilla. 'Ellie, just to say that I've offered to have

Felicity stay here for the time being, but she won't hear of it. She had a nap this afternoon and since then she's been out in the garden helping Rose. Roy's phoned twice to see how she is, and though she didn't take his calls I am not displeased with the way things are going. I couldn't make out if she was really in danger or not. On the whole, I think it would be good to take precautions. Better safe than sorry.'

Click went the phone.

Bill ringing again. 'Ellie, did you get my message? Seven o'clock sharp. They live near me. I do hope you're not off on another of your wild goose chases. Well, see you this evening. The time is now ... oh, two p.m.'

Click.

Diana. 'Mother, I know I said I could look after Frank this afternoon, but something's come up. It seems his father doesn't get back till tomorrow, now. So inconsiderate. But luckily, Frank likes coming to you. I'll pick him up about six, all right?'

Click. Ellie groaned. It was after six now, so presumably – hopefully – Diana had checked with the school and retrieved her son in time.

The phone rang again as she was halfway up the stairs. She hesitated about returning to answer it, and decided to let the answerphone take a message.

Roy this time. 'Ellie, are you all right? My

meeting's only just finished, and I'm on my way home. Mother says Felicity's had a good rest and is looking much better, but I don't think she should be alone in her house until things are sorted out, do you? I'm going to suggest I take us all out to supper somewhere local, and then I'll doss down with her for the night. Pick you up about quarter to seven?'

Click.

Ellie took a deep breath and tried to sort out her priorities. If Roy was looking after Felicity, then she could go out with Bill – which she ought to do, anyway.

She found her mobile phone, and dialled Bill's number. This time it was his answerphone that clicked in. 'Dear Bill, sorry I didn't get your message till just now – the time is ... er ... just after six. Yes, I'd love to come, and I'll be ready as near seven as I can make it.'

Next she rang Aunt Drusilla. 'Aunt, Roy's been on his phone to me, I gather he's on his way home at the moment. He suggested we all go out for supper somewhere but I've got a date...'

'There is absolutely no reason for him to take us out,' said Aunt Drusilla, who obviously didn't want to be bothered going out for the evening. 'Rose is preparing a special treat here for us tonight. Are you sure you can't make it?'

'Quite sure. But would you tell Roy that I think I've discovered where Mrs Alexis lives. She was working at the retirement home till this morning but has left that job. The only address they had was her old house – Felicity's house. But she works for a woman called Ruby Hawthorne, who runs a dress shop in the Avenue, and it's thought she lives in one of the big houses in the Butts, in Hanwell. I don't know whether or not the police are ready to move in this matter, but perhaps if he told them where to find her...?'

'Good thinking. I'll see that it's done. Oh, here's Felicity, wanting a word.'

Felicity's pretty voice took over. 'Ellie, is it you? I've had a lovely time here, but helping Rose in the garden just makes me think all the more about what I can do with mine when I get back. I'm determined to sleep there tonight, but ... you will be with me, won't you?'

'I believe Roy intends to act as guard dog again, so you won't need me, will you?'

'If you don't mind, Ellie, I'd rather have you and Roy. Rose says he sleeps like a top and is difficult to wake, and that's the last thing I want if someone's going to start creeping around the house at midnight. Besides, I don't want to be alone with him in the house, do I?'

Felicity was trying to joke, but Ellie could hear the fear in her voice.

331

'Very well, my dear. I'm dining out with some friends of Bill's and will come on to you after that, all right?'

'Bless you.' Felicity hung up.

Before the phone could go again, Ellie rushed upstairs, stripped off and jumped into the bath, wishing there was time for more than a quick shower. Splash, splash. Run the dryer over her hair.

What to wear? She'd met Bill's younger partner on several occasions, and liked him. What was his name, now? David something. David Webb. So far so good.

How décolleté did one go when dining out in the summer? Not very, perhaps.

In any case, there might be gnats in the evenings down by the river, and she was sure to get bitten because if anyone was going to be bitten, it would be her.

Perhaps she ought to have bought something suitable at Ruby's boutique. Or perhaps not. Black didn't really suit her. She pulled open her wardrobe door, and tugged various garments out. The rose pink was too warm for a summer's evening.

A pale blue with splodgy flowers on it ... no, it made her look too pale.

A good white blouse with a bit of a plunging neckline never comes amiss, dressed up with some jewellery ... a string of good pearls, rather old-fashioned but they suited her, her engagement ring. Her favourite floaty dark blue skirt, cut on the bias. The outfit looked a trifle too severe, perhaps? Well, tough. It would have to do.

High-heeled sandals. Bother, was that a ladder in her tights? Oh well, knee-highs would have to do. Better than tights in this hot weather, anyway. Where are the knee-highs? Mustn't try to rush putting them on, or they'd be laddered for sure.

Brush out her hair. Dash on some pressed powder and that rather pale lipstick that she was trying to remember to replace with something a little darker ... she did hope Diana managed to collect Frank from school...

Bill sounded his horn and she snatched up her evening bag, thrust necessaries inside, and ran down the stairs, clutching at the banister so she didn't fall over in her high-heeled shoes. Only seven minutes late.

'Dear Bill, what a lovely surprise date.'

He welcomed the peck on the cheek that she gave him, but was clearly annoyed that she'd kept him waiting. 'I thought I said seven o'clock.'

'You did. Sorry.'

She didn't like this. She'd spent half her married life apologizing to people because she hadn't measured up to what they wanted. It was a trap which was far too easy to fall into, even now.

'Never mind,' said Bill, patting her hand. 'I

know most women like to keep a man waiting now and then.'

The words 'but don't make a habit of it'
hung on the air, unuttered but understood.

David and his wife Janetta lived not far
from Bill on the river. Their garden didn't
actually go down to the Thames, but in all
other respects it was delightful. The house
was rose-red brick, Georgian or early Victorian, with high ceilings and sash windows.
There was no evidence of children around,
and no expense had been spared in the
décor. Ellie was reminded of Felicity's next-
door neighbour with her minimalist furniture and swimming pool in the back garden.
David's wife also reminded Ellie of skinny-
thin Suzie, even to the glass of red wine in
her hand.

'Lovely to meet you at last,' gushed Janetta,
air-kissing Ellie's cheek while assessing every
item of her clothing and deciding it definitely wasn't from Harrods. Janetta was wearing
something so flimsy it looked as if it might
take off any minute, and Ellie realized that
she was under-dressed for the occasion.

There was another, similar type of fortyish-
woman-trying-to-be-thirty, possibly divorced since she was wearing rings on her right
hand but not on her left. 'Come and meet
Cilla,' said Jannetta. 'And this is a neighbour
of ours, another Bill, I'm afraid.'

'Bill Two,' said Cilla, showing over-large

teeth.

Ellie felt dizzy. 'Second Bill?'

Everyone except Bill Two and Ellie laughed. Both of them smiled politely.

'Sorry we're late,' said Ellie's Bill. 'I'm afraid Ellie was off on one of her wild goose chases.'

'Oh, do you shoot?' said Janetta, looking almost interested. 'Red or white for you, Ellie? I know what Bill likes.'

'No, I don't shoot,' said Ellie. 'May I have a soft drink? It's been such a hot day, and I'm really thirsty.'

'Do you play bridge, by any chance? We're looking for a fourth for next Wednesday.'

'Sorry, no.'

Bill tapped her arm. 'You'll learn quickly enough. There are classes for beginners.'

Ellie made a mental vow never to learn to play bridge. Hadn't she enough on her plate already?

'It was so hot at Wimbledon,' yawned Cilla. 'And the tennis was deadly dull. I don't know why I bother to go before the Finals.'

Tennis became the subject of the conversation. Ellie was not particularly up on tennis, but knew that you only had to listen with rapt attention to someone on their hobby horse, to be considered a delightful guest. So she listened. From tennis they passed to cricket, and these two subjects lasted them till supper, which was served in a garden

335

room at the back of the house. Candles were lit on the table as Janetta conjured up dish after dish from the kitchen to oohs and aahs of appreciation.

'A few of my favourite recipes,' said Janetta, modestly.

Ellie cast her eye over the food, spotting that it had all been ordered from Waitrose. Clearly Janetta was no great cook. But what did that matter – so long as she didn't try to pull the wool over her guests' eyes? The portions were small, but that was fine by Ellie. Conversation flagged.

It was then that Bill Two asked the fatal question. 'So what sort of goose chase were you on today, Ellie?'

Ellie's Bill had had several glasses of wine while they waited for supper. He was pleasantly relaxed, and ready to poke fun at her. 'Someone played a practical joke on one of Ellie's friends, and she fancies the role of private detective.'

Ellie knew she'd blushed, but managed to keep calm. 'No, of course I don't.'

David Webb showed interest. 'Now wait a minute. Didn't you get mixed up in something nasty some time back? A case of poison-pen letters?'

Her Bill rolled his eyes. 'This isn't poison, but it sounds as if it involves an emetic. Big deal.' The others laughed.

Ellie lowered her eyes. 'This mousse is

delicious.'

'Intriguing,' said David, pouring wine lavishly all round. 'Tell us more.'

'Yes, do tell us,' said Janetta, her attention elsewhere. Was that a wasp hovering around?

Ellie's Bill was not displeased to play the role of indulgent sponsor. 'There was a mix-up with some bread rolls at a church function, and now everyone's in a blind panic that they're going to be poisoned, or murdered in their beds. Isn't that right, Ellie?' He was belittling her in front of the others. How could he!

'Are you frightened of being murdered in your bed, Ellie?' asked Cilla, amused and a little disdainful.

Ellie recalled Mrs Alexis staring at her across the road the previous evening. These people hadn't seen the woman, and didn't understand. Bill ought not to have made fun of her like that. He knew her better than anyone and he knew that although she could be a bit silly at times, she had seen something of the dark side of life in her time, and Mrs Alexis was as dark as they came.

She squared her shoulders, pushed aside a full glass of wine, and took a sip of iced water. 'Very well, if we're going to tell horror stories, let me tell you how this one started. One evening last autumn, a rich tycoon found a pizza on his doorstep. He ate some of it, disliked the taste, threw up. His dog ate some, and died. There were sufficient sleeping tablets in the pizza to kill more than one man. That's Act One, Scene One.'

The rest of the table fell silent, as Ellie told them what efforts had been made to find the perpetrator, how suspicion had fallen on a certain woman, who had then disappeared leaving no forwarding address.

'Then came the incident at church. Senna, possibly? Or something similar in the bread rolls, just as Bill said. Trivial? No. An elderly man, who had a weak stomach, died. A woman miscarried. There was no evidence at that point that the two incidents were linked, except...'

Ellie went on to tell of Felicity's fear, the false trail that had led to Mrs Rivers, and then the information Ellie and her friends had gathered about Mrs Alexis' past.

'Husband, father, sister, gone. The dog, poisoned. The handyman Paddy, dead. Mrs Alexis has a motive for persecuting first Felicity's husband, because he turned her out of her house. She has perhaps even more motive for persecuting Felicity, who's taken it over. She's haunting the place.

'Now we think we've found out where Mrs Alexis can be found – she has a live-in post as a housekeeper – and we're just waiting for the police to analyse the bread rolls. And then ... well, that's it, really. I'm no detective and don't try to be. All I do is talk to people and sometimes they tell me what they know.' Though she'd failed to get through to Ruby Hawthorne, hadn't she?

By this time Janetta had cleared away the dessert dishes and put cheese on the table.

Bill helped himself to more wine. 'Well, I'm glad you haven't asked me to be involved this time, Ellie. It seems to me there isn't a single piece of evidence to convict this poor woman.'

Cilla shuddered. 'Poor creature, hounded from pillar to post.'

David Webb concurred. 'There's nothing in it, Ellie. No wonder the police aren't rushing to act.'

'I disagree,' said Bill Two in his quiet way. He'd drunk less than the others. Ellie still didn't know what he did for a living, but he had a look of understated competence about him, and she thought that he was probably very successful. 'I think Ellie's friend has every right to be worried.'

Janetta scoffed. 'What, on the grounds that someone might have put a laxative in her bread?'

'No, on the balance of probabilities. You can take each case on its own and dismiss it ... but remember that in none of these cases have the police been called in. Suppose they had been? Would the verdicts still be 'Misadventure', 'Accident' or 'Natural Causes'? Each time Mrs Alexis has had motive and opportunity to kill, and so far she's got away with it.'

'The husband gassed himself,' said David Webb. 'The father had gastritis, the sister fell down the stairs, Paddy took too much to drink...'

'And the dog died of sleeping tablets. So let's start with that death.'

'Not proven, not proven,' chanted Janetta.

'True, but the balance of probabilities is that she did poison the pizza ... do you agree?'

Everyone nodded, some reluctantly.

'Good. Then add the death of the husband. Does that improve the odds? How about if we add the deaths of husband, father and sister? What do the odds look like now?'

'Don't forget the handyman,' said Cilla, pertly.

'Include the handyman. Include the second batch of rolls dumped on Felicity's doorstep, include the fact that she seems to be haunting the place. What are the odds?'

'I'm hopeless at maths,' said Ellie. 'But I think what you're trying to say is that the balance of probabilities tips more every time you add in one of the "incidents" surrounding her.'

'I could easily convince a jury that she did it,' said Bill Two. 'All of it.'

Ellie looked at her watch. 'You're saying

that Felicity is in very real danger. I've promised to stay with her tonight, just in case. So I ought to be going, I'm afraid.'

Bill Two said, 'If you survive the night in one piece, Ellie, go straight to the police in the morning, tell them everything you've told us, and insist that they get those rolls analysed straight away.'

'We have been trying to get them to move but, yes; of course, they haven't had the full picture, have they?' She looked around at the others, who seemed set for the duration. 'I'm sorry to break up the party – lovely meal, quite delightful – but perhaps I could ring Felicity, see if she can drop by to pick me up. Or get a taxi?'

Ellie's Bill got to his feet with difficulty, looking disgruntled. He'd expected Ellie to be laughed at, and instead she'd been commended. Ellie wondered if he really liked her having taken the limelight for once. 'The night's young. You don't have to go yet, Ellie.'

'I'll just crack open another bottle,' said David Webb.

Janetta pouted, shrugged, smiled. 'If you really have to go ... what a shame!' She didn't really mean it.

Ellie put some warmth into her voice. 'It was a really lovely evening. Thank you. Dear Bill, I'll speak to you tomorrow, shall I?'

Janetta and Bill accompanied Ellie to the

hall. As soon as the door was closed on the others, Ellie heard them burst into raucous laughter. Laughing at her? That hurt. She knew that if she'd left her own friends, they wouldn't have laughed at her behind her back. Bill's lips were twitching, but that may have had another reason. He made an inarticulate sound and lurched towards the downstairs loo. Ah. Bladder trouble?

'Can you manage?' asked Janetta.

Ellie said, brightly, 'Of course I can. No need to stay with me, you know.' She fished out her mobile phone, trying to get through to Felicity's mobile. Switched off. She tried Roy's. Ditto.

'No luck yet?' Janetta attempted to look as if she cared. 'Shall I phone for a taxi for you?'

'No, thanks. I'll try my aunt's landline.'

Janetta hung her hip on the hall table. 'My dear, if you'll accept a word of advice ... if you're going to marry Bill then ... well, men like their women to fit in, don't they? I mean, there's no need to let yourself go, is there? A touch of hair colour would work wonders...'

Ellie wanted to die. Luckily Miss Quicke picked up the phone. 'Aunt Drusilla, Ellie here. Have Felicity and Roy left yet? No? Well, tell them I'm on my way home to change and will get to Felicity's in about ... oh, half an hour.'

'Taxi?' said Janetta, inspecting perfect fingernails.

Ellie nodded. 'I'll get a cab to pick me up. No need for you to wait here, Janetta. Unless, of course, I can help you with the washing up.'

Silly of her. Of course Janetta would have a dishwasher. Also, she wouldn't want Ellie to see the discarded supermarket packaging from the meal.

'That's all right,' said Janetta, and disappeared into the kitchen.

Bill came out of the toilet, and seemed surprised to find her still there. 'Shall I run you home, Ellie?'

'No, no, Bill. You've enjoyed your wine, and we don't want you being picked up by the police, do we?'

Ellie got through to the cab firm she always used, and said she'd be waiting outside on the doorstep. David Webb came to the door, calling for Bill to tell them some tale or other. Bill hesitated.

'You go back in,' said Ellie.

'Are you sure?' he said, looking relieved.

'I'm sure,' said Ellie. 'It was a lovely evening. The taxi will be here in a minute.' She went and stood outside till the cab came.

Mrs Alexis was puzzled. The old man had fallen asleep with the television full on. Well, there was nothing unusual in that. But he didn't wake up

343

to have his supper, and that was unusual. His bottle of sleeping pills stood on his bedside cabinet as usual. She picked it up. Had he taken one early, by some chance? She couldn't be sure because she'd never counted them.

Ruby had come back to the house earlier on, but only stayed long enough to change into another of her evening outfits and check on her father before leaving again.

Perhaps he'd asked Ruby to get one out of the bottle for him earlier. The cap was difficult to remove, although he could manage it, if he tried hard enough.

He was still in his big chair by the window. Mrs Alexis drew the curtains, and wondered what was best to be done. If she left him in the chair, he might fall out of it and bump his head. Or even break a limb. Old people had fragile bones.

She pulled back the duvet on the bed, and with some difficulty manoeuvred him across the room and tipped him on to the mattress. It was lucky she was stronger than she looked. He snored gently as she lifted his legs into bed, and covered him over.

She left his soup handy in its thermos, so that he could drink it when he woke in the night.

There was something else she had to do before she went to bed. She lifted the handset of the telephone in the hall and dialled 999. 'Police,' she said, disguising her voice. When she got through, she made her voice go high and panicky. 'Oh,

344

please do send someone. There's some horrid boys in the park playing with matches, and I'm afraid they'll set fire to the litter bins, oh dear ... who is it calling? Lady Kingsley, of course! I live just opposite the park!'

Mrs Alexis killed the call, and sat there, laughing. That had set the scene nicely. The police would go looking for some youths playing with matches, if all went as she planned.

Oh. She'd just remembered that she hadn't used gloves when preparing her final weapon of destruction. She must go down and wipe the bottle clean before she went to bed ... not that she'd be there for long, of course. Two o'clock, two o'clock and all's going to be well.

Seventeen

Ellie arrived at Felicity's just after eleven. She'd been home, checked on Midge, turned off the water sprinkler, closed all the windows, changed into a light sweater, comfortable skirt and shoes, and packed a change of clothes to take with her.

The night was still warm and there was a full moon, which turned the park opposite Felicity's house into a setting fit for *A Midsummer Night's Dream*. In the daytime you'd

345

see the usual graffiti and discarded litter, but by night it was a place of delight. And so quiet. Ellie fancied she could almost hear the big city breathing, though of course what she was hearing was traffic on the A40 not far away.

All the curtains were drawn at Felicity's, and the garage locked up. As Ellie walked up the drive, security lights came on.

Roy let her in. She heard a burglar alarm chime as he opened the door. Then he cut it off.

He'd changed his clothes, too. He was wearing a long-sleeved shirt in a pale green over well-cut grey trousers, with a greeny-grey cashmere sweater thrown round his shoulders. He doubled-locked the front door behind her.

'Felicity's having a bath. To relax her, you know. Care for a cuppa?'

They went into the kitchen and sat down at the table. Roy was very calm. She thought he'd done a lot of hard thinking these last few days, and maybe a bit of growing up. About time, really.

He made a pot of tea and put it on the table.

'I've made the place as burglar-proof as possible. All windows and doors locked. Burglar alarm in place. Normally on a warm night like this Felicity would leave her bed-room window open, but I've persuaded her not to, tonight.'

Ellie nodded. She'd noticed the curtains were drawn at the back of the house, too.

'What haven't I thought of, Ellie? You're good at putting yourself into other people's shoes. Can you think like her?'

Ellie shivered. 'It's a mean, nasty mind. Her first thought is poison, but if we're locked up right and tight...'

'I keep telling myself we've taken every precaution, but somehow it doesn't help.'

Felicity came in, wearing a fluffy white towelling robe, with her hair loose around her shoulders. She looked about fifteen years old. Roy poured three mugs of tea.

Felicity sat beside Roy, not touching but close. 'I feel in my bones that she's going to try again. You agree with me, Ellie, don't you? Yes. Of course it may not be tonight. It might be tomorrow or the next day. The police might catch up with her, and we'll look back on this night and wonder why we got so worked up. But just to make sure, I'm going to suggest that we take it in turns to sit up.'

Ellie repressed a sigh, but nodded. Roy nodded, too.

Felicity said, 'I was lying there in the bath and trying to relax. What kept going through my mind was that if something does happen, there won't be another chance to sort things out.' Here she looked at Roy, but kept both her hands around her mug. Her body language was saying: I'll talk, but don't touch me ... yet.

Roy shifted slightly on his chair to face her. 'You know how I feel about you.'

She dropped her head so that her hair half-covered her face. 'Yes. But. Arthur said he loved me, too. He didn't mean it, of course. It was just what he thought he needed to say, to get me to marry him. I'm no good in bed, you know.'

Ellie had been thinking it was more than time that she withdrew and left them to it, but Felicity's hand shot out and fastened on her arm. 'No, don't go, Ellie. Help me out on this. Am I being stupid, not wanting to have sex without ... well, without having talked everything through?'

Roy smothered a laugh with his hand. 'My dearest girl, I am not Arthur, and perhaps with me...'

'Oh, I realize that,' said Felicity. 'And of course I hope ... well, if you didn't want me to do some of the things Arthur made me do, which made me feel...' She shuddered. 'I'm sorry. I really hated all that, you know. That's one of the reasons I never wanted to get married again. That, and not being able to have children.'

Roy looked grim. 'I don't give a damn about not having children, and as for the other, we could always give ourselves a chance to...'

She shook her hair back. 'I thought about that, too...'

Ellie picked up her mug and removed herself to the hall. The others didn't seem to notice. She sat on the hall chair, sipping tea and trying not to listen. Well, she wasn't trying very hard, perhaps.

Felicity was saying, 'We could go upstairs now and you could try to make me feel less like a block of ice and perhaps it would work and perhaps it wouldn't. But it would be ... somehow ... not quite right, even it's what most girls would do, isn't it?'

'I did that first time round and got my fingers burned,' said Roy. 'I'm not looking for an instant fix here, Felicity. After what you've been through...'

'And you, too.' Felicity repeated herself. 'And you, too.'

From where she sat, Ellie couldn't see their faces, but she could see their hands, both clutching mugs.

'I thought I'd never get over it,' said Roy. 'But with you ... it's ... well ... different. I trust you, and I hope you trust me.'

Felicity gave a gurgle of laughter. 'Well, I think I can trust you not to jump on me before I'm ready.'

'No, I won't do that,' said Roy, and both his listeners heard the dedication in his voice.

'Mummy says I should get you to sign a pre-nuptial agreement, but...'

'Your mother,' said Roy, 'is a pain.'

'Yes, I know. I told her you were worth a fair bit, as well.'

'Probably not as much as you. Of course I'll sign,' said Roy. And again they heard the commitment in his voice. 'I'd better take out some insurances as well, make sure you're covered, whatever happens to me.'

Ellie was riveted. She saw Felicity's hand leave her mug, and start to make circles on the table with her forefinger, round and round. 'Where would we live? Always presuming that we get that far?'

He kept both his hands on his mug. 'I'm happy. Wherever.'

'Here?' Felicity's forefinger almost went as far as Roy's hand, but drew back just in time. 'Double garage, two bathrooms. We could do a loft conversion as well, I suppose. Then you could have the coach-house as your offices. Always providing...'

'Always providing,' agreed Roy, flexing his fingers on his mug, but not removing them, as her finger made bigger and bigger circles.

'Although, of course, my taste in décor isn't yours. I go in for pretty, whereas you've got some stunning modern pieces. You'd have to teach me to like them.' Somehow, in the last of the circles she was making on the table, her hand accidentally touched his, and stayed there. To his credit, he managed not to cover her hand with his, but stayed rock still.

Silence. Neither of them moved.

Ellie eased a leg which had gone to sleep. It was no good. She'd got pins and needles and would have to stand up and stamp her foot. They probably wouldn't notice. She stood, and they looked up with identical bemused expressions.

'I think,' said Ellie, 'it's time I went to bed.'

'First watch for me,' said Felicity, leaving her hand next to Roy's, but looking up. 'You and Roy go to bed. I'll wake you at one, Ellie, right? Roy can sleep till three.'

Ellie stamped her foot hard, got the feeling back in her leg, and took her mug back into the kitchen to wash it up.

Someone rang the doorbell and used the knocker. All three of them froze, and then switched their eyes to the kitchen clock. Nearly midnight.

Roy cleared his throat. 'I'll go, shall I? You stand by, ready to dial 999 if it's her.' He tried to make a joke of it, but neither Ellie nor Felicity could summon up a smile, and both followed him into the hall when he went to peer through the spy hole in the front door. They could all see the security lights had come on outside. 'It's the police!'

Roy turned off the burglar alarm, unlocked

the door, and opened it, but kept it on the chain.

Peering around Roy, Felicity and Ellie held hands as they glimpsed a true blue, really truly policeman standing on the porch. 'Excuse me, sir, but we've had a complaint by a Lady Kingsley about youths larking about in the park.'

'What?' Felicity went to stand by Roy, who took the chain off the door and opened it wide. 'Come in. What's that you said? I haven't made any complaint about ... what did you say? Youths in the park?'

A stolid policeman stood there, notebook in hand. They could see a police car outside in the road, with a policeman inside it, watching them. A routine patrol?

'Some youths playing around with matches in the park. Are you Lady Kingsley?'

'Yes, but I haven't made a complaint. What sort of complaint?'

'A telephone call.'

'I haven't made any call to the police this evening. Yes, of course there are always lads playing around in the park, but they're harmless enough.'

'You didn't make a complaint?'

'No, I didn't. When was this?'

'Well, if you didn't ... and there's no sign of any youths doing anything they shouldn't in the park...?' He ducked his head and made off down the path to the road, saying, 'Hoax call,' to his mate.

Roy closed the door and double-locked it.

'Matches?' said Ellie. 'Did you say matches?'

'Fire!' said Felicity, going pale. 'Do you think—'

Ellie caught hole of Roy's arm. 'Quick, call them back.'

Roy looked surprised but got the door open again, only to see the police car driving off.

Felicity sank on to the bottom step of the stairs. 'It's her, isn't it? Making a hoax call to get it into the minds of the police that there's a group of youths going around, playing with matches. She's changed her method. She's failed with poison, so she's going to try fire.'

'I'll ring the police and explain it to them,' said Roy, shooting home the bolts on the front door and checking the alarm system was operating.

Felicity threw out her arms. 'They'll think it's another hoax call. At this time of night, there'll be no one there in authority.'

'Nevertheless,' said Ellie. 'If Roy calls, they might get the word to the patrol cars to come this way more often.'

'I'll take first watch,' said Roy, lifting the phone. 'Flick, you look all in. You go to bed, now. Get some sleep. I'll get Ellie up to relieve me at one, right?'

Ellie was poking around in the cupboard

under the stairs. 'Where's the fire extinguisher kept? Or haven't you got one?'

'Certainly,' said Roy, dialling. 'Where did you put it, Flick?'

'Broom cupboard, kitchen.' Felicity hugged herself. 'Am I dreaming? Is this really happening? I can't think straight. Ought we to stay here, if she's going to attack the house? We could go to a hotel, or back to Ellie's...? No, we can't. I won't let her drive me away. But I feel so helpless. What can we do to stop her?'

'Stop dithering, and go to bed, Felicity,' said Ellie, hoisting the fire extinguisher into the hall from the kitchen. 'I've found a fire blanket as well. A good thing Roy knows how to protect his houses.'

'Is that the police?' Roy spoke into the phone. 'We've just had a call from...'

Ellie took Felicity's arm, and pushed her up the stairs. 'You ask what we can do. Well, first we pray. And then we go to sleep. And trust to wake up safe and sound in the morning. Everything will look better in daylight, believe me.'

Felicity slept in the master bedroom at the front of the house. Roy had cleverly contrived an en suite bathroom for it, over the rebuilt garage. The curtains had been drawn some time ago. Ellie propelled Felicity in, turning on the bedside light as she did so. There was a big, king-size bed. Good. Roy would like that, when ... if ... he managed to get Felicity to the altar.

'Pray?' said Felicity. 'A fat lot of good that will do, if she wants to burn the house down tonight.'

'We've taken all the precautions we can as humans. Now we ask for His protection as well. And believe me, it works.'

'I wish I had your faith.'

Ellie pinched in her lips. So did she. Sometimes she felt absolutely sure that God loved her and would never send her a trial that she couldn't overcome with His help. And sometimes she was very much afraid that He'd let her muddle through on her own. This was not the moment to say so, though.

She could hear Roy still on the phone as she went through to the second largest bedroom at the back of the house. She had a good wash, but didn't change into her nightie, so she wouldn't have to dress again when it came to her turn to keep watch. She realized she'd forgotten to bring her Bible. Again.

Well, that didn't stop her praying, did it? Praying calmed you down. Gave you courage. Might even help you to sleep for a while. She needed a good night's sleep, and if she had to be woken at one ... in less than an hour. She probably wouldn't get any sleep at all, knowing she'd have to be awake so soon.

Dear Lord, help us through the dark hours of

the night. We are so much afraid, perhaps with reason, perhaps not. Watch over us. Protect us from evil. You know, better than us, what we have to be afraid of. Look after Felicity and Roy ... and please keep an eye on Thomas, helping other people even on his day off. And I suppose I ought to pray for Bill as well, although...

Well, tonight showed me once and for all that I can't marry him. I was dithering before, wasn't I? Seduced by the lifestyle which he was offering me, and his kindness and his need. But I really don't want that lifestyle, do I? I'd rather be like Thomas, trying to do my best for others ... even on my day off.

She shed her shoes, lay down on the bed, pulling a corner of the duvet over her feet, and lay back, relaxing. Turned off the bed-side light. Sighed. Wriggled around a bit. Turned over. Slept.

Someone was shaking her shoulder. Her bedside light had been turned on. She blink-ed, blinded by it. Realized it was Roy who had roused her. Behind him a glow of light showed that the landing was still lit.

'Ellie.' He was keeping his voice low.

She nodded. Squinted at her watch. Ten past one. She must have slept for an hour. Yuk. She struggled to keep awake, not to fall back into sleep.

'The police?' she asked, pushing back the duvet and swinging her feet to the floor.

'They've promised to send a patrol car round at least once an hour. They've just been round. I watched them from the window. They stopped, used a flashlight up and down the path, saw nothing amiss and went off again.'

'I don't suppose she'll come.' Ellie ran her fingers through her hair, yawned, made herself stand up. 'I'd better make myself some coffee to keep awake.'

He nodded, disappeared, moving silently.

She found her shoes and still yawning turned off the bedside light and went down the stairs, holding on to the banister. She heard the light click off in the smallest bedroom, and hoped Roy would sleep tight. What was it her mother used to say? 'Goodnight, sleep tight. Don't let the bed bugs bite.'

When were bed bugs last to be found in a modern house? Don't answer that question, Ellie. There's always squatters and people who ... yawn ... can't look after themselves properly.

She shut off the landing light and found herself in darkness. Oh. She felt for the hall light, and switched that on. Then thought that if Mrs Alexis was going to attack the house, she'd be expecting to find it in darkness at that hour of the morning, so ... was it best to have the lights on ... or off?

Well, if she switched off all the lights and

sat in darkness waiting for something to happen, she'd probably fall asleep again.

But if she did leave the lights on, then ... would it be a deterrent, or not?

Did she want it to be a deterrent?

Wouldn't it be best to get it over and done with? Let Mrs Alexis attack the house, which would be proof positive that she was a criminal...?

Ellie put both hands to her head and gave it a shake. This was ridiculous.

Ellie, pull yourself together. Make yourself a coffee because you need it. You're on duty till three o'clock, remember. One thing at a time. Concentrate. Put the light on in the kitchen. Turn the hall light off. Close the kitchen door so the light doesn't shine out through the front door. Fill the kettle. Switch it on. Where's the coffee?

The kitchen had been decorated in a dull yellow with matching tiles. Blond wood furniture. The units were stainless steel and cream. The accessories were clear glass and cream. Not particularly modern in look, but it pleased the eye and made it a pleasant place in which to work.

Felicity had been right in thinking Roy might want her to update her furnishings, but what she'd done so far was to make a comfortable home. Perhaps that was better than being an up-to-the-minute minimalist.

Ellie made herself a mug of black coffee

and took it to the table which would – when the blinds were drawn back – look out on to the garden.

Perhaps this was the way Mrs Alexis would attack. She could walk down the path at the side of the house and set fire to the kitchen extension – with Ellie in it.

Yuk. Ellie shivered. The temperature had dropped since nightfall.

Think like her, Ellie.

The moment Mrs Alexis steps off the road on to the driveway, the security lights will come on. So all I have to do is keep watch in a room at the front of the house. When – if – the lights come on, then I'll wake up Roy and ring the police and that will be that.

The only problem is that we've got nothing on her at the moment. Ought we to let her take some action, before we call the police? How much rope can we let her have? How much damage do we allow her to inflict?

Don't know, don't know, don't know. *Please, Lord. Help. I'm really, really stuck on this one. Please look after us. I feel so stupid … so helpless.*

She shut off the kitchen light and groped her way into the small study at the front of the house, which had once been Mrs Alexis' dining-room but which now func- tioned as Felicity's office. A computer and printer occupied most of the window space. There were blinds at the window, instead of curtains. One of the blinds hadn't been pulled all the way down.

Because of that, and the street lights outside, the room was not completely dark. Ellie tugged the blind right down and it flew up with a muffled crash. She set her teeth, hoping the noise hadn't woken the others. She pulled the blind down again, right to the bottom, and again it went up a few inches. Ellie shrugged. If that was how it felt about it...

She looked around for somewhere to sit. She could make out darker patches of furniture against the light cream walls. A vase of sweet peas on the desk scented the room.

Ellie sank into a comfortable chair and leaned back. Oh, that was good.

She made herself get up, and sit on a high-backed office chair instead.

A car drove past, slowly. She shot upright, wondering if it was a police patrol car ... looked at the digital display on the computer, realized it was only a quarter to two, and relaxed again. Too early for the patrol car.

It went past, anyway.

It was very quiet. She could hear a clock ticking somewhere in the house. Probably the kitchen clock. Another car went by. It didn't stop.

She began to count back from one hundred, to keep herself awake.

Another car ... slowing ... turning off the road ... lights flashing this way ... voices, slammed car doors. Ah, Suzie and her husband returning from some party or other. It was only two o'clock. Not late for their sort of party.

Ellie wondered if the party had broken up yet at the Webbs'. What cheek that Janetta had, trying to pass off supermarket dishes as her own cooking. And we won't think about her remarks as to my having a make-over, will we, Ellie? Colouring my hair, indeed! Bill really wasn't sticking up for me, was he? I suspect he realized that I wasn't really going to make him the sort of wife he wanted, as soon as he put me in his social group.

Yuk. Double yuk.

It would have been nice if we could have gone to Kew Gardens this afternoon...

I wonder if Roy and Felicity will have a big wedding ... in church, of course. Maybe I'll be asked to be matron of honour. That would be a turn-up for the books. But I'd like it. I really don't feel hurt about his turning to Felicity. No, I really don't.

I'm glad I don't. I wish them well, I really do.

She grinned. Fancy Felicity saying she didn't want Roy to jump on her. It's like Little Miss Mouse saying to the Big Big Pussy Cat, 'Please don't chase me ... or if you do, don't hurt me too much!' And Big Big Pussy Cat is being very good about it, I must say. Perhaps he really is growing up.

Two o'clock. She sighed. How slowly time went when you were dying to go to bed and sleep. She'd be wrecked in the morning.

Someone walked along the road outside. She tensed. Waiting, listening.

During the day you never noticed if someone walked along the road outside your house, but in the middle of the night you heard it, all right. The footsteps paused. Ellie crept to the window and looked out through the four inches below the bottom of the rackety blind.

It was a man walking a dog. The dog had paused to investigate something, and the man stood there, gazing out over the moonlit park. Waiting.

The dog moved on, and the man followed.

Ellie returned to her chair. How much longer before she could wake Felicity? Half an hour? No, less. Good. Nothing was going to happen tonight, was it?

She didn't hear the whirr of the bicycle, but suddenly the security lights outside flashed on.

Someone had stepped off the road into the garden. Ellie's heartbeat went into overtime. Her mouth was dry. She stood up, slowly.

Ellie imagined what would happen next: stealthy footsteps up the path to the front door, the flap of the letter-box pushed up and a flaming rag dropped inside...

She must get the fire extinguisher.

Where had she put her mobile phone? She hadn't left it upstairs, had she?

Should she shout for the others?

Would they hear her?

There was a crash, an explosion right in front of her. The burglar alarm went off. The blind flew up. The window cracked from top to bottom.

A sheet of flame shot skywards.

It was like looking into the face of hell.

But the petrol or whatever it was had landed a little short of the house and the flame was dipping, spreading sideways ... and through the flames Ellie could see another face. For a split second she thought she was looking into a mirror and she was looking at her own face, distorted with horror. But it wasn't her face that she was seeing, though the face she did see was also filled with horror.

Through the flames, she looked at Mrs Alexis ... and Mrs Alexis looked at her.

Eighteen

Ellie was terrified of fire. She cowered, expecting to be engulfed by flames any minute ... and then she would writhe and die.

The burglar alarm was so loud it blotted out all thought. She couldn't move.

The flames, the roar...

Yet the flames seemed to be lower, spreading to right and left along the front of the house. And still the heat didn't reach her.

The woman's face outside wavered and dissolved. Even as Ellie watched, Mrs Alexis turned and fled back to the road. She mounted her bicycle and rode off.

She could hear someone shouting over the clamour of the burglar alarm. Slowly, painfully, she made out some words. 'Ellie? Are you all right?' Someone was trying to make themselves heard over the burglar alarm.

Someone else was screaming. Felicity?

Ellie didn't understand it, but for some reason the heat of the flames wasn't reaching her. They were outside the house, not inside.

She unstuck her tongue, and shouted back. 'It's all right. She threw something at the window, but ... there's no fire inside. It's all right.' She realized she probably couldn't be heard. She staggered to the hall.

Roy was coming down the stairs, hair tousled, wearing nothing but his jeans. He cupped his hands over his ears, and shouted what might have been, 'Has she gone?'

Ellie nodded.

He fell on the alarm and silenced it. Blessed silence.

'Fire,' said Ellie. 'I was in the study. There was an explosion, like a bomb going off, and flames. Outside. Not inside. I don't understand it, but there's no fire inside.'

Felicity appeared at the head of the stairs, pulling on her towelling robe. 'What happened? It sounded like a bomb.'

Roy put his head inside the study. 'Ah, the double glazing kept it out. I don't think there's too much danger, girls, but just in case, get your handbags and a warm coat and go and stand in the back garden.'

Double glazing? Ah. Roy had done a thorough job of remodelling the house, and of course he'd installed expensive double glazing units in all the windows. Whatever it was that Mrs Alexis had thrown at the house, it hadn't penetrated two layers of heavy-duty glass.

Felicity couldn't resist going into the study.

She wrung her hands. 'Oh, my poor garden, the roses ... everything's so dry.'

The pergola outside had caught fire and was burning brightly. The flames were spreading along the woodwork, setting fire to the rambling roses and clematis.

'Come out of there,' said Ellie, trying to drag Felicity away from the window. The woodwork around the window burst into flame. Flames licked and ran along the bottom and up the sides. Soon the inner glass would go.

Roy was on the phone, summoning police and fire brigade.

'Don't look, come away,' said Ellie once more. 'Come on, Felicity. We must do as Roy says. Get our shoes and handbag and something warm to wear, and we'll go and stand in the garden.' She got Felicity as far as the hall, and closed the door on the study to slow down the fire.

'Was it her?' Felicity wouldn't move from the hall.

'Yes. I saw her quite clearly. I think she was as horrified by the flames as I was. Where are your shoes, and your handbag?'

'Out, both of you!' said Roy, thrusting them towards the kitchen. 'Outside, now!'

'No shoes,' said Felicity.

'Then I'll have to carry you out!'

Ellie ran up the stairs, collected her handbag, darted into Felicity's room for a pair of slippers, anything, a pashmina ... and down again.

Felicity had got as far as the kitchen door. 'How long will the fire brigade be?'

'Not long,' said Roy. 'The flames seem to be dying down. I wonder...' He went into the study for a moment. He said, 'It's very localized. I wonder if I could tackle it with the fire extinguisher.'

'No!' shrieked Felicity. 'You'll be hurt. Leave it for the fire brigade.'

'I'll be all right,' said Roy, who had never lacked for courage. While Ellie thrust slippers at Felicity, Roy unlocked and unbolted the front door, and went out, closing the door behind him.

'Oh, no! Stop him!' moaned Felicity.

Ellie thought their little fire extinguisher probably hadn't a chance, but you couldn't stop men if they thought they knew what they were doing. She said, 'We ought to go into the back garden.'

Felicity took no notice, but ran to the front door and peered out through the glass panes at the top. 'Why do men have to be so brave!'

Ellie thought that sometimes 'brave' meant 'stupid', but didn't say so.

The wail of a fire engine could be heard in the distance, coming closer. There were signs that neighbours had been alarmed, and were coming out of their houses to see what was going on.

As it drew up outside, Roy opened the front door, brandishing the empty fire extinguisher. 'The house is safe now, I think. They can deal with the rest.'

The pergola was still burning merrily, and the fire had blackened and destroyed all the planting around it, but though the front of the house around the study window was still smouldering there was no more active fire there.

A police car rolled gently to a halt in front of the fire engine. It was manned by the same two policemen who'd called earlier.

'Now for the explanations,' said Roy.

Ellie said, 'I'd better put the kettle on.'

Mrs Alexis pedalled home in a state of shock. She'd never had to use fire before. It was a horrifying method. And that woman had seen her! Had locked eyes with her! What to do about it?

She couldn't think straight.

Woosh! It had gone up like ... like a rocket. Like a sheet of lightning. It had been wonderful! And then she'd seen that face peering at her through the window! She'd lost her nerve, then and fled. If she'd stayed, she'd have seen the fire engulf the whole house, and that woman would have gone up with it. The only witness. Mrs Alexis laughed to herself. The beauty of it all was that even if the witness survived, no one knew where Mrs Alexis lived.

She reached the house, and received a nasty shock, for a police car was parked in front, while a man and a woman were being let into the house. There were lights on in the hall and upstairs. Whatever could have happened?

Her heart beat faster. Had they had a burglary?

She mustn't be found outside. She negotiated the side door with care, so that it wouldn't creak and betray the fact that she'd been out. She didn't bother putting the bicycle away properly, but left it at the side of the house. She got out her torch to help her find the lock to the kitchen door, and used the key to let herself in.

There was no light on in the kitchen or back passage, but she could hear movement and voices up above. With any luck, she'd be back in bed before her absence was discovered. She crept along to her bedroom at the back of the house.

Putting on the bedside light, she shed her clothes and donned her nightgown. The time was a quarter past three. She'd been out for less than an hour. Pretty good going, if she said so herself.

She was just about to get into bed when she hesitated. There was quite a lot of noise going on above. Footsteps. Voices on mobile phones. Could she have been expected to sleep through that? Would it be a good idea for her to appear at this point, saying she'd been woken up by all the goings-on?

Someone knocked on her door. A woman police officer.

'What's the matter? What's going on?' asked Mrs Alexis, trying to behave as if she'd just been woken up.

'We'd like a word, if we may.'

Mrs Alexis said, 'Why? What's happening? Is it a burglar? This is the middle of the night. I don't understand.'

And she didn't understand for quite a while. Two of the police, a man and a woman, sat her down in the kitchen – her kitchen – and questioned her as if she'd done something wrong.

What time had she last seen Ruby's father? Had she gone into his room then? She'd helped him to bed, had she? And what then?

'Well, nothing. He was sleepy. I went to bed.'

'You went back again, though, didn't you? Don't deny it. We know you did. On your first visit you put a sleeping tablet in his hot drink, didn't you? Don't lie. We know you did. There's a clear set of fingerprints on the bottle ... ah, you admit you gave him a tablet, then?'

'I handled the bottle, yes. He was sleepy, as you said. I wondered if he'd taken one himself, although he did have difficulty with the cap. What's all this about?'

'You went back later, though, didn't you? Don't bother to lie. His daughter checked on him when she went to bed and he was all right then, though it worried her that he was sleeping so heavily. Then at half past two she woke up and decided to check on him again. And found him dead, with a pillow over his face...'

'No-o-o!' Mrs Alexis rocked to and fro.

'We know you've a real way with you when people upset you,' said the policewoman. 'Admit it. Husband, father, sister ... You've done away with all of them, at different times. But why get rid of this poor old man, who's never done you any harm? Did you think to get some money from his will?'

'What? No! I was fond of him. He could have gone on for months. I tell you, it wasn't me!'

'Ruby says otherwise.'

'It's a pack of lies! I've never heard of such a thing.'

'Ruby knows all about the others you've killed.'

'What?' Mrs Alexis went pale. 'How could she? I mean, it's not true.'

'Someone told her. She'd never suspected you of anything before that, but once she'd started worrying, she couldn't rest. That's why she checked up on the old man in the night.'

Mrs Alexis began to be really worried. Who could have told Ruby? 'It's not true. She's making it up.'

'It's going to be easy enough to check it out, isn't it?'

Mrs Alexis eyes switched to and fro. The house was in the old man's name. Ruby avoided looking after him, was prepared to pay someone else to do so. If the old man had to go into a home, the house would be sold to pay for his stay in a retirement home, and Ruby would lose out. It *was perfectly clear to Mrs Alexis that Ruby had killed her father, to save her inheritance.*

'It was her that did it,' said Mrs Alexis. 'She wanted him dead, not me.'

The police laughed.

'It's true. He was alive when I saw him last. She must have gone in when she thought I was fast asleep, and put a pillow over his head.'

'Why should we believe you, and not her? You've done this sort of thing before, haven't you? How did your sister die, eh?'

'That was different. She fell down the stairs. Anyway, I wasn't here last night.'

'Oh, come on! You can do better than that.'

'It's true. I was out,' said Mrs Alexis. 'It was a hot night. I couldn't sleep. I went for a ride on my bike. I've only just got back.'

'Oh yes, that's a really good alibi, I must say. Can't you do better than that?'

For a moment Mrs Alexis wavered. She tried to work out what was best to do. If she said she'd been setting a fire over by the park, she'd be prosecuted for that. Maybe a couple of years inside for arson? But if she didn't claim that as an alibi, then she'd be done for a murder she hadn't committed. She'd been fond of the old man, and she didn't see why Ruby should get away with it. No, she was not going to let Ruby get away with it.

'I cycled round by the park and started a fire at my old house.'

'Really? You can prove it, too, I suppose?'

'Yes. There was a woman inside the house. She saw me. She's a friend of Lady Kingsley. She recognized me.'

'What time was that? One o'clock? Two?'

'About twenty past, twenty-five past two. I set my alarm for two, got up, dressed and rode over there, which takes about ten to twelve minutes. You can check with my alarm. And my bed hasn't been slept in.'

The two police looked at one another. 'So...'

'Ruby did it,' said Mrs Alexis. 'She wanted him dead, not me. He was a nice old man. All he wanted was his telly and his hot drinks, and an arm to help him to the bathroom. I hope she rots in hell.'

That wasn't the end of it, of course. The police didn't want to believe her. They had her down for other murders, so why not this one as well?

Mrs Alexis began to pray that the only witness to the arson had survived.

In the immediate aftermath of the arson attack, Ellie, Felicity and Roy spent most of Saturday at the police station, giving statements.

When Ellie was allowed to leave, she couldn't think what to do next. It was turning out to be another hot day. Too hot to think straight. She found a seat on a bench near the police station, and phoned Bill. She felt shaky and disorientated. The police had said she'd have to go back to attend an identity parade. It was the last thing she wanted to do. She wanted Bill to come and pick her up in his big car, and take her somewhere nice, to make much of her and tell her how wonderful she'd been.

She wasn't going to admit how frightened she'd been, of course, or he'd come over all heavy and say it served her right and she shouldn't interfere in other people's business.

So when she got through, she started off by telling him that it was nearly all over, that they'd caught Mrs Alexis and everyone was very relieved. She said she'd managed all right by herself this time, thank you very much.

But he'd only just come in from playing golf, and wanted to tell her all about that, instead of listening to her. She could have screamed. She cut him short, saying she'd love to hear about it some other time, but just at that moment she was so tired she couldn't concentrate properly.

'Well, don't forget to be ready tomorrow morning, will you? We won't want to be late for church.'

Until that moment she'd forgotten that she'd agreed to go to Bill's church on Sunday. She said that yes, she'd be ready, because she couldn't think of a good enough excuse to get out of it.

She tried to phone Thomas, to tell him why

she wouldn't be in her usual place at church the next day, but had to leave a message on his answerphone as usual.

She gazed into space for a while, then summoned up enough energy to ring for a cab to waft her over to Aunt Drusilla's.

The old lady answered the door herself, and took her through to the big sitting-room at the back of the house. Two huge fans revolved from the ceiling, keeping the room at a pleasant temperature.

'I'm glad you dropped by,' said Aunt Drusilla. 'Perhaps you can give me a coherent account of what's been happening. Roy had to hare off to a meeting somewhere and all I could get out of Felicity were blushes and sighs and testimonials to my dear son's thoughtfulness in providing her house with perfectly standard doubleglazing.'

'Where's Rose?' Ellie suddenly felt hungry, and Rose could always be relied on to produce food on demand.

'Rose has gone with Felicity to help clear the burned plants from her garden. I said they should wait for the insurance people to have a look first, but no, they had to be at it. Are you hungry? She left me some soup and a sandwich in the kitchen, but I couldn't be bothered to fetch it. Doubtless there's enough for two, or even three, knowing Rose.'

Ellie found cold summer soup and some

smoked salmon sandwiches in the fridge, neatly cling-filmed and ready to eat. She took them through to the living-room and, around mouthfuls, gave her aunt a blow-by-blow account of what had been happening.

Miss Quicke nodded approval. 'Although of course I do not approve of arson in general, this little incident does seem to have brought matters to a head for my family. Well done, Ellie.'

Ellie was too tired to laugh out loud, but she felt her ribs ache. 'I didn't do much.'

'Don't tell me they'd have got where they are now if you'd folded your hands and done nothing. You steered them with a touch here and a touch there, and the result is highly satisfactory. I'm pleased with you. I'm also pleased with Roy, who seems to have matured through having to think about someone else for a change.'

'It's not over yet. They arrested Mrs Alexis but they've no real proof, unless I can identify her as the person who fire-bombed Felicity's house. I have to attend an identity parade to see if I can pick her out. I dread the thought of it. Suppose I don't recognize her? I've only seen her a couple of times before, and on neither occasion was I really looking at her; once when I went round her house, and once in the Post Office, and that was just a glimpse. And then last night...' She shuddered.

'You'll remember her all right.'

Ellie polished off the last sandwich and leaned back in her chair, beginning to relax. 'Do you know, I'm almost sorry for her? Her husband beat her up, and she contrived his death. Then the money ran out and she loved her little house so much that she helped her elderly father into the next world. Oh, I know it was dreadful, but I can understand it, in a way.'

'You're not going to tell me that you're so fond of your own little house that you'd kill to stay there?'

'No, of course not.'

'Or that you'd turn down an offer of marriage, if it meant leaving it?'

'No, I'm not going to say that.'

'You're not going to marry Bill, are you?'

'No, I don't think I am. Not because I'm so fond of my little house that I don't want to leave it, but ... let me try to think straight ... because I don't think I love him enough to put him before my house and garden and friends and way of life. He's a lovely man. But.'

Aunt Drusilla settled back in her chair. 'Pass me that light rug, will you, dear? I rather fancy a nap before Rose comes back. I told her to be back by five. I won't have Felicity wearing her out over there.'

Ellie unfolded the rug and laid it over her aunt's knees. 'Nothing wears Rose out, when she's working with plants.'

Aunt Drusilla patted Ellie's hand. 'You're a good girl. You're looking peaky. Why don't you go and have a nap, too?'

Ellie considered that the best advice she'd had all week. If only she could follow it. But first she must tie up some loose ends.

She took a cab back home, and let herself into the hall.

Blessed silence.

The answerphone was winking. As usual. Midge came to greet her. She picked him up and huffed into his fur till he objected and she had to put him down. He demanded to be fed and she obliged.

She threw open all the windows, and the door on to the garden. She could hear Kate talking to Catriona in the garden next door.

She fed her goldfish, something she'd neglected to do for a few days. They didn't seem to mind if she did forget to feed them. Happy creatures.

She put the sprinkler on in the back garden, and watered the plants in the conservatory. Nothing much seemed to have suffered from her absence.

The grandmother clock in the hall ticked solemnly away.

If only she could collapse on her bed ... but first she must check on Diana and little Frank. It was nagging at her that she hadn't been in touch for days. Had Diana actually collected him from school the other day, or had he been left weeping in the playground? Of course the teachers would have looked after him, but...

She punched in Diana's mobile number. 'Diana, is that you?'

'Mother, where are you? I've been ringing and ringing. I've even called round a couple of times, but since you've locked me out I wasn't able to get in even to leave a note for you, and as for the times that I've phoned you...'

Ellie tried to keep calm. 'Yes, well, I was away for a few days, but...'

'You're home now? Good. I'll be round in five minutes.'

'No, don't do that!' But Diana had already put the phone down.

Ellie tried to see the funny side of things, and failed. She put the phone down and went through the rest of her phone messages.

Diana ... Kate, wanting to know if Ellie was all right, and should she continue to feed Midge and water the plants.

Dear Mrs Dawes, from church, wanting to know how Ellie was doing. Mrs Dawes had missed seeing Ellie at choir practice, and hoped she'd be back soon.

A sales call. Diana again.

Thomas, just a quickie to see how she was doing. Diana again.

Ellie sat down to take the calls, and shuffle through the pile of mail which had been delivered in her absence. Midge came to sit on her lap.

An old friend from the other side of London, ringing to see when they could meet. Diana again. There were some bills, some circulars. A library book that she'd ordered had come in and was waiting for her to collect it. A letter from another old friend on the South Coast. Two holiday postcards. A hand-written note from someone who'd heard her house was for sale, and wanted to know when they could view it.

A note from Diana in screaming capitals, underlined. RING ME.

She hadn't missed much while she'd been gone. She pushed them aside ... and had a moment of déjà vu so horrible that she gasped. She was back in Felicity's study, while a sheet of flame went whoosh! In front of her. And then she was looking through it at the contorted face of the arsonist.

Ellie shuddered. Yes, she'd know the woman again.

The doorbell rang. A babel of voices outside. Midge leaped from her lap, streaking for the back of the house.

Ellie opened the door only to be pushed back by what seemed like a horde of children all under the age of ten, who rushed through her hall and kitchen into the conservatory at the back after Midge.

There stood Diana, smugly smiling, with little Frank looking scared behind her. Behind them stood a man who was also smiling, and whom Ellie thought she recognized.

Shrieks from the conservatory announced that Midge had made good his escape. The shrieks died out as the boys – however many of them were there? – dived out into the garden after him.

'I know you, don't I?' said Ellie, letting the adults and remaining child into the house. 'You came round to look at the house the other night, and were very understanding about everything.'

'Yes, indeed,' he said, still smiling. He pushed Frank further into the hall. Frank was behaving in uncharacteristically quiet fashion, but then he must be much the youngest of the group who'd just rampaged through the house. The man lifted his voice, and bellowed, 'Boys, play quietly, now!'

Diana went through into the living-room and flounced down on a big chair. She yawned. 'This is Denis, and those are some of his brood out there. We're joining forces, work-wise. He's setting up a new estate agency, and has invited me to be a partner, provided I can raise enough money to pay the first year's rental of some premises. He's got four kids already, so his wife can look after Frank as well, when necessary.'

Ellie ignored the screams and yells from her garden, knowing that Midge was a brilliant escape artist and would be a couple of houses away by now. What she couldn't ignore was a cold, sticky hand thrust into hers, and a thin boy's body pressed against her side. Diana and Denis might look on their plans for the future with satisfaction, but little Frank was seeking Granny's help. Rumbustious he might be on his own. Annoying, frequently. Naughty, now and then. But what chance did he have against four boys, all older and bigger than him? None. And he knew it.

'So you see,' said Diana, smoothing the lapel of her smart black suit, 'it's all worked out for the best.'

'Providing,' said Denis, continuing to smile, 'that you can come up with the first year's rental.'

They both looked at Ellie, whose first instinct was to get out her cheque-book, and whose second was to refuse to do so. 'One thing at a time. Wasn't Frank due to go back to his father's on Thursday?'

'Chickenpox,' said Diana. 'They want me to keep him for another week.'

Ellie could understand that. 'I see. So how are you planning to raise this first year's rental? From me? Surely not.'

Diana and Denis didn't even exchange

glances. It seemed they'd come prepared for some initial difficulty. Diana said, 'I thought you'd be pleased not to have to babysit Frank, especially if you're thinking of getting married again.'

'Whether I am thinking about getting married or not,' said Ellie, 'I wouldn't want to miss out on my grandson's company.' Little Frank looked up at her with the look of a condemned man being reprieved from the gallows.

Diana was not amused. 'I thought you'd consider it a fair exchange.'

'You mean that I'd pay you so that I didn't have to look after Frank now and again? Oh, Diana. You can't have thought that.' Ellie gave a light laugh.

Diana reddened. 'Mother, this is my whole future.'

'Tell you what,' said Ellie, 'You know I have nearly all my money in a trust fund. Why don't you apply to the fund for a start-up allowance? If the other trustees agree, then we can draw up suitable financial terms, how much to be advanced, and how it is to be repaid. But remember, this would be a proper business arrangement, enforceable in law if necessary.'

Nineteen

The clamour outside had faded. Presumably the boys had found their way out of Ellie's garden and either down the alleyway past the backs of the houses or on to the Green around the church. Neither Denis or Diana appeared worried about what the children might be up to, and Ellie wasn't going to remind them.

Denis was thoughtful. 'I suppose that might do, Diana. On easy terms. I assume, Mrs Quicke, that you'll let us put a For Sale board up outside your house for a while – just to get our names known in the area.'

Ellie was beginning to distrust his smile. 'You assume wrongly. A business arrangement is all I'm prepared to offer. Take it or leave it.'

'I'll take it,' said Diana, with a poor grace. 'Come along, Denis. We've got work to do. Best dump the kids back at your place first. Frank, do you want to stay here with Granny?'

'Ess,' said Frank, pressing even closer to Ellie.

Ellie stroked his forehead. 'He can stay the night, but you'll have to collect him by ten tomorrow, as I've arranged to go out for the day after that. Frank dear, go and get yourself washed, and we'll see what we can cook up for supper, shall we?'

Diana shrugged. Denis thanked Ellie for all her help, and still smiling, wafted himself down the garden, calling for his boys.

'Kiss, kiss,' said Diana to Frank, who permitted the peck on his cheek, and then ran upstairs, presumably to get out of the way of the horde of boys who presently came rampaging back up the garden, through the house and out of the front door.

'Bye bye,' Diana said to Ellie, and slammed the front door after her.

Peace and quiet. Ellie sank back into her chair and closed her eyes. The sprinkler outside made a soothing sound. Midge came back, to sit on the coffee table and give himself a good wash. Presently she heard the muted sound of little Frank playing on his games console upstairs.

Life was gradually returning to normal. Mrs Alexis' face flashed before Ellie's eyes once more, and once more was driven back. It wasn't over yet.

Even after a good night's sleep, Ellie felt sluggish. Some younger folk might be able to take getting firebombed in their stride, but

Ellie was not one of their number. Frank perked up no end, but Ellie had to struggle to appear bright and cheerful.

Felicity rang, to ask how Ellie was and to say that she and Roy were planning to speak to Thomas about their wedding after the service today. It would be a small affair, Felicity thought; just a few close friends, with a reception at Miss Quicke's, which that lady had insisted upon. Felicity said she rather thought of asking Kate to be matron of honour, which was obviously the right thing to do but gave Ellie a twinge of regret.

'We know it's all thanks to you,' said Felicity. Which made Ellie feel better.

What she really wanted to do was to sit in her garden, doing nothing and trying to think of nothing, but instead she had to cook a proper breakfast for herself and Frank, and see that they were both clean and tidy, ready to be collected before ten o'clock. Luckily Diana called for him dead on time. Without being reminded, for the first time Frank lifted his face for a kiss on leaving, and said, 'Thank you for having me.' Perhaps there was hope for him yet.

As Diana drove away, Bill drew up in front of the house. Ellie picked up her bag and pulled the front door to behind her. It seemed all wrong to be getting into Bill's car and driving away from her own church, but she'd agreed to go, and she wasn't the sort to break her promises.

Bill asked her if she'd tidied up her last little adventure satisfactorily, and she said, 'Almost,' and that was all he wanted to know about it. She knew that if she married him, she'd have to give up interfering in other people's lives. At the moment she felt that would be a good thing, but she suspected that tomorrow she'd feel differently. She hoped that tomorrow she'd feel differently.

Bill's church was older than the one she had gone to most of her life. It was beautiful, very up to date inside, with individual chairs and a look of prosperity. It had a paid choir and a better-than-usual organist. The church was pretty full and the sermon was thoughtful.

The congregation were mostly well dressed. It was a very smart church.

Everything was as it should be, and nothing felt right. Ellie told herself that it was all her fault that she wasn't getting anything out of it. She was out of sorts. Tired.

She longed for the slightly muddly choir that she'd been singing in since Frank died, and the worn, slightly dusty pews of her own church. She missed the eccentricities of some of the older, less well-off and sometimes plain dotty parishioners. She missed the warmth. No one at her church minded if someone came in wearing odd shoes – but they'd be worried and try, tactfully or otherwise, to find out if anything was wrong and even try to do something about it.

Of course, 'trying to do something about it' usually meant asking Thomas to have a word with ... whoever.

Thomas, who was on call even on his days off.

Bill took her elbow at the end of the service and steered her into the church hall where they had coffee in good china cups – how posh! Ellie smiled and smiled, and said 'hello' and all the right things. David Webb and Janetta were there, and made all the right noises. Bill Two wasn't there, nor Cilla.

'Now for lunch,' said Bill, indicating they should make their way across to the restaurant. 'I've asked David and Janetta to join us, returning their hospitality.'

What could Ellie do but smile and say 'How delightful!' while wishing he hadn't done it. If he'd asked her first ... but there, that was men all over. Her late husband had always assumed she'd go along with his plans, and so had Roy during his half-hearted courtship of her.

And now she knew – even if Bill didn't – that she was going to shed yet another aspirant for her hand in marriage. Ay di me!

She smiled through lunch, and listened to the men talking, and wondered how Janetta contrived to keep an even tan all over. Did she visit a sun-bed emporium or whatever they were called? Didn't they give you skin cancer? Did Janetta care, so long as she looked good?

Bill took her home. 'Come in for a bit?' she asked, meaning that she wanted to talk to him, quietly, at her own pace.

He checked his watch. 'I thought I might get in a round of golf this afternoon.'

'Ah.' It was the last straw. 'Well, what I wanted to say was, that this is not going to work. I'm very, very fond of you. But I'd like us to go back to the way we were, seeing one another now and then, going out for the day together sometimes, that sort of thing?'

He turned in his seat to face her. 'But Ellie, I thought we were doing fine. You know I've wanted to marry you for years, and we're only just beginning to explore a deeper relationship.'

'What I think is, that you want to marry the woman I used to be when Frank died. Only I've changed since then. I've grown up a bit, I suppose, and made new friends, made a busy life for myself, and – let's face it – you really wish I hadn't changed and that I didn't have anything else to do but be your companion in life.'

'Well, you'd hardly continue chasing criminals once we were married, would you?'

'There's two criminal trials coming up, Bill; those of Mrs Alexis and Ruby Hawthorne. I've got to attend an identity parade tomorrow. Then I'll be a witness in both cases. I can't get out of any of that, can I?'

'Well...' he pinched his chin. 'No. But you could promise me not to get involved in anything else of that kind in future.'

'I can't promise anything of the kind. I got into this because my friends were involved. Suppose another of my friends gets involved in something in future? Would you really want me to walk away, to say it was none of my business?'

'Well...' He would, really. But it was not going to be possible for him to say so.

Ellie added, 'You've moved on, too. You've got your own circle of friends, your own pastimes. Golf and the Rotary Club and all that. Let's face it, I'm just a simple little suburban housewife who helps out around the church and parish. I loved going to the Ritz – I hope you'll include me in some other outings like that – but that's a treat for me. It's not everyday fare. To put it bluntly, Bill: I don't fit in.'

'You could at least try to—'

'Learn how to play bridge, and dye my hair and diet till I'm skin and bone and think about nothing but how to spend money? I can't, Bill.'

He sighed. 'But that's why ... hang it all, Ellie ... it's what made me love you in the first place.'

'You may like that about me, but at the

same time you'd like me to have a make-over and look like Janetta, wouldn't you?'

'No, not really.' He ran his hand over his eyes. 'Yes, I see what you mean. But Ellie, I really do value you as you are. At least, if you were to give a little bit...'

Ellie smiled. 'You see?'

'You could learn to play golf. If I let you off the bridge...'

She laughed, and got out of the car. 'No, Bill. I'm far too busy for that. Give me a ring when you want a day out sometime, right?'

She let herself into her house with a feeling of enormous relief. So, that was that. A road had opened up before her, and turned into a cul-de-sac. She felt some regret that it hadn't worked out. It had been lovely to be praised and flattered and taken out to nice places. But the bottom line was too steep for her.

The following morning Ellie went down to the police station, and attended an identity parade. She was assured that the people behind a certain window couldn't see her, although presumably they knew who was going to be looking at them.

She prayed a bit, waiting for the moment to arrive when she had to confront Mrs Alexis again. If, indeed, Mrs Alexis was there.

'Ready? Take your time.'

Ellie spotted Mrs Alexis straight away.

There were other women there, all about the same size and all dressed in dun colours. Mrs Alexis was looking straight ahead of her ... and then some instinct made her glance to the left. Ellie knew that the glass in front of her was one-way but she fell back a pace and caught her breath. It was exactly as if the woman was looking directly at her.

'That's her. Mrs Alexis. She firebombed Lady Kingsley's house and I saw her there.'

'Are you sure? She can't see you, you know.'

Ellie tried to laugh. 'She looks as meek as a mouse, but she's no mouse, believe me. What are you going to charge her with? She won't get bail, will she?'

'Arson, to start with. And no, we'll oppose bail.'

Betty Alexis was charged with arson as soon as Ellie had identified her, and at that point the police began to delve into her background in earnest. They obtained permission for the exhumation of the body of Paddy the handyman, which revealed the fact that he had enough sleeping pills in his body to tip his alcohol level over from high to dangerous. In the end Mrs Alexis was never brought to court with his murder, nor with those of her husband, father and sister, because it was felt that there was simply not enough evidence to convict.

However, when they analysed the rolls Mrs Alexis had left for Felicity, they found cytisine, the alkaloid which can be obtained from laburnum seeds, in sufficient quantities to have killed two adults. The chain of proof leading back to Mrs Alexis was not fool-proof but they might have prosecuted on that if they hadn't got her for arson. In the end, the charges of murder and attempted murder were left on file, because they knew that, with Ellie's evidence, they could get Mrs Alexis for arson with intent to endanger life. Mrs Alexis had been wrong about only getting a couple of years for it – she got life.

Ruby Hawthorne was charged with the murder of her father. Her barrister argued plausibly that his client was as white as blinding snow, and that the jury should look instead at the background of Mrs Alexis, her housekeeper, who was a proven arsonist. He urged the jury to give his client the benefit of the doubt, which they might well have done if Ellie hadn't given such a damning testi-mony which proved Ruby knew how to get away with murder. As a clincher, the police found an acquaintance of Ruby's, who testified that her friend had been complain-ing bitterly in the wine bar about the hor-rendous cost of putting her father in a home, because it would wipe out the money she expected to inherit on his death.

The gossip about Mafia connections was,

of course, nothing but a rumour, but it transpired that Ruby was heavily in debt. The lease on her boutique was sold and it became a dry cleaner's, which Ellie felt was rather apt.

All that was in the future. After the identity parade Ellie returned home feeling shattered. The weather remained balmy, and she was looking forward to sitting down in the garden, in the shade of a large parasol, and drinking some iced tea. She'd made a large jug of it that morning and it was sitting in the fridge waiting for her to get back.

She let herself into the house, greeted Midge and fed him, and opened the back door to go down into the garden. There were two reclining chairs under the big parasol on the lawn. Two, because Kate often came over for a chat. From the top of the steps, Ellie could see that one of the chairs was already occupied, and not by Kate. She put the jug of iced tea and a couple of glasses on a tray, added the tin of biscuits, and went down to join him.

'Hope you didn't mind,' said Thomas. 'Kate said you'd be back soon. She's taken Catriona swimming.'

'Fine by me. Iced tea?'

Thomas lifted a can of beer from the lawn. 'Brought this, but I wouldn't mind a biscuit. Had a bad day?'

Ellie grimaced. 'Might have been better. And you?'

'So-so.'

Ellie sank into the other chair and sipped iced tea. It was good.

Silence. A few butterflies were clustering on a buddleia halfway down the garden. Bees were investigating some thyme which had come into flower.

Thomas produced a Get Well Soon card and handed it to her.

'What's this?' said Ellie. 'I haven't been ill.'

'It's from the choir and some other members of the congregation, asking you to come back. They held an indignation meeting over coffee after the service yesterday morning. Mrs Dawes happened to have a couple of cards in her bag; I understand it was a choice between "Get Well Soon" or "New Home".'

Ellie opened the card, which had a picture on the front of a hippopotamus with his head tied up in a handkerchief. There were a lot of signatures inside. Ever since Reggie had thrown her out of the choir, there'd been a nasty hard place inside Ellie's chest. Now, it melted away. She wanted to cry, but managed not to.

'I bet Reggie didn't sign.'

Thomas pointed to a tiny signature. 'Jean stood over him till he did.' Jean was four foot ten, and Reggie was six foot. Ellie giggled.

'Jean said that you were a pillar of the

church, and he'd no right to keep you out of the choir.'

Ellie laughed out loud at the idea of her being a pillar of the church. 'I suppose she'd be short of someone to help with coffee, if I went. But honestly, Thomas, I haven't much of a voice, and I really don't know why they should want me back.'

'You've a sweet voice, you use it to praise God, and you care about people,' said Thomas. 'I quote, of course. From Mrs Dawes, among others. You were missed yesterday.'

Ellie fidgeted. 'I went to have a look at another church yesterday, but I probably won't go again.'

'Good.' He took the last biscuit, turning the tin upside down to make sure he'd got all the crumbs.

'Thomas, you shouldn't eat so many biscuits. You ought to go on a diet.'

'Don't blame me. It's your fault for giving biscuits to a poor lonely widower with no one to look after him.'

Ellie gave him a sceptical look. He must know that he could have half the widows in the parish inviting him in for meals, if he wished. Then she remembered that moment in her hall when she'd gone to him for comfort and ... well, best not think about that.

He folded his hands over his tummy and closed his eyes, the very picture of bliss personified. 'Of course,' he said, 'I may be moving on soon to another parish. What do you think?'

She nearly dropped her glass of tea. 'What? But you've only been here five minutes.'

'I thought it might get a bit awkward, between me and thee. And if it did become awkward, then I'd best make a move. The bishop's agreeable. Said he could find me something straight away. It's up to you, really.'

Ellie shot upright, experiencing shock, followed by outrage ... how dare he put it all on her! Then came an urgent need to laugh.

She remembered Felicity's forefinger describing circles on the table top, getting ever nearer to Roy's hand. Here was Mr Mouse playing the same game.

Only Mrs Pussy Cat was not going to be pushed into saying Yes or No. Mrs Pussy Cat had come to the conclusion that her life was all right as it was, thank you very much.

Of course, life with Thomas would never be dull. It would be a useful life. And a very full one. She was extremely, warmly fond of him. Fonder of him than of Bill? Well ... probably, yes. And what's more, Thomas still seemed to be functioning in a particular area where Bill wasn't. But he hadn't actually asked her to marry him, had he?

Oh, no. Mr Mouse wasn't going to risk that. He was going to poke his whiskers out of his hole and see if Mrs Pussy Cat wanted to pounce, or to walk away.

She didn't know whether to kiss him or hit him.

She said, 'I'll have to think about that. In the meantime, you could give me your mobile phone number, right?'

'Will do. How about Kew this afternoon?'

'This isn't your day off. If we go to Kew, will you turn your mobile phone off?'

She awaited his reply with interest.